Luna of the Bastlings

Journey to the Upper World

Luna of the Bastlings

Journey to the Upper World

A Novel

D.L. Richards

A Conscious Shift Publication

Conscious Shift Publishing Registered Offices: Saint Petersburg, FL 33710

Library of Congress Control Number: 2017940548

D.L. Richards

Luna of the Bastlings (Journey to the Upper World)

ISBN 0997955236
ISBN 9780997955231
Published in the United States of America

Cover design by Ellen Kaltenbacher

Dedication

This book is dedicated first and foremost to the Oneness, The All, and to the Christ Consciousness of that unending Love…

For Luna, whose elfish magic started the whole thing…

For Morgan, my inspiration and the Star on the stage of my life…

For Dan, thank you for Morgan…

For Dad and Mom, who always believed this day would come…

To the Dreamers and the Weavers, never stop refilling the creative cup from the endless magical fountain of this universe…

For my Native and Welsh Grandmothers and Grandfathers, thank you for the DNA…

For all my relatives in the Sacred Hoop, may we always remember we are all woven together…and may the bond always be strong…Mitakuye Oyasin…

For Chris, thank you for the love and support…

For Tracey and Mary, whose excitement and hard work made all the difference every day…

Table of Contents

Chapter 1

The Shrouded Corridor

There is a place far from here, in a world below worlds, beneath all things green and fair. Under twigs, roots and the richest of soils. It is a place where shadow chases light and light seeks the truth. Drawn out by the breath of the Oneness, forged into existence by the Sacred Fire, Elan cloaks itself in shadow waiting defiantly to return to its natural state, when truth will rule supreme. The first of the eight lower worlds of Mother Earth, Elan is a place of duality, and it is from this polarity two races were birthed. As to their order of birthright no one can say for certain, yet there is one definitive knowledge about these two rivalries, there are many against the one, Luna of The Bastlings. A singular, barely breathing piece of life fluttering within the walls of Elan, she scurries for refuge from her opposition, the Dreglings.

The little Bastling lives by her wits and will to survive, struggling to make sense of a world gone so wrong. Searching Elan for any clues that might indicate where she came from and what her purpose for existence really is, Luna is constantly pursued by the dark Dreglings. Their reason to give chase is nothing more than malice and greed. It is told that when the Bastlings disappeared from existence they left many rich artifacts that would transform the gray, cavernous world of Elan back into the mecca of wonder and power it once was. The kind of power that in the hands of the Dreglings would surely spell disaster for the other worlds.

It is said in the Times Before Times, Elan and the other seven worlds were interwoven in perfect harmony with each other, until the Dark Storm came upon them. In an instant all worlds were transformed, links were lost, and barriers raised, with Elan suffering the greatest casualties. Which brings us full circle to dear Luna. The brave Bastling searches endlessly for the answers that elude her while the nasty Dreglings hunt for her in hopes of finding clues to the Bastling bounty. Although Luna pleads a lack of knowledge of any lost treasure, it has fallen on deaf ears or more aptly put, deaf souls. Therefore Luna, armed only with her faith, methodically travels the gloomy caverns and halls of Elan in search of her prize; the truth of her existence. The only answers she receives are from obscure statues and barely visible wall paintings in what was once the Great Hall. These sullen, chalky, gray statues hold orbs, books of knowledge and other various talismans in their grasp raised high as if praising some invisible deity above them. Each proud Bastling statue also carries the mark of their race, the very mark that adorns Luna's forehead; a flame encircled by a crescent moon. A birthmark whose meaning has eluded Luna as much as the meaning of her own existence. Two symbols that even have great meaning in other worlds and realms, but to the Bastling, it is a constant reminder of her solitude and abandonment. So that is where she is left, struggling to get to the heart of it, the very deepest part of her existence.

On a day like any other, Luna quietly made her way back to the Great Hall, nothing was abnormal or out of its usual dull place, yet there was something in the air that the little Bastling could not put her finger on. Her sleek Bastling ears moved in each direction with radar precision honing in for any peculiar sound, yet nothing. As she entered the vast chamber Luna made her way to the center statues amidst the rubble. Her long arms dropped to her sides as she gazed up into her ancestors' faces, "What is it that could have possibly made you leave so suddenly?" Luna's eyes fell to the ground knowing she would never hear an answer. There were far too many questions that deserved answers, like how did she survive all by her lonesome? Of course, there was no doubt in her mind that there was not a single Dregling who would have cared for her, let alone raise her. No, they were far too unloving, full of greed, hatred, and heartlessness. Yet with that certainty known, the question remained, how did Luna endure all this time in Elan without family or love or companionship? Food was an easy find. It didn't take much to fill a Bastling belly, unlike her Elanian counterparts who possessed a ravenous, rarely satisfied appetite. Grisly meat and heavy ale was not Luna's idea of a healthy meal, root vegetables and leafy greens filled her plenty. Besides, cooking in any form would attract those nasty Dreglings which was what she was always trying to avoid.

The Bastling plopped herself down on one of the large concrete slabs that at one time shone above her in the decorated ceiling of the Great Hall. She gazed lovingly at the statue to her left, a graceful Bastling woman smiling as if proud to know the secret Luna sought. Within the woman's grasp was a book simply entitled, *The Truths*. Luna jumped to her feet to get a more distinct view of what lay within the concrete pages. But alas, as always, she was left empty. The ancestral statues were ones she visited often knowing full well the Dreglings tended to avoid them. It was not that they wouldn't go within the Great Hall, it was that there arose an uneasiness about them when they did. The Dreglings felt it, and Luna noticed it. Thankfully this provided a restful reprieve for the Bastling and she was glad to be amongst the old ones, even if they were made of stone.

Luna looked up at the beautiful Bastling again, admiring her long flowing curls and stunning features. The braid that rested gently alongside her face was tied with jewels and ribbons. Luna presumed it to be one of the many that used to fill Elan, then again, she doubted these stories were true. After all, they came from the mouths of the Dreglings.

Luna peered up at the stone book in the hand of the beautiful Bastling once again. Her eyes following the raised lettering as she read *The Truths* aloud. She scanned the cover for any other symbols or smaller words she may have missed, but, nothing. Moving on to the next statue, Luna's eyes fell upon a man who appeared to be standing proud aside his female counterpart. Luna preferred to think of them as happy together when they lived, if they had ever lived at all. For all she knew they could have always been statues and nothing more, but deep within her heart and soul something stirred giving rise to the belief that these two Bastlings were once very real. Luna's gaze darted to the book he held in his hand, *The Way*. She scoffed, throwing a small rock, "Wish I knew the way, the way outta here!" The silent hall and stone figures echoed her words back reminding her once again she was ultimately the only Bastling in the room. The rock ricocheted off the remains of the final stone Bastling. Its head had been smashed off the body and was nowhere to be found, nor was the left arm. The right arm had somehow remained intact as it still clutched a book titled, *The Light*. Luna dropped her head in quiet desperation and gave way to sobs. Tears fell from her big, brown eyes, "Why did you leave me? Why? I just want to be where you are wherever that is, I just want to go home." Her voice was barely audible above the mournful weeping as an uproar arose from outside the Great Hall door. She knew at once it must be the Dregs. She instinctively rose, but then immediately assumed a crouching position behind the enormous statues. Her heart froze as the giant doors swung open, revealing her fierce rivals.

There they stood in all their treacherous glory: the Dreglings. Each one a sad imitation of the next, it was as if they had all been created from the same ugly mold. None, of them birthed, all of them made.

The frightened Bastling stayed low to the ground as she heard her nemesis approach. Looking up to her granite companions she prayed, "If you were ever real, please help me. Help me to find a way out of this horrible situation." With the last word of her plea, a gray, boney hand grabbed hold of her, yanking her to her feet. There she stood in the middle of an ungodly circle of venomous wretches. Their poison all for her. They clamored around, sniffing her as if it would reveal more than what appeared. Luna held her breath terrified of what might happen next. One of the Dreglings grabbed her, tying her hands behind her back with thick black rope, "Let's take her back to the camp and see what Lord Derkaz wants to do with her. He will be well pleased that we have finally captured her." Luna struggled to break free from her enslavement but it was no use. She was surrounded and the ropes were too strong.

As they pushed her forward she looked up one last time at the statues and sneered, "That was some answer to my prayer." Head held high, she followed behind the first group of Dreglings as the second group kept in close proximity.

As they made their way into the Dregling encampment Luna took notice of a dark entrance to a corridor she had never seen before. She asked her captors, "What is that corridor?"

Fylgan, one of the more brutish of the bunch shoved Luna causing her to trip over her own feet as he spat in the direction of the dark corridor. "That is what we call the Shrouded Corridor. They say it leads to the Upper Worlds but nobody knows for sure. Anyone who has ever gone in never comes back out," he growled at Luna, stopping the procession. Despite her terror, Luna pretended to be unafraid.

She retorted, "Maybe they made it to the other worlds and didn't come back."

Fylgan and Luna locked eyes as she desperately tried to hide her fear, her chin rose in insolence. He then shoved her shoulders back, his gray, scaly face jutting into hers, "Well Miss Barely Bastling, that very well may be except every time someone has gone in, they hit the Black Pool screaming and never come back to the surface. Besides, everyone knows the other worlds aren't accessible anymore, not since the Dark Storm. That's why our camp is right near that entryway, we always keep guard in case someone does try to get into Elan, we can stop them. There's all kinds of treachery above us and we don't want anyone stealing our goods or our land."

Luna muttered sarcastically under her breath, "Not really much to steal."

"What did you say Bastling?!" Luna's eyes dropped as she fell silent. She waited for the troop to commence towards the camp and started scoping out her surroundings. She knew every nook and cranny of Elan except this part, never daring to enter for fear of being caught and never again being free. Now it looked as though her fears materialized.

Once deeper inside the world of the horrid Dreglings, Luna was thrown into a dusty corner near the fire chamber. Landing on her head and shoulder, it took her a moment to get herself upright, as the Dregs teased and laughed at her graceless position. Although guards were placed on each side of her, they didn't seem to watch her as closely as she watched them. She noticed that the Dreglings always travelled together, never alone.

After hours of Dreggie watching in silence, Luna was well versed in their comings and goings. Their routines consisted of puttering, rambling and mindless business that seemed to go nowhere. There were only three prominent habits. Groups coming and going strictly in charge of treasure expedition, other groups that ate ferociously, and a third group that was charged with keeping watch over the Shrouded Corridor. The latter was a small group that did not venture too close to it, but kept watch nonetheless. This group held Luna's interest the most. She watched as these creepy little Dregs would walk towards the doorway, come to an abrupt halt and retreat again. Luna knew her only chance for freedom would be to make a run for it when a guard retreated. She planned on heading into the one place the Dregs would never dare go, the Shrouded Corridor. As Luna kept vigilant, she also tried to peer into this mysterious doorway. There seemed to be nothing out of the ordinary as far as she could tell. It just looked like a dark corridor that presented a far better alternative to Luna than being a slave or worse to the Dreglings.

"Eh! Bastling, you ready to tell us the way to the bounty?" Luna swiveled round on her knees to find a nasty Dregling staring into her face. His eyes piercing red, with breath like mold and a smell so putrid her stomach began to turn.

"I told you all before, I don't know where any treasure is and if I did I certainly wouldn't tell you." She was as defiant as one could be standing on their knees.

He responded by grabbing her by the scruff, "Oh, you are going to tell us or it will be the end of the Bastlings forever." He forcefully threw her down to the ground and marched off toward the others. Luna searched desperately for something to cut the ties that coiled her hands like black, ropey snakes.

As Luna scanned the ground, a slight movement caught her attention. From the Shrouded Corridor, two eyes gazed out at her. Then without warning, the ropes holding her hands hostage dropped to the ground as if some invisible force had loosened them. Panicking, her eyes darted to see if anyone noticed, and they hadn't. Without hesitation, in one fateful move, Luna made the greatest decision of her life and darted so quickly from her holding cell that the lazy and disheveled Dregs didn't have a chance to respond before she was at the entrance to the Shrouded Corridor. She slowly backed up into the darkness that lay behind her as she dared not turn her back on the Dreglings. They crept towards her, inching carefully so as not to enter the dark territory engulfing her.

Fylgan was the first to speak, "Listen Bastling, we're not playing around. If you go into that Corridor it will be the end of you. Now personally, I don't care if I ever see you again. But you are the only one who can lead us to the treasure, and I don't want to tell Lord Derkaz you escaped on my watch. So, I am going to tell you only one time to get over here. When we find the treasure, you can go wherever you want here in Elan." His sarcasm was evident in his smirk that revealed hideous brown teeth dripping with saliva.

Luna cringed as he ventured closer to the doorway, "Stay back!" she yelled glancing behind her for the glowing eyes. "Do you think I'm stupid? I know very well that my end would be the day you ever found the treasure, but you won't find it because there is nothing to find. Your frustration would be my end as well. I'd rather take this chance and die by my choice than die by yours." Fylgan lunged to snatch her arm, only to have her bolt suddenly in the direction of the darkness. Fylgan fell to the ground smashing his already distorted face. The others rushed up behind him with torches just in time to see the Bastling fall head first into the Black Pool below.

Plummeting into the onyx waters, Luna flailed her arms to make way to the surface. Panic followed confusion as couldn't find her way to the top. Darkness swallowed the little Bastling. Water trickled into her lungs as consciousness escaped her and fatigue became a friend.

Back above the surface, Fylgan rose and scurried back to the rest of the Dreglings, grabbing one of their torches. As he gazed into the waters, a set of glowing eyes became prominent in the foreground. Seeing this, the other Dreglings did what they did best. They fled, leaving Fylgan alone. He cautiously followed her splashes and ripples like a cat stalking its prey. When his gaze finally fell upon the glowing eyes, he dropped his torch and ran. As his feet touched the Shrouded Corridor's entrance a howl emanated in every direction. Fylgan dove over the threshold of Elan crashing into the other Dreglings. They hurried to their feet scattering like paper in the wind, as a hand reached into the waters and pulled a now unconscious Luna to the surface, placing her lifeless body on the other side of the Black Pool.

Luna woke to the sound of her own breathing, a great relief as the last time she had tried that her lungs were filling with water. She quickly sat up looking around, confused. Although still soaked, she was lying in a comfortable bed. The dimly lit room cast shadows on the wall as Luna barely whispered, "Hello? Is anyone here?" The two glowing eyes appeared again in the darkness outside of the room and suddenly the eyes became shadow and the shadow took form.

Standing in the doorway was a small-statured man with the same glowing eyes Luna had seen in Elan. "Allow me to introduce myself, I am Eldred of the Selvz, Magician, Sage and all around fairly nice guy." He bowed very formally and then quickly resumed his standing position.

Luna fumbled for her words as she jumped to her feet and bowed awkwardly, "And I am Luna of the Bastlings, very nice to meet you." Her weak body stumbled backwards and flopped down on the bed.

Eldred chuckled, "Very good! Introductions have been made and now we shall tend to the job of getting you dry. I will give you some clothes as yours hang by the fire." Luna shyly agreed and thanked him.

The old Magician led her into the next room. Although oddly shaped as a circle, it bore an air of familiarity. Luna brushed the feeling aside knowing full well she had never been there before. Eldred burst into laughter as he hobbled towards the fireplace, "One can never be so sure of these things!"

Luna stopped as puddles began forming at her feet, "Excuse me?"

Eldred swirled around surprisingly fast, "The feeling that you've been here before, you can never be too sure of these things."

The confused Bastling exclaimed, "That's impossible, I've never been anywhere near the Shrouded Corridor let alone here and I certainly would have remembered that Black Pool!" Eldred held his belly from the bellows of laughter. Luna stood still, perplexed by the Sage's statement and the fact that he knew her thoughts.

"Oh, that is just one of the charms of my people, the Selvz." His laughter came to a halt. "You see Luna, every one of us has charms regardless of what race we are from, each in its own specific way has shaped who we are. It is a gift, a very precise piece of our DNA that was activated long ago just waiting for us to discover. Every race has its charms, telepathy just happens to be one of mine." He smiled, rubbing his hands by the fire. Luna sat silently staring into the embers dancing and soaring like fireflies in the night.

Sadness filled her heart, "I don't know what any of my charms are, and I am the only Bastling."

The old sage turned very serious, "It is indeed a privilege to know and understand who we are and where we come from, to know exactly why we are here. But it is a greater honor to seek these truths for ourselves. The journey to discover these realities makes the answer far sweeter when we find it."

His voice softened and a loving smile filled his face. But Luna, being the stubborn little Bastling she was, did not feel satisfied by his answer. "The only journey I have taken is through the world of Elan, only to find faded ghosts from the past who would not utter a word to me."

Eldred raised himself up to get the two of them a warm drink of Elderberry tea and some food. "Perhaps they did not speak, but they certainly were listening; your ancestors that is. After all, you are here aren't you? So begins the journey to uncover your Bastling truth."

Frustrated by his words, Luna said, "How can I discover charms, truth or anything about who they were and who I am if I'm not even in Elan anymore? The answer to those questions obviously lie where they once resided, not elsewhere." Her irritation melted into tears as she buried her head in her hands.

Eldred compassionately made his way to the sobbing Bastling, "There, there my child. All is not so lost as you believe. There is still a way for you to embrace your charms." He patted her on the back and continued, "It would be a great undertaking however and I'm not sure you are ready for such an expedition. It is not for the weak-willed. It is filled with peril, but it is the only way I know for a being such as yourself to find the answers you seek."

Luna slowly looked up from behind swollen eyes eager to hear more, "I don't care whatever it takes, just tell me what I have to do," she pleaded.

Eldred of the Selvz' eyes glistened even brighter than before, "It is not so much of what you must do, but instead it is where you have to go. There are only two ways to discover who you are. One is by the Elders teaching you the ways of the Old Ones, or you can make your query to the Tree of Answaru. Since the first doesn't exist, your only choice is the latter."

Luna leaned forward, her breath hanging on his every word.

"It is a tree that contains knowledge of all things and is as old as The Great Mother planet herself. They say that

Answaru was there from the very beginning of the Times Before Times. Legend has it that when The Great Mother planet was forged from the breath of the Oneness, the tree appeared simultaneously along with her. And there it has held true as the greatest of all Scribes knowing all the workings of all things, creatures and races that turn within the Great Mother carefully recording all within the life of this beautiful place." He gazed upwards as if some invisible window was above them allowing him sight of the tree. He wistfully smiled and pointed in the same direction of his stare, "The way to the Tree of Answaru is not an easy one, you must pass through the seven Lower Worlds above Elan to reach the Upper World where the tree resides. There at the gate you will find that great and glorious leafed being, waiting to bring you the truth you seek. It is an arduous climb to the top, but once there, all will be revealed to you." Luna sat mesmerized, her mouth half open in amazement at the thought of making this incredible trek. Excitement welled inside her as she took in all Eldred said. The great magician understood her anticipation, but sternly warned her, "You must not take my words lightly, the seven worlds are filled with many things, some dangerous, some beautiful, you must never let your guard down. I fear your innocence could be your undoing if you are not careful. You will have many tests along the way, as the truth is glorious. It comes at a price, but it is a price seekers of truth are more than happy to pay."

Luna sat upright as her mind caught up, "Wait, I thought the seven worlds above were no longer accessible since the

Dark Storm. I was told that they were all once connected to each other but that it is no longer true."

Eldred smiled again, confident in his knowledge. "It is true there was indeed a great storm so powerful that all of the inhabitants did their best to survive. With the instinct to persevere came an end to many relationships of worlds that were once entwined. Soon the focus of existing at all, became so imperative that connection with the races of the other worlds was simply an afterthought. And then the day came, that awful lapse in time when all communication ceased to exist, the moment frozen when all life stopped being consistent. It was a day filled with sadness and great remorse, for then all worlds realized that whatever they had been before had vanished in a blink of an eye."

The Elanian Bastling wondered how such a great tragedy had happened. Eldred responded, "That has been a question on every great thinker's mind in every world since the Great Storm. 'What transpired within this storm that caused all of us to be disconnected?' But alas, not a one could give an answer. Every great philosopher, genius, artist and poet has tried desperately to solve this great riddle, some with purposeful intent, others naively channeling answers from above; yet not a one solving the whole puzzle."

Luna blinked hesitantly for fear she would miss some invaluable piece of information if her eyes sat closed for too long. "Oh, oh I understand everyone had a small shard of the broken window, yet none could put all the pieces back together. Perhaps there is still a way for the lower worlds to be connected again."

The old Sage smiled wryly, "Well perhaps you can figure that out as well on your way to the Upper World." He began laughing almost falling backwards and Luna couldn't help but get caught up in his giggling and soon the two were in full-blown hysterics.

Once their frenzy of laughter subsided they took up the plan for Luna's adventure upwards. Eldred jumped to his feet and went into his old wood cabinet that sat in the far corner of the room. He scrambled through drawers, occasionally glancing behind him careful that she could not see what he was doing. She sensed his secrecy and leaned forward, her Bastling ears twitching as her nose rose high attempting to sniff out what Eldred was doing. "Never you mind Luna, I will reveal all of this to you in a few moments."

He quickly closed the drawers and swung around with a rawhide bag that was most unappealing. Luna thought it quite drab and wondered how old it was and of course, what it contained. He plopped himself and the ancient bag at the round table in the center of the room and beckoned Luna to sit with him. "Now young Bastling, this is your Bag of Borrowed, it contains all things you will need to help you on your journey. You must never part with this as it will save your life many times." Eldred haughtily wagged his index finger at her as he continued, "Now each item has a special meaning and purpose and all the items in this Bag of Borrowed will help and guide you on your journey into the seven worlds and beyond. They are to be used sparingly and with great care. You will know when to use each one. Never let this bag out of your sight and never let anyone else use it or look inside. The magic contained within it is for you and you alone. Each will prove to be your greatest friend in time of need." Eldred pulled out the first item, "A pen that will aid you with a great deal more than writing." He handed it to Luna and she studied it carefully. It seemed like an ordinary pen with a brown feather tip. She especially liked it as one of her favorite pastimes was writing, she imagined how many fantastical stories she could craft about her amazing adventures. He continued, retrieving another item, "A knife to cut away all things that bind you." It was small, but long-bladed and its handle was silver and ornately embellished with ruby jewels. Luna thought it beautiful but it showed no other signs of magical powers. Eldred placed it gently on the table, "Ah young Bastling, the magic contained within that knife is one of a kind, no other blade can do its work." Luna chuckled to herself at his telepathic abilities, but continued to listen earnestly.

The next article he pulled out was a beautifully decorated orb. Although encased in gold, it shimmered ever so softly with all colors of the spectrum. Luna was drawn to its splendor. "This orb will only work for you when it is set in the right place, only then will its power be revealed." Luna had no idea what he was talking about but Eldred continued, "You will know when the time comes." He smiled warmly and continued, "This is a jewel that has only one home." He held up a small citrine stone that was shaped like a tooth. She thought this the oddest of all. "Do not be afraid of the bite of this tooth." Reaching his hand in again he pulled out two emerald stones, "You will remember these two when the dogs bark." Luna uneasily shifted in her seat.

Completing his presentation, "The rest of the contents include clothing, a torch and oh yes! The most important thing of all, the map!" He pulled out an antique rolled parchment held tightly by a hide string. As he carefully unrolled it, it revealed tears, scripts, and pictures. He took the feather pen and placed a mark on the map representing where the two were in Eldred's cave. "This passageway to the left is the path you must take when you leave here. All the worlds were once connected by passageways but now must be forged, and as you can see each world is located directly above the one that proceeds it." Luna studied the map following the outline of each world with her finger. They were all represented as a circle encompassed by a bigger sphere that connected to roots of a great tree. Above the roots was the Grasslands and the words, *The Upper World.* The stalks met with a trunk and further an enormous tree. Written across the leaves, *The Tree of Answaru.* It sat as big as life to Luna.

"How hard can it be? It looks like a straight path through the worlds above to the tree."

Eldred watched her false confidence building. "Do not underestimate these travels Luna or you will be met with great misfortune. You must be dedicated, wise and use all of your awareness to survive." Her confidence quickly plummeted. "I don't tell you these things to frighten you my dear, but to enlighten you in the hopes you will find your way home." Luna's anxiety eased. "Well I suppose that covers it, there isn't much more I can tell you. Everything else you will learn as you go." He searched deeply into her eyes. Luna quivered uncomfortably, he knew more about her than even she did.

The two sat quietly for the rest of the evening watching the fire gleam on the walls of the Selvish cave. When it was time for sleep Eldred left her with a cot, blankets and her thoughts. It was the longest night she had ever spent. Tossing and turning she wondered if she was strong enough to do it, yet there was something small stirring within that told her she could. That was her last thought as she finally drifted off to sleep.

When Luna awoke she believed for a moment that the happenings of the previous day had all been a bad dream, and expected to wake in Elan. She instead found Eldred standing at the wooden table making breakfast. Reality came flooding back as he spoke, "Good morning my child, and no, it is not a dream, it has all been very real." He kept his back to her as he prepared the food.

Luna gathered herself up off the cot, "I did think it was a dream until I saw you standing there."

The ancient magician chuckled looking back at the weary Bastling, "You finally got some sleep."

Luna nodded not shocked by his knowledge of her insomnia. "I finally did nod off but not soon enough. Can't I just stay here a few more days with you to catch up on some sleep?" She was testing Eldred to see if he would bite, he didn't.

"That is a good try Luna, but you are on your way today. There will be no benefit from hiding from your fate." She felt lovingly scolded as if by a father. It touched her.

The two shared breakfast, conversation, and more instructions for her journey. Her nausea made it difficult to eat, but she forced it down knowing she would need the energy. They finished their meal and Eldred signaled it was time to go. Her body felt a fiery flash of fear. She walked over to her cot and picked up her Bag of Borrowed. They stood at the entrance to the cave to say their goodbyes. Eldred cupped her shoulders with his hands, "This is where your journey begins. I wish you all the best and hope I have given you all that is needed for you to succeed."

Luna's eyes flooded with tears, "Thank you for everything, I don't know how I can ever repay you for all you have done." She wiped eyes that were overflowing with gratitude. Flinging her arms around his wrinkled neck, she knocked him off balance.

Regaining his footing he returned the embrace patting her gently on the back, "There child, everything will be just fine. My repayment will be you achieving your goal." Realizing his own eyes were welling with tears he let go and cleared his throat, "Now you must be off! There is no time to wait!" He ushered Luna down the passageway to the left.

She proceeded a few feet then turned to ask one more question, "Eldred, will I ever see you again?" Her big green eyes filled with innocence.

Eldred smiled and announced loudly as if there was more than just the Bastling standing there, "One never knows when the Selvz will make an appearance. But enough of this chatter! Off you go! There's no time to waste!" His bellows echoed throughout the stone hall. Luna continued walking, smiling all the way. Eldred called out again, "Soon Eldred will be a distant memory! Soon there will be others to occupy your time!" Luna doubted she would ever forget the wise old man. "Remember Luna, the time has come to unweave and rethread! Ahead lies your tomb of awakening! The greatest of warriors accept everything and yet, accept nothing at all!" Chills traversed the Bastling's spine. She turned around to Eldred but the magician of the Selvz had disappeared. Once again she was alone, but this time it was not in a familiar world of Dreglings. It was a passageway that would lead to her destiny, if she was lucky.

Chapter 2

The First Step

Luna trekked along the empty corridor until she came to an opening with a path on either side. She stopped in her tracks. Unsure of which way to go, her knees began to quiver. As panic started to overtake her body, she remembered the map and flung the Bag of Borrowed off her shoulders. She pulled the map from her bag and lit the torch illuminating the scroll and her surroundings. Luna focused her attention on the map beneath her, not wanting to look ahead into the unknown. The lone Bastling's mind began spinning with all sorts of imaginings as she tried to stay focused on the map. Two paths lay on both sides of her each connecting to a set of stairs. The path to the left connected to yet another set of steps that led around the canyon oddly named the Stairs of Siloth. The set on the right led to a high cliff wall that showed no sign of further advancement. Luna picked up her belongings and methodically made her way to the long staircase to the left.

The stairs seemed to stretch forever, narrow and swirling. Her heart raced as doubts of her abilities plagued her. Reaching the first descent she saw that the staircase tunneled through rock to meet a small pond at the bottom. Luna sighed with relief and gazed at her map again finding the small blob of water, *Pond of Possibilities*. The pond was extremely small and even the weakest of aerialists could jump across to reach the greater Stairs of Siloth.

The slow and steady sound of dripping water reverberated against the walls. As Luna began to make her way, she quickly realized how narrow the steps were, leaving no place to rest along the way. It was a daunting task and tears began to well in her eyes. She had barely started the journey and was already giving up, "I don't know if I can do this." Her voice echoed eerily back. She was used to feeling alone but even the cruel Dreglings gave her some odd comfort of company. As her mind raced back to Elan and all that took place there, her mood resonated with a new determination, "I can't go back." Luna's feet carried her with renewed speed and she quickly reached the dark tunnel and hesitated only to wait for her eyes to adjust to the sudden change. As she traversed the channel her hand found rest on the smooth archway dipping down toward the pool. To her right was revealed what she could not see from her previous vantage point. The pool was engulfed in a foot-high rocky circle that divided it from the bigger waters of Bilogh. A gurgling echoed alongside the dribbling water. Luna stood perfectly still as her eyes darted to the right capturing nothing in their periphery. Everything remained mysteriously calm causing the tiny hairs on the back of her neck and arms to stand at attention. She quickly rubbed away the uneasiness from her arms bringing her focus back to the ledge, "Come on Luna, you can do this." She massaged her arm nervously again, "Even if you can't you have to try." She inched closer to the edge of the pool, checking each direction once more. The water was busy in the tiny pond but the Bilogh was eerily calm. Her eyes fell into the *Pond of Possibilities* catching her own reflection. She watched as it mimicked her every twitch with ripples of liquid. As she gazed into it, her face began to change shape and form. A flash of wings jumped out at her causing her to fall backwards. Her eyes darted upwards expecting to see a winged creature flying, only to find silence again. Rising, she carefully placed one foot in front of the other onto the ledge and cautiously stepped across. She spied movement darting in the corner of her eye and with one swift leap, Luna's body moved faster than her mind. Before she realized what she had done, her sleek frame was midair diving towards the first steps of Siloth. Crashing hard on the rocky surface of the stairs the little Bastling instinctively scrunched her eyes shut waiting for an attack that never came. Instead, it was her own anxious breathing that besieged her. She peered back at the spot she had just flown from and began laughing at herself as it echoed back, piercing the darkness and the waters below. Reclining back on the steps, the Bastling of Elan was quite pleased with herself.

After a few moments of basking, she eagerly hopped to her feet and turned once again to face the steep steps of Siloth. Gazing high above her head, the enormity of the task loomed, but with it a renewed sense of confidence. She chuckled as she initiated the ascent and the Waters of Bilogh began to stir.

As she methodically made her way up the steps they started to narrow even more and soon their width did not even hold hers. Turning sideways, Luna slid her way upwards, the Bag of Borrowed in front while she held her balance with her back to the walls. After an arduous uphill climb, Luna's journey brought her to the plateau at the top of the canyon that led to an old wooden door, illuminated with a scarlet hue.

The waters of Bilogh stirred and swirled in thousands of circles. From the plateau, Luna could hear the currents below and as she stared down into the watery depths, a swirling eddy of bubbles caught her sight. As steam rose from the surface of Bilogh, Luna darted for the door, ignorant of the boggy bubbles now making their way up the walls, dividing and becoming an army of millions.

Luna peered back at the precipice across from her. The entrance where she had stood when she first walked in, now sat quietly watching from across the way. The canyon wall below it was moving, the army of watery bubbles also moving precariously toward the top. Her eyes circled the entire canyon, the liquid army was coming up all around her.

Panic surged as she grabbed the old iron handle of the door, pushing the latch and throwing all her body weight into the task. Driving drops of water were now coming up over the top wall. She trembled as she tried pushing and pulling the door, searching for another latch or lock, but there was nothing. Her eyes scanned and rescanned the perimeter of the door for an answer when a minute hole peeked out at her, from directly underneath the handle. Encircling the tiny opening was an old script, barely legible, *What takes flight will come down, round and round, round and round.* Alarmed, Luna cried in despair as the water rushed the canyon walls. "A riddle?! I seriously don't have time for this!" The sound of the bubbles rang through the air, cascading into her ears. Desperation flooded her as she searched for what the rhyme could mean. Frantic, she stuck her hand in her bag to grab anything that could open the door. She opted to disregard the riddle for a moment, and attempt sheer force of will against the old door. Eldred's feather pen caught her grasp first. She sarcastically muttered the riddle under her breath, *What takes flight will come down, round and round, round and round.* Holding the pen up, its tiny translucent feather glistened like a beacon. "Of course!" She stuck the hollow tip into the hole and turned it four times. Just then the deadly droplets reached the plateau, rushing towards Luna. She backed up to the door as far as she could go. The ground beneath her began to shake violently. She watched the floor crack as the watery creatures were almost upon her. Her bag on the ground started slipping into a fissure. She quickly scooped it up, just in time to see the ground give way as the liquid creatures ran over them. The earth ripped open forming a vast hole, as the army of water bubbles sank to their demise. At that very same moment the door gave way taking Luna's balance with it. She fell backwards through the doorway and rolled away to freedom. The door immediately slammed shut behind her allowing no reentry. Her feather pen lay on the ground a few feet away. She slid herself up against the walls of safety. The hall was short and lit with a torch propped in the wall. At the opposite end of the hall was another door far different than the first. Emblazoned with gold and rubies, this entrance was more regal than its predecessor. Exhausted from her ordeal Luna slumped down, grateful to be alive. As she pulled out the map to check the next passage, she felt her eyelids flutter, and before long she was asleep.

Luna awoke to find the map still in her hand. Having lost track of time, she looked around confirming it was not a dream. Her eyes fell again to the map. The next spot was marked, *Halls of Redios*. Forcing herself back to the present, she got up brushing herself off. Fearful, but curious about what lay ahead, Luna crossed through the golden gateway and into the next world.

The hallway beyond the door was red brown in color, a nice change from the grave and sullen walls of Elan. There were speckles of ruby and garnet in the layers of the stone enclosure and a comforting heat arose from the surface of the crimson ground. Just ahead was another door that offered no hole or riddle. She cautiously pushed it open and walked through, stopping abruptly at the entrance of an old gray room. It was made entirely of slate with high ceilings. Dust lingered in the air like ghosts clinging to life. It also covered the floors like an old, musty blanket. It was obvious nobody had set foot in the room in a long great while. As the dust shifted beneath her, pictures were revealed on the floor, images of wise and majestic beings. They were undersized with short hair to match. Huge bellies protruded beneath robes of red. Flower wreaths adorned their temples, tiny jewels in each bloom. Above the sparkling cluster was a coiled snake appearing ready to strike. Luna thought it odd as the room was otherwise barren. What once had great life, now lay in dusty death. She walked across the room to a set of slate double doors.

Luna approached with caution, unsure of how to open the doors as they were as tall as the ceiling. Yet to her surprise they gently moved open as she pushed. When they opened completely, Luna could not believe her eyes. A room so strikingly beautiful she gasped. Made entirely of gold with ruby and garnet patterns embossing each section, this hall bore magnificent artistry. The high arched ceiling was laden in gold with garnet flowers delicately posed around the ceiling's perimeter. She marveled at what talented beings could have done this. Along each wall's bottom edge were plants, vines and flowers stretching the entire length of the wall. Luna had never witnessed such a stunning collection of gardens. "How beautiful they are," she whispered, fearful of waking them. In the center of the great gold room were pictures emblazoned on the floor just as in the previous room. This time they were uncovered and fresh. The scenes were far different than the first ones. These beings were happy and joyful in celebration. They all victoriously held a jewel in their hands high atop their heads.

While pondering these scenes, a noise caught Luna's attention from behind as she darted around to find nothing out of place. What she hadn't noticed was the vines from the garden inching ever so slowly from their place at the wall. They slinked their way over the garden and onto the floor. Luna moved towards the door at the other end of the room and turned to see vines all over the floor around her. They moved quicker as the Bastling ran to the doors. As she reached for the handle, the vines reached around her leg and pulled her down. She slid back from the golden doors. She kicked frantically, but the more she did, the more entangled she became. She reached for her bag as it slowly slid away from her. Again, and again she reached, each time more vines wrapped around her small stature. They were now at her throat, once, twice, three times around her neck. Luna gasped for air and with one last effort she reached out for her bag, breath no longer entering her lungs. She reached in and grabbed the knife Eldred had given her and stared cutting away. With one swoop, she put the knife under the ropey necklace and cut outwards, freeing her throat to breathe again. Quickly she cut at the vines that ensnared her feet and hands. They screeched and howled as they dropped, dying on the floor. She jumped up, grabbed her bag and raced for the door, fleeing the pile of vines that lay slumped beneath her. Luna glanced back to see more vines coming from the garden. Swiftly turning forward again, another set of vines caught her in the face, reaching out like wire hands to steal her breath. She thrashed furiously, killing them over and over. Each one fell to the floor screeching louder than the one before. On the doors were paintings of the same beings victorious in their delight of jewels. This time she noticed the dead and lifeless vines behind them in the background. Luna quickly turned around once more to see more vines slithering along the floor. Gazing at the dead ones, she got down on all fours and began scuffling through the leaves and plants. At last she found a solitary bulb on the end of a lifeless branch. She peeled back the layers of crisp, red petals. In the center was the most exquisite crimson jewel.

She carefully pulled it from its nest and held it up to the light. As she did, the vines began to screech and howl, the sound was deafening. Luna cupped her ears, never releasing the jewel. As her hands rose to her head, beautiful music emanated from the jewel, the most poignant she had ever heard. The vines fell quickly to their death. Satisfied, she rose and headed towards the door once more, this time jewel in hand. Luna looked up at the immortalized beings in the pictures knowing full well their conquest. She smiled and opened the doors.

Once on the other side she stood staring at another hall, "I am really getting sick of these rooms!" Pausing to see what else could be jumping out at her, she noticed that this next hall was different than the previous two. The only similarity was that they were dressed in garnets and rubies with gold inlay. There were no paintings, plants, and no markings. There was one unlit torch on the wall. Aside from the jewels, the room was dark and dreary. Luna wondered why such a pretty room would be so dimly lit. These three rooms were a mystery. At the far end of this one sat a ruby pulpit. A familiar heat washed over her as a movement caught her sight from behind the podium. Luna tightened her grip on her bag, ready to defend herself again, "Who's there? I can hear you! Step out where I can see you!" Luna surprised herself by her own bravery. Muffled sounds echoed through the room along with the sound of papers being flung.

A head popped out and back again from behind the pulpit. "Yes, yes! One moment! I'm in the middle of an out and out crisis! I cannot find my papers for the next meeting! I am giving a very important speech tomorrow and cannot find them anywhere!" Stepping from behind the pulpit was a woman. Stout, with a round faced and belly to match; short, messy silver cropped hair framed a sparkling set of mischievous eyes. Her features echoed those in the paintings of the previous halls. "Pleased to meet you, I am Notty from the Clan of Baze, at your service!" She smiled quickly sticking her hand out and retracting it back before Luna had a chance to shake it. "I'm not in the business of games, so what do you want? I'm awfully busy! I am indeed a busy Bazer. If I can be of assistance, make it quick…haven't got a lot of time."

Luna felt put on the spot. She fumbled for words, "Well, uh I um…"

Notty huffed, "Well get on with it, spit it out!"

Luna's sudden irritation flushed out the words, "I'm Luna of the Bastlings. I'm from Elan and on my way to Redios. I am on a journey to the Upper World." She felt satisfied with her answer.

Notty stood with arms crossed tapping her foot, "Upper World, eh? What reason are you going there?" She eyed Luna, sizing her up and down as the Bastling's shyness came back.

"Well, I'm not exactly sure. I mean I know why I'm going but I don't know what I will find there. I'm looking for some answers to very important questions." Notty started rocking back and forth on her feet.

"Oh? What kind of questions?"

Luna explained, "Questions about me, who I am, where all the Bastlings have gone to."

"Those my dear are the toughest ones of all. So, you're a Bastling, eh? I should have known by those pointy ears. And only a Bastling could have made it through those Gladarian vines, aside from a Bazer. Got yourself a stone from those vines, did ya? You know one of those stones contains a secret, but will only reveal it to its true owner." Notty went silent sizing her up and down again. She circled around her twice as if confirming her identity, "So a Bastling, eh? Well, why didn't you say so?"

Luna's head cocked to the side, "I did tell you, I told you…"

Notty slapped her leg, "Oh now, now, enough of this nonsense. I'm a very busy Bazer you know! Come, I'll take you through and you can stay the night with me and in the morning you'll be off." Away she toddled towards the door. The pudgy woman was quite speedy for toting so much weight.

With one swift movement from her short and stocky arms the door swung open. Wasting no time, they crossed through two more halls. Luna was almost running to keep up with her. "You seemed to do that quite easily."

Luna observed almost out of breath. "Do what?" Notty maintained her pace.

"The way you swung those doors open as if they were weightless."

Notty laughed, "Oh don't let the size fool ya' my dear, I'm a Bazer. It's one of our charms, strength that is, they say it's from a long line of Bazers having to quarry all the stones in our world. The whole of Redios is covered in it. Never used to have to quarry the way we do now, but since the Great Storm happened, we've been digging ever since. Generations of us have been doing it, twenty to be exact. I've moved quite a few stones in my day, you know. I'm a piece of me old man, I am!" She raced ahead never pausing once, but Luna was panting. "It was rumored that my old man could lift three times his weight in stone. And that was on a bad day!" Luna laughed at her rough and hurried mannerisms. "What are you laughing at?" Notty demanded keeping her eyes straight ahead.

The Bastling replied, "Oh I just think you're really funny, that's all."

Notty replied, "Fun! I don't have time for fun, I'm a very busy Bazer!" Luna reined in her laughter.

"What is it you do here in Redios, Notty?"

The Bazer sniffed a big breath of air making her chest bigger, "Why I'm the person in charge of making sure everyone is in order!" Notty flipped her finger in the air. "I make sure everyone has their sense about them." She pointed to her head and heart, "It's impossible to be good Bazers if we aren't coping well now, isn't it?"

"No, I suppose not," Luna stated agreeably, unsure of what she was in agreement about.

Notty detected Luna's uncertainty, "Look, it's like this. If you're going to be the best Bazer, you can't have all this emotional weight dragging you down. That's what I'm here for. I can listen to whatever is bothering them and guide them to the right answer." Notty was pleased with her statement.

"Oh, I understand! So you tell them how to deal with their problems the right way." Notty shook her head disagreeably.

"Heavens no! That's not what I do at all. How is anyone supposed to learn if the answers are given to them? No, no... what I do is simply give them a chance to see it for themselves. It's hard for some Bazers, being strong and all. Sometimes they have issues about that strength. Sometimes our gifts can be a burden as much as a blessing. So I just help them figure out what is gnawing at them, listen and wait for them to tell me their answer, you know, give them a chance to speak about it. They usually come to their own conclusions once they verbalize it." They arrived at another set of doors. Notty stopped and faced Luna, "Well, here we are! Welcome to the world of Redios!" and with that flung open the giant doors. Luna's mouth fell open. For miles in every direction there were huge towers, homes, and buildings of ruby and garnet, traversing the landscape as far as she could see. Everywhere, there were Bazers quarrying gemstones from the ground as Luna followed Notty down a smooth, garnet path that wound through the heartland of Redios.

Still racing, Notty stepped quickly into the throngs of Bazers that covered the streets of the heartland. Some were buying, some were selling, and others were trading in the streets. Notty carried on through the traffic, "This is where all the Bazers work in one way or another, it is the heart of Redios. Most Bazers live just outside the city, but some do stay here where they can be close to their work. Most get along, there's the odd scuffle, but nothing really comes of it as Bazers are content and dedicated to what they are doing. That's where I come in. I keep them grounded." Luna was tripping and getting caught up in the crowds shuffling by. Notty wasted no time, never pausing once. In the distance, there were two towers exceptionally taller than the rest.

She yelled to Notty, "What are those towers?" Notty was far ahead now, beyond the crowd.

"Come along, hurry up! No time for that, I'll explain later." Luna ran to catch up with her, still eyeing the red giants in the foreground. Their spiral staircases wrapped around them. At the top was a ring of rose colored stone that encircled the entire diameter of the towers themselves, with guards posted every so many feet. Luna felt as if in a dream. Nothing Eldred said could have prepared her for this.

She followed the Bazer up the path to her house, it was tiny and glistened with rubies that were set in the roof. The frame of the house was made of garnet.

"Wow Notty! This is the most incredible house I've ever seen!"

Notty scuffled to the door, "Oh never mind that, I have work to do!" Notty was almost panicked. The two rushed into the foyer to find a crowd of Bazers all talking quite disagreeably. All eyes turned Notty, paying no attention to Luna at all. They drew around the Bazer chattering away about things the Bastling could not decipher. It was impossible to follow one story or voice. Just as the pitch of the conversation was at its peak, Notty yelled at the top of her lungs,

"Alright everyone, calm down! I will get to all of you one at a time!" Notty was the one person Luna could hear perfectly well. "Luna, come with me." Notty beckoned with her hand as Luna started through the crowd of frustrated Bazers making her way to a door that read, *Calming Room.* Notty opened it and led Luna through to a much quieter place. It was immediately relaxing and Luna felt welcomed. "Now listen my child, I have many people to see today so I want you to relax, enjoy the music, think, sleep, and do whatever you like. If you're hungry there's plenty of food in the pantry. I'm sure you can find that. When I'm finished we'll have dinner and talk in greater length." Notty smiled and hurried out of the room. As the door opened Bazers began shouting upon seeing her return. The old Bazer started yelling once more, "Right then! I'll see Angorius first, the rest of you be patient!" The door slammed and Luna was left to focus on the quiet room. It was simply furnished, cream-colored walls, a few trinkets, pictures and candles, yet very comforting. There was an energy within the tiny walls that soothed. That same energy radiated from the stones of garnet and ruby that sat on the mantle above the fireplace. There was something else that occupied the stone shelf that Luna did not recognize. Two strings of metal were beautifully interwoven with a crimson filament that twirled in unison, appearing to be infinite. Soft music played as it turned on a golden case. It was so enchanting that Luna soon fell fast asleep.

Her Bastling spirit bounced off to another realm where dreams live and strange beings whispered at her. A woman in white appeared, her chestnut hair flowing in harmonious waves. She beckoned Luna and after a long pause she spoke, "What do you not see? What do you not know? Only in icy willowing shadows do lonely hearts grow." With another flash, she disappeared into a haze of white light with the sounds of wings fluttering, jolting Luna from her sleep. Sitting up, she pondered this woman in white and the riddle she posed. It was not the first time she had encountered this beautiful being. Luna didn't understand the dreams or the riddles, but they refused to leave her mind. The room was still quiet. Luna assumed she hadn't been asleep very long as she looked over again at the trinkets on the mantle.

Suddenly the door opened and Notty walked through to find Luna studying the musical instrument. "I see you are enjoying my harmonic. Yep! It was passed down to me by my grandfather, who acquired it from his, twenty to be exact, dating back to when the serpent first disappeared. It was created as a symbol of hope for the day when we would find her again, a day when she would return."

Luna turned to Notty, "The serpent?"

Notty responded longingly, "A long time ago Redios used to be quite different. We once worked with the serpent of fire, a wise and beautiful being who used to occupy and share Redios with us. As a matter of fact, its den was at the bottom of this world. It had a trail that wrapped around the outer edges of each of the Seven Lower Worlds that led all the way to the Grasslands of the Upper World. On the day of the Great Storm, she just disappeared. Nobody knows why, but because of this unfortunate event we Bazers got to work searching for her. We've quarried for twenty generations now to find her, but with no luck. We have our suspicions that the Braiggs have something to do with it, but we Bazers try to keep our distance from them. They're not too friendly. They live on the ice flats just outside of Redios before the Fire Mountains, but nobody ever goes there. It used to be the crossover point into Orangelis, the next world above here but since the Great Storm it has been covered in ice. Once we've quarried to the bottom of Redios and we cannot find the serpent, we will have no choice but to try and quarry through to the ice flats, but we are hoping it doesn't come to that."

The story gripped Luna. She too wanted to know what happened to the serpent. "So that's why the Bazers quarry stones all the time! Why would the serpent leave though? Especially after the Great Storm?"

Notty shook her head in despair, "I really don't know. Nobody does which has made our lives very hard, everything changed for us Bazers after that. You see, before we didn't have to do that, our sole purpose as Bazers was to help her. We kept her den opening clear from the jewels that would constantly grow and in return she let us keep the gems. I'm sure the other worlds have suffered from the loss of her as well. She gave each world an energy source that was unmatched by anything. Her life force fused with each world every time she moved around them. Now we dig in the hopes of finding her again, we haven't lost hope yet." The old Bazer's face went stern, but held sadness as she quickly changed the subject, "Well my work is done for the day! Another endeavor to save Redios from the very people who live in it! What a blast! Those Bazers will give you a headache if you are not careful! Full of spunk they are!" Luna laughed at Notty's words, she made her do that quite a bit even if she wasn't trying to. Notty spun around and headed for the kitchen, and yelled back to Luna, "Are you hungry? Did you find anything to eat while you were waiting?"

Following the plump Bazer, "No, I fell asleep and woke just before you came in but I am hungry, I must admit."

Notty had already reached the kitchen and was busily rummaging through the pantry for food, "Well I'm starving too after all that nattering today. Those Bazers do a lot of talking for having so little to worry about, you'd think they were being tortured the way they carry on!" Notty's hands were waving furiously in the air.

Luna chuckled, "Do you need any help Notty?"

The Bazer's arms stopped flailing, "No need my dear! I am fully capable of preparing it all, you just have a seat and talk to me while I get it ready." Luna plopped herself into the chair Notty was pointing to. The Bazer arranged her food on the counter and took out her knife, "So you're going to the Upper World to find out the answers, eh? Let me get this straight, you want to know who you are and why you are the only Bastling? Those are some big questions Luna. Are you sure you are ready for the answers? Once you pose questions like that, it changes everything, and once you move your feet in the direction of finding those answers things get really crazy. Look at how your life has already changed just from acting on it." She turned and smiled at Luna. The little Bastling hadn't considered that before but she agreed with the old Bazer, it had indeed turned her life upside down. "It's all right though Luna, that's what it's all about. There's no reason to exist at all if there isn't a purpose in your day. Do you have any idea of what your purpose might be?" Notty swirled around to face Luna.

"I believe I have a purpose like no other. Sounds pompous, doesn't it? I don't mean it that way but I just have this feeling that there is something I'm supposed to do that nobody else can. It speaks to me all the time, ever since I can remember but I can't make out the words. It's as if I hear it in whispers and I'm always leaning in for a better listen, but the wind takes it and it's gone until the next whisper. I feel it in me like a huge rush of water just about to overflow out of me but I am drowning in it and blinded by the current."

Notty cocked her head to one side. "Out of all the Bazers I have ever listened to and all the years I've been doing this work, I have never heard it put in such a way. Do you write Luna?"

The Bastling's face lit up, "Yes I do." Notty was impressed.

"The reason I ask is sometimes I tell my clients to try writing to better understand themselves. Do you find it helps?" Notty's demeanor, changed from gruff around the edges to a soft, mothering quality.

Luna answered happily, "Yes, I suppose it does. Sometimes I don't even know where it comes from, it seems to flow from another place outside of me and then through me." Luna smiled, softly feeling content and magical when she talked about this charm she had. Notty continued cooking the dinner.

"You should be very proud Luna, not everyone has this ability to express their heart in this way. Never let it go. Besides, scribes are some of the most important beings of any world, below or above. They have the ability to walk in two worlds:

this one and the world of Spirits." The old Bazer paused for a moment and gazed upwards, "How did you feel being in Elan?"

Luna didn't have to think about her answer, "Lonely, sad, like I never belonged there even though I know it was once where the Bastlings lived. Now there are just statues of them and rotten Dreglings."

The Bastling's head fell as Notty twitched her nose, "I know they definitely are a rotten bunch. It's too bad the Bastlings aren't there anymore but perhaps you will discover the answer to that one along the way or when you reach the Upper World." She continued on with her work cooking the food as Luna considered her words.

Soon the two were sitting at the table sharing the homemade meal. Notty studied Luna's face while she ate, "There is an innocence in you that I rarely see. You mustn't lose this and you must protect it at all costs. She is the magic within and also the most vulnerable to attack by others who do not have kindness as their goal." Notty's wisdom transported her. The Bazer's observations allowed Luna to see herself differently for the first time in her life.

Luna finished her dinner and shared something she never thought she would tell another soul, "You know Notty, I have had these strange dreams, they are so vivid and real. It is as if when I come out of them that these beings come through to this world." Notty listened intently as Luna explained the dreams, especially the last one.

Luna paused as Notty dropped her head to the side, "Luna I have never met someone such as yourself, a young soul to have so many spiritual conflicts, visions and questions, you are indeed special. I wonder after everything you've told me, if you are on quite a different journey than what you believe it to be. Make sure to stay open to all possibilities." Luna smiled.

"You know Notty, you just reminded me of Eldred when you said that, he gave me similar advice before I left him."

Notty slapped the table with her hand, "Well I can't believe it! After all these years that old bugger is still alive! How is he doing anyways?" Luna was shocked at Notty's revelation,

"You know Eldred?"

Her mouth gaped open as the Bazer continued, "Of course I know him, he and I go way back! How is he doing? Does he still live in that dingy old cave?" Notty slapped her thigh this time instead of the wooden table and Luna laughed knowing Notty was back to her old rough and tough self.

"Yes, he does, actually Eldred saved my life. He pulled me out of the Black Pool outside of Elan." The Bastling thought wistfully of her sage, old friend. Notty barreled over laughing.

"Yep, that sounds like Eldred all right!"

Luna questioned Notty again, "So how do you know Eldred?"

The old Bazer quickly changed the subject, "Well Luna we'd better be off to bed, it's going to be an early morning and a long day."

Luna watched as the Bazer tried to pry herself out of the chair, "Do you have another full day with the Bazers?" Luna asked innocently. Notty finally got her round belly out from under the table and stood up.

"Not only do I have all those Bazers to see, but I have to help you get out of Redios!"

Luna was surprised to hear her answer, "I don't expect you to do that, I have the map, and I'll be fine."

Notty scuffled off towards the hall, "Nonsense my dear, I'll show you to your bed and plop into mine. I will see you in the morning and we'll be off! I'll not hear another word about it! Goodnight!" Luna sat shaking her head at the table. She had a big spot in her heart already for the pushy Bazer. In the span of a day she quickly became like the mother and friend Luna never had. The little Bastling jumped up from the table and hurried after Notty down the hall as the Bazer came to an abrupt stop. She swung around, "This is your room for tonight! I will see you first thing in the morning." With that, the busy Bazer rushed off to her room down the hall and disappeared through its door. Luna fell into her bed welcoming rest once again. The little Bastling stirred before Notty, mostly due to the snoring sounds emanating from the Bazer's room. She decided not to wake her, but instead went to making her bed and double-checking her things. It didn't take long considering there was very little in her bag. Once finished, Luna brought it with her to the kitchen table and pulled out the map. It was a long time before Notty appeared in the doorway.

"Why didn't you wake me? I don't have time for sleep. I am a very busy Bazer and still have to see you off!"

Luna's eyes peeled away from the map, "I'm sorry Notty, I just thought you would like more time to sleep."

"Nonsense!" Notty snapped. She pulled the chair out, squeezing her belly between it and the table.

"What are you looking at?" Notty asked.

"I'm looking at the map Eldred gave me. It shows here the mountains just beyond the ice flats like you said. Are they called the Fire Mountains for obvious reasons?"

Notty began fidgeting in her chair, "Ahem, well they are indeed fire mountains. Very dangerous, very dangerous. I would recommend another way, but as you can see it's the only way into the next world." Luna peered again at the map. Notty was right, it was the only way into Orangelis.

Luna looked into Notty's face, as the old Bazer's eyes darted away nervously. Luna had yet to see this kind of reaction from this tough woman, "What is it you're not telling me Notty?"

"Hmm, oh nothing, I just get a little jumpy when I think about climbing all those mountains, very rough terrain you know. It takes talent, skill and agility to make your way through those narrow passages. Obviously, that is not a talent of a Bazer." Luna didn't trust the answer and knew there was more to it, but resigned herself to the fact that perhaps she was better off not knowing what made Notty so nervous.

Luna rolled up the map, tied it, and returned it to her bag. "So, we will be going through the *Door of Withou*, the company will be nice before we say goodbye."

Notty chimed, "Of course I said I would, just allow me to make some adjustments to my schedule before we leave. I have to cancel my speech for today. Better off, it needed work anyways!" Notty pried her plump body out and made her way to the room down the hall, "I'll meet you outside my dear!" Notty's voice echoed through the hallway to the kitchen. Luna shrugged and made her way to the front of the Bazer house. She opened the door to the noise of busy Bazers on their way to the mines. As they rushed past, they glanced long enough to recognize her, but not long enough to stop and chat. She hadn't been in Redios for more than a day but every Bazer knew who she was and where she was from although none spoke to her.

Notty stepped out behind Luna in her usual frenzy. As soon as the Bazers saw Notty, one by one they began to gather around her. "Alright, alright! Enough, I am very busy! I am assisting someone right now. This darling Bastling needs my help, the rest of you will just have to wait!" The Bazers assembled around them both, all chatting incessantly.

Notty began yelling at the top of her lungs. "Hold it! Hooold it! I am not available today, I am taking our friend out of the city to the Door of Withou." Gasps broke the babble which was followed by silence. It made Luna's heart skip a beat. Now she was truly scared.

In a matter of seconds her mind flooded with questions, "What are they so scared of? Isn't there any other way to Orangelis? What is so terrifying about the Door of Withou?

Notty saw the reaction in Luna's face. She turned to the Bastling, put her hands on her shoulders and spoke calmly, "Luna my dear, it's not as bad as it seems. I know you are scared and our reactions haven't helped. It is true there is no other way into the next world, however I trust Eldred implicitly and if he believed in you enough to send you on your own, then I believe you will be perfectly fine." Notty chuckled, throwing her hands in the air, "My dear there are many things you don't know! What is important is that you know you can do this! You must do this! This is your journey and however daunting it may seem at times this is what you must do to become whole and that is worth risking everything. If you are not whole and don't endeavor to be so, then there is no point in existing anyway." Notty's profound words flowed through Luna. She realized it as truth and calmed down considerably.

The rest all stood waiting for her answer, "Well then, I have no choice but to go through the Door of Withou and into the Ice Flats and Fire Mountains. But if I must go, you have to tell me all you know without holding back." Luna couldn't believe she had just said that. Another part of her lingered not wanting to know. It screamed at her. Luna brushed away the panic.

Notty cleared her throat and stepped back, "All right, it's a deal." Luna and the crowd of Bazers gathered even closer to hear every word. Notty wrapped her fingers around her suspenders as if about to deliver a great oration. "First we must take you to the Door of Withou. It isn't a far trek, but long enough. Once through the door, you will be standing on the Ice Flats. These flats are a long stretch and at the far end of them lie the foothills of the Fire Mountains. The Ice Flats are by far the most dangerous part of the journey. Once you make it to the foothills you must continue and never stop, it is imperative."

"Are you going to tell me why Notty?" The old Bazer looked around at the deeply concerned faces of her people.

With a nod to the others as if an agreement was between them, she answered Luna.

"I feel it is better to take it one step at a time. Once we get to the Ice Flats I will give you the rest of the details." Luna was satisfied with that answer. She had already come to know one thing about Notty, when she wanted to speak she would, and if she didn't there was good reason. She trusted the old Bazer. Luna stepped into the crowd pushing her way through. "Well if we are going to do this, we should go now before I lose my nerve." She was beginning to sound a lot like Notty.

The frumpy Bazer smiled and followed Luna through the crowd, "Coming through, coming through!! No time to dilly dally! We have a very important task at hand." The two began walking through the street of Redios. It was usually much busier, but since most had been standing at Notty's front door, there were no miners' tools clanking, no yelling from the shops. There was no rush of Bazers nearly running into each other through the garnet streets. Luna realized it wouldn't be Redios without all those crazy Bazers mixing up the place. The oddly paired explorers were chased by the entire flock of Bazers who had been on Notty's front steps. The old Bazer was first to notice, "What on earth! Where do think you're all going? Get back to work! You're all late!"

One of them stepped forward and spoke up on behalf of the group, "We'll not see our most esteemed Bazer go through the door alone. We're all going with you; no offense to you Luna."

The Bastling nodded, "None taken my good sir."

Notty's arms were folded in front of her. She scowled, "You are doing no such thing! I appreciate your loyal gesture to protect me, but I fear it is only for the enjoyment of driving me crazy!" Luna couldn't hold her laughter in. Soon they were all laughing. Notty stopped and throttled another command, "Alright, if you insist on going there is one rule. You do as I say without question!" She waited for their reply as they promised in unison and started walking towards their fate. Luna caught sight of the giant towers and their watchmen again.

"Are you going to tell me what those towers are now?"

Notty huffed, "Simple! They keep watch for the serpent and of course invaders. They are always on watch."

When they reached the Door of Withou, it was as Luna expected it would be, just as elaborate as the big doors that led into Redios. This set of doors were considerably thicker and larger. It would take the entire group to push it open. Luna was grateful they were all there to help. With all their Bazer might, they slowly pushed the doors open. From the other side, a wall of cold air hit them. They grumbled in unison. It was a sudden and unwelcome change. Stepping over the threshold first, Luna felt her feet pinching from the bite of cold that hissed at them. She looked out into the distance, the Ice Flats were just that, cold, white, and hard. Far off beyond the flats the Fire Mountains spewed red. Luna noticed something peculiar in the icy ground. Every so many feet there were huge holes burrowing down into the ice. Luna surmised at least five Bazers could fit into one hole. She turned around to the group, "Well I guess this is goodbye." The Bazers were all shivering but Notty.

"Well, I don't know about that, the more I look around the more I think we should walk you in a little further." Luna was surprised at Notty's assessment.

"No Notty, I don't want any trouble for any of you."

The old Bazer scoffed, "We Bazers know our limits. Besides, I think it would be a good test of our Bazer strength! What do you think fellas?" Notty turned to see them all quivering. She smiled, "Just as I thought, they're all in agreement with me." Luna's teeth chattered as she laughed.

"OK, we'd better be off then."

The frozen group walked reluctantly into the barren ice fields. It was cold, dismal, white and empty. There were rocks every so many feet and aside from their presence the flats seemed a lonely, lifeless place. Luna noticed a movement to her left. She thought her eyes were playing tricks on her. The others stopped, noticing it as well. Without thought, one of the Bazers walked towards it to get a better look. A frosty hand reached out and grabbed him. The huge rocks that sat in icy clumps began moving all around them.

Notty yelled, "Run!! It's the Braiggs!"

The little Bastling and the group of Bazers started to run, slipping and sliding with every step. One by one they were scooped up by the horrible ice creatures that had disguised themselves so well. Luna was the only one who remained free. She ran as fast as her feet would take her until she realized the Braiggs had given up on her and turned all their attention to their already captured prisoners. She could hear Notty yelling as they carried her away to their tunnels below, "Put me down you big block of ice!" Luna felt a furious determination to find her friends. She found another opening not too far away and jumped down. She wandered down one of the cave openings beneath the ice. Dark and cold, the caves gave way to the reality that the Bazers would not last long. She listened for the Braiggs, but her ears were met by an eerie silence.

Three tunnels over, the Bazers were being dragged to their jail chamber, most of them too frozen to yell or speak. Notty began kicking the Braigg that was carrying her, "Don't think old Notty is going down without a fight! I'm not going down as easy as the rest of them." The old Bazer lashed out furiously at the Braigg leaving her knuckles bruised and near bleeding. The Braigg let out a yell into her face letting her know of his displeasure with her. The ice surrounding them began to crack from the vibrations of his screams. The others commanded him to stop yelling in their frosty and indecipherable language. Notty was silenced but only for a moment, "Put me down you blockhead!"

Luna slid through the other tunnel, frantically searching for her friends. As she skated her way down, a dark object caught her attention. It was a piece of garnet sticking out of the ice above her head. Looking around, she reached for it to find it was stuck in the hardness of the ice, its beauty evident. Luna was mesmerized by its splendor. As her eyes continued upwards, she noticed more of the same, their dark, red eloquence peeking through the ice, shading the frozen water on top of them.

As the Braiggs threw the last Bazer into an icy cage, Notty's voice could be heard from the pile of round bellies, "You're not going to get away with this! You'll see, you thick-headed bricks of ice!" The angry frozen army walked away single file as if not hearing her threats at all, and headed to meet the others at the surface. As they made their way, they connected to another burrow, the tunnel Luna was in.

She continued to stare up at the vibrant red gemstones beneath the ice, wondering how far they went. She was excited and scared all at once. Suddenly, her feet were moving with a vibration. Luna thought it was the ice breaking from a quake, but then realized it was something far worse, the Braiggs. Panic gripped her as she darted from one side of the tunnel to the other, "Where can I go?"

The Braiggs approached the turn in the passageway where Luna had made her discovery. They stopped, putting their noses up in the air, smelling something that was not of their world; the little Bastling. They began roaring at the top of their lungs. Loud and boisterous, their cries carried for miles. It was painful to Luna's ears. They turned every which way, but the more they searched for her, up and down and all around, the more frustrated they became.

Luna shivered frantically within the walls of the passageway, hoping they would leave soon. Her shaking became violent and she wondered how she would light her torch, which would be her only chance of escaping from her hiding place. When she heard the Braiggs coming, she darted behind the curve of the wall. It was a corner that was only a couple of feet deep. Luna quickly realized it was far too shallow a hiding place, but since there was no place left to go she made it work to her advantage.

She grabbed her torch, lit it and brought it as close as she could without extinguishing the flame. She melted a spot just big enough for her to fit inside. By the time she squeezed herself in, the cold had frozen the puddle of water that pooled on the ground where she stood. She looked down, "There's no way those Braiggs could reach a thick hand around to reach me." There was certainly no way for them to even peek their block heads to see her poised inside. She hadn't however counted on them picking up her scent.

An eternity passed as she waited to see if they could find her hiding spot. The more she shook, the more frantic they seemed to become. With each shiver, a ripple of her scent went out. They moved closer to the area where they sensed her. They screamed out, indicating they were right beside Luna. She tried to still herself as much as she could but it was no use, the frigid temperature had taken control of her body. They sniffed, snarled - increasingly agitated. Suddenly a bellow came from a Braigg further down the passage, and he signaled for the rest to follow him to the surface. They stomped off leaving the icy corridor empty again. Luna waited another minute before attempting to make her way out. She knew it would be impossible for them to remain quiet if they were there.

When she finally released herself from her frozen hiding place with her torch, her mind went back to her imprisoned friends. Luna knew she had to act fast. There was no telling when the Braiggs would return for their jailed Bazers. Worse than that, if she didn't find them soon they would perish from the cold.

She made a sharp left and ran down the cold corridor, deeper into the Braigg's world and deeper into danger. She came to a fork that divided three paths, the one she was coming from and one to either side of her. Instinct made her follow the path to her left. She approached the intersection carefully, peering around the corner, and when it was clear, ran as fast as she could, trying not to slide. As she raced down the path a thought occurred to her, "What if they have a guard on them?" Luna pulled out her torch.

"Shut up and quit your bellowing! It's not going to help us and might agitate those blockheads! Besides it's irritating me more right now!" Luna smiled and almost screamed aloud, it was the feisty Bazer's voice. She wanted to run even faster but the slippery terrain wouldn't allow it. Besides, she needed to side with caution, thinking the Bazers might not be alone. She crept along the hall now. There was no real shadow in the icy world below, yet it gave off a strange glow. Not enough to alleviate her directional confusion, as it was hard to tell where tunnels were. A quick turn took her directly to where the Bazers were imprisoned. Luckily there was no Braiggs on guard for she would have run right into them.

Some of the Bazers looked shocked to see her and others were too frozen to give any expression except one of painful cold, but Notty didn't look shocked at all. She looked like she had been expecting the little Bastling.

"Let's get a move on my dear! This old Bazer is not going to meet her fate in an icy cell! Nope, I have a lot of business to take care of yet!"

Luna laughed heartily, so happy to see her plump friend alive and well. Luna quickly put the torch to the ice, melting the bars, "Hurry everyone it won't stay melted for very long." The Bazers tried to hurry despite their frostbite. Once they were all out, they stood shivering trying to shake off the cold. "Here's the situation Notty, behind us there are three tunnels. The one I just came from leads right up to the surface, but if we go down that path we stand the chance of running into the Braiggs again."

Notty looked up as if listening to voices from beyond, "Nope, there's no other way, we'll have to take a chance. We'll have you stay at the back Luna, if we are captured again, you'll have the best chance of getting us out." Luna felt sick at the thought of meeting the Braiggs again, but agreed with Notty's plan.

Luna and the group made their way back down the tunnel where she had been hiding. They did indeed find their way up to the surface with Notty leading the way. When they reached the opening, Notty put her hand up for everyone to stop. She announced to them she would go up first. When the old Bazer crawled up, a few Bazers tried to help her, "I need no help, I'm tougher than most of you!" Luna chuckled from behind. One by one they all reached the surface with Luna being the last to come up. They stood staring in every direction looking for Braiggs, but none were found. The only sight and sound was that of the Fire Mountains burning and spitting in the distance.

Luna hopped up next to Notty at the front of the group on a pile of rocks. She felt she had earned the right to be there next to the eccentric Bazer. Nobody protested, not even Notty. The Bazer spoke, "I think we should try and make it to the Fire Mountains." Luna looked at Notty then back to the mountains.

"Maybe you should all turn back and head for Redios, I'll go on ahead. I know I can outrun those frozen blobs." The rest of the Bazers mumbled in agreement with Luna.

Notty bounced around to face her, "I've heard enough! We decided to take you in a little further and that's what we intend to do. A Bazer never goes back on her word." Notty stuck her head up in defiance indicating her decision could not be swayed. The others rolled their eyes in hesitation. Luna knew as well as the others it was pointless to argue with the stubborn Bazer. She reluctantly conceded.

They moved along as fast as they could, hiding behind rocks that framed their path, hoping that none were a Braigg in disguise. Luna spoke to Notty who was of course at the front of the line, "I firmly believe if we can get close enough to the mountains we'll be safe from the Braiggs."

Notty kept on her course. "Those blockheads can't take the heat!"

Luna interrupted, "I agree that they wouldn't get close to the heat but if you all go with me to the Fire Mountains, how are you supposed to get back?"

Notty replied without hesitation, "I already thought of that my dear, that is why we need to figure out how to get rid of them for once and for all." Luna laughed out loud.

All the while they were being scented by their enemies. Before long the Braiggs were once again on the trail of the

Bazers and the lone Bastling. The Braiggs conversed back and forth as they followed the trail. They had just discovered the empty prison and were furious. The leader pointed straight ahead giving orders. The rest of the Braiggs peered towards the rebel group that was trying desperately not to be seen, but, it was too late. In unison, the Braiggs let out a battle cry and began running after the little ones. The ground beneath the Bazers and Luna began cracking. They had no need to look back as they knew who it was. Running as fast as they could with Luna in the lead, the Bazers desperately raced to reach the foothills of Fire Mountains. As the Braiggs gained distance on them, Luna picked up speed, "Hurry everyone! We can make it!" She heard screams coming from the Bazers behind her as one by one they were scooped up again. Roars of victory slashed from the Braiggs' hardened mouths as Luna stopped for a moment not knowing what to do.

She witnessed the last of them being picked up, her dear friend Notty screaming and kicking once again, "Luna! Go to the foothills! You'll be safe there. I know you'll figure a way to get us out, this time for good but you had better not be too long! You know how soft these Bazers are! No backbone!" With that, her captor covered Notty's mouth.

Luna shrieked back, "I swear to you I will come back for all of you!" The remaining Braiggs were gaining on her as she turned quickly and sped up, focusing her attention once again on the Fire Mountains. Luna put all her heart into her feet and raced faster than she had ever raced.

Hurdling the icy ditches and holes along the jagged path, Luna met with sudden warmth, greeting her like an old friend. "I'm close, I'm almost there." She muttered under her breath, barely audible through her panting. She finally hit solid rock on the path which gave way to more heat. "I made it." The Bastling slowed down and looked back to see the Braiggs stopped dead in their tracks. One Braigg could not halt in time and was instantly wiped from existence. Defeated, they roared in anger that echoed through the mountains as they turned to catch up to the others. Luna resolved to fulfill Notty's wish and stop them for good. She turned towards the spewing giants hovering over her on the dirt path, mesmerized by the enormity of the mountains and by her daunting task. Luna gazed around to scan for any more unexpected guests, yet there was nothing but the warm terrain and the tiny rivers of lava running through it. She hadn't a clue how she was going to save the Bazers, but her instinct told her the answer lay all around her. The closer Luna came to the foothills, the hotter it became. She found a place to sit on a small crimson boulder that gave her a view of the entire place. She let out an exasperated sigh. It was the first time she had rested since being in this strange land between lands. As Luna looked out she could see the Braiggs in the distance carrying the Bazers. She surmised they would be taken back to the original place they were held underground, and most certainly be guarded this time. She assumed they would wait for her to return, but she had no intention of doing that...yet.

She peered all around her at everything over and over, "How could this place be like this, frozen and fire all in one? How could two extremes exist in one place?" Luna scanned around hoping the land would reveal the answer. She spoke aloud to herself again, "Perhaps there is something we missed?" Yet the land offered only the same strange opposition as before and it puzzled her to no end. "What happened here?" Her thoughts wandered back to the red shadows beneath the ice ceilings in the passageway. "Maybe Notty didn't tell me everything, but why would she hide anything from me?" Luna jumped down and walked back to the path. She returned to the spot between fire and ice, between cold and heat. She stretched out one arm toward cold while the other hung in the warm air of the Fire Mountains and continued to wave her hands between the two climates. A tension fell between her fingers. It was faint, so light that she hadn't noticed it before. Scrutinizing her surroundings, she knew she was close to an answer. Her mind wandered back to Eldred and his words in the cave the night before she left, "The greatest of warriors accept everything and yet accept nothing at all." She carefully considered his words. She spoke aloud as if the old sage were standing with her, "I see half of this place cold and ice and in its opposite direction, heat and fire. Somewhere between these two there is one's beginning and another's end -- a common ground. And this spot would be a medium where the two exist as one." She stepped back and forth. "It is a place where the two exist equally not only sharing space but each other!" Luna brewed with confidence. She found that space between, the neutral ground and sat down within it. Her Bag of Borrowed fell off her shoulder and opened, spewing its contents on the ground. The stone from the Gladarian vines rolled out and hit her foot. Picking it up, she noticed colors within its compartment for the first time, a fiery red and an icy blue. In the very center of the stone was a marking. The same mark as on Luna's forehead. "Impossible, how could that be? Why did I not see this before?" Her mind raced back to her first conversation with Notty in the Great Hall, 'Got yourself a stone from the vines did ya? You know one of those stones contain a secret, but only reveals it to its true owner.' Luna's body felt a familiar quiver of confirmation, "Why is it showing me this?" She got up and instinctively walked through the narrow middle ground further down than she had before. She only had to walk a few more feet before discovering a perfect blue stone circle with a ruby flame carved into the center of lava rock, the very same as her Bastling birthmark, "There it is!" Luna ran back to grab her bag and returned to the circle and placed the stone within its diameter. "Nothing! Why isn't this working?" Her frustration rose, "This is useless! I'm wasting valuable time when I could be sneaking in to find the others." She looked up with slouched shoulders, not knowing what to do next.

At that very moment across the ice flats and beneath the layers, the Bazers were losing consciousness one by one. There were several Braiggs near the gate keeping watch. Even stubborn Notty was struggling to stay awake. The rest of the Braiggs had stayed above the surface to wait for Luna, time was running out for everyone.

As Luna walked away frustrated, she tried to put her mind back to the problem at hand, freeing her friends. She looked down in disappointment at the stone. It flickered with reds and blues. Even the marking glittered as if it were alive. Luna stopped abruptly, "Wait a minute! I've got it!" She swung back around and ran over to the circle. She towered over it placing her bag down again. The stone remained in her hand as she stepped into the circle. Taking a huge breath, she sat down and held the stone at eye level. Bright colors began swirling in a haze around the mark within the stone. A bolt of color shot out at Luna's mark on her forehead. It magnetized itself by her linking them together. Energy and colors of red and blue swirled out of the stone and surrounded her in the circle. In one clear swoop, the energy lashed out in every direction as far as the eye could see. Vibrations from the energy field shook within the fire and ice kingdom. The once narrow stretch of energy that lay between the two extremes expanded outwards, melting the icy terrain and reaching the Fire Mountains, snuffing out the blaze that frothed from the top. Within seconds the Braiggs were nothing more than a pile of water melted to the spots where each stood. As they perished, a roar could be heard throughout the land. The warmth reached the tunnels and caves where the Bazers lay nearly dead. The Braiggs that guarded them disappeared as their jail vanished. Notty was the first to wake from the rush of warmth that embraced them.

"What in the world?! What happened? Wake up you lot!" The old Bazer began smacking the others. They slowly began to regain consciousness as groans were replaced by gasps. Above them and all around them where the ice once lay, sparkled layers of giant rubies and garnets. They jumped to their feet and ran down the path in amazement. There was no end to the beauty of the red stones. They climbed out of the now crimson hole and onto the surface to see fields of rubies and garnets once more. Notty was the first to point out that the Fire Mountains were now inappropriately named. They were instead silent and dormant, but covered with the same beauty as the fields and burrows. The Bazers started down the path to find Luna. They found her at the foothills in the circle, unconscious. They carried her to an open space, her hand still clutching the stone that started it all.

The Bazers sat quietly until she awoke to their smiling faces. Luna smiled back weakly, "You're alive, all of you."

Notty pushed her chubby body a little closer, "Well my little Bastling, I knew you could do it! I had the utmost faith." Her finger went up in the air as always to emphasis her point. The old Bazer crossed her arms and pushed her nose up in extreme pride, "The prophecy came true after all!" Luna sat up bewildered. Notty smiled pleased with herself, "All those years ago when the serpent disappeared, the old grandfathers wrote down the prophecy and put it inside the harmonic I have sitting on my mantle. It states that three generations from his, a young one would come up from another world, a different being, not of our own race and would free the serpent from her prison." Luna and the rest listened intently. "When this one comes she would usher in a new time of prosperity and abundance for the Bazers. It looks to me as if that time has arrived." Notty stretched her arms out to the dazzling fields around them.

Suddenly a vibration from underneath them broke the trance. They shook uncontrollably as the ground gave way to the sound of a thousand rattles being shaken. In the far distant fields, a mound began to grow. The top of the mound erupted as a head rose, pushing its way to the surface. At once Notty and the Bazers began cheering, "It's her, she's alive! She has returned! The serpent is alive!" Luna watched in shock as the mighty and majestic serpent rose to her freedom, peering around at her fields of red gems and throwing her head back in victory. Her tongue spoke a language all its own as did her whole body, but the Bazers understood every word. Luna was being jostled by the whole group, grateful for her bravery. They hailed Luna as the prophecy come to life.

The snake peered around once more and went back into her den to begin her work again. Notty turned to the Bazers, "I need a moment here alone with our friend Luna. The rest of you go and tell the others of what happened here today! There is a great deal of work to be done!" Notty's happiness quickly turned to sternness. The Bazers said goodbye with handshakes and hugs for Luna. Notty waited until they ran off, "Now listen dear child, and make sure those pointy ears take in everything I say. You know that I believe in you. I know you are special and have charms to match. I don't know exactly what that entails and I know right now you don't know either. I have learned how powerful you are, surely you must see this too. I'm sure there are others like you out there somewhere." Luna listened to her words and wondered if she would ever meet the others. "Listen carefully little Bastling, you must take extreme precautions with an energy and gifts as powerful as yours. It can be used either way, for creation or destruction."

Notty went silent staring at her and Luna smiled, "Don't worry Notty, I won't do anything silly." Notty was afraid the Bastling didn't comprehend the severity of the warning. Luna's eyes began to swell with tears. Her heart filled with sadness. Notty had become like a mother to her literally overnight, something she never had. It was difficult to say goodbye. Luna gave Notty an endearing hug, "I'm going to miss you so much. I'm starting to feel that maybe I should stay here." Notty pulled away from the embrace and put her finger in Luna's face.

"Oh, no! You have a great responsibility ahead of you and I'm not going to be the old Bazer who stops that from happening! Besides I'm far too busy! I'm a very busy Bazer! Now we have to figure out how to help the serpent reach the other worlds again." Notty's boisterous voice was cracking and gave way to sobs. She grabbed her friend and hugged her tightly again, taking Luna's breath with it. The two cried and it was a long time before they released each other. Notty finally cleared her throat, "Well I must get back to those Bazers! They'd be lost without me, just useless without my guidance!" Notty's voice softened, "Thank you Luna for all you have done, it will never be forgotten."

Luna blinked away more tears, "Thank you Notty for all you have done. You have helped me so much and I will never forget you. You have a special place in my soul." Luna put her hand to her heart and picked up her bag. "How do I get out of here Notty?" The old Bazer explained the entrance to the next world was around the base of the extinguished Fire Mountains. Notty wiped her old Bazer eyes as she watched the Bastling walk toward the entrance to the next world of Orangelis.

Chapter 3

House of Changes (Morgan the Beautiful)

Luna crossed through the Fire Mountains and turned back to look for Notty, but couldn't see her anymore. Her dear friend had disappeared over what was once the Ice Flats. It was hard to believe that a few short hours ago the spot where she stood was filled with lava rock and fire. She reached for her map which showed the ascent into the next world. It appeared to be nothing more than a long upward reaching tunnel. "Well that seems straightforward, which means it's probably going to be really hard." Luna smirked at her own sarcasm. Feeling tired and still out of sorts she tried to push away her longing for Notty and plodded on.

As she approached the gateway to Orangelis, Luna noticed dark vines curled around the frame. They were not of the Gladarian type. The door itself was light in color, lighter than those of Redios with their grandeur and ornate decorations. Instead, this one was light and billowy. The crescent-shaped door handle turned with ease and in a moment, Luna was transported to the other side. There was a distinct difference in the atmosphere, a hazy warmth hung in the air, like soft pillows against the skin. The corridor's long and sleek walls were made of pale white moonstone whose incandescence shimmered with blues, greens, and pinks, a delight to the eyes. Luna's hands followed along its path until it came to its end. Luna studied the tiny opening and peeked through to the other side, "Another tunnel made of moonstone, I might as well give it a try." The Bastling pushed against the miniscule opening. She tried putting her arm through to find a latch or handle on the other side but found nothing. She pushed again and again to no avail. Panic set in. Despite her doubts she attempted one more time, which only served to add to her frustration.

As Luna stubbornly refused to give up, eyes fell upon her. "Oh no," she muttered under her breath. Gulping down the fear, she turned to face what was behind her and was shocked to find nothing. The feeling of being watched persisted and a movement caught her eyes as she swiveled her head sideways to catch a glimpse of her observers. Within the moonstone walls, along both sides, rose beautiful beings in white flowing gowns who were waving slowly to her. Their big brown eyes were kind, although their faces held no smiles. Each one a replica of the other, their looks penetrating, but calm. "There must be hundreds of them," Luna mumbled in disbelief. In unison, they raised their hands and remained poised until the closest one to Luna smiled and motioned to the tiny entrance. Luna looked at the gate and then to the silent guardians. She stepped back with her shoulders pressed hard on the gate, nothing. The mysterious woman motioned again while the others remained with hands in the air. Luna fought to understand what she was saying, mesmerized by her methodical movements. She realized she had seen them before. This was the woman in white from her recurring dream. The ones floating before her now were smaller versions of this elusive other-worldly woman. Luna leaned on the opening still holding the edge, but crashed to the floor with a hard thud. The gate had opened wide. She tried to hurry to her feet but before she could, it closed on its own. "I get it! I've been pushing too hard." Sweet laughter was coming from within the walls. Luna felt embarrassed, but determined. She approached the door with gentle kindness this time and simply touched the opening, circling her hand around it. With ease it opened, allowing her full passage. Luna reached into her bag to grab her map satisfied with her accomplishment, but was interrupted by the sweet laughter once again. They were on the other side with her following in the walls, pointing downwards to the end of the next tunnel. Luna followed without question as they floated and guided her all the way down to the end. She reached it only to find a solid wall made of the same moonstone. Luna threw her hands up in the air, stamping her foot, "Oh no! There's nothing here!" She wanted to be angry at the spirits in the wall but when she turned to them they were smiling so gently and calmly she couldn't be. Once again in unison they began shaking their heads. "Well if I went the right way, where is the door?" She waited for a reply from her ghostly helpers. They pointed to the wall. Completely frustrated, Luna bellowed, "There's nothing here! There's no door, no opening, nothing!" They continued to smile and point in the same direction. Luna stood with shoulders hunched, defeated by her lack of understanding as she walked up to wall and pushed with all her might. Grabbing her arm and rubbing it she backed away from the wall, "Forget it, I don't understand what you're saying!" I'm going back out to look for another passage!" Waving their hands slowly back and forth and passing it through the other they smiled at her. Luna's face began to change from anger to understanding. "Right! I think I get it. If I don't do this right, don't laugh." Luna stepped back, focused and began breathing deep. She slowly walked towards the moonstone barricade. Closing her eyes and keeping a gentle pace she simply walked right through the wall. Coming out on the other side she opened her eyes with astonishment. "I did it! That was amazing!" She turned back to smile at her ghostly helpers but they were gone and she was left standing on the periphery of Orangelis.

Luna stood on the threshold of another world, the second realm above Elan. She looked down at her feet and the path that lay beneath them that rounded off to her right. Her eyes followed it around and behind a beautiful dark forest. It disappeared for a moment and then peeked out to her left, meeting up at the spot where she stood. It was a dark world shrouded in mystery, yet the dimness was not scary, it lent to the beauty of the light of fireflies that danced above the trees. She didn't look at her map. Luna knew the only way must be through the enchanting forest. She stepped across the path and into the great unknown of the woods, veiled by a low hum that was strangely soothing. In the distance, Luna could see a fountain and in every direction from within the center rose a bloom of brilliant colors. Orbs of pinks, reds, oranges, and yellows flowered, lifting high for a moment then falling back into the base of the fountain. The fireflies dove up and down and all around her as she walked.

Luna reached the fountain and stopped to rest, watching the spectacular light show. Sitting down, she peered into the water at the base of the fountain to see her own reflection. She smiled and laughed, it had been a long time since she felt good about herself. Luna liked who was gazing back at her and was proud of herself for having made it this far. Without warning her reflection disappeared. The light emptied and darkness intruded. In an instant, beams of light shot out from the center of the fountain. Streams of fireflies and butterflies followed with a great burst of flight and then she appeared. Rising from the center, it was the one being Luna had always wanted to meet, the woman in white. There she stood, no longer a fragment of a dream, but alive and tangible. Dressed all in white just as Luna recalled in her visions, her dark hair flowed endlessly and her sparkling russet eyes stared into Luna's soul. A moonstone crescent jewel sat proudly on her forehead, contrasting the stark amber stones that hung from her belt in the middle of her waist.

"I am Morgan the Beautiful, Enchantress of Orangelis. You must be Luna." She smiled warmly. Luna was shocked that Morgan knew who she was.

"How do you know me?" Luna asked, flattered.

"I know all who enter my kingdom." Luna watched Morgan admiringly. She was so confident it emanated from every part of her. "Luna, we are all more confident in our own kingdoms." She seemed hauntingly familiar not just from her dreams but as if she had known her, her whole life. "You are passing through Orangelis to go through to the next world. This I know, I have been waiting for you. I have tried to reach you many times in your world, hoping you would heed the call. It has taken longer than hoped, but nonetheless you are here." She waited for Luna's reply but the Bastling was taken aback by her words.

"Why were you trying to reach me? Why did you want me to leave Elan?"

Morgan chuckled at her naivety, "To come and do your work of course. Why else would I beckon you?" Luna was more confused than ever.

"I'm afraid I don't understand. What work are you referring to?"

The beautiful woman's face was empathetic, "Are you still that far from yourself that you don't know who you are?"

"That's one of the reasons I took this journey, to find out more about myself, my destiny, who I am. It is also why I am here in Orangelis, to pass through to the next world until I reach the Upper World."

Morgan's expression washed over with a melancholy smile, "Unfortunately, anyone who passes through this world has only one way out and that will bring you to the House of Changes. Have you ever heard of this house?" Luna thought perhaps her map listed it, but she hadn't bothered to look at it since entering the tunnels of Orangelis.

"No, I'm afraid I haven't. Is it very far from here? This doesn't seem to be a very large world so I assume it cannot be too far." Luna glanced around as if she might have missed it on her walk in.

"No, this world is not very big. However, many great things are often contained in small spaces, don't you agree?" Morgan's face was calm and pleasant. She didn't wait for Luna to answer, "Walk with me a while Luna. It will do your soul good to be here. It is a place of magic and reenergizing power. I wish I could share this world with more beings, but we are what we are. Most will never set foot in here despite its beauty. For some kinds of magic are too powerful, it is a universal energy gathered in a confined small place. Let's just say it is a very charming place." Morgan's words penetrated Luna's soul, confirming it as truth.

"This House of Changes, is it the only way through to Yellao?"

Morgan smiled, "Yes. You must pass through the house to leave my kingdom. It has been done this way since the beginning of time, and I suspect it will never change." As they walked under the Water Drop Trees Luna felt the enchantment of Orangelis, the dark mysterious beauty, and its peacefulness. Morgan reached up and touched a branch of one of the trees, causing it to rain as it sang, "So tell me Luna, what is it that you are looking for that would make you risk everything to find it?"

"I am searching for who I am, what my purpose is." Luna watched the captivating woman for a reaction.

"So, you are searching for your true heart." Morgan stared straight ahead, "Once we find our truth we must live in it, and it will never let you forget once it makes itself known to you. In order to live in the truth, one must first be baptized by fire. It is a power unto itself, and the only way to find this power is to journey within, through all the pain and joy of it, through all the darkness and light." Her words flew into Luna's soul and fluttered down softly to rest.

"I have always wondered how I lost it, my truth that is, or if I ever had it at all, and how to get it back."

Luna looked up to Morgan who was peering into the distance, "It was never lost, only sleeping." Luna was comforted by her words. "There is a stillness that can only be seen by the truest of hearts and it leads us to where we are from, where we are now and where we must go. You cannot afford to lose another moment in the wilderness of the world without yourself. Time waits for none of us. It is a strange thing, time. It brings everything, and yet is far too impatient. It passes, leaving only footprints. You cannot afford to linger any longer, it simply will not wait." The two stopped at the end of the path and Morgan turned to face her, "My dear, you are at the crossroads of your destiny and although you may not realize this, it is as true as you and I stand here now." She put her hand in Luna's, "You can search for the truth in all things around you but in the end, you will be lost and barren. You must never forsake yourself. The truth is always within, it never strays from you. It is only a matter of knowing how to listen to the voice inside." Morgan raised her hands to the tree and parted the branches revealing a white mansion hidden behind them. "That is the House of Changes where you must cross through to leave this world." Morgan looked deeply into Luna's eyes, "Remember all the answers lie within." She watched as the house breathed with life. "Yes, this is a world within a world." Luna's attention was broken by her words. The beautiful woman in white smiled gently, "This is as far as I go with you for now, but know I will always be with you and I will see you again. I am so pleased you have finally reached this sacred world. We have all waited a great long while for this moment. For in uncovering and facing our truth we not only help ourselves but help others as well." The enchantress put her arms out to Luna and held her close, "I am always with you." Her whispered words echoed through the trees as she disappeared from Luna.

The little Bastling stood grasping the air, confused and wanting to say more to the ghostly woman, "Morgan! Morgan, where are you? I have so much more to ask you!" The only answer came from the Wonderlings giggling in the treetops above. Luna bent the branches back as Morgan had done to look at the house again. "She's gone, disappeared just as she always did in my dreams." Luna started off towards the house, uneasy about what awaited.

Stepping into the foyer, its quiet walls seemed ordinary. She opened a door that led to the rest of the floor. Stepping inside, buzzing and flittering fireflies bombarded her. There were hundreds, perhaps thousands of them endlessly flying in random patterns around her head, revealing a fury of beauty.

"Whoa! Come here you!" A young girl bounced into the room where Luna stood surprised. "I've been trying to catch them for the longest time! I will one day though, I've almost figured out their pattern of flight!" The young maiden jumped furiously up and down grabbing at the tiny lights racing through the air. Luna studied the girl as her long chestnut hair bounced along. She was the picture of perfection. Her eyes sparkled with lights that equaled the ones she was chasing.

"Hello there, why are you trying to figure out their flight?" Luna waited for the maiden to answer.

"Well, I might as well! There's nothing else to do today!" The maiden screeched with childlike laughter. Luna became frustrated waiting for the maiden to stop jumping about.

"I wonder if I could get your help for a moment. I need to find my way to the back door. If you could just point me in that direction, I would appreciate it."

The maiden stopped abruptly, "You can't just leave here." She seemed offended that Luna would ask such a question.

"Well how can I get out then?" Luna stood in panic and confusion. The maiden walked over to Luna and became quite serious.

"You have to clear that with the queen and believe me she's tough, she won't let you get away that easy." The maiden rolled her eyes in sarcasm. Luna wasn't sure how much she liked this maiden but tried not to judge her.

"Well, where can I find this queen?"

The girl smiled coyly, "It's Queen Mader and she's on the second floor." The maiden pointed up behind her to the staircase. Luna glanced up around the corner into the next room. It was a huge spiral staircase made of glass that danced with color. "What is your name by the way?" the maiden queried.

"I'm Luna of the Bastlings."

The maiden showed a devious grin. "I'm Megden and by the way I'm not going up there with you. I've had enough of talking to her today!" The young maiden's rebellion took Luna aback.

"Well that's fine, you don't have to go with me. I can find it by myself." Luna's tone was just as biting as Megden's. Luna had already made up her mind to go, she had had enough of the company of the sarcastic, spoiled girl, "I'll see you later." The maiden began jumping up and down attempting to capture the poor fireflies, having already forgotten about her guest. Luna made her way over to the stairs and began the ascent to meet the queen.

Once atop the grand staircase, Luna navigated left. The blood red carpet was extremely thick and plush. The walls were adorned with pictures of regal, proud and majestic women, previous queens who had once ruled in this magical place. Luna's thoughts ran back to the maiden downstairs, "Why did she seem so bitter and resentful about this particular queen?" She looked back to the gallery of ancestral rulers. Their faces were strong and noble, their eyes revealing a gentle compassion. Luna caught a glimpse of light flowing out like water from an ocean beneath the door ahead. Luna knew this must be the queen's room. She entered the room quietly for fear of disturbing her, "Hello, are you there?" Luna's voice matched her soft walk.

"Come in." Luna opened the door and stepped slowly unsure of what she might meet with. "Luna, welcome to our House of Changes, I presume you've met Megden?"

Luna answered, "Yes I have, although I wasn't sure how to take her."

The queen laughed softly, "Megden is a sweet girl but she has a great deal to learn about becoming queen. It is a responsibility not to be taken lightly." Luna was surprised and her reaction showed in her face. "Oh, I see, she did not tell you she is the heir to the throne. Yes, one day this House of Changes and the kingdom will be under her rule, although I fear it may take longer than previous maidens. She is stubborn and refuses to grow up." Queen Mader shook her head in disgust. Luna chuckled to herself. She had only very recently become acquainted with the young maiden and could already understand the queen's frustration. Luna quickly regained her composure.

"Queen Mader, I know it must be difficult for you right now and I do sympathize with your plight, but I came up here to ask a favor of you. I wonder if you could point me in the direction of the door so I may pass through to leave."

The queen laughed heartily, "My dear, there is no way out of the House of Changes until a new queen is crowned and a new orb placed upon the Scepter. Only then will the door open long enough to allow you to exit."

Luna's heart sank straight down to the floor, "Are you sure? Perhaps there is another way, something I can do to allow me to go?" Luna's voice cracked with emotion.

The queen became very serious, "As a matter of fact there is something you can do for me. You can help Megden understand what it is she needs to do to become queen." Luna's shoulders took the weight of the disappointment.

"I don't know the first thing about this house and what becoming queen entails. What could I possibly offer that stubborn girl downstairs?" Luna wanted to walk out of the room that instant and make the girl downstairs understand the situation even if she had to shake it out of her.

The queen understood her frustration, "Luna, I have given Megden a riddle. Perhaps you could help her solve it, although the true work must come from Megden herself or it will be fruitless and she will remain a maiden." To herself, "A riddle? Are you serious, a riddle?" Luna turned and started walking out the door when the queen spoke once more, "Luna I feel you should know something else. I am the queen but there is also an old queen on the third floor, now holding the title of crone. She has long passed her throne to me and waits patiently for me to take her place once again, this time as crone. For that is the way it has always been since time began. The crone waits for her time to end here and make the crossover to the other side. Each one of us has our roles and responsibilities and when we reach the chair of the crone it is our final step before leaving here. She is old and tired, but cannot go until the maiden fulfills her destiny and takes my seat."

Luna melted with compassion for this old crone and was now facing the queen again in the threshold of the door, "Well, since the only way for me to leave is to have the doorway opened, I really have no choice but to help Megden. Although I doubt it will be any small feat if our meeting was any indication of her character."

"I must tell you, there is something very similar about you and Megden."

Luna didn't want to hear that, "With all due respect your majesty I fear you are dead wrong on this one." The queen was still laughing as Luna made her way back down the hallway to the spiral stairs and back downstairs.

Luna dropped her bag on the floor, causing Megden to stop jumping for a moment.

"So, did you have a nice visit with the queen?"

Luna noted her sarcasm, "In fact, I did. She has requested my help. She wants me to help you solve a riddle. Then I will be able to cross over out of this weird house." Luna's voice was full of disappointment.

"Do you want to hear it?" Megden queried. "The riddle the queen gave me?" Luna nodded and stepped closer. "Alright, but I have to go get it from my room, come on," Megden beckoned Luna with a hand to follow. The two walked into the next room as Megden made her way over to a door that was attached to the far end of the room. Megden turned the knob slightly then paused, "This is why I don't want to be queen. I have far too much fun here." With that she threw open the door. Luna gasped. A garden, the most splendid one she had ever seen. A grassy carpet of emerald greens, flowers sprouting forth from it in the most wondrous explosion of color, and a twisting, rolling tree that stood in the very center of it all begging to be played on. Ivy rose in every direction and climbed along the cobblestone walls of the magical compound. Stardust sprinkled as tiny fairy bees busily whorled fulfilling their duty as keepers of the grounds. Luna understood why she didn't want to grow up, her playground was paradise. She also realized the duty Queen Mader had given to her was far greater than initially imagined. How could she ever convince this maiden to leave here? She watched as Megden chased the fairy bees, screeching with delight, "Come on, this is fun!" Luna forgot her mission and ran over to the tree and climbed onto its inviting limbs. She perched herself at a high vantage point to see everything in the garden, it was awe-inspiring. Luna laid back against the mighty limb and closed her eyes as Megden ran crazily chasing the light spawning bees. Luna had almost fallen asleep when Megden's voice brought her back to consciousness again, "So do you want me to tell you the riddle now?" She was staring up at Luna from the ground as flowers fell all around the child from the blooms of the tree. Her youthful beauty radiated from under the cover of petals.

"Sure, let's hear it." Luna poised herself in anticipation.

"Three contained in three, absorbed into one, what am I?"

Luna was stumped, "That's it? There's nothing else to it?"

Megden laughed and began swirling round and round, "That's it, I haven't given it too much thought but when I have I come up with nothing!" With a carefree burst of laughter, she ran over behind the flowering bushes. Luna jumped down and ran to find her. When she caught up with her, Megden was sitting by the side of the pond.

"I didn't see this here when I was in the tree."

"It wasn't there when you were in the tree, I just made it now." Luna stood confused.

Megden saw the bewilderment and explained, "I can make this garden however I want every day, every minute. All I have to do is think of what I want and it appears." She smiled proudly at her creation.

"That's incredible! Luna exclaimed, "Can anyone do it or just you?"

Megden was quite adamant, "Oh no, only I can create in here, because it is my garden. It belongs only to me."

Her answer gave Luna an idea, "Tell me the riddle again."

Megden rolled her eyes and reluctantly and began to say the words: "Three contained in three absorbed into one, what am I?"

Luna's eyes widened with understanding, "How many of you are there in this house?"

Megden gave the answer without hesitation, "Me, the queen and the crone." They both jumped up and down and Luna started pacing back and forth mumbling under her breath. Megden waited for her response.

"I need to go see the queen again."

Megden became frustrated, "Why can't you tell me? Tell me the answer!"

"I don't have the answer yet, I just think I'm on to something, but I have to ask the queen." Luna walked to the door and turned back to Megden, "Do you want to come with me?"

Megden huffed, "No I'll just stay here and wait." Luna chuckled at her stubbornness. Reaching the top of the spiral staircase once again, Luna pondered the riddle. Her thoughts came back around to her journey. It had been a long one already and she wasn't even halfway there. It was a daunting task, one she wasn't sure she could accomplish, but despite her self-doubt, Luna proceeded down the hall to see the queen once again.

As she approached the doorway the familiar voice carried through the air, "Come in Luna, I had a feeling you would be back soon." Luna peeked around the door to see the queen sitting on her throne once again.

She waved her in and Luna followed her hand, "I wanted to ask you about the riddle. The first part states, "Three contained in three," this represents the three of you that reside in this house, does it not?"

The queen tilted her head and smiled, "Luna I am impressed that you could come up with an answer this fast. Do you have the entire riddle solved?"

The queen fidgeted in her chair as Luna took notice of her discomfort, "No My Queen, I do not. I only came to ask you some more questions. The first line is all we have worked on."

"Well I cannot tell you if you're right unless the whole question is solved."

Luna smiled knowing more than she revealed, "I see, well that's fine. I will have it done before too long. Tell me, do you fear leaving the throne?"

The queen lashed out, "How dare you ask me such a question!"

Luna retorted, "It is not out of disrespect that I ask, however it did cross my mind that perhaps Megden's immaturity has been a good excuse for you not to step down. Perhaps you lack the faith in her that she needs in order for her to be ready to take your place."

The queen was furious, "You pretend to know anything about me or my kingdom?! I am greatly insulted!"

Luna pressed on, "Tell me Queen Mader, do you have a garden room?"

The woman's eyes softened, "A garden room, yes, I do. Why do you ask?"

"Well I was just admiring Megden's downstairs and I thought perhaps you had one as well, and if you did then I assumed it would be much grander than hers," Luna smiled and let her eyes do the pleading.

The queen looked over to her left where a door stood waiting to be opened, "Come, I will show it to you." Luna and Queen Mader walked slowly to the golden door whose center carried a moonstone oval jewel with a crescent shape on either side. Thousands of butterflies came fluttering around their heads as they entered the royal garden. The queen's grass was not only the same emerald green as Megden's, but it glowed from underneath. Sounds that Luna had never heard before seemed to be coming from the velvety lawn. Flowers bloomed in every corner. A mixture of tangerine, yellows, and blood reds infused the mass display of plants. There were several trees, the largest was in the center. There was a lake behind stone seats that stretched as far as the eye could see. Birds happily played above while fish frolicked in the waters below. The butterflies danced joyfully as new ones were being born every few seconds in the trees above.

Luna turned to the queen, "What is that sound I hear?" The Bastling looked around for its source.

"That sound is life Luna. All around it is growing, expanding, and living. All things are connected and alive, therefore all things have the song of life within them. Most cannot hear this song. It is comparable to a blindness, just because someone cannot see you, does not mean you do not exist." Luna was stunned once again, not only by the queen's wisdom, but the beauty that surrounded them. She admired the queen and her soft, female features. In her eyes shone her insight framed by tiny lines that showed years of experience. Amidst the lines a young girl smiled back at her.

"I wonder Queen Mader, how I will be able to help Megden. She doesn't seem to have any interest whatsoever in being queen."

The queen strolled under the trees that danced with life, "I suppose we all were like that at one time."

Luna questioned her, "Who is we?"

Queen Mader laughed, "Well, the crone and I weren't always this age you know. We two were once like Megden, although I believe she is a fair bit more stubborn than we were. Then again, perhaps I am just forgetful in my years now."

Luna looked over the water's surface where brightly colored fish jumped in their watery playground. "Would I be able to go speak with the crone?"

Queen Mader turned to Luna abruptly, "Of course you may, but I am not sure how much information you will get from her. She is old, and wishes for the most part to be left alone."

Luna had already resigned herself to seeing the old woman, even before the queen had finished talking. "Well that's it then, I'll go see her now. Perhaps she can shed some light on this problem for me." Luna smiled at the queen waiting for her response.

"I wish you all the luck in your trip upstairs Luna, but I will not be surprised if you leave empty handed." Luna made her way back to the door with Queen Mader following behind.

As they exited, Luna looked back one more time at the luscious gardens, "It really is a beautiful place, Queen Mader."

The regal woman closed the door behind her and took her place on the throne, "I will be expecting to see you when you are finished." Her face reverted to its original sternness.

Luna walked into the hallway, "I will definitely tell you of my meeting when I am done. Which way is it to the crone?"

With an unyielding profile, "Left down the hall, up the next flight of stairs, first door on your right."

Luna smiled, "Thank you and I will see you soon, wish me luck." As the queen sat staring after her visitor, her face revealed her sadness.

When Luna reached the top of the stairs, there was no denying she was no longer in the presence of the queen's domain. This level of the house was entirely different, it seemed more lifeless at first glance. There was a dim light that penetrated every corner creating a still and calm atmosphere. She found the door and stood before it, natural wood with an elegant crescent moon. She rapped lightly and the door creaked opened. Luna stepped inside to see a barren room, no throne, no gardens, just four walls. She made her way to another adjoining door and knocked gently.

A voice met Luna, "Come in, child." It opened, revealing an old woman sitting comfortably in a huge throne. It was weathered and worn to match the woman's complexion. She was tiny and frail, but her eyes glistened with youth. She forced a smile and shifted in her chair, "I've been waiting for you, I knew you would come."

Luna wasn't surprised, "It seems everyone is expecting me. How did you know I was coming?"

The old woman laughed, taking a great deal of energy out of her, "Oh, you'd be surprised at what I know."

Luna got straight to the problem at hand, "Well I need to find a way out of here, but apparently the only way I can is to help the maiden downstairs solve her riddle." Luna waited for an answer but instead the crone's cackling laughter rippled through the air. Luna didn't find anything funny, "I was just wondering if you could help me. I'm sorry I didn't get your name."

The crone stopped laughing abruptly, "Oh my name is Morel, Crone of the House of Changes. I have been here for many years now, waiting to leave, but unfortunately neither one of my consorts seem to be able to reach into themselves to let me go. They are both stubborn. They use their energy in all the wrong ways." The old woman began coughing and waved her hand as if to scoff. Luna felt sorry for her. "Don't feel sorry for me dear, feel for those two and yourself. Your leaving depends on them and I fear you may be waiting a long while."

Disappointed by her words, Luna said, "Well that's why I came to see you, I thought perhaps you might be able to shed some light." The old woman quieted and listened to Luna. "You see, I understand what the three are, it's the three of you, but as for the rest of it well, even if I got it I need Megden to as well."

Morel laughed, "Megden is just a younger version of Queen Mader, the answer lies with her. If she would just help the young maiden, we would all be freed."

Luna thought back to when she spoke with the queen and how uncomfortable she looked. "What if I brought the queen here to speak with you? Would you let me do that?" Luna hoped the answer would satisfy her.

The old crone sat up, "Yes, I would like that very much. I have a great deal to tell her. Nobody ever comes to see me you know." She leaned in to whisper to Luna, "It's because they're afraid of me. They see my wrinkled skin, my gray hair, my frail body, and know that I am a reflection of what they will be one day. No beautiful woman wants to look at that, or face it, but it is inevitable, every one of them will be a crone one day."

Luna, flooded with compassion, "Do you like being where you are? As crone that is?" Morel beckoned Luna to come closer and sit on her velvet stool. The Bastling obliged and sat poised, ready to take in all her words.

"Being a crone, an old woman has more advantages than disadvantages. I look into the mirror and see so many years of life on my face, yet my eyes and heart are still those of a young maiden. If I were to fall in love, I would feel it just as strongly if not more as a young girl does for the first time. I have learned many lessons over time and look back at years gone by and see so much of what I could have been, I see what tomorrow can still bring." She smiled and a light glowed all around her.

Luna spoke softly, "Are you afraid to die?"

Morel began to chuckle and sighed, "Ah my dear, I have died a thousand deaths already. That is the circle of life. It is nothing more than birth and death contained in one big circle we loop through. Each time we change and grow, we gain insight into ourselves and others, we die and are born again. There is never an end, only beginnings. I don't fear death or leaving this mortal body, it is only a vehicle, a shell to bring us around the circle. There will be a new birth of some sort just as soon as I die in this one." She pointed to herself and her body. Luna felt as if she were sitting with the wisest of all women. Morel looked intensely into her eyes, "What is your circle Luna? Where are you from, and where are you going?"

She wasn't expecting those questions but thought about it, she wanted to be very clear to the old woman as a sign of respect, "I have come from loneliness and a solitary life in many ways. Yet as I make my way, I find I am learning so much more of what is inside me. I find I have strengths I never dreamed I had. I am seeing myself in a different light." She was honored to be in the presence of this woman, soon to be stardust.

"That is the only way of gaining insight and wisdom in any world you live in, we must experience things, all things, as much as we can. We will fumble, fall, make decisions that aren't always the best for us, and some choices we make will be absolute and right, but we cannot know that unless we take the risk. Life comes out fine in the end if we let it. We mustn't try to stubbornly push things, we must let it flow all the while standing strong in the light of that which we truly are. That is the most difficult part of the journey, but worth every second of it. So, you see Luna, those two beneath me are simply doing what I say we mustn't, they are fighting their own death. They must accept it, claim it, for it is theirs and theirs alone, and how much can we say that about things in this world or any other for that matter? How much are things really our own?" The old woman clenched her fist. Luna admired her, wanting to possess her same wisdom. The old crone smiled and put her hand on Luna's head, "You do have it my dear. It has been inside you all along, you must simply listen to this," she pointed to Luna's heart. "The key to everything lies there little Bastling. Now, go do what you must and listen to the wisdom of your heart as you do it." She sat back slumped and exhausted from her talk.

Luna got up to leave, "Thank you for sharing all you have with me Morel, I will never forget what I learned today."

The old woman smiled weakly, "That is the wisest thing you have said." Morel laid her head back, chuckled and closed her eyes. Luna walked out, feeling changed for good.

She walked back to the queen's room and stopped to look in at her as she sat doing needlework on her throne. Luna came right out and ask her the question, "Queen Mader, may I have another moment of your time?

The regal woman looked nervously at Luna. "Yes, what is it? I am very busy though I must tell you."

"Well I would really like you to come and visit the crone and to be honest, she would like it as well. It is an open invitation from her and I am the messenger." Luna smiled freely knowing she had cornered the queen.

"What does she want to see me about?"

Luna smiled nervously, "Well she said she wants to share some things with you in light of the situation at hand." Luna waited for the queen's reply.

"I don't see how I could possibly help. There's nothing any of us can do until Megden solves the riddle. That is the way it has always been done. It's not going to change now." Her look was commanding yet fear was etched beneath the queen's facade.

Luna waited for the queen to get up from her throne but she didn't. Luna prodded, "Well we had better be off now, the crone doesn't look well and her frailty may cause her to never say what she intends, we should go." Luna motioned to help her up.

The queen stood haughtily and brushed down her dress, "I am fine, I need no assistance getting to my feet." She threw her head to the air in defiance. It was then that Luna realized the crone was right, Queen Mader and Megden were similar in their stubbornness.

She followed behind Luna, back up the stairs and to the room where the crone sat waiting. The moment they entered a voice came through the room, "Come in Mader, I've been waiting for you. I am glad to see you have done as I requested." Her voice was weak but her spirit was strong.

Luna hesitated at the doorway, "Perhaps I will just wait out here in this room. This is probably a private conversation."

The queen agreed, but before she could confirm, Morel bellowed, "No Luna! You must join us! This has to do with you and besides, I need a witness in case the queen decides to have selective hearing." The queen looked offended and surprised that the crone would belittle her in front of their guest. Luna brushed it off so as not to make the queen feel any worse than she already did and stepped forward. There the crone sat just as Luna had left her, weak and slumped in the chair. She coughed and gasped for breath, "Come, come and sit down here close to me." She looked up at Luna, "Be a dear and bring that other chair closer so you can sit too." Luna obliged. Both the queen and Luna sat down and waited for the crone to speak, "Mader, you have not come to see me in a long while, and I know why. You fear what I have to say, you fear me, the way I am."

Fidgeting in her chair and clearing her throat, "I beg your pardon dear Morel but I am not afraid of you. I have great respect for you. I am not afraid."

The old woman began cackling again, "Oh you always did try to put on an aloof air, but you cannot fool me." Morel shook her finger at the queen. "The reason you fear me is because I am what you will become. I am what you are destined to be and for that you fear me." The crone's laughter faded and her wrinkled face softened in pity for the queen, "It isn't as terrible as it seems my dear. Life has a way of comforting us at any stage of life. It cradles us and we come to accept it in time. We mustn't fight these things, we are all destined for change and growth, that is inevitable. I remember when you became queen, you were young and beautiful, full of life and so naive in the ways of responsibilities. You didn't always want to become queen, remember?"

She smiled at Mader and it was returned with a fond chuckle, "Yes I know, I do recall feeling very scared and unsure of myself. I didn't know if I could enter the role of queen and follow in your gracious footsteps." The queen looked away, "Such a foolish young maiden I was."

Morel cocked her head to the side, "And here you sit with me, a beautiful charming and respected queen for many years now, and you are faced again with having to change, grow and move on to the next responsibility, the next stage. I see here before me an older version of the scared maiden you once were." The queen began to cry, her head falling forward, it was as if they no longer remembered Luna was in the room.

The queen spoke through her sobs as she clutched her handkerchief, "I am afraid, but I don't want to hurt your feelings. I have been feeling this way for some time now and I just didn't know how to tell you. It is my vanity I suppose, my ego. I fear that I have been of no assistance to Megden in her ascension to the throne. Every time I speak with her it fills me with fear and I find my frustration outweighs my wisdom." Mader was crying full force now as the old crone's face washed with compassion.

She leaned forward, patting the queen's arm, "There now, it's all right Mader. Now that you have faced your fear, you'll be a great help to Megden. What you must remember is your own ascension to the throne, the fear of the unknown. Being crone is the same as being queen in many respects, but better. You will have days of not knowing if the decisions you make are the best but life always helps you along the way, guides you in the right destination. The wrinkles, and feeble body come in the end, it is a gradual decline, but not a decline into death alone, it is a transition to a higher place, a new life. There is nothing to fear about this stage of the process. Like the queen, it is filled with wisdom and laughter. There is no shame in being old, there is great pride in it. Growing to my age has its own beauty. I am a living reflection of all who have passed before me, I am a testament to life itself. Look at me Mader, look into these old eyes of mine." The queen and Luna both leaned forward to peer at the face of this wise old woman, "Tell me what you see?" As the two drew closer they were pulled to the old woman's eyes. Swirling amidst the wrinkles, they were set in youth, vitality, a young girl's thoughts dancing, a world all unto itself, a world where light met darkness and all things were revealed. Luna and the queen were speechless. They leaned back slowly, stirred by what those eyes revealed. Crone Morel chuckled, "You both looked so shocked! It's great, isn't it? I've been waiting so long to put that look on your face! Oh, ha, it's priceless!" She was slapping her own knee now as Queen Mader sat looking on, stunned by it all. Luna watched as the old woman continued laughing and soon she couldn't help but catch the feverish laughter. The queen sat dumbfounded for some time and then she too was swept up in the frenzy of giggles.

After they had all calmed Luna posed a question, "So what's next, what do we do?"

The crone slumped back down, "I think that will be up to the queen." She smiled and gave her a wink.

The queen put her hand over Morel's, "Thank you so very much my dear, sweet Morel. I know exactly what I must do now." She patted her hand and embraced her. Both she and Luna stood up to leave.

Luna hugged her as well, "Thank you for all your help."

The old woman tapped Luna's heart as they broke away from each other, "Don't forget, that is where your wisdom lies." Luna promised she would always remember her words.

The queen, now poised at the doorway, "Crone Morel, if I do not see you again, have a wonderful time on your new journey." She smiled a warm, loving smile.

The crone waved and smiled back, "I will my dear, and one day I will see you again."

Luna and the queen made their way back down the stairs. The sovereign broke the sounds of their footsteps, "Well Luna, I must make a special trip to see Megden now. It is long overdue," she said, her head held high. Luna followed Mader to the lower level where they both looked for Megden, who was nowhere to be found. They knew at once she was in her garden. The queen confidently opened the door to the garden room, where she saw Megden sitting under the tree being rained on by falling blossom petals. Looking up to the petals as they cascaded around her, Megden appeared to be in deep thought. Luna followed quickly behind the queen, "Megden I see you are enjoying another rainfall of flowers." Queen Mader smiled generously as Megden looked over, shocked to see the queen in her domain.

She jumped to her feet nervously, "What are you doing here? You never come in here." Megden looked at Luna suspiciously.

"Don't worry Megden, Luna did the right thing. She has taken me to, well let's just say a new level of understanding. May I sit down?"

"Sure, if you want." Megden was barely able to speak.

The queen sat down gracefully under the blossom tree and let the petals shower her face. She looked over at Megden and smiled, "See? I can still do it too."

She began laughing and Megden was suddenly eager to sit with her. "I didn't know you could do that!"

The queen looked over to Megden, "Well there are many things you don't know about me." She began to laugh again and motioned to Luna, "Come Luna and sit with us, we'll show you how queens make it rain flowers." Luna willingly sat down with the present and future rulers of the House of Changes; it was a remarkable sight. Queen Mader laughed as she looked up at the tree. It began to grow and twist, causing the branches to touch the water of the pond. Luna and Megden marveled at her talents. She looked to Megden once again, "You know when I was your age I was terrified of becoming queen, I used to get a queasy stomach just thinking about it."

The young maiden's eyes grew wide, "You did? Honest and truly?" She could hardly believe what she was hearing.

The ruler continued, "Yes, and for a long time I fought against the old queen, I tried everything in my power to defy her wishes. I simply didn't want to grow up. Then one day I realized something, I had to grow up. There were those around me who needed me. As we both know, there are more than the three of us in this world. There are other races that look to us for guidance. That is a very great responsibility, but a great honor indeed." Megden was listening for the first time. Luna noticed she wasn't sarcastic or uneasy, even the fireflies fluttering around Megden's head did not hold her interest.

She was glued to the queen's words. "Tell me what it was like when you were crowned queen." Megden rested her chin on her hands in anticipation of the answer.

"That day was glorious, but I was so nervous that I felt like my crown was slipping off my head which made me drop my scepter!" The two started laughing together sharing a moment that only they truly understood. It was at that point Luna felt as if she shouldn't be there.

Megden asked the queen, "When you sat on throne for the first time, did you feel like a queen immediately?"

Mader thought about the maiden's question for a moment, "No, not right away. It takes time to feel comfortable in a new role. No, it was quite a while before I felt like a queen, but I remember the exact moment when I did." The queen reflected for a moment, catching a spiraling petal in her hand, "It was a moment when I realized I could laugh and still be the girl I was, and that all those experiences would help me be a better queen as well, but I could make firm decisions from a place of strength and my truest, noblest self. It was an inspiring moment." The queen and the maiden smiled at each other.

"Do you think I will be a good queen?" Megden's face was genuine with concern.

The queen smiled and caressed Megden's hair back from her face, "Yes, I believe you will make a wonderful queen for Orangelis, a dignified and wise one." The young girl blushed with embarrassment and pride. The queen rose to her feet, "Now Megden, it is time for you to complete the riddle so we can all make our transitions. Will you do that for me, for all of us?"

"Yes, I will My Queen," Megden smiled softly and stood with the monarch. "Luna, I expect you will continue to help us in this beautiful House of Changes, so we may live up to the name."

Luna beamed, "I certainly will." The queen said her farewells, and quietly closed the door. Luna turned to Megden, "Well, we better get started. Why don't we have a seat in your tree for some inspiration?" Megden raced to the tree and began climbing, "Sounds good to me!" Luna scurried up the trunk behind her.

The two sat in silence for a long time, when Luna decided it was time to hash it out. "How about we throw some ideas back and forth?"

Megden agreed, "So far all we have is the first part, representing the three of us in the house, I go blank after that. I feel so frustrated!" The maiden slunk down and back against the limb.

"Let's look at it this way, you know that the three are you, the queen, and the crone, right?"

"Yes, but what are they contained in that's also three?"

Luna looked around, "Well, let's think about it." Just then a butterfly glided down in the tree on a branch below the two. They watched as it flaunted and spread its wings in even motion, up and down.

Megden smiled, "I love the purple ones the best."

"Yeah, they sure are pretty, aren't they?"

Megden peered at Luna through the bright tree colors, "Did you know that butterflies will migrate for hundreds of miles, even without knowing their parents? Only instinctively understanding the way they must go." Luna watched it closer and closer as Megden sat mesmerized. She noticed a caterpillar weaving its cocoon on the branch above.

Luna sat up straight, "Megden what is that?" She pointed to the caterpillar slowly weaving its cocoon on the branch.

"Oh, that's what a butterfly looks like before it has wings. The caterpillar spins a cocoon for itself, and sits within it and emerges as a butterfly." Luna was enamored by this creature. As she stared at the caterpillar and then to the butterfly, another movement caught her attention.

"Megden what is that?" Luna pointed to another branch where a tiny creature was eating leaves.

Megden rolled her eyes, "Well that's a larva, it's the initial stage of a butterfly, you know, before the caterpillar becomes what it is." Luna stared again at all of them as something began to occur to her. Megden sat poised looking at Luna's smiling face, suddenly the maiden understood what had not been said, "Of course! Luna that's it, isn't it?"

Luna clapped her hands, "Yes that's right!"

Megden jumped up to the next branch and crouched, "I've got it! The three contained in three are maiden, queen and crone contained in the three stages of womanhood! Yes, that's it!" The two jumped down and began dancing around in a circle.

Falling to the ground, Luna was near breathless from the celebration, "So now we have one last part. Yes, no doubt it will be the hardest of them all. Alright Megden, let's hear it again."

Megden gathered her breath, "Three contained in three absorbed into one." Megden looked hopefully at the Bastling.

Luna pondered it over and over in her head, "Hmm, that's a tough one, I just don't know. Maybe we should just clear our heads for a while and come back to it."

Megden agreed. They lay in companionable silence watching the colorful show before them, the fireflies, butterflies, and flowering petals. All was silent except for the sounds of creation in the garden. "So, Luna, where are you going after here anyways? Better yet, where did you come from?"

Luna smiled and repositioned her hands behind her head, "Well I'm from Elan and I'm on my way to the Upper world."

Megden continued her questioning, "How far is Elan from here?"

"It's two worlds away, the very deepest of all of them. I just came from Redios."

Megden sat up on her arm and side, "What was Redios like?"

Warmth shot through Luna, "It was beautiful and magical."

"Was it more beautiful than here?"

"Well so far I think each place has its own beauty, so you can't really compare." Luna felt very satisfied with her answer.

Megden sighed, "Yes I suppose you're right. What do you think you'll find there in the Upper World?"

Luna watched as the butterflies gracefully filled the air above her head, "Well I hope to find the answers I've been looking for my whole life, at the top of the tree that is."

Megden got excited, "What do you think the other worlds will be like?"

Luna laughed, "Let's put it this way, I hope there are no more riddles!" They laughed together at Luna's sarcasm.

"I think it's really neat you are doing this Luna, all those worlds and adventures!" Megden gazed wistfully into the tree.

"It's not as great as it seems, it's pretty scary at times, especially when you're by yourself."

Megden looked back at Luna, "I'll be here my whole life, and I'll never see other worlds."

Luna sat up and faced Megden, "Even though you'll never go there, you are still part of them and they are a part of you. You and these other realms make up what is called the Lower Worlds, and because we have met I will always remember you, therefore when I make it to the Upper World, in a way you will be there too."

Megden perked up, "What did you just say?" Her face was full of anticipation.

"I said even though you don't go there, you are still a part of everything."

Megden bounced to her feet and jumped up and down excitedly. "That's it Luna! You're a genius!"

Luna was trying to figure out where the maiden was going with all this, "What do you mean?"

Megden paced back and forth grabbing her hair, "We have to go tell the queen. I can't believe we got it!"

Luna stood up, "No, as far as I can tell you got it, whatever it is!"

Megden grabbed Luna by the shoulders, "Three contained in three Luna! Absorbed into one! Maiden, queen and crone contained in the three stages of womanhood, absorbed into everything, the universe, all of life!" Luna stood stunned trying to analyze the riddle Megden had just solved. "When the crone dies she is absorbed back into everything, life itself!"

Luna knew in that instant the maiden was right. "Congratulations Megden, you got it!" The two joyfully pranced in a circle again.

Megden was the first to halt the dance, "We better go tell Queen Mader the good news."

Luna followed Megden up the stairs to the second floor. When they reached the threshold of the queen's door, Luna thought it best if she waited there. Megden agreed and walked in to Mader's room. Luna watched as the queen sat silently listening to Megden's explanation of the riddle. When she finished the queen nodded in approval, and Luna felt very happy, not just because it meant she would soon be free to go, but because her new friends had been victorious.

The queen beckoned Luna inside, "My dear Luna, Megden has solved the riddle and now we will prepare for her crowning. I will notify the crone. I am sure she will be pleased. In three days the ceremony will take place, and during that time

I would be very grateful if you could assist the maiden in her preparations."

Luna smiled and bowed, "It would be my honor."

The queen's voice became a little weak, "Then it's settled, we shall begin immediately." She rose and went to her garden door, "I have much to prepare for as well." She smiled and disappeared.

Luna spent the next couple of days helping Megden get ready for her crowning. They spent most of their time in the garden room downstairs creating and gathering flowers that would be made into the maiden's coronation dress. It was the custom in Orangelis for the new queen to make her own dress, a symbol of her new creative authority in the House of Changes. Tiny birds helped as well, weaving threads and bouquets together. It was a light and joyous time, and soon the entire world of Orangelis buzzed with anticipation. The Wonderlings, the ghostly women and Morgan herself had preparations to do. Crone Morel had been notified by the queen and was grateful her time in the House of Changes was soon to be over. She was tired and sat quietly with eyes closed awaiting the coronation. The queen spent most of her time in meditation within the walls of her garden room. Morel summoned Queen Mader one last time on the eve of the coronation for a private conversation.

The following day Luna stood in the middle room of the main floor waiting for Megden to emerge from her garden room. She watched as the firefly orbs flitted around in anticipation. The door opened and the maiden stepped out into the light of the room. She was a vision, beaming with youth and vitality.

"Oh Megden, you are so beautiful," Luna exclaimed as her flowering gown and long train flowed across the room. As Megden walked, the flower petals opened and closed. The fireflies buzzed around the maiden's head, no longer afraid of her childish behavior. Luna fell into place behind her lifting the train to assist her up the stairs, "Are you ready Megden?" The anxious Bastling tilted her head to the side to catch Megden's expression.

"Yes, I'm ready Luna. Thank you for all your help. I couldn't have done this without you."

Luna blushed, "Oh Megden I really didn't do anything. You already had the riddle solved inside yourself, you just needed a nudge to remember what you already knew."

The two friends smiled knowingly at each other, "I will never forget you Luna of the Bastlings."

Luna nodded in agreement, "As I will never forget you." They continued their ascent to the throne room. There was an undeniable vibration of change in the house that day.

When they reached Queen Mader's room, she stood in full regal dress, glowing with an eternal wisdom and confident vitality. "Megden, you look radiant."

The maiden bowed, "Thank you My Queen, as do you." The two embraced for the first time since Luna had been in their kingdom.

Mader turned to Luna, "I must thank you on behalf of all of us in Orangelis as well as the future rulers to come."

Her garden room door swung open as Morgan the Beautiful entered and embraced Luna tightly, "I am so happy to see you again. I knew somehow the magic of who you are would inevitably bring us to this moment." Tears were in Luna's eyes as she longed to stay with Morgan in Orangelis. The breathtaking woman spoke, "I told you we would see each other again and so we will yet another time. Know this, I am always with you regardless of where you are and I will be watching over you." She gently wiped Luna's tears from her face.

Morgan stepped back allowing the queen to speak, "Once the ceremony begins you must be ready to cross through with the crone." Luna's heart fell in disappointment as she had hoped to see her friends make the transitions. Queen Mader sensed her dashed hopes, "Don't worry Luna, you will know the exact moment Megden receives her crown and scepter."

"I wish I could see it but I understand."

"Speaking of which, I must inspect the royal treasures before we begin the ceremony," said Queen Mader. Picking up the scepter she stopped, "Oh no, this can't be!" She turned to the group with shock.

"What's wrong?" asked Megden.

The queen's voice was quivered, "This has never happened, the orb is cracked, we cannot have the ceremony without it."

Morgan stepped forward with a smile, "I told you this Bastling came for a reason aside from her own. I am quite sure she has an answer for us."

They all stood staring at Luna, "Who me? I don't know the first thing about royal scepters! What could I possibly do?"

Morgan continued to grin, "Perhaps you have something in that bag of yours."

Luna was about to deny it when her time with Eldred came back, "Hold on, I think I just might. She reached into her bag and pulled out the orb he had given to her, "This orb will only work for you when set in the right place!" She laughed as she imitated her old friend. Luna handed it over to the queen who quickly changed it out with the damaged orb. As she placed it gently within its resting place sparks gently ripped around it and down the staff.

All of them smiled. "Why on earth would you have that?" Queen Mader asked the Bastling.

Luna shrugged, "I guess Eldred knew before we did." They all laughed as she turned to Megden, "Well I guess this is it, time to say goodbye."

The two stared into each other's teary faces as the queen gently interrupted their difficult farewell, "Come on, let's not make this harder than it needs to be, focus on the task at hand."

The soon-to-be crone gently choked back her own tears as Luna made her way back to the doorway, "Good luck with the new position Megden, and you as well My Queen, as the wisest of all in Orangelis."

Luna reached the third floor where Morel sat waiting. Luna knocked gently and entered, "Are you ready Morel?"

The old woman grinned, "Oh yes, I've been ready for quite some time. Thank you, Luna, and never forget what I told you."

The old woman used Luna's body for leverage to pull herself to her feet as Luna assisted, "I won't, I promise."

Morel stood straight, "Now, when I tell you to go, do it quickly. There is only a fraction of a moment in which you can leave." Luna nodded nervously.

In the throne room, the queen and maiden stood face to face, "Well my child, shall we begin?" Megden agreed quietly. Queen Mader lifted the crown and music began to fill the kingdom.

Luna looked up and around as the old crone whispered feebly, "It has begun." Mader walked over to Megden and placed the crown on her head as fireflies began flying frantically in every direction. The glorious fountain near the entrance churned and bubbled as the trees of the forest began a hypnotic dance.

As the two women stood in the throne room each of their gardens began to fade, "The crown you will wear as a symbol of your sovereignty in the kingdom and world of Orangelis." Megden's head rose in pride. The entire world clapped with thunder as Luna shook from the energy all around her. Morel hung onto the Bastling even tighter as she was losing strength rapidly.

Queen Mader then took hold of the scepter, "A symbol not only of your power as a fair and just queen, but also your part in the great cycle of womanhood. May you always hold it with gentle strength." Mader placed it in the hand of the new queen as Megden nodded and turned to take her place on the new throne.

As she stood before the grand chair she turned to Mader, "I will always do my best to be fair, gentle and strong. My only hope is that I will be half the ruler you have been." As Queen

Megden took her seat, the entire world of Orangelis began to shake. The new queen's scepter glistened as the glowing orb emerged, a beautiful moonstone with a crescent moon of silver on each side. As the glow radiance from the scepter grew steady and strong, a million sparks of light flew in every direction. They travelled at the speed of light throughout every space within the walls of the house and made their way downstairs to where the firefly orbs were, and began giving chase.

Megden watched the fantastical light show as the old queen began to make way up the stairs to the third floor. The crone began to shake uncontrollably as Luna tried to hold her steady. Lights began to shudder from the heart of the old woman as Luna stared in disbelief.

Downstairs, the sparks continued their pursuit of the firefly orbs as rays of never ending lights spewed forth from the fountain. Morgan the Beautiful raised her arms high above her head, "Let the new cycle begin!" In that instant, all things ceased movement creating an aura of anticipation. A spark of light suddenly continued its course catching a firefly orb as the two merged. Form took hold and the new maiden stood in the lower level of the house that once belonged to Megden. Spotting the door to the old garden room, she excitedly ran over and threw open the door. Sizing up her new playground she squealed with delight and ran inside.

Crone Mader bowed to her predecessor as the lights flashed in an orchestra of color. Morel staggered back from Luna's clutches, her entire body now engulfed in the light of change that opened as a gateway, "Go Luna, go now!" The terrified

Bastling shook her head and looked to the new crone who nodded in agreement. Luna ran, diving into the light-filled exit hoping it wasn't a mistake. As she approached, the light caught her and pulled her forcefully towards it and what was left of Morel. Luna was sucked into the gateway along with the old crone. In an instant, the light exploded and vanished. The Bastling was catapulted through a tunnel towards the next world's entrance as Crone Mader took her seat on the third floor.

Queen Megden arose from her throne and ventured into the hallway, gazing over the railing of glass as the young maiden played below, "Hello there little one, come sit with me a while up here, I have a riddle for you." The young girl looked up nonchalantly as the new queen smiled.

Chapter 4

Sacred Fires, Moving Mountains

Luna flew fast and furiously through the light that streaked with the old crone's voice buzzing around her. In a flash, the blur of phosphorescence had vanished and with it the ancient woman, gone to her new mansion. The Bastling was left standing in a long narrow tunnel of citrine, sparkling like lemon water and diamonds. It arched upwards towards a door at the far end. Luna approached her ascent, mindful of the new challenges that lay ahead. As she quietly moved toward the entrance to what she assumed was the new world, thoughts of the previous one and its new rulers flooded her. She began to cry. Luna was happy and excited to once again be moving on to a new realm bringing her one step closer to her destination, but was grieved to have left yet another set of friends behind. She was quickly learning how much life was changeable, forever turning and inevitably destined to transform. Although it was the truth, it was difficult for her to accept. After all, she had spent most of her life alone and her new, yet short-lived friendships had made a deep impact. She thought about Notty and her friends in Redios and of the beautiful women of Orangelis and how they did indeed have a place to call home. She enviously wondered if she would ever have such a place.

Luna's tears ceased by the end of the golden tunnel as the old wooden door stood defiantly before her. It bore etchings of an alphabet she didn't recognize, and a circle in the center in which three pictures were artfully carved, a gold and red phoenix bird with feathers outstretched above a wolf's head that contained a single citrine tooth. Below that, a red and gold fire-breathing dragon's flaming projection encircled them. Luna stood in awe of the masterful hands that had created such a fine work, yet as her eyes scanned the door she realized there was no latch or handle. She slumped against the sunshine-colored wall scratching her head, studying the old wood door over and over. Her eyes caught sight of the wolf again, his one citrine tooth glistening against the lights of the tunnel. It was then that Luna laughed out loud and dug into her Bag of Borrowed to retrieve yet another tool for the journey, "How could Eldred know everything I needed, surely he must have made this journey before!" She carefully placed the missing citrine tooth into the mouth of the wolf and waited for the door. When she heard the click, Luna gently pushed it open.

Her first steps into Yellao proved uneventful, there were no Braiggs waiting to grab her, no beautiful faerie beings pointing the way, it was simple and calm. In the distance, there were sounds of life and a lingering sweet smell in the air that was vaguely familiar.

Before her shimmered a lake that stretched out as far as she could see; green, wild and untouched. Idyllic. Sparse trees dotted the landscape, inviting her to set up camp amidst the tall pines. Luna laid her weary head down on a small round of grass. Sleep took her swiftly and within minutes she was fully immersed in a dream. She flew recklessly in her sleep among the trees of this new land, diving and swooping until a growling caused her to turn around. As Luna's spirit plunged to take a closer look she spied a magnificent creature, a gray and silver wolf. His head fell back as he howled his song into the air as an enormous shadow took shape over him. Luna fearfully peered upwards to see a red and gold phoenix cast its flight overhead. As it circled, its screech echoed throughout the dream time lands. Her spirit was pulled away as she abruptly awoke to the soft melody of nature and nothing more, no wolf, no phoenix, just a memory of them and the sound of her tree friends gently swaying above.

For days Luna stayed amongst the quiet of the land thinking and dreaming. There was nothing else to do but listen to the winds, watch the small animals, and talk to the trees. She welcomed it as she was in no hurry to venture inland. Interrupting thoughts would intrude often however beckoning her to move on, but Luna would do her best to ignore them, she felt extremely peaceful in this world as such solace typically eluded her.

Luna lost count of the days, but awoke one afternoon from a nap to hear sounds coming from the water. Her eyes followed it to the lake. On the opposite side of the shore stood a man, tall and bearishly husky. The lone Bastling made her way around to the other side of the small lake as he threw stones across the water, "Hello, you wanna play too?" Luna was surprised he knew she was there. "It's all in the wrist you know, the key to a perfect glide." He threw another stone and Luna watched as it skipped on top of the water and finally plopped down below the surface. He finally turned around sizing her up hiding all expression from his face, "I'm Lakota, what's your name?"

Luna had to tilt her neck back to see his face, "I'm Luna. You're the first person I've seen here in Yellao. Are you the only one or are there more?"

He smirked, "Oh no there's more, they just don't like to venture out too much like I do, they like to stay around the camp beyond the trees over there." Lakota pointed to a small forest in the distance, "They're friendly but they like to stick to their own, if you know what I mean. They don't mind new people but they are a little leery now since the Dark Storm. I'm a little different though, I like giving people heck!" He laughed heartily at his own joke but Luna felt like she was missing the punch line. "What are you doing here in Yellao anyways?"

Luna cleared her throat feeling intimidated, "I'm on my way to the Upper World, so I had no choice but to pass through Yellao to get there, I hope it doesn't upset anyone that I'm here."

Lakota shrugged his shoulders, "Heck no, they don't mind, they're not like that, you're more than welcome to be here."

Luna posed another question, "I was wondering what those symbols are on the door back there."

Lakota chuckled, "Oh you mean the wolf, the dragon, and the phoenix? Well the people of Yellao believe that the wolf will always lead you to your true path if you're willing to follow, and the other two are mighty symbols of our people here in Yellao." He skipped a stone and watched it jump three times changing the subject, "So where are you from originally? Where do you get your blood from?"

Luna couldn't decipher whether his expression was suspicious or arrogant, "I'm from Elan. As far as my blood goes, I'm not sure what you mean."

His expression turned genuine, "Your blood is your race, your heritage."

Luna blushed embarrassed of her ignorance, "Oh, that's what you mean, well I'm a Bastling by birth but that's about all I really know, there isn't much else to tell, I don't know of any others like me. I spent all my life living with another race, the Dreglings. My origin is a mystery, there are only hints of who I really am."

He nodded his head and turned away to skip another stone, "That's why you're going to the Upper World, you're looking for the truth."

Luna quickly contemplated his comment, "Well I want to know who I am and someone told me the only way to find out is to seek the counsel of the Great Owl atop the Tree of Answaru."

Lakota continued throwing stones, "Well whatever it is you seek, I'm sure you'll find it up there, the owl knows all."

Luna perked up, "You know the owl? Have you met him before?"

"I haven't met him, but my people have communicated with the owl for many years -- through their dreams that is. The Old Ones, the Elders they know all about the Owl, the Upper World and other things of course. They know all things about the Times Before Times." His head rose in confidence. Luna suddenly realized his expression wasn't arrogance, it was pride. Envy growled within her. She wanted to feel that way about her people but she had nothing to place it on, she didn't know who they were, there were no relatives, only ghosts of the past who were out of reach. Her heart fell into a familiar void of loneliness, but the silence of sadness was broken by her new friend's voice, "So you are from Elan?" His head nodded as if quite impressed, "I know of Elan, the Elders talk a lot about that world. Maybe you could talk to them about your bloodline, I'm sure they could tell you quite a bit."

Her heart raced faster as she reluctantly agreed, "When do we go?"

Lakota smiled, "Well first I'll have to tell them about you and when it's time I will bring you to meet them." Luna thought it a strange answer, but she didn't want to wait, she craved the answers and certainly didn't want a delay, but if she had to wait she would.

Picking up rocks herself and joining Lakota, she probed further, "So I guess you'll come back and tell me when it's time?" He continued staring straight ahead, "Yep." Luna sighed and returned an obligatory, "Okay." He ceased throwing, dropped the rest of his rocks and began walking toward the trees from where he came. Luna watched as he swayed back and forth from side to side his body adjusting to his enormous size with each step.

When he reached the edge of the tree line he called back loud enough for her to hear, "Don't bother trying to follow me either. If they don't want to be seen, they won't be. I'll be back in a while." He disappeared into the greenery just as mysteriously as he had come. Luna turned back to practice her rock skipping.

When she awoke on the third day after meeting with Lakota, Luna began to wonder what he meant by "a while". It had been far too long for her liking and doubt began to fill her as to whether he was indeed coming back. She decided to wait a little longer before going into the trees after him, when suddenly he appeared exactly where she had last watched him leave. She jumped up and ran towards him, "I didn't think you were coming back! I was just getting ready to come in there after you!"

He smirked, "I told you I'd be back in a while."

Lakota seemed slightly annoyed by her impatience as Luna defended her position, "Yes, but you said in a while, it's been days. I assumed you meant a few hours, but after yesterday I didn't think you were coming back."

He just looked at her and shook his head, "We don't live by everyone else's time, we live on Huma time." She stared at him, her mind trying to comprehend what he had just said. "You ready to go now? We got a long trek through the woods to get to the camp. We can make it there tonight if we move quickly enough. Everyone is waiting to meet you. They were ready a long time ago for this, they knew you were coming." He turned and started walking back into the trees. Luna grabbed her bag and ran to catch up.

After a long stretch of land through forests, open fields and rocky terrain they finally came upon the camp. Nestled in the yellow of the fields, it reflected Yellao itself, simple with very little furnishings, but rich in nature. The grounds flowed with earthly delights as tiny cone-shaped houses sparsely decorated the landscape, all gently puffing rings of smoke from their peaks. The peaceful atmosphere immediately calmed her. In the distance, a faint drumming echoed, reminiscent of one of her dreams.

Although nobody could be seen in any direction, Luna sensed the Huma presence intensely. Lakota headed towards one of the homes as Luna quietly followed behind. He stepped up to the flap that lay across the opening. A voice from inside called out, "Come in Lakota." He opened the little door, crouching to fit through the small opening. Once on the other side, Luna's eyes had to adjust to the darkness lit only by a small fire pit in the center. A Huma, much older than Lakota, sat staring into the fire, never once lifting his eyes to greet Luna's. It made her feel uncomfortable and she began to wonder if it was such a good idea that she came. An overwhelming feeling of not belonging washed over her as she fought back tears. Luna's heart filled with love and sorrow and although she tried to make sense of all the emotions flooding her at once, it was useless.

They swirled around inside her like the smoke rings that puffed out the top of the tiny quarters. The Huma motioned for them to sit down, "I was just sitting here asking the Great Mother Planet and Spirit of All to guide us and help us to understand the next stage of our journey." Lakota nodded in understanding, while the Bastling sat wondering if introductions would be made. They weren't. She looked around at the inside of his little house. It was scantily decorated with plants, leaves and flowers hanging from vines just as Eldred had in his house, putting her more at ease. Feathers of different shapes, sizes of brown, black and white were affixed to head bands and sticks that sat reverently against the wall of the circular domicile. The two Humas talked about many things as Luna's attention flowed in and out.

Her emotions ran from sadness to self-pity as she thought to herself, "I don't understand why I was brought here if nobody even wants to talk to me."

As if reading her mind, the old Huma finally spoke directly to her, "So you are journeying to the Upper World? It is a place very different from our worlds below. One must be ready and wise." He smiled and nodded.

Luna was happy to finally be addressed but curious about his words. "Have you ever been to the Upper World?"

Luna expected a different answer than the one he gave. "I have many times, in spirit."

Lakota finally spoke, "Luna, this is Mediwin. His family was one of the first families in Yellao."

Luna's curiosity gnawed at her, "First families? Where did they come from originally?"

Mediwin smiled, "That is a very good question with a not so easy answer. We come from a place far from Yellao. Like all Huma, we were placed here. That is what our name means. Yet what is far more important than where we really came from, is where we are going. All Huma believe, as taught by our Elders and passed down through each generation, that our sacred heritage must stay alive, and our responsibility to the Great Mother be upheld." Luna felt a bolt of truth race through her veins as her body responded with goose bumps. Mediwin continued, "Long ago we came to this world, this sacred Great Mother. Our people always talked of a time when we came from the stars and made a new life here." He looked into her eyes for the first time. She saw his, dancing and sparkling with sincerity. Luna nodded in agreement as Mediwin's revelation was washed away as he turned to Lakota, "Go tell the others to prepare for the ceremony." With that, the conversation was over leaving Luna wanting more.

Lakota rose to his feet, hunching over again to avoid knocking the conical house down as he turned to the Bastling, "Come with me Luna."

He made his way out and she followed, looking back in Mediwin's direction, "It was very nice to meet you."

He simply nodded his head and stared into the fire again. The two stood outside letting their eyes adjust back to the light, "Well I better go tell the others to get ready." He started off for the other houses and Luna carried close behind. She felt safe with Lakota, although her fear was not of being in a different world, it was of the feelings that brewed within her. The more she tried to understand them, the more confused she became.

After wrestling with conflicting thoughts and emotions, she surrendered to the feelings, and decided to let them take her where they wanted her to go. As they went to each little house, Lakota announced the ceremony as Luna stood bashfully outside. Excitement could be heard brewing amongst the Huma. It was obvious they knew far more than Luna, but she surmised there was no use in trying to find out. It was already apparent to her that the Huma didn't rush things, they went at their own pace and believed when something was to be known, it would present itself in its own time. Luna respected their way of thinking and living. It was refreshing and a welcome change from the ways of the Dreglings, who were the most impatient group of beings she had ever known.

After Lakota finished spreading the news sent by Mediwin, he and Luna went down to the water's edge of a second lake in Yellao that lay directly behind the Huma village. Far bigger than the first lake, Luna's eyes searched for a natural end to its body as the two sat for a long time silently listening to the water gently wash against the shore. In the distance, Luna could hear the same drumming she had upon her arrival and assumed it was some of the Huma playing. "Do they play the drums like that all the time?" Luna innocently peered at Lakota for an answer.

His puzzled expression matched his reply, "Do "who" play the drums like that?" His face gave no hint of sarcasm, he was serious.

Luna was unable to conceal her surprise, "You can't hear those drums right now?" Lakota shook his head. She paused listening for a moment, "There, right there! Now they're singing."

Lakota raised one eyebrow at her, "You're hearing the old ones. They're playing for you. They don't play for everyone, and certainly not for everyone to hear."

Luna shivered. "What do you mean by the 'old ones?'" knowing full well the answer that was coming.

Lakota looked to the dunes that lay to the far left, "The old ones are the Elders who have passed, the first of our people who watch over the lands. They are the protectors, the watchers."

A tingle pinched her Bastling belly, "You're sure you can't hear them right now?" she queried Lakota once more. He shook his head again, and continued to stare at her suspiciously. Luna's self-consciousness rose but secretly gave way to honor that she could hear the old ones drumming. They sat watching the water dance for a while longer, as the ghostly elders serenaded. In that moment Luna was at one with everything, perhaps for the first time in her life.

The two returned to the camp to find the Huma running around excitedly as they readied themselves for the ceremony. Luna turned to Lakota as they walked through the people, "What is this ceremony and what is it for?"

Lakota continued staring straight ahead, "You'll see. Boy, you like to ask a lot of questions. Just wait, be patient." Luna felt frustrated by his refusal to answer, little did he know she was holding back so many more questions, but it was fruitless to ask as he would evade those too. Instead she began to question herself, and wondered if she was indeed too impatient. She was still thinking about it when Lakota stopped in front of a house that was far different from the rest. Constructed of wood, this dwelling was long and square. Lakota entered with Luna close on his heels. Once inside she found herself standing at a long table filled with faces staring at her. She immediately felt self-conscious. Lakota spoke up, "This is the Bastling you've all been hearing so much about." He pointed to her as their stares continued.

"Where do you get your blood from?" The Huma posing the question looked stern and proud.

Lakota spoke up, "She comes from Elan, from the old ones' race, as Bastlings and that's all she knows." Voices around the table muttered in shock. Luna blushed, unsure of their reaction as one of the bigger Huma stood up.

He was not quite as tall as Lakota but he was extremely muscular with a face that was proud and fearless, "I'm Nantan, one of the Warriors." He pointed back to all the male Humas sitting at the table. Their stoic heads nodded in unison. The female Humas sat expressionless, yet their eyes glittered with a thousand tales. Nantan sat back down and looked over to one of the warriors, "Now let's see, my grandfather told me stories of the Bastlings. He used to say that there were none left, wiped out completely, said they used to have markings on their foreheads, flames with a star in the center. Some of the Huma have remnants of that same mark." Luna scanned the table and found the faint star on some of the Huma, while others' foreheads revealed an almost invisible outline of flames. They all turned to look at Luna again. This time she proudly perked her head up for all to see as Lakota grabbed a chair and nodded for her to sit. He pulled another up for himself and began talking about what he had been told about the Bastlings. Lakota and the others recounted legends of great Bastlings and their works. The Huma were especially impressed by the healers of the once great Elan, exceptional at communicating by telepathy with each other and other realms, and being able restore one to health with a mere touch. The story that intrigued Luna the most was how they first came to be. There were many different theories and stories tossed around the table but one factor was clear, they didn't originate in Elan. Luna was fascinated by this and wanted to know so much more.

Nantan was the first to acknowledge the thirst in Luna, "We can't know it all in a day, but now we know one more thing about our great ancestors, they were very impatient!" Nantan chuckled and soon the rest followed suit including Luna. It was freeing to be able to laugh at herself, and she realized that despite their first stoic appearance, they were a fun-loving race with an incredible enthusiasm for life. Just when her comfort level reached its peak, the ceremony was called and Luna's nervousness returned, piercing her belly like an arrow.

The Huma made their way to the center of the village where a huge house was set up. It was cone shaped like the rest but could seat everyone in the village comfortably. There was a smaller round-roofed house in front of the large one. Smoke plumed quietly from each one. Drummers started playing as everyone turned to watch Mediwin enter the center, his silver hair waving. He was dressed from head to toe in great feathers and hides and strode with the confident gait of a warrior. Luna knew immediately by the reactions of those around her that he was highly honored. He said nothing but went straight into the house. Everyone stood still while the drummers continued and a procession of warrior dancers entered the center as well. Both men and women were dressed in gold and red, the colors of the phoenix bird. A few wore a phoenix feather of the same hues in their hair, but nobody had more than Mediwin whose feathered headdress reached the ground. The flap on the house closed, and one of the warriors went and stood in front of the house. He waved his hand and soon people began lining up in front of him to enter the tent. One by one, the Sacred Elders went first with the old grandmothers leading the way, then all others followed suit, entering to see the noble elder briefly, retreating quietly to crowd behind the line. Luna asked Lakota what was happening. "Everyone goes in to receive a blessing from Mediwin, he's our sacred Elder, the one who knows the spirit way. After everyone receives a blessing, we'll enter the Hot House. Take this with you and give it to him."

He handed her a small soft pouch that was tied at the top with a piece of hide, "What is it Lakota?" She peered down at the tiny parcel.

"It's our sacred plant here in Yellao, Arawak. It has many uses for ritual and healing, and we always present it to an Elder when talking to them.

Luna looked around, "What do we do while we're in there getting a blessing?"

Lakota smiled staring at the big house, "You'll know exactly what to do when you get in there."

Lakota was next to go in leaving Luna to watch anxiously as he left her side. Her nerves took control and she began shaking. She felt short of breath. Lakota soon came out from behind the flap door, it was her tum. She hesitated, her feet frozen to the ground. The warrior beckoned her forward with his hand. When his summoning did nothing to move her, a gentle nudge from behind successfully urged her forward. She made her way slowly to the entrance as the warrior moved the flap back for her to enter. Luna stepped inside as her eyes adjusted again to the firelight's dim glow. Ghostly shadows danced on the walls as if entranced by the drums from outside. Gazing at Mediwin, with great certainty she observed a small phoenix sitting on his shoulder, but upon inspection again there was no indication of any such thing. He stared into the heart of the fire, "Sit down for a moment child." His voice was serene to match his expression. Luna awkwardly sat and waited for the next instruction from him, but there was none. Instead he held his hand out and poured herbs into the other hand while Luna's butterflies increased. Her heart pounded in perfect time with the drums. He swirled his finger into his palm and his eyes dove into Luna's. Although she was uncomfortable she couldn't look away, as if a cord stretched between the two. Without warning, he quickly closed his palm again and spoke, "I will go into the spirit world to speak to those who know you, your ancestors. I will ask your divine council what your spirit name is from the beginning of time." Waiting without breath, Luna leaned in closer. There was a breeze now spinning around them while the once imagined bird reappeared and ghostly figures flew with great speed around their heads. The drumming pitched to a frenzy. Then as if an invisible hand paused life itself, suddenly everything stopped. Mediwin opened his eyes wide and glared at Luna. He spoke in his Huma language, his face full of surprise and disbelief. "You are Wabun Ahnung!" With his face still set in shock, he rose to greet Luna as if meeting her for the first time.

Luna stumbled to her feet unsure of what was happening. He grabbed her hand and spoke feverishly in Huma to her. There was no sound coming from outside, all was quiet save the sound of his voice. Luna's eyes darted around for any signs of the once flying spirits, there was stillness, not even shadows dancing from the fire's light. She wished to understand his words, but they flew at her only revealing his excitement. Mediwin led her to the door and stepped out into the silent crowd. Gasps filled the air as Luna felt awkward with all the eyes of the village upon her. She looked to Lakota who stood close by. He made his way to her side and whispered, "They are shocked right now because Mediwin never comes out before everyone has been blessed, something has happened." He spoke in Huma to the crowd and Lakota translated for Luna, "He says today is a special day for the Huma! Today we welcome our new friend and relative, Wabun Ahnung!" The crowd gasped again and followed with cheers and claps. Lakota gazed at Luna with surprise. She had no idea what it all meant but she was naively grateful for the friendly welcome. Soon everyone was coming up to her and patting her on the shoulder. When every Huma had welcomed her in their way, Mediwin motioned for her to follow him and Lakota trailed closely behind. He took her behind the semi-circle of tents and stood her in a quiet place among the grasses, pulling a sandy herb out of his bag he carried on his side and began sprinkling it around in a circle. He brought her to his side and held up his hands as they turned to face each of the four directions. Lakota translated again as he stood in each way, "Great Spirit I thank you and welcome your daughter Wabun Ahnung back to your heart. Thank you for sending her into our world of Yellao, we are honored. Mediwin turned towards the east, "Spirit of the east watch over this young Bastling and illuminate her path with your light. May the phoenix always carry her prayers to you." He turned to the next direction, "Spirit of the south, tread lightly with your lessons for her on the path she walks. May she learn the way quickly and gently from your son the wolf, who always leads us home." Luna began to cry as he continued, "Spirit of the west, great bear spirit, give this child of light your strength every day that she walks the good road, so she may face her struggles as a true warrior." He turned once more coming full circle, "Spirits of the north; buffalo, may your wisdom always shine on her path with the knowledge of the old ones who walk with her." He turned to Luna and put his hand on her shoulder as Lakota once again interpreted, "Wabun Ahnung, you come from an ancient and honorable race full of many sacred charms. Their blood runs through your veins and I am grateful to the Great Spirit to have met you. Yellao will always be home for you if you wish, but I know that your journey has just begun as the old ones have told me. We will soon be saying good luck to you on your travels. As you walk your path always remember who you are, and know you are never alone. I bless you with love, wisdom and courage." As Luna stood listening to his words, light rolled through her spirit, like a gentle wind kissing her soul, changing her forever. Tears flowed down her face as Mediwin smiled with compassion. He wrapped her with his arms, enforcing the feelings of belonging and loving acceptance of who she was. He patted her back, and then motioned for her and Lakota to face the crowd of anxious Humas in the distance. As the three returned to the awaiting crowd, Mediwin nodded to the drummers to begin again, the ceremony was to continue.

The blessings of each Huma were completed as Luna and the others waited for the ceremony to begin. As the last Huma exited with Mediwin from within the Sacred Elder's domain, the others lined up as they awaited the water to be poured on the rocks inside the round ceremonial mound. Luna stepped in line with the others, and one by one they reentered the large Hot House to sit down in the humid darkness. It was extremely hot within the walls of the Huma-made sauna and Luna welcomed the cool earth beneath her. All were blind with the blackness until the last person entered, Mediwin. She strained her eyes to watch him as he sat across from her on the other side of the hot rocks that smoldered with life. Mediwin grabbed a ladle of water from a bucket that sat beside him, and poured it over the rocks. Steam rose over their heads and up into the tiny hole at the top waiting to escape. Everyone's breath echoed through the hot house. The Huma holy man began reciting prayers in his native tongue. She listened, closed her eyes and took in his words, hoping the emotion would interpret for her. He began pounding on a small drum he had brought in with him as a change in the atmosphere came over the earthen house. All were silent as Mediwin began chanting along with the beat of the drum in. She opened her eyes for a moment to see flashes of blue, yellow and orange lights streak above their heads. A hand touched her shoulder and held itself there. Her eyes now adjusted to the darkness, searched for its origin, finding none. The Humas on either side of her were still as the other-world music continued. Luna heard a voice in her ear whisper, "Close your eyes and still your mind." She followed its instruction without hesitation. The instant she closed them she saw a flash of light, brilliant and fast. A tree appeared in her mind's eye. It moved closer and with its movement a star burst forth overhead and stayed fixed above the foliage. She focused on the vision, not wanting to lose it. With her next breath, a wolf appeared at the base of the tree looking up to the star. Tears of bliss fell from her eyes. Her emotional vision was interrupted by a few of the Humas leaving the hot house. Luna was determined not to leave, regardless of how uncomfortably hot it was. There would never be another opportunity like this. She closed her eyes to readjust to the incoming light from the others' exit. She loved where she was and the contentment it brought, it was all she really needed in that moment.

When the ceremony was coming to an end, Mediwin began drumming and chanting louder. Upon the finale, those who were left slowly got up from their seated positions and crept towards the door, exhausted. Weak from the temperature and meditation, the fresh air from outside hit her nostrils, cooling her heated body and reinvigorating her spirit. The light from outside broke her eyes once more and she shielded her face as the others did. They were all handed towels as they were drenched from the warmth of the hot house. Lakota found her and smiled, "You good? Did you like the ceremony?"

Luna excitedly answered, "Yes!"

She was about to bombard Lakota with all the details of her experience and visions but he quickly raised his hand, "Don't tell me anything, that was your sacred time." Luna's excitement diminished slightly, what she experienced had been magnificent and she wanted to share it with someone. Feeling special, she wiped herself down and breathed in long and deep. She looked down and noticed black markings on the towel. Lakota reassured her, "Don't worry, that means the ceremony worked, it's supposed to rid us of the impurities that reside in our bodies over time. It's not just cleansing of the spirit you do in there, it's cleansing for the body as well." He started to laugh in his hearty manner. Luna was still focused on the gritty towel. Her hands let it fall completely open, disbelief captured her, a perfect image of her vision drawn into the towel from the black smudge. Lakota stopped laughing and cocked his head to one side, "Hey, now that's cool." He smiled at Luna and didn't ask anything. He just looked away and searched the crowd, "Now we eat!" They feasted together as a community, eating generously and laughing a great deal more. Everyone loved each other with friendship and a bond from the ceremony they just shared.

Sleep came easily that night and when morning came nobody was eager to wake up early, except Luna. She rose and walked out of the little tent that had been made for her, finding her way to the open grasses where her only companions were the little animals and sweet song birds. She was in high spirits, so happy it could have burst forth from within her chest. Luna reflected on her journey up to that point, and marveled at how far she had already come, no longer the lonely little Bastling from Elan, scared of her own shadow. She loved her new-found pride, and even more, she loved the faith that swelled within her chest. For the first time she knew that wherever the path led her it would always be the one she was supposed to be on. That much she had learned from her Huma friends. She felt respect for her ancestry and hoped to one day fully understand what it meant to be a Bastling. A noise from behind her in the grass drew her out of her reflections, it was Mediwin and Lakota. The old Huma motioned for her to stand up and she jumped to her feet with a smile as Lakota stood looking half asleep. Mediwin looked to Lakota while pointing to the Bastling.

Lakota once again began translating, "Luna, I am very pleased with what the spirits have told me about you. Your journey ahead is great and you have already shown your warrior spirit. There will be many more things to come, a great deal more to learn and understand but remember this, you are chosen, there is nothing you can do about this, it is written in the stars that guide all in the Upper World. It is written in the pages of time. Hold fast to what no eyes can see, faith and honor. Remember always in the face of greatest trouble and deepest despair your greatest ally is your own heart; the heart unlocks the door to everything. Accept this not as a gift, but as an honor for me to be able to present it to you, it is rightly yours, a symbol of your own people's spirit and faith in you. With it, comes great responsibility to your people. I believe you will make us proud." He took a huge red and golden feather from his staff. An aura of violet hue embellished it. He handed it to Luna as she stood at a loss for words. Lakota's mouth fell open. The old Huma smiled, nodded and walked away.

Lakota turned back to her after he watched Mediwin get some distance away, "How did you get one of those? Warriors wait years to receive a phoenix feather!" Luna felt extremely humbled and a little uncomfortable. She didn't want her friend to be upset with her, yet at the same time she felt warmth around her as if great wings were embracing her. It was knowing that this gift came from the Great Mother Ahki herself.

Luna replied to her friend, "I don't know why he gave it to me. He didn't say anything to you about it?" Her question was sincere and Lakota recognized this.

He stared blankly, "No, he didn't, but when Mediwin does something he does it for a reason and there should be no questioning it. Come on, let's go see what's going on in the camp."

Luna's tensions began to ease as the two started walking back into the center. By the time they reached the middle of the village some of the Huma were now awake and moving about. They stared in disbelief at Luna's gift. She tried her hardest to be nonchalant about it, but was finding it more and more difficult as the Huma came out to see. Closing in on her tent, she placed it lovingly inside her Bag of Borrowed and returned to

Lakota. Changing the subject with Lakota, she questioned him about the rest of Yellao, "Are there any others here?"

Lakota casually replied, "Yes there is another village you must cross through before leaving."

Luna was surprised by this new information, "How far is it to the next village?"

Lakota stopped and sat down on a bench, "Hmm…it's about a day's journey. You'll be meeting the Kumrai at the foot-hills of the mountains in the valley, from there the Kumrai will show you the rest of the way to the gate." Luna paused looking over to the mountains far off in the distance. She was not so willing to go as before, she had found true companionship with the Huma. Yet she knew, as much as she wanted to stay, she must go on wanting to make Mediwin and the rest proud.

Looking into the crowd of smiling Humas, she was at home, but that was about to come to an end, it was unavoid-able. "Lakota, do you have any Arawak with you?"

He reached into his bag and retrieved a small pouch, "Here, it's all yours."

She smiled and set off to seek out Mediwin with Lakota. Luna found him sitting alone, watching his Huma with great pride and contentment. She turned to Lakota as he sarcastically replied, "I know, I know, you want me to translate." He smirked as he plopped down in front of the sacred elder. Luna joined him and began to ask her questions as Lakota translated.

"When you gave me the feather, I was so grateful and deep-ly surprised and I want to thank you for that now." As Lakota spoke, Mediwin nodded in understanding. "I also wanted to ask you about facing each direction and praying, can you explain that to me, so I have an understanding of what it was all about?" Luna waited as her words were explained to Mediwin, hoping she wouldn't offend him.

He looked back at Lakota and began to speak heavily in Huma, "Yes, Luna. I will tell you some things every Bastling knew and the Huma as well. For as long as we have been here in Yellao, we have been taught these things. It was told by our grandmothers and grandfathers many times before us, that a star being came here and gave us these sacred ways to follow. It is told she came from the same star our own ancestors did, the Bastlings. With her, came the wisdom of the four ways, or directions, east, south, west and north. It was told that each direction carried with it multiple meanings and lessons. There is a sacred spirit that sits with each. They also represent the four races of the Great Mother seeded here."

Luna was confused, "I don't understand, there are far more races than those existing here in and on the Great Mother Ahki, why does it only represent four?"

The old Huma responded after Lakota explained, "I didn't say there were only four races, every group that exists now came from the original four. Like four leaves from the same tree, they too will fall and disperse themselves among the soil, changing and creating new life of their own." Luna nodded in understanding as Mediwin continued, "The directions also represent the four quarters of the universe from which our ancestors came. They are a reflection of the cycle of life itself, four stages from birth to death." Luna smiled humbly thinking about how small she was in the grander spiral of life. Mediwin instructed Lakota in Huma again, "When you need to speak to your ancestors, and spirit helpers, when you need strength, all you have to do is face them in this sacred circle given to us and speak. Give them some Arawak so they will know your true heart's intention."

Mystified, Luna inquired further, "Is that all she gave our people, did she bring more?"

Mediwin smiled as Lakota explained her question, "Yes, she gave us many ceremonies, one of which you participated in. There is a great deal more for you to know when the time is right, when many things have come to pass. For now, I will tell you this, she brought us seven sacred ways to live, and we continue to uphold all of them although the Bastlings are but one now. She also told us that she would come again one day, to a time when the Bastlings needed her the most. It would be a message and a signal for all to know that a time of great peace, light and understanding was upon us. I have always held great hope in my heart that I would see this day, and now more than ever I feel that I will." The entire time Mediwin talked, energy swirled deep inside Luna's spirit.

He spoke one final time before getting up to go, "Luna, I filled your mind with enough for now. It will take far longer than even you can imagine for it to sink in. Perhaps in the next lifetime it will be clear." The old Huma walked away, head held high. Luna watched him leave wishing she could hear every story he had to tell.

Lakota rose to leave as well, "You're coming back into the village center?"

Luna softly laughed to herself, "Yes I will in a minute, I just need to sit here for a moment longer."

Lakota shrugged, "Suit yourself, I'll meet you back there." As he strode away, Luna sat thinking of Mediwin's words, he was right that it would take a lifetime for her to comprehend them, but she knew she would have time on her journey as she was once again faced with the reality of having to leave her friends. A task that was becoming increasingly harder each time. Luna made her way through the Huma saying her good-byes as they all wished her well. Luna hoped to one day come back to see them, but her instinct told her it may never come to pass.

Mediwin was the last to greet her as Lakota stood nearby to translate, "Wabun Ahnung you have a great journey ahead of you. Remember your responsibility, remember your heart song. Listen to your ancestors singing, it will guide you home. One day you will understand all that has happened here and the rest of your journey. The ceremony has prepared you for the next part of your journey here in Yellao." Luna didn't understand, but Mediwin explained, "In order for you to leave here, you must have permission from the Phoenix and Dragon. They are the keepers of Yellao. You have proven yourself worthy of the Phoenix, now you will need the Dragon's approval as well." He smiled, "For now I will not say goodbye, instead I will see you on the other side of the stars." Luna's sadness flowed like water onto the grasses beneath her feet. She loved the Huma and all they had given to her, heart, mind, and soul and hoped they all knew how much. Mediwin nodded quietly and stepped back to open her pathway. She started through the line of Huma with Lakota. He had promised to walk her to the first valley side. They walked some distance until Luna turned back to wave once more. Hands waved back lovingly as Luna's eyes filled with tearful goodbyes.

The two headed towards the direction of the massive mountains with Lakota leading the way. They walked in silence for some time until he turned back to Luna, "I'll take you where I said I would but then the rest is up to you. You sure you're gonna be all right?"

Luna shrugged off his question with a brave facade, "Oh sure, I'll be just fine."

The two friends reached the valley quickly and Lakota stopped dead in his tracks, "Well this is as far as I go."

Luna looked across the basin and back to Lakota. "Why can't you go any farther?"

Lakota laughed and shoved her lightly, "You are scared, aren't you?"

Luna quickly recovered, "No I'm not scared!" She brushed off her clothes, "I just wondered why it seems so definitive."

Shrugging his shoulders, "It's just the way it has always been. Our two races have lived here for a very long time but it has always been an unspoken rule that we keep our distance."

Luna threw out her arms, "But why? Where did that rule come from?"

Frustrated by Luna's need to question everything, he snapped back, "It's just the way it's always been. I really don't know, we've never warred, we've always been peaceful, just distant." Luna's mind tried to reason it out, but her instinct told her there was something more to it than that.

Regardless, she put it in the back of her mind and leaned in to give Lakota a big hug. She knew she annoyed him at times with her curious mind, but she also knew they had a true friendship as well, "Thank you, for all you've done, especially teaching me patience."

He ruffled off his embarrassment as he let go of her embrace, "It's all right, that's what friends are for."

His discomfort persisted and Luna recognized it, "Well I'm grateful for it just the same." She put her hands to her waist and looked out again to the mountains, "I suppose I won't be back this way again, but if by chance I do, I'll come and say hello."

Lakota stared out into the distance to some faraway place as well, "Just be good and be careful." He looked into her eyes and smiled.

Luna started walking down the valley side to cross the stream that divided the land. When she made it through to the other side of the valley, she turned back towards where Lakota stood watching her. He was now a tiny figure in the landscape, not the massive friend she had come to know. She bellowed out to her companion, "Lakota, straight up the valley side and down?"

He cupped his hands around his mouth, "Yep! Straight through! You can't miss it! See you!" He waved his hand and disappeared over the top of the valley's ledge.

Luna waited a moment to see if he would reappear, and when she was satisfied he wouldn't she looked down into the water at her reflection, "You are a mystery Luna of the Bastlings, especially to me." A smile and a tear waved back from the water's surface.

Her feet carried her up the valley side until she was on top with a full view of a new valley wall. Turning back, she could see the faint outline of the Huma village, now specks against the land. Looking forward again, she watched as tiny smoke plumes sputtered out into the sky in the distance. The mountains behind the tiny village in the distance sat as great silent watchers, their full bodies now completely visible to Luna. It was breathtaking and Luna stood mesmerized. When she finally broke from the mountain's trance she looked down again to where the smoke rose. She realized why Lakota said it was a day's travel to reach the Kumrai, the valley below was massive. Luna decided to sit for a while and take in the beauty of the green that surrounded her. As she studied the mountains once again, they spoke their own language. Her eyes gazed up to the top of these rocky emerald giants. Tiny figures moved back and forth along the peak. Shaking her head, Luna focused again thinking her eyes were playing tricks on her. Once more she riveted her attention to the top. This time upon inspection there was nothing but a gentle sway of a stray bush or two. She scoured the landscape attempting to study the village below. It was impossible, it was too far away to make any sense of it. When she gathered herself together again and reflected long enough on the experience with the Huma, she rose to meet the new people of Yellao. Apprehension and excitement swirled within her little Bastling body. She could not shake the question of why these two peaceful races could not exist together.

Luna's travels carried her down into the valley and when dusk fell she decided to make camp for the night. Lakota had assured her that no harm would come to her as the others were peaceful Ahki people as well. She found some old dried wood lying scattered about, and gathered it together with dry weeds and plants. She started a small camp fire for herself, and sat down leaning against a lonely rock. As Luna stared into the fire a noise from behind caught her attention. Twirling around she saw two yellow eyes riveted on her. They sat focused on her for a long time. She didn't dare take her own eyes off them, for fear she may be attacked. Then with a rustling of grass and snapping twigs, suddenly the eyes were gone. It didn't make her feel any better. She fought sleep for what seemed like an eternity until her body lost the battle and her eyelids collapsed with exhaustion. Luna awoke to the smell of dew and morning mists. It was a magical sight in the valley. Watery spirits danced above her in the moist air and among the greens of the grasses as the mountains silently watched the life below. She packed up her Bag of Borrowed and made sure the fire was completely out, before walking on again.

As midday approached, Luna finally reached the top of the other side of the valley. The Kumrai village was straight ahead. Thatched roof houses were now plainly in sight, as people were scattered about looking busy and alive. Singing filled the air of the plush greens making her feel instantly welcome. At first, she walked into the circular village undetected, until a man whose eyes sparkled like diamonds dancing on water approached her directly with a look of disbelief, "Hello young one, I recognize you. You, you are the one in my dreams all these years. I am honored to finally meet you, in person that is." He stuck out his hand, and cupped his other hand on top of hers to emphasize the welcome, "I am Dewin, Spirit Keeper of the Kumrai and you are a Bastling. Does this Bastling have a name?"

Luna smiled in relief that she was welcomed so kindly, while surprised he knew who she was, "Yes, I am Luna."

He released her hand from his grasp, "We Kumrai have been here in Yellao as long as the Huma. It has been a very long time indeed. I imagine you have just come from the other side of the valley. Did you enjoy your stay with them?" His question was sincere.

"Yes, I did. They are a very peaceful, beautiful people with so much to teach. I have learned a great deal in the short time I stayed there."

Dewin smiled and turned his back to Luna and began walking away, "Well I hope the Kumrai will have such noble words spoken of them as well. Come I'll show you the village." Luna hurried along to catch up to him. She made her way to his side and listened carefully to all he had to say as her eyes watched the singing Kumrai. "We are a working people, taking care of the land as the Huma do but in a slightly different way. We are also a ceremonious bunch with a great love for the arts." His voice was as powerful as the mountains, and as deep as the valley beneath their feet.

Luna looked up at him, "What do you mean by the arts?"

Dewin pointed to the center of the village, "Come, I'll show you." The two veered off to the left and made their way through the people. Luna had already noted a difference between the Huma and Kumrai, the Huma gave her full attention upon entering their world, whereas the Kumrai left her feeling virtually invisible. She didn't know what to make of that, but decided to leave that question for later. She followed him to where a rock slab stood. It was at least four times as tall as the people and had symbols and writing etched into it that Luna couldn't read. Dewin pointed to it, "There is a belief, a saying here among the Kumrai as old as time itself: *A people born with a song in their heart, words in their blood, and magic in their souls shall never perish.*" Dewin's head went up in dignity, "It is our pride, our life line to the sacred source. We are a hardworking people whose art and words flow through us with ease. We are all born with it and each one of us develops those charms to hone them and increase their power."

Luna was surprised, "You know what charms are. That is what the Huma say as well; regardless of what world I've been in so far, they all know what they are.

Dewin chuckled, "Well of course everyone knows what a charm is, besides the Huma and Kumrai are from the same bloodline, why wouldn't we use some of the same words?" Luna was intrigued. "Just as the Huma are descendants of the Bastlings, we Kumrai are also the grandchildren of the once great and mighty race."

Luna stood puzzled, "How can that be?"

Dewin laughed heartily, as his voiced boomed through the air, "It's quite simple really, we and the Huma were once a single race which were the Bastlings, as time went on we parted ways and became the Huma and Kumrai, still carrying the Bastling charms within each lineage." He gazed at Luna with compassion, and hope. "That is where you come in my dear Luna. You are the prophecy come to life."

His words weighed heavy on her shoulders, "I am no prophecy, I am just a Bastling a long way from home." She looked away in defeat.

Dewin picked up on her state instantly, "Luna, you underestimate yourself too much. Every single trial and tribulation on our path is for us to understand to increase our strength, it is not a weakness to be ashamed of. If you had not felt so lonely and out of place, you would not have made the journey to begin with."

Her eyes swiveled to his, "How do you know that about me?" Her question was filled with suspicion.

His expression became very serious, "Luna, you still don't get it, do you? The prophecy states that a Bastling still true of heart as the old ones would be born into Elan, where she would be a stranger among those who inhabit there. Her Bastling ways would be shunned by those around her, causing her to be forced out and flee into the other worlds. This Bastling's journey would lead to her immersion into the Upper World. Once there, her fate would bring a new way of life for all who dwelled below, and above, ushering in a beautiful dawn of peaceful existence. Luna, you are that Bastling. You must be, you are the only one. We were also given a sign, an indication of your arrival. The eyes of the red dragon would shine once for the Kumrai on the eve of her arrival. Last night I not only saw the eyes of the dragon peering at me in the darkness, several of the people saw them last night as well. You are the prophecy fulfilled."

Luna shuddered knowing she too saw the yellow glow of eyes upon her the night before. Goosebumps flared throughout her body, a definitive sign that the truth was being spoken. Then doubt fogged her, "Yes, but Dewin, I don't even know how I came to be at all. There are no other Bastlings in Elan, why is that? How can I exist when no others do?"

He put his hand on her shoulder just as Mediwin did, "My friend, my sister, do you not see the magic in that? In a world full of Dreglings a single Bastling could be born at all? It is very purposefully done, don't you agree? One day you will remember your soul's true purpose, how you came to be and when you do all will be clear, but for now you must rely on faith, and your charms of knowing." Luna felt his words slash through the doubt like a knife cutting away weeds. Her body became lighter, as she felt something shift in her being. Dewin looked around at the Kumrai, "That is why nobody dares look at you right now, they are in awe and really don't know how to be, for they know you are the Bastling we've been waiting for." Luna gazed around at them all working and singing, but never a glance from anyone came to her. Dewin walked to where a small platform was, and ascended the steps, "Attention everyone!" He raised his hands for everyone to stop what they were doing. "Please lend me your time! There is a visitor among us as you all very well know, and she will be staying with us for a short while. Her name is Luna of the Bastlings. Yes, I said Bastling. She will be here for the festivities tonight and I encourage you all to speak with her, get to know her as she wishes to know you as well." Luna sheepishly watched as the crowd gathered around them. Dewin stepped down and moved towards Luna and the other Kumrai. Soon she was barraged with Kumrai shaking her hand, and greeting her with warm welcomes as if she had returned home from a long time away. Just as when she visited the Huma, in the Kumrai she saw faint reflections of her Bastling birthmark, and once again she was filled with the sense of belonging. Dewin broke into the group as he informed the crowd they must ready for the festivities in the evening.

The people slowly returned to their work as Luna questioned Dewin, "What are the festivities for?"

He looked around lovingly, "It is because we have been blessed with the dragon's presence. It is to honor him for revealing his energy to us once again. He told us you were coming."

Luna's thoughts flew back to Dewin's words about her fulfilling the Kumrai prophesy, she simply had a hard time believing that she was the one they had been waiting for. She pushed the opinions away and resolved herself to the practical side of the matter. "Dewin, is there anything I can do to help for tonight?"

He looked behind, "You can come with me for a while and help me gather some things." Luna felt extremely comfortable going with him, as if she had known him all her life. As she observed and listened to him, she sensed a familiarity between Dewin and Eldred. She followed Dewin behind the standing rock and the platform to a small thatched house. He quickly went inside, as Luna scurried close behind, "We'll gather some things here first and then we can go to the Feathered Forest." His house was small and simple containing many unfamiliar plants hanging from the ceiling. There was a fireplace in the center of the wall to her left, with a huge black pot hanging there, just like in Eldred's cave. "What do you need to do for the festival tonight?" Dewin was busy going through the house checking his items. "Well I need to gather some more plants for my part in tonight's events." As he focused on going through the herbs that hung from strings along the wall, his face was set in a permanent smile. She followed his fingers, studying them closely as they sorted the plants lovingly as if each one had an intimate relationship with him. He spoke as if knowing her thoughts, "These plants are very good for you, they help cleanse the system, give energy and are used in ceremonies to bring in the good spirits. They don't like too much handling, they prefer to grow independently." He glanced sideways at the Bastling, "All plants have a distinct purpose here inside the Great Mother. Actually, everything has a distinct purpose, there is not one thing that has been accidentally placed." Luna pondered his words as her eyes followed the stone rows that lined the walls of Dewin's cottage. He continued his sorting, "I sense you have many great charms as your ancestors. I hear the words swirling around you, waiting for you to pull them down and allow them to come through you. Being artistic whether it is writing, or painting is a generous charm to have, it is a way for us to not only connect with the divine, but to share the light of the source of all life with others. As I said earlier, everything has a distinct purpose, if someone is gifted with the charm of art, it is a blessing that one can share with those who do not."

Luna tilted her head, "I never considered that before." She looked out his little window and watched as the children ran up the side of the valley. "It's happy and peaceful here in Yellao."

Dewin let go of his plants and set a bunch on the table in front of Luna, "Where there is a sense of purpose there is always peace. Shall we go now to the forest? I'll show some magnificent trees." He threw a satchel across his chest, "Ready to go Luna?"

She raised herself from the chair, "I am really looking forward to tonight, there's an excitement in the air." Dewin was tickled by her enthusiasm. He patted her back as he let her out first, "Spoken like a true Kumrai."

The two walked back through the village that teamed with life. The people were all feeling that same sense that was brewing within Luna. "We'll head straight across to the other side where the trees are." Dewin pointed to the forest that danced with a life all its own.

"I've never seen trees look so alive, as if there were a thousand birds fluttering their wings." Their magnificence caught Luna's breath.

Dewin clasped his hands behind his back, "Yes, they are a beautiful race of beings. That is why it is called the Feathered Forest. The trees carry a great wisdom, they are the secret keepers. They have been witness to all the events here, they have seen all." Luna's mind fell onto the Tree of Answaru, "That is what Eldred said. I hope I find the answers I'm looking for in

Answaru." Her eyes studied Dewin's face for anything he might be concealing.

He continued his pace and kept his eyes straight ahead, "Ah yes, the Tree of Answaru, a noble and precious tree, by far the wisest of all." Dewin stopped and turned towards Luna, "All trees carry wisdom of the ages, but this tree contains all the wisdom, every event, every thought and action, every memory of the Great Mother, of life and the universe itself."

He continued walking again, but Luna remained stationary, "Why Dewin, why is it like that? Why do I have to travel all the way up the top of this tree to get the answers I need? Why can't I find it here or in another world? Why does it have to be all the way up there? I may not make it, and then all this traveling will have been in vain." Her face set in a childish pout.

The elder continued walking, "Nothing on one's journey is in vain, and if you don't make it up to the top in this life, then you'll be all the wiser for the journey in the next life."

Luna pondered this wisdom as she caught up with him on the approach to the Feathered Forest, "So what are we going to get in here?" She hurried along behind him. He took a sharp left off the path and began gently walking through the tall grasses and plants so as not to disturb them.

"We are gathering some special plants and herbs for tonight. We will use them in the ceremony for offerings and cleansing." He stooped to reach down for some of them. He pulled dried herbs from his bag and placed it down before the plant. He paused and then gently pulled the herb out of the ground. Grabbing a cloth, he wrapped it and placed it in his bag.

Luna watched his every move, "What is that for?"

Dewin rose and continued walking, "It is an offering to the plant that is giving itself for us to use. We must always be respectful of any life that gives to ours. Whether it be an elder or a plant. You probably already knew that being with the Huma." Luna thought back to the Arawak Lakota had given to her. He continued, "These festivals and ceremonies serve to remind us of who we are, where we came from and who we will become. It is a mirror allowing us to look at the old and new. That is why it is such an honor for the Kumrai to have one of our ancestors in our midst. You are far more important than you realize Luna, you are a living legacy of our ancestry standing before us. I am sure the Huma felt the same honor." They headed closer to the center of the forest as Luna fell deeper into the depths of her identity. "Look over here little Bastling." Dewin was pointing to a bush that was decorated with glowing yellow berries, "The most sacred of all plants to the Kumrai. It is the Dragon's Bush, filled with great magical properties. It is used in healing, visions, and ceremony." Luna stared down at the berries watching them pulse with amber light, their power could be felt without touch. Silently mesmerized by them as well, Dewin continued, "Legend has it that long ago this bush had dark berries, inedible, lifeless. One day the Dragon noticed the bush and breathed on it and put its own essence on the berries. Now each bush carries the power of the Dragon." Dewin' s eyes blazed with fascination as he once again left his herbal gift before carefully choosing which berries would go in his bag.

Luna angled her head in curiosity at the magical berries, "So each bush grows with that same energy of the dragon?"

Dewin turned to walk back towards the village, "Yes. Each and every one forever carries that power." He smiled broadly to himself.

When the two returned to the village center they found the Kumrai even busier than before with real organization to their preparations. Luna was reminded of the Bazers in Redios, how they worked together to forge new things, and complete old tasks. She followed Dewin to the door of his house again, pausing to look back at the scenery, the motherly mountains, the people bustling back and forth, and the indistinguishable feeling of a presence greater than what her eyes took in. She felt pride swell within her just as when she was with the Huma, yet it was a different kind of pride and although diverse peoples, she knew she belonged and was a part of both.

Dewin ushered her inside to his table once again. She watched him work as she tried to guess his age. He and Mediwin were much the same, both showing age through the wisdom they carried, yet both so alive with vitality that an endless youthfulness shone through everything they did.

"Luna, hand me those dried herbs over there." She quickly fetched them wanting to help in any way she could. He mashed them into a bowl with other mysterious ingredients as she posed a question, "Do the Kumrai have their own language as the Huma do?"

Dewin continued his work, never looking away, "The Kumrai's language had nearly disappeared, but there are those of us who hold it close, still passing it down through the generations. The history of our language lies in the stars, it is told by our ancestors that it is the language of the star people. Perhaps one day it will flourish again, perhaps by way of a Bastling." He finally looked up at Luna revealing the sparkling dance in his eyes. Compassion rose in Luna for the Kumrai and their loss of language, but was as hopeful as Dewin that it would return. Luna let out a wide yawn, fighting hard to conceal it.

"Luna, go into the back room and have a sleep and get some rest, you're going to need it."

Luna felt uncomfortable fearing she would offend him, "Oh no I'm all right, it's just been a long couple of days."

He smirked, "I know, and that is why you must rest now. There is a great deal for you to do later and you'll need your senses about you." He continued working the mixtures into a paste. He jerked his head to the side giving directions with them, "Go, you'll only be bored watching me mash plants. Straight back, there is a bed there, I insist."

Luna finally gave in to Dewin and her fatigue. "Okay, but if you need me just wake me and I'll help out in any way I can." He smiled, "Good enough."

Luna found the bed and quickly fell into a deep sleep. What seemed like hours later, she awoke from her dreams feeling extremely well rested. The little thatched cottage was quiet and empty. "Dewin? Are you here?" Silence. She looked out the window next to the fireplace and found Dewin and the others huddled in a circle. Luna walked out to join them, "Hello everyone, I hope I'm not interrupting anything." She became shy fearing the possible truth of her words.

Dewin and the others looked over her way, "No of course not! We were just discussing some last-minute preparations for this evening, but everything is set otherwise." Luna relaxed, "So what's next?" Dewin looked around over everyone's head, "I suppose we can all go to the ceremony site now and meet up with the others."

Luna followed the group listening to their conversations while taking in all the rugged beauty of Yellao. The mountains surrounded them like a mother nestling her young. It was a strange, new comfort but she welcomed it all the same. Dewin was the first to acknowledge their arrival, "Here we are, the sacred site." Huge stones stood as guardians to an enormous circle that encompassed a great deal of open ground at the foot of the mountains. Symbols marked the path along the outer edge of the giant circle indicating the stone sentinels' history and ancient posts. The groups of Kumrai were all around the stones keeping to themselves. There was very little of the bustling she had seen before, now they calmly awaited the festivities.

Dewin walked to the center of the circle of stones, "We are here, gathered as fellow Kumrai, young and old alike to honor not only the spirit and fire of the sacred dragon, but the presence of our newfound relative and friend." The crowd began to clap and cheer as Dewin outstretched his arm to Luna. Embarrassment flushed her Bastling body, making her want to hide behind the mammoth stones, "Luna, please come join me in the center." Dewin and the others waited as she slowly made her way past the crowd to Dewin's side. He looked at Luna with pride, "Tonight as always, we celebrate our heritage and remember why we are here, why we exist at all. I'd like our guest to say a word to everyone before we begin."

Luna was seized with fear. She didn't know what to say, and she certainly didn't want to make a fool of herself. Panicking she shook her head at Dewin, as he leaned over to calm her, "Luna just say what is in your heart, after all that is what the Kumrai do best." He winked and began clapping, as the rest of the Kumrai joined in.

She cleared her throat, "He-hello everyone, it is so good to be here among you tonight. I am deeply touched by your generosity and welcoming ways. I'm not used to speaking like this at all, but if there's one thing I've learned since my short time here, it is that to use your voice if you have one is highly regarded, so bear with me." She gave a halfhearted smile and the people began to chuckle and clap. Luna's tension eased. She spoke for a while longer as Dewin suggested, what was in her heart. She told them of her wishes, hardships, and journey thus far into the worlds above Elan. Her speech concluded with the cheers and song of the Kumrai. Luna felt deeply honored.

The people began the ceremony with Dewin in the lead making magic with his herbs. He made fire dance and light sing and the people were in awe as if they had never seen it before. Of course, they had, but every time was new as one of the Kumrai had explained to Luna. Then others followed, artists bringing life to blank canvases right in front of everyone, poets dancing their dreams aloud for all to hear, and singers whose voices echoed off the tops of the mountains. Surely if there was a dragon he would have clearly heard and seen all the beauty and creativity that took place there for him that night, and he would have been impressed.

When the last artist finished painting, and the final poet chanted with the end of the singers, Dewin took to the center once again. "Now let us give thanks for our charms, for our existence, and our eternal time." He raised his hands and turned to face the eastern quarter. In clockwise rotation, just as Mediwin had done, Dewin gave offerings of sacred plants, honored the four spirits and all the Kumrai before him, with him now and to come. He walked over to Luna and sprinkled herbs around her, "Thank you for the blessing of our Bastling sister. I pray that her journey through life be long and fulfilling with peace always on her heels. Guide her to her true path." Dewin smiled and hugged her. "Now we feast!" The Kumrai spiritual leader clapped his hands and laughed.

They all joined together in the center for the feast, and by the end of the night Luna was full on friendship, community and food to last what she thought was surely forever. There was only a few Kumrai left when everything ended and Luna sat staring into the fire that burned before her. Dewin came and took a place beside her, "Well young Bastling did you enjoy yourself?"

Luna continued her stare in the flames, "Oh yes, I am quite full, and am overflowing with the hospitality and sacred ways you have all shown me."

Dewin interrupted her, "But I know, I know it's time for you to go."

Luna nodded her head and glanced at him, "It's true though Dewin I do have to go, but you already knew that." They sat and laughed companionably.

Dewin broke the lightheartedness of the moment, "Luna I feel I must encourage you to stay one more night, get a good rest and leave tomorrow. I must also tell you that there is no easy way out of Yellao." He gently grimaced.

Luna felt her heart sink, "I knew this was coming. Somehow there is never an easy way out of any of the worlds, even in Elan I couldn't just make up my mind to walk out of there, they threw me out." Her head slumped down in defeat.

Dewin chuckled, "Well there is no easy way out of anything that needs to go." His gaze shifted to the mountains in the background, "There is never the same exit twice in Yellao. The door to the next world always shifts and it is up to the one searching for that door to find out where it lies. The only way to do that is to sleep at the top of Draig Mountains. There, the seeker will wait until daybreak when the new gateway shall be revealed."

Luna sighed with relief, "Well that's not so bad, not too fun sleeping alone in the dark at the top of a mountain but still, I can think of worse."

She rose to her feet as Dewin followed, "I must also tell you one other thing Luna, there is a legend here among the Kumrai, a person who goes up the Draig Mountains either comes down a madman or a poet. It depends on whether the dragon feels you are worthy of its presence."

Luna gulped as fear shot up her body. "Well, I guess I will need my sleep then won't I? Better yet, why don't I just stay?" Dewin's laughter rose heartily as he slapped her on the back. Luna joined in, not revealing her serious sentiments.

The Bastling awoke to the smell of food cooking and a choir singing. She sat up in the bed and looked around drowsily. Dewin was busy making her breakfast in the kitchen when she entered, "Good to see you're up and ready to go."

Luna groggily replied, "I'm up, but I don't know if I'm ready to go." Dewin giggled and slid her plate onto the table, "Eat up Luna, the village is waiting to say goodbye." Luna plopped down and dug into her food. She finished, helping Dewin clear away the dishes and gathered her things. She exited the little thatched roof house and said goodbye in her mind. The Kumrai were all waiting as Luna reluctantly bid her farewells.

When all the villagers had dispersed, Dewin offered to walk with her to the foothills of the mountains. "Thanks, Dewin but I think I'll just go by myself, I need to get used to it." She smiled wryly.

Dewin sensed she was hiding her fear but didn't push the issue, "Well then I guess I'll say goodbye to you here. I want to tell you Luna, you are far braver than you give yourself credit for. I also want to tell you that it has truly been an honor to have you in our midst. This tiny village of Kumrai has forever been changed because of you."

Luna politely refuted, "But I haven't done anything, I just stayed and visited and learned about your ways, you taught me."

Dewin grinned, ""You have done far more than you realized, you have renewed our faith in our people, given us hope that tomorrow will be better than today." He looked away deep in thought.

Luna, scrutinizing his mannerisms, "What are you not telling me Dewin?"

He looked back at the village and then to Luna, "I have told you all that you need to know now. The rest will come later, when it is time."

Luna was frustrated, "But I'm not going to be here later." The Kumrai's spiritual leader just laughed. Luna's heart sunk, "Well Dewin, I will go now." She leaned in and gave him a hug. He reached into his robe and pulled out a bag, "Here, have these tonight when you get hungry." It was a bag full of Dragon berries. "Thank you Dewin, I will." With that Luna turned and started her trek towards the mountains. Dewin couldn't see it, but Luna was sobbing like a baby.

It took Luna all day to reach the summit of the Draig Mountains. When she felt satisfied with a spot to set up for the night, she sat down and rested as she watched the village from high above, longing to be there. She thought she could see Dewin's figure in the distance, looking up at her, but it was too far to tell for certain. She hunched over her knees, resting her chin, oscillating between boredom and anxiety. Luna tried to push out all the fearful images looming in her mind, even wishing from time to time that she could be back in Elan, wallowing in loneliness. That kind of loneliness was easier to deal with, before she knew all these wonderful people she had to constantly keep leaving behind.

She soon became drowsy so laid out her things to get more comfortable. Thus far, the experience on top of the mountains was uneventful and Luna hoped it stayed that way. She considered how she would find a doorway that changed all the time. She had no idea how long it would take to find it, how it would reveal itself and if she would discover it at all. She simply resolved herself to act as quickly as she could and follow through to the end. She had come this far and although she sometimes wished she wasn't enduring this journey, deep in her heart she knew it was the right path. Her stomach began to rumble from hunger and remembering the berries Dewin had given to her, she pulled them out and ate heartily. Soon Luna fell into a deep sleep, forgetting her worries.

Luna dreamt feverishly, her spirit bouncing between many worlds. Suddenly she was flying over the Kumrai and their sacred circle stones, her soul longing to be there still. Without warning she was drawn back to the reality of the mountains. Opening her eyes slowly, she tried to focus in the black pitch of night. Suddenly there were eyes following her from every direction, yellow, glowing ones. Luna jumped to her feet but there was no place to hide. She didn't dare run for fear of falling of the mountain cliff. Terrified, she shook as her breathing increased, and the eyes darted quicker. She watched as a shadow began to show itself in the darkness, glowing green. It loomed closer as she backed up and tripped backwards landing face up. The giant figure revealed itself, the mighty dragon of the Kumrai. Luna screamed in fright but it was useless, nobody would hear her. Without warning the dragon roared and directed a huge breath of fire right at Luna. It struck her in a steady flow to her chest. Luna felt the heat surge through her body, the pain unbearable, as she lost sight and consciousness.

The Bastling opened her eyes only to find she was still in darkness. She grasped at her chest as the memory of the dragon came flooding back to her. Her search for burns, or wounds turning up nothing, no scar remained. Luna thought perhaps it had been a very vivid dream. As she sat up for a while thinking about the dream and its intensity, she reached into her bag for more berries. Luna finished off the bunch and fell to sleep again.

Once more Luna flew through times and places fast and furious. Her spirit soared over the village of the Huma and watched as they performed their hot house ceremony. She felt a pull and longing in the dream wanting to drop down and join in. As she breached the incline of the land she caught sight of Mediwin, he looked as he always did. Standing in the grasses, he peered up to Luna's spirit as it approached. He waved and lifted the other hand to blow dust at Luna as she flew in. At that moment she woke, suddenly snapped back into her mountaintop world. A cry resounded through the air, the screech of a bird unlike any she had heard before. Luna searched once again for the origin of this night stranger. At first it offered no revelation of its source or location as Luna sat breathless. All was quiet for a moment and then the cry resonated once again, shaking her and the mountains themselves. A shadow appeared over the cliff stretching as far as the land itself. It was the largest bird she had ever seen, the phoenix. It reached flight high over the mountaintop as its red and gold glow illuminated its path. Luna's head fell straight back as she watched. It turned its regal head and looked down towards Luna as it changed direction and began its torpedo race towards her. Luna braced frantically frozen to the spot in fear. The phoenix dove straight at her heart. When it hit Luna, she could feel a surge of power and electricity go through her as she too now glowed with the same red and gold hues. Her body fell back as the bird disappeared into the night. Luna lay bewildered and confused.

Morning broke as Luna sat clutching her bag for comfort. A peace came over the land, and whatever had transpired through the night was now history. Luna rose to her feet and began searching for the illusive doorway. She didn't know where to look, the mountains held walls all around her. She walked over towards the side that faced the Kumrai village, all was quiet. It was strange as she had expected to see the people working and singing but instead it looked abandoned. She walked back to the other side that held a round of walls that connected to the other smaller mountains as her eyes scanned the walls again. Finding nothing, she decided to go back to her sleeping spot and gather things. Once she had put all her belongings into her Bag of Borrowed, she noticed something glistening a few feet away. On further inspection she found a gleaming emerald dragon next to a red and gold statuette of a phoenix. Luna shuddered, as the incidents of the night before were confirmed as real. She looked around as she picked up the items, and quickly placed them into her bag. She smiled and instinctively walked towards the edge of the mountains and followed the pass into the canyon walls below.

When Luna reached the bottom, there was still no sign of any doorway. She began to doubt her decision, perhaps she should have stayed atop the mountain. A noise dragged her from her thoughts. Just then a wolf stepped into her path, gazed into her eyes, and disappeared behind bushes next to the wall of the mountain. Luna immediately followed his path. She lost sight of the wolf but discovered something else, a familiar symbol; a wolf head howling up at a dragon and a phoenix. She let her fingers run the surface of the stone symbols. There was no evidence of a doorway or any cut in the rock itself. Her hands fell over the dragon and the phoenix as they brought revelation. Luna grabbed the two figures from the Bag of Borrowed. She studied them, the dragon and its powerful claws and fire, the Kumrai people. A tear rolled down her cheek. Next she gazed at the phoenix, its everlasting power of transformation, the Huma. She wept clutching the two objects in her hand. Luna laughed through her tears, and then very carefully placed the dragon and the phoenix into their respective places. The earth beneath her feet began to quake as the mountains shook. Blazing green red and gold lights shot out in every direction. Suddenly a doorway burst open where the symbols once were. Luna walked through and turned around to watch Yellao disappear. When the wall became the stone of the mountain again, she began her journey to the next world.

Chapter 5

Anchors Away!

Luna trekked through the mountainous corridor, marveling as it began to swirl with greens and pink hues. The vortex made it increasingly difficult to keep her balance. She stumbled often from her disoriented view and was forced to close her eyes momentarily. Once she regained her equilibrium, she hurried to exit the corridor. Without warning the streaming circles of color ceased and she was immersed in a peaceful passage of luminous pinks, calming her. Her pace slowed, as her thoughts reverted back to Yellao and all the important lessons she had learned. A low rumbling pulled her away from her peaceful thoughts. A vibration was now pulsating throughout the calming corridor, reverberating from the ground beneath her feet. Curiosity seized her as Luna started towards the door at the end of the corridor. The rumbling's volume increased and she knew at once whatever it was that lay beyond that door was powerful. She loosened her bag quickly, found her knife and pulled it from its sheath. An eerie light flowed from beneath the gateway and the vibration was almost deafening. The door itself chattered like teeth on a cold, dark night as Luna grabbed hold of the knob. She realized her method of sneak attack would be hidden well by the sounds coming from within. With that in mind she closed her eyes, thrust open the door and stumbled blindly into the next world.

When she opened her eyes, Luna was awestruck. Her knife clattered to the ground. Her mouth gaped open, eyes fixed on the scene in front of her, it was heaven. In every direction, water streamed in a torrent of waterfalls. It hung as a mist in the air above her head, swallowing itself on the banks of the rocky shore, it trickled from cavernous walls that were continuously sprayed with iridescent fluid from the waterfall's fury. A glow emanated from the flow of great waters, matching those of the vortex corridor, increasing with intensity in the water's depth. Beneath the waterfall that lay in front of her, was a narrow path barely visible from the mist that led beyond the falls, refusing to reveal its destination. Luna felt an urge to press on but her heart longed to stay in this watery paradise. She eased herself to the rocky ledge and let her entire body be doused with arrows of moisture. She lay beside the little rivers that rippled between rocks. They were shades of emerald. She lay down, putting her hands behind her head and leaned back on the wet rocks taking in the realization that she was in the heartland of all the worlds. She observed the power of the many faces of the water, wondering if there were any faces of a race here in this new world, Centros. There was only one way to find out and Luna knew she had to begin her journey into this water wonderland soon. She decided that the trip could wait as she enjoyed the mysticism of this wet land.

For longer than she was aware, Luna lay engulfed in the beauty of the waterfalls. Her knife caught her attention as it lay on the ground where she had dropped it. She retrieved it, replacing it back in its sheath and into her Bag of Borrowed as the decision to poke around a little further kept her from returning to her rest. Luna hoped there would be food here amidst the water's fertile ground as she followed past the falls to find a lovely patch of untouched soil tucked silently away from view. She crouched down and entered its domain, it was loud yet held so much peace, drowning out all her thoughts and fears. As hunger pains started tearing at her stomach, her eyes caught sight of a bush twinkling behind small rocks beyond her. Green and pink berries fell from its leaves from the power of the waterfall. She hurried over to grab some of them hoping they were edible. She plopped one in her mouth, delicious. Then another and another, soon she was unable to stop eating them. All her aches and pains disappeared. The fears and anxieties that had plagued her were extinguished. They had a taste all their own and before long, she craved it day and night.

Time passed, she was uncertain how much. She lingered in that small private place until the day the berries started to turn on her, once giving her euphoria and pleasure, they now made her feel sick, turning sour in her stomach. Yet her consumption didn't cease. Luna's frustration turned to rage. At times, she would scream out from behind the torrent of the falls, as it drowned out her cries of pain. The passion had turned to poison and soon she had forgotten why she was there, where she had to go next, and she really didn't care. All she knew was her little clearing by the waterfalls and the berry bush behind it. One morning Luna began crawling on all fours to get a drink at the water's edge, too weak and confused to stand. As she knelt over the water, her reflection offered no signs of anything she recognized. The face staring back at her was bitter and twisted, drawn and tired; no longer the Bastling she once knew. She cried falling backwards as she lay there for hours sobbing. Exhausted, she fell asleep and a dream came upon her. Luna saw herself standing in front of a stone so rare and beautiful its brightness was blinding. She was blissful and content. A flash of light raced across the scene and she saw herself again, this time she was standing in what was the Upper World beaming as she stood in front of the Tree of Answaru. She held in her hand a sword that glistened in the sunlight. Luna awoke startled. Looking around, everything was as it had been before her sleep. Exhausted and emptied, she had cried everything out, no more tears were left. She pondered her dream feeling a renewed sense of purpose, and although she didn't understand it altogether she knew what it meant to be standing in front of Answaru. To Luna that was worth more than gold and if she dreamed it she knew she could still make it a reality. Right then and there she resolved herself to leave the seclusion of the waterfall world and venture further into Centros leaving her berry addiction behind. She took out her map and briefly studied it and found only one entrance into the heartland of Centros, through the trees that lay just beyond the waterfall.

When Luna regained her strength from her long, dark, berry time, she rose to see what was on the other side of the waters.

She knew she had wasted a great deal of time there, but tried not to be too hard on herself. Grabbing her bag, she made her way through the forest. When she had ventured through the trees without incident, she came upon a lake. Far in the distance she caught sight of people on the shores. Hesitation plagued her, as Luna wondered if she should outwardly approach or sneak in first to get a better look. Upon reflection of the map once more she saw no way out of Centros directly, leaving her no choice but to make direct contact with the people to find out. Onward she went in search of the answer.

The people noticed her approaching, one stood. He was a tall man, tough yet regal looking. He greeted Luna with a stern, curious look. His face covered in lines that reflected a lifetime of hardship. Luna smiled feeling unusually confident with the stranger, for although his facade was tough, she sensed a softer interior. She waved her hand, "Hello there! I'm hoping you could help me, my name is Luna. I've been in the falls for some time and I came through the clearing back there. I saw you folks, and thought I'd come over and introduce myself. I hoped you could answer a question for me." She stuck out her hand.

He did not reciprocate the greeting but instead eyed her suspiciously, "Where did you say you're from?"

Luna put her hand down, "Oh I didn't, I'm originally from Elan but I left quite a while ago now in search of the entrance to the Upper World." He stared at her forehead as if her eyes were there. Luna became self-conscious, "That's my birthmark. I don't know exactly why I have it, but I do. Are you going to introduce me to your friends?" She pointed to the circle of people who were sharing food. He looked back down to her eyes.

"Well I don't know yet, that depends on what you want here in Centros." Luna was taken aback by his coldness.

"Like I said, I'm on my way to the Upper World, so I'm just passing through." He bellowed, almost howled. His belly shook as he slapped his knee. "You're just passing through, eh! Well that would be a first! Come on, I'll introduce you to the clan." The man waved his big paw that resembled a hand in the air. Luna followed as his curly red hair bounced as he walked. Worry set in and she immediately began to think her assumption about him having a soft side was incorrect. She walked into the circle with the gruff man as everyone stopped eating and began whispering as they gazed at the visitor. He thumbed back to Luna, "This here is Luna and says she's just passing through Centros to the Upper World." The entire group of people started laughing uproariously as Luna looked for something to hide behind. Embarrassment flooded her as she looked over to the lake hoping it would wash away their cruelty. Anger filled her heart for this place and its people. Tears began to well in her eyes.

Her voice was a bare whisper, "I'm sorry I have to go, I made a mistake coming here." Luna ran back towards the trees. Panic and comfort in the familiar convinced her that if she could make it back to the waterfall area she would feel better.

A woman's voice called out from behind, "Wait! Luna is your name?"

She stopped still facing the place of her intended refuge, "What do you want? Just let me go."

The woman pleaded, "Wait, I'm sorry everyone did that to you." Her voice was soft and nurturing like a sweet song, "Please let explain why everyone was laughing." Luna wanted to listen but her pain was too great so she started off on the rocky path of the forest again. As her feet began to pick up the pace, again the berry bush came to mind. Hopelessness filled her heart ushering in old agonizing thoughts of Elan. Just as the powerful sound of the waterfall came rushing in, Luna heard her name being called again, the woman had followed her. "Luna, do not go back in there, don't do it please. If you go back to those berries you may never be free again." Luna stopped dead.

Swiveling around, Luna shrilled, "How do you know anything about me?! You couldn't possibly have *that* much audacity!" Luna was furious as the gentle woman smiled and drew closer.

Her dark hair was pulled back from her face showing the beautiful contours of her middle-aged profile, "I don't know you Luna, but I do know that anyone who stays here too long gets lost in those bushes and the euphoria it brings, but it isn't real, it's just a way to escape for a while. And I also know this: if you want to pass through Centros, you need to stay as far from this part as you can." Her words were honest and painful to hear. Luna was humbled and she began to cry. The woman put her arms around her and patted her gently, "There, there, you just let it out." Luna succumbed and released what seemed like a million tears that flowed like a river. She felt safe and warm as this stranger comforted her, but was surprised she allowed her vulnerability to show. Even in a moment of pain, Luna's mind could never stop asking why. As her crying subsided, she released herself from the gentle stranger. The woman spoke softly, "My name is Cheelah, and if you let me, I'll explain to you why everyone was laughing." She lovingly brushed the hair from Luna's eyes. "And pay no mind to Captain Maskel, he's been far too long on the waters of Donloom. Too many days locked inside himself and too little time with anyone else. He's forgotten how to be civil in matters of the heart." Luna's pain began to ebb as she listened to the motherly woman, "Come and sit with me on the other side of the trail." The two walked out again past the trees, and found a rocky ledge. "Luna let me explain about Centros. Long ago we Sentients were a flourishing tribe of people. We lived here, close to the beauty of Donloom. The waters were plentiful then and we respected the life it gave. Then one day, a war was waged, we were attacked by a group of beings called the Scavengers. We had no idea where they came from or why, only that we stood in their way. Our fishing fleets were nearly destroyed leaving us but one remaining vessel, the Erudition. The ships were our lifeline and our only prized possessions, created from special materials from the Heart Stone."

Luna's intrigue was peaked, "The Heart Stone?"

Cheelah smiled softly in reminiscence, "Yes, at the far end of Centros stood an altar and upon it sat the Heart Stone. It guarded the gate of Centros which led into the next world above. Yet it was so much more than a guardian of the gate, it was the heart of the people. Prior to the Great War which was brought on by the Dark Storm, the Sentients were gifted healers, loving and unafraid to feel emotion, helped others and lived in a world of mutual respect. Then everything changed. The people became withdrawn and afraid, not only of another attack, but of not surviving. You see Luna, these Scavengers stole the Heart Stone from the altar and when they did, and they stole the heart of the Sentient people with it." Luna's heart filled with compassion melting her defenses even more revealing only sadness and pity for the people of Centros. Following her empathy came anger that rose like a mighty tidal wave. Cheelah stared back towards the waters, "Legend has it each Sentient carries a source of the Heart Stone deep within them forever linking us to its sacred energy, and as long as it is gone from its special place, so we Sentients are lost too."

Luna was even more curious, "But what happened to it?"

Cheelah sighed, "When the Scavengers came in and raided Centros, they methodically planned their attack so it would lead them to the stone's resting place. When they took it, Centros shook with earthquakes, and fire spewed forth from the Island of Trygall which had never happened before. The scavengers then fled to the island where they have been ever since."

Luna was shocked, "They're still there now? Why don't you go get your stone back? It's yours! It belongs to the people here!" Luna was furious and bewildered by their reticence.

Cheelah explained, "Some tried over the years, but alas never returned, leaving us to assume only the worst. Time and time again we would attempt the stone's rescue, but to no avail."

Luna pieced the story together in her mind, "Wait a minute! You said the stone sat at the gateway to the next world, does that mean the gate is no longer there?" Luna sank back not really wanting to know the answer.

"I'm afraid it does mean that and now you know why everyone was laughing when you said you were passing through. Whoever sits in Centros, sits here forever."

Luna slumped even further back against the rocky chair, her mind racing as she spoke to herself, "Surely there must be a way out. Eldred wouldn't have sent me all this way to be stuck here forever, I just know it." She reached in her bag for her map. Quickly unrolling it, she laid it down on the ground, "Let's see if this map shows us another way."

She frantically searched as Cheelah replied, "It's no use Luna. Every inch of Centros has been scoured for another gate. We Sentients once thought if we could escape we might find refuge in another world, bring back an army to help us retrieve the stone, but there is no other gate to be found." Luna continued looking despite Cheelah's hopeless response. "Where did you get that map Luna? I've never seen one like that before." Luna knelt to take a look, ignoring the question as her fingers and eyes roamed every spot in Centros. Just as her new friend predicted, the only gateway marked was where the Heart Stone once sat. Luna rolled the map up quickly and slapped it back and forth in her hand.

The Bastling exclaimed, "Well then, the only choice I have is to go to the island myself and get the stone."

Cheelah pulled away, sitting back with astonished eyes, "Luna! You don't realize what you're saying! That island is no place for the dead, let alone the living. The most seasoned of trackers never made it, what makes you think you will?"

Luna wasn't listening to her warning, "You don't understand Cheelah, if I don't leave here then I don't make it to the Upper World, and that is a far worse hell than dying on an island trying." Cheelah was taken aback by her answer, unsure if it was strength or insanity. Luna grabbed her bag and turned to Cheelah, "Will you come with me to ask them? Petition to them for me, on my account…please Cheelah. What do you have to lose?"

The Sentient stared at her still in disbelief, "I'll go with you Luna, but I can't make any promises." Luna smiled.

The two walked over to the group as the circle of Sentients watched them approach. Luna walked right up to the captain, "Don't you ever laugh at me like that again, it's rude!" He glared at her as Luna continued, "Now that that's out of the way, I need to ask a favor of you. I need you to take me to the island." She stood with arms crossed waiting for his reply.

Nobody in the group laughed this time, they just stared waiting for the captain's answer, "No I will not."

Luna was relentless, "Why not?"

Captain Maskel was equaled in his determination, "I don't have to give you a reason."

Luna snapped back, "Again you're being rude. Why won't you take me?"

He was getting aggravated by her tone and yelled back, "Because I don't feel like dying today!"

Luna shook her head at him and snapped, throwing it right back, "You don't feel like dying today, so you'd rather sit here wasting away, instead of being a hero or dying with dignity."

The captain threw down his food and stood to confront her, "Don't tell me about being a hero. Nobody talks to me that way!" The two forces stood their ground, both staring into the other's face.

Luna fought back, "Well I just did!"

The captain was on the verge of lunging at her but instead held his restraint, "That's it!" He turned and stomped off in the direction of one of the makeshift shanties that dotted the beach. All eyes were now on Luna as she took it upon herself to grab a seat in the circle of people, all still shocked from the scene that had just taken place.

Luna looked around confidently and more determined than ever, "Well, now that everybody knows my intention, does anyone else know how to get to that island?" The people began mumbling to themselves.

One of them pulled at the bread that was in his mouth while he spoke, "I think you're crazy."

He looked at her disdainfully as Luna bit back, "Why, because I'm willing to at least try?"

The young man retorted, "Like the captain said, you don't have a clue what you're talking about." He stood up to storm away but a hand caught him and pushed him back down, it was the captain.

"You are right, she is crazy, but she's also right." He looked Luna's way, "And yes, the answer is I would rather die a hero instead of rotting here another moment. I'm not getting any younger, and as far as I can tell, neither are any of you!" He pointed around the circle of Sentients. They all hung their heads in shame. He bellowed at them again, "Why didn't any of you say this to me a long time ago?! None of you had the guts! Then along comes little *Miss Whoever You Are* who kicks me square in the teeth! I don't like it much but I do respect it. So on that note, we'll gear up tonight, and set sail in the morning. We'll see what our little mate is really made of then!" He laughed, nodding his head at Luna, and then headed off away from them towards the ship Erudition, the last great vessel of the lost fleet. Luna secretly cheered for her triumph, but also realized she had to live up to her bravery. The group that had made up the circle now became the crew, jumping to their feet in defense of why they shouldn't go, running after the captain, arguing the whole way down the beach. The captain turned around, "You better all be on that ship in one hour to gear up, or you face me." They all ceased their bickering and dispersed to their shanties.

Cheelah smiled at Luna, "Very impressive Luna. Now impress me even more and bring yourself and everyone back in one piece." She started to leave, "You can sleep in my shanty tonight." Luna followed the tender Sentient, hoping she could fulfill her wishes.

When morning came, it was easy for Luna to get up, as she hadn't slept all night. Tired and restless, she readied herself for the trip and when she was finished, she and Cheelah headed down to the ship to meet the captain and crew on board. After arriving, the small group of Sentients that remained stood on shore watching the last-minute preparations. Captain Maskel was hollering at a crewman, "Watch it! We haven't even left yet and you've already nearly got us killed!" The rest of the crew laughed, making fun of the mate.

The last of the supplies were being loaded when Cheelah put her arms around Luna, "I know we just met, but I feel like I've known you forever. Please be careful and if there's any piece of advice I can give as a Sentient, it's this: *Listen to your heart, it will never take you down the wrong path.*"

Luna smiled warmly, "You know a few very wonderful people gave me that same advice recently." Luna walked onto the ship's ramp. She turned towards Cheelah and the others waiting on land, "Don't worry, I'll see you again, very soon!" The crew pulled away the ropes and lifted anchor. The ship rocked and swayed slowly as the sails were raised to full mast. The Sentients on shore waved. The brave Bastling waved back as the Erudition set sail.

For what seemed like hours Luna stood on the deck looking back at the shores of Centros. The island was straight ahead. While visible from land, it seemed like they hadn't gone far at all. Captain Maskel came up from behind, "Are you feeling sick?"

Luna answered quickly, "No, not at all. I was just wondering why it seemed like such a short distance from land, yet now that we're on the water it seems so much farther."

The captain chuckled, eyeing the waters ahead, "Yes well, the waters of Donloom are deep and mysterious. It plays tricks on the eyes, or maybe it's the island that does. It's been a long time since we've been down beneath the water to get a better look. It used to be clear green, but ever since the Scavengers came, well it's dark down there now. Too many ghosts I suppose, or maybe like I said before, the island's powers stretch further than we think." His thoughts drifted off like a lost boat at sea, and then snapped back to the moment. "Speaking of ghosts, you must have come from Yellao to get into Centros, how'd you like all those ghosts in there?" Luna's confusion was evident so the captain continued, "What, you didn't realize that it's filled with two tribes of ghosts? Yep, it's been that way since the Dark Storm, that damn storm changed everything."

Luna reeled, "I don't understand! I lived with them, did ceremonies with them, how could that be?"

Captain Maskel shook his head, "One never knows the strange things that happen in these Lower Worlds, maybe you just needed to see them. Well, I best get back to the helm. Can't leave them alone too long, they might sink us before we even get there!" He smacked Luna on the back as if she were one of the crew, and walked away.

"Captain Maskel, is there anything I can do to help?"

He answered, "You could go down into the galley and see if Furst needs some help." He continued walking away leaving the Bastling to contemplate this stunning information about her friends in Yellao.

Luna stepped down into the galley to find a crewman working on the floor. "Are you Furst?"

He looked up nonchalantly, "Yeah, why?"

"I came to see if you needed any help."

He stopped and sized Luna up in a glance, "Yeah, all right you can help me, have a seat." He pointed to the spot next to him.

"So, what are you working on?"

He continued weaving the wire as he spoke, "I'm making a wire trap. I love to snare things and it always comes in handy when you're hungry." Luna felt uneasy about Furst but she tried to push it away, after all he was someone to talk to. "Have you ever made one of these before Luna?"

She replied shyly, "No I haven't." He smiled as he wove the wire, "Well stick with me then, I'll show you the ropes."

After a while watching Furst, Luna felt confident enough to give it a try. "Okay, let me give it a go." She grabbed hold of the wire as he directed her.

"Take it real slow now; feed the wire into the hole and wrap it tight." Luna achieved the technique on the first attempt. Soon she was quickly knotting along with Furst. "So how long have you been doing this trapping Furst?"

He shrugged, "Well, all my life really, it's the only life I've ever known. My dad did it all his life and his dad before him. I'm very proud of my family."

Luna detected a defense in his voice, "Well you should be, not everyone can even boast about having a family."

He looked at Luna, "You don't have a family?"

"No. But I'm also starting to realize that family doesn't have to be blood. I think on our journey we are given all the family we need. I've met some very special beings, people I'll never forget, and as wonderful as any family I could have been born into."

Furst cut her off, "Hey! You missed one."

Luna retracted her fingers, "Oh sorry, I thought that was your weave."

He looked back to the trap, "No it was yours." The two carried on weaving but when Furst made a mistake, he blamed it on Luna, which really irritated her.

After the fourth time of being accused of what she knew was his mistake, she lost her patience, "Alright, that's it, I've had enough!"

He smirked, confident in his manipulation of her. "Look, just sit down and I promise I won't do it again." She was quickly calmed and gave him one more chance. The two weaved without incident for a while and then again, he accused her, she had decided she was done and would do no more with him, and again he appeased her, manipulating her, and winning the situation at hand. Once more he promised he wouldn't accuse her any longer. Luna and Furst sat quietly for a while before working. Once they resumed he accused her again. Luna had grown tired of his games. She didn't allow the next lie to come, her mind was made up.

"Furst, I'm not going to help you anymore, I'm done."

She got up to leave, "What, come on, we're almost done!" Furst threw down his wire in a temper tantrum, "Look, I promise I won't do it again." He was confident he would be able to get her to sit down again. His eyes were pleading, but it was too late. Luna could see through the game he played and no longer wanted part of it. She watched him expressionless and then replied, "No Furst, no more." She walked up the galley stairs, feeling freed from that one simple act of speaking her truth.

Luna made her way on deck to where Neehst was working on the masts. He looked over his shoulder, "Hey, how was it? I saw you go down there earlier." He laughed as directed his attention back to his work.

Luna felt embarrassed, "Well it was interesting. I'm really not sure how I feel yet, I'm still trying to take it all in, but I'm pretty certain that guy is crazy." Luna looked away wanting to forget what had happened with Furst, she felt stupid for being manipulated like that.

"Furst is a different character. Here, grab hold of this rope." Luna started helping Neehst, happy to forget about the wire trap maker. They got along quite well as if they had been friends for a long time. Luna laughed as he told funny stories about the crew's fishing adventures. "It sounds like you guys have a lot of fun. I wish I could have that much fun all the time."

Neehst laughed and then quickly lost his humor, "Yeah, it's fun but we'd all still rather have Centros back the way it was before." Luna could not empathize more.

Suddenly, Neehst leapt over Luna's head. She darted around just in time to see Furst coming at her with a club. Neehst dove on top of him and wrestled him to the deck as a couple other crew members came running over to help. Furst wriggled screaming that it was all Luna's fault, "She'll be the end of us all! You watch!" Captain Maskel rushed around the corner to find Furst pinned to the deck, screaming frantically.

He ordered him down into the galley for the remainder of the trip. Luna stood startled, yet relieved Neehst was there to save her from the attack. The two finished their task and resumed their friendly conversation. When the mast work was completed, Neehst wanted Luna to help him on the next task, but she decided to take a little break, and look at the island from the other end of the ship. Guilt plagued her for wanting to leave but Luna's sense of adventure got the better of her. She asked Neehst if he wanted to join her for a while, but he had no intention of leaving his post. She was disappointed but understood they both needed to do what they needed to do.

Luna walked around the deck to an open spot and stared out at the water and the mysterious island that lay ahead on the watery path. Luna was aware of the heartache that cursed the Sentients, but something was serene about the waters of Donloom, and intriguing about the island. She looked back to the others on board, there was an unspoken pain that loomed over the people of Centros, like a misty fog. It was so obvious to her but she wondered if they were aware at all, of its power. The shores of Centros were barely visible now as she wondered what Cheelah was doing and if the others would be all right. Luna's heart warmed thinking about Cheelah, and her emotions reassured her that the Sentients would be just fine. "Good day for a sail, isn't it?"

Luna turned around to see one of the mates standing there. His head almost touched the pole he was standing under. His brown eyes sparkled with irresistible mischief as he dipped his hands in the pockets of his worn attire. She smiled, "I'm Luna."

He stretched out his hand, "I'm Feallan, we didn't really have a chance to talk yet so I thought I would come over and say hello. It's pretty crazy what you did with the captain. Nobody ever talks like that to him." He shook his head as if he was still in disbelief.

"Well maybe I just felt I had more to lose if I didn't." She smirked and looked out to the island again. She was pretending to be brave but inside she was frightened as the island loomed closer.

Feallan stepped closer to the rail, "It's going to get pretty nuts once we get there I'm sure." Luna walked over and leaned on the rail next to him.

She looked back to the sailor, "Do you like being on the waters like this?"

He shrugged his shoulders, "It's all right, but sometimes it can get pretty boring just sitting on this ship day after day waiting for food that never comes. There's not really anything to do anymore. Fishing takes so long and the catch is rarely a feast." She studied his face as he described his daily life in Centros. Through his eyes, Centros was a boring, ratty place. "That's why I take a few of these every day." He pulled out a sack from his ratty shirt, "It helps with the boredom." He reached in and pulled out some berries. Luna shrunk back from the all too familiar berries from the waterfall. "You want some?" He put his hand under Luna's chin.

Her hand caught his and pushed it back, "No I'm okay, I don't need any. They made me feel weird.

He laughed, "Oh, so you've already had a taste. So, they made you feel weird? You just couldn't handle it that's all." His smirk was off-putting.

Luna chimed in defense, "No really, they were good at first but then started to make me feel sick more than they made me feel good." He looked over his shoulders to make sure nobody could hear him.

He crouched down and whispered, "They work you to death on this ship, sometimes it's the only way to stay awake some days." Luna thought about what Feallan said. Looking out to the water, she searched for a sign or any kind of answer.

She teetered back and forth in her mind, "Well I am really tired. Stop it! You don't need it, you've been fine without it. Well, one couldn't hurt." Her inner strength kicked in and the Bastling ran to get away from Feallan. She ended up on the other side of the ship, this time only to find another crew member. Aside from Neehst, she was beginning to think they were all crazy.

She swirled around to step away quietly but he caught sight of her, "What, you afraid of me or something? Not many consider me handsome but I didn't think I was that hideous," he laughed at his own joke as he gazed out towards the water. Luna stopped turning around while she searched for a good excuse, "No of course not, I just didn't want to interrupt you."

"Nonsense, you're not bothering me at all." He stuck out his hand for introduction, "I'm Ardor and I already know who you are." Luna smiled shyly as her face turned a bright red, "Have a seat on that crate, I'll grab another one." Ardor returned and the two spent the entire night talking instead of sleeping, they shared their whole lives with each other and by the time morning came they had forged an unbreakable bond and the truest friendship she had found since boarding the Erudition.

As day broke, Luna and Ardor headed in the direction of the bow to find the captain. When they found him at the helm, Luna yelled out, "Captain! Is there anything we can do?"

He laughed, "Yeah, you can make sure we live through this little adventure. We're here!" He pointed to his left as the island loomed larger than life. They had approached the island in the night hours while her and Ardor talked.

Her stomach fluttered, "My, it is ominous looking, isn't it?" She could hardly breathe as she said it, feeling insecure with her decision to travel there. Trygall was dark and eerie producing unnatural noises as a thousand invisible eyes leered out at them in the water.

Captain Maskel hollered to the crew, "Drop the anchor and tie the lines! Let's get her secured!"

The crew scurried off the ship as the captain ordered. Once on the island they decided to set up camp on the shores of Trygall to give them time to figure out which way to go. Once settled in, Luna pulled out her map which caught the captain's attention, "Let me see that map for a minute." He was flustered, "This map is amazing, it even details the island! But how is that possible? Where did you get this from?"

Luna shrugged her shoulders, "From an old sage who lives on the outskirts of Elan. That's what Cheelah asked me, what's the big deal?"

The captain explained, "Well it's just that I've never seen a map of all the worlds post-Dark Storm, even in Centros. It has the island on it, the island wasn't here before the storm. How could it be possible for someone to know all this?"

It was a very curious thing indeed and Luna's thoughts turned to Eldred as she questioned it herself now, "Maybe Eldred travelled the Lower Worlds before and the Upper World as well."

The captain gave her a puzzling look, "Now how the hell would he do that? He wouldn't have made it out of Centros and yet here is the map of all the worlds. Did he ever tell you anything about the island?"

Luna sat bewildered, "No, the only thing he said was the map was accurate and needed to be followed as such. He said everything in all the worlds is as it is on the map and any hidden pathways or alternate routes would be marked."

The captain rolled it back up and handed it to Luna not taking his eyes off her, "Listen up crew! We stay here and rest and in the morning, we head into the forest. We need two sentries at all times, we'll rotate shifts."

Luna and the crew sat silently on the shores keeping constant watch all around them as the captain fell in and out of snoring bouts. She chuckled to herself as Ardor spoke up, "His snoring can get pretty unnerving after a while." They all quietly chuckled. Ardor continued to stare into the fire, "You know you've caused quite a stir around here, I admire it though, it takes a lot of guts to do what you did." Luna smiled at him, she liked the kindness in his eyes.

The rest of the crew slept without incident and woke with a sense of purpose. Anchoring just off shore, they loaded up the row boat and headed into the Black Forest with Captain Maskel and Luna leading the way. As soon as they stepped into the trees, Luna understood why it was given its ominous name, every tree looked as though it had been burned, with leaves to match the sullen trunks and branches, showing no signs of life. Their tendrils were as black as night and crept over each other creating a dark canopy where no light could be found. Luna looked ahead to the opening in the distance where the forest ended, daylight was barely visible; slowly disappearing altogether. Soon they were hardly able to see one another. Luna's eyes were playing tricks on her, dark shadows began to dance around her veering from side to side. A noise startled her from behind, "Captain are you still there?" Her voice was in a low hush.

"Yes." His gruff voice tried to be quiet but it was fruitless. At the back of the group Furst followed as closely as he could, too fearful to utter a word. Something in the darkness reached over his mouth as he was quietly pulled up and away.

Neehst and two others stopped for a moment, "Did you hear that?"

Neehst listened closely, "Yeah I did. Furst, are you all right?"

The sound of silence closed in on Neehst and the other two mates. Suddenly they too felt darkness cave in on them and were carried away. Feallan and three others heard the muffled yells and started to run. "Get out of my way!" yelled Feallan. But it was too late, the five mates were swiped away as well. Luna, Ardor, the captain, and the remaining three began running to find an exit in the pitch. Captain Maskel took the lead as he and Luna stayed on the narrow path using only their feet as their guides.

A pinhole of light could be seen ahead, "There! Follow the trail to that light!" Captain Maskel hollered out. They fled as fast as they could and in one fatal swoop Ardor and the three were scooped up in the darkness as Luna and Captain Maskel dove into the light and fell out of the Black Forest. The two sat on the ground and waited to see if any others were coming. The captain got up and peeked back in, "Hello, anybody in here?"

Luna shook her head, "It's no use, they're gone. She began to cry, "This is my fault entirely."

He turned around, "Don't say that, we all knew what we were doing when we came in here. They just weren't quick enough. Let's keep moving. We'll take a look at the map when we get a little farther ahead." Luna wiped her tears and followed the captain wondering how he could brush the incident off without feeling. When they reached a wall of slate rock, they consulted the map. Pinpointing their location, they found a diagram of their position with the words: *What has been lost to the Forest Black can be salvaged and brought back. When you enter the three long caves, the lives of the lost ones can be saved.*

Luna looked at the captain waiting to hear any advice. "Well, we may as well get busy finding the entrance." He handed her the map and started looking along the rock.

"Wait a minute! Aren't you a little curious about what is in there? I mean it could be a trap or something!"

He stopped and glared at her, "So what are you saying? That your friend there in Elan would send you to your death?"

She took offense, "No! Eldred would never do that! But he never did say it would be harmless or easy, and so far, it hasn't been. Who knows what may be lurking in there!"

The captain just smiled sarcastically, "Well then I guess we'll just have to be ready, won't we?" Luna stomped her feet as she followed him knowing it was useless to argue another moment. "If I can help save our crew, then that's exactly what I'm going to do." Within minutes they had found the entrance to the three long caves, and began their journey in.

Before long, completely immersed within the walls of the caves, they came upon a crossroads of paths. Luna threw up her hands, "Great! Now which way do we go?" The captain didn't answer but studied each path carefully. He leaned in listening for something that only he understood. When he reached the third entrance, he listened a little longer than he had the rest.

"We go this way." He pointed down the last corridor. "Why that one?" Luna was curious as to how he came to that conclusion.

He huffed, "Because there was no noise coming from the other two."

"That doesn't make any sense to me." Luna was confused.

He looked back at her surprised she didn't understand, "I trust noise, I don't trust the quiet, or do you forget what happened in the silence of the forest back there?" Luna realized he had a good point. They followed the dim cave hall, hoping for the best.

When they neared the clamor of voices they hesitated. Captain Maskel reached for his knife. Suddenly the laughter they heard ceased and a voice yelled out, "Who's there?"

A second voice called out, "Reveal yourself, now!"

Luna and Captain Maskel looked at each other as the female voices continued their demands. "Let's go Luna, it's now or never." They stepped around the comer into the light of the flames. There sat three old, decrepit women, frail, ragged and hideous. One sat rocking just staring blankly into the flames, the other sized up the two as the third played with an animal that was no longer distinguishable.

"Hello, we are hoping you can help us," Luna halfheartedly smiled trying to banish the sinking feeling in her stomach. The two women began cackling as the third chimed in when she noticed the others.

The captain was getting impatient, "Look, we mean no harm we just want to free our friends."

The old lady who was staring towards the fire spoke, "I may be blind but I do know two fools when I see them!" Her laughter resounded through the grisly cave. She continued, "We are the sisters three. I am Ele, this is my sister Maul, she cannot speak, and this lovely woman here is my sister Eyra. She is deaf but can hear all things in a different way." She quietly chuckled under her breath. Luna felt instant distrust for them as the captain looked around him as if waiting to be pounced on. Eyra made grunting sounds at the others and motioned with her hands. Ele turned her head in the direction of the captain accusingly, "How dare you think that of us! We mean you no harm, we have been waiting for you. Sit down and speak with us. We'd love to talk for a while and help, it isn't often we get company." She smiled coyly revealing her black rotting teeth as she extended her hand in courtesy.

Luna and the captain reluctantly took a seat in front of the fire. He moved to seat his back against the wall. Eyra mouthed something to the others that only they could understand and Ele replied, "Yes, he is very stubborn, isn't he?" They laughed in unison.

Luna interrupted, "Look, can you just tell us how to save our friends? Please." They all stopped and looked at each other with fear.

Ele replied, "There is only one way to save your friends, you must release the captive Heart Stone. It is the only thing that can save them now." Luna stared at the flames hoping another answer would leap out of the embers. The old woman continued, "We know Luna, we know why you came here to begin with, but what you search for is so perilous, so elusive that you may lose your life striving to get it." They all laughed again and then peered in the captain's direction, "And you Captain Maskel have a lot of courage coming here. It may be your last sail as well." He looked away pretending not to hear their message.

Luna spoke in defense of the captain, "Just leave him alone, he's not the one you want, it's me. So, let's get on with this, just tell me how to find the stone."

The three were quiet for a moment, talking to each other telepathically. Luna waited anxiously for their reply. Finally, Ele spoke, "The stone is locked and hidden away in the Castle of Wreckage. There the Maimed King and Savage Queen have it guarded day and night. It is fiercely protected as it is the weapon the dark Sovereigns have over the world of Centros."

Luna replied suspiciously, "How can we tell that what you're saying is the truth? How do I know you're not lying?"

Ele snapped, "How do you think I lost my eyes! How do you think my sisters are deaf and mute?" Luna stared at each one. The old witch continued, "When the stone was stolen we were taken as slaves from the shores of Centros. We once lived there as healers among the Sentients. The king and queen stole us too, and used our healing abilities for wrongful doing, but what they didn't realize was that once the stone had been removed from its rightful place, it began to change. It turned on whomever held it, touched it, and looked upon it, almost as if it knew the user's intention. We never wanted to take part in their dark plans, but our charms were far too weak for them. Once the stone turned on us, they banished us to these caves to die a slow death. So here we sit waiting all these years for you to find us. You see Luna, if you find the stone and free it from the dark grips of the Castle of Wreckage, you will set us free as well."

The three old witches sat silent again, all rocking back and forth. Captain Maskel was astounded at their story. Luna turned to him, "Is this true Captain? Have you ever heard of these three women?" Luna didn't really need an answer, she already knew in her heart it was true.

He looked up and away from them to Luna, his eyes big and wide, "Yes, I have heard of them, but the legend has them perished. Nobody ever said they had been taken and survived. I had no idea." Pity washed over him and for the first time since entering the cave he stopped being so untrusting.

Luna asked them one more thing, "You said the Heart Stone was in the castle, but where?" Ele, Maul, and Eyra all looked at the little Bastling.

Ele spoke on all their behalf, "It is rumored to be held captive, locked away from the eyes of all in the tower. It is guarded by menacing beasts, and it is thought to be impossible to defeat as well as three obstacles that will block your path before reaching the castle itself. Yet we believe you can retrieve it Luna." They looked at her with disdain, not believing their own words.

Luna picked up on their doubt, "Why do you say that when you don't really believe it?" She crossed her arms in defense as she did with the captain when they first met.

He watched, rolling his eyes, "Oh boy, here we go again." He slapped his head.

Ele responded quickly, "We just see many things inside you that may prevent you from accomplishing this most incredible feat. We can see your pain, your fear, your heartache. You do not speak your truth most of the time, you hear only what offends your sensitivity and you are blind to your own power. If you can understand all this, then perhaps we will see you succeed." The three witches turned away from the captain and Luna, "Go now, before the darkness takes over us again and we do something we may regret." They began to shake, growl and fidget as Luna and the captain slowly backed up out of the cave.

Luna and Captain Maskel followed the path back out into the open musty air of the island. They saw the path that wound around the caves and deeper into the island center.

They traveled quietly for a long time and then Luna asked, "Do you think I can do this? Do you think we'll get our friends back?"

He stared straight ahead on the path always keeping an eye on their surroundings as if waiting for a surprise attack. "I think it can happen, but if what those three witches say is true, then you've got a lot of soul searching to do." He glanced over at Luna as he held back branches to clear the path for her. Luna felt the burden growing, and she wasn't sure if she could carry it. Suddenly the captain put out his hand to stop her, "Listen, you hear that?" Luna paused, she could hear a faint noise in the distance, barking.

She looked to Captain Maskel, "What should we do?"

He shook his head with uncertainty, "Well, it could be the first obstacle or it could be a trap. We should sneak up and check it out." Luna agreed and they started off following the sounds.

When they were close enough they veered off the path and hid behind the trees to get a better look. They watched as two dogs sat guarding a beautifully decorated caravan shrouded in gold, scarlet and ginger silken clothes. Luna thought it an odd thing to see on such a dark island. She decided to go ahead and approach. She started to walk out, but the captain grabbed her arm, "What do you think you're doing?"

"I'm going to go talk to whoever is in that caravan."

"Have you lost your Bastling mind?" His gruff voice rose catching the attention of the two dogs, who began to bark and snarl in their direction.

A voice called out from the caravan, "Who's there! Come out, I know you're there!"

Luna's eyes darted at the captain in defiance, "Yes, hello! I just want to talk to you for a moment!" The dogs began frothing at the mouth as they barked, showing their fang-like teeth.

The voice called out again, "Well state your case then!"

Luna stepped out from the shadow and shelter of the tree, "I am trying to get to the Castle of Wreckage and I'm wondering if you could tell me how to get there."

"You think I'm going to give you that information?! Nobody passes by me and my caravan! You will not pass any farther beyond this point!"

Angered by the disembodied voice's words, Luna retorted, "Who are you to tell me whether I can pass or not? I have no problem with you, I just need to see the king and queen."

"Well why don't you tell me what you want and I can send the message to them? I am one of their council." Confused, Luna turned to the captain for assistance.

He rolled his eyes again, "Look, whoever you are, we'd just rather talk to them in person if you don't mind so could you just call off your dogs and let us be on our way?" He felt confident the voice would follow his request.

"No! Rivkah doesn't allow anyone through!" The dogs barked even louder as if in agreement. Luna stood frustrated and defeated slinking back against the tree she had been hiding behind as Captain Maskel looked at the ghastly dogs.

"What are we going to do now Captain?" Luna peeled bark from the tree root beside where she sat.

"I don't know but we better think of something fast, my crew's lives depend on it." The dogs started to calm down again as they were before the two strangers' arrival.

Luna watched the guards carefully as she whispered to the captain, "You know, if we got rid of those dogs we might have a chance to get by her." The two sat smirking at each other. They got up and started looking around for anything to use to distract the dogs. Immediately the two guards began growling at their movements in the trees. Luna went left and the captain tracked right. As Luna trudged through the brush she toppled over something hard. She turned over after her fall looking back to see what she had tripped over. There, underneath the leaves and grass stood a statue, a dark grey dog with its teeth bared as if ready to attack. Luna crept up closer, studying it carefully.

She was nose to nose with it when the captain's voice broke the spell, "Hey where are you? Are you all right?" Luna turned back, "I'm over here!"

He came up behind only to stop and stare at the statue as well, "What is that?"

"I don't know Captain, but I bet it can help us." She smiled and looked up at her friend as they reviewed the newly found treasure. "Do you know anything about this in your people's lore?"

He shrugged his shoulders, "There isn't much to tell about the island before the stone was stolen. It was a beautiful secluded place where animals were free and happy."

"What was the island called before the king and queen renamed it?"

He scratched his head, "Let me think. I wish Cheelah was here, she would have known." Luna pulled out her map from the bag, looking for the island again. She found the name of the island, Trygall. She scanned the map to find their exact spot. A name etched in the trees read, *The Silent Dog.*

Luna looked at the captain, "Does the *Silent Dog* mean anything to you?"

He thought about it and then shook his head, "No, I can't say it does." He pondered it further, "Wait a minute, now that I think about it, the island was happy and peaceful, maybe that has something to do with it."

Luna looked at the dog again, "The animals were peaceful, and this is the Silent Dog." She was trying to make a correlation. Scraping away the rest of the grass, Luna revealed writing at the bottom of the statue, *Faithful and loyal my stare is true, with anger or rage I would never harm you.* She fell back on her feet wondering what this could all mean. Luna glanced up at the eyes of the statue again. This time she noticed there were two holes where the eye sockets should be. "Maybe something goes in there." She felt around on the ground looking for anything to put in them. She stopped suddenly, realizing what she had just said. Luna hurriedly reached into her bag fumbling for two things Eldred had given to her, the two emerald gemstones. She pulled them out and placed them in the eyes of the Silent Dog. Captain Maskel studied her but said nothing. As the second stone was placed, a wave rushed forward pushing the two back on the ground. They could hear nothing but the sounds of the guard dogs in the near distance yelping in pain. They got up and ran over to where the caravan sat. By the time they reached it the dogs had stopped yelping and lay asleep. The caravan, still and silent as well.

Luna went to run over again to the dogs but the captain grabbed her arm again, "Let's make sure." He threw a rock in their direction but the guard dogs didn't move. "I can see they're breathing, so they must be in some kind of deep sleep." He smiled at Luna giving her indication to step forward between the dogs and knocked on the caravan door.

"Hello, Rivkah! I want to talk to you now." Her voice was full of sarcasm.

"Go away! Don't you come near me, where's my guards? What have you done with my dogs?" Rivkah's voice was now full of fear.

"Come out Rivkah, I need you to answer me!" Luna didn't wait for a response, grabbing the door, she opened it, ripping the silken cloth with it. A scream penetrated the trees as Luna and the captain stood in shock. It was a tiny mouse sitting in the enormous caravan, scared and alone. It squeaked and ran off into the forest. Luna and Captain Maskel began laughing, at themselves as well as the mouse. She picked up the cloth to examine it, but found nothing more than thread. They began walking over the mess of what had been Rivkah's post, and continued down along the path.

The two traveled further into the center of the island, laughing about how silly they felt about Rivkah being nothing more than a mouse, "I can see that the witches were right Luna, you do let your fears get the best of you." He laughed heartily.

Luna became defensive, "Well I don't know why you're laughing so hard, you didn't know it was a mouse either." She snubbed him and walked ahead. His laughter ceased as he realized she was right. They didn't walk on much farther before they came upon another obstacle, just as the witches had predicted. The path narrowed and became walled on either side.

Blocking the path was a man-beast. It turned to face Luna and the captain. He jumped up and down laughing, "Look at you, you're so ugly!" His poisonous laughter echoed in the pathway. He was pointing his fingers at Luna, "You have the biggest ears I've ever seen! Oh, and those legs! Hey, that mark on your forehead is a beauty!" He fell on the ground laughing hysterically at Luna.

When it seemed as though he was calming down, Luna spoke, "Well I'm glad you think I'm so funny but we need to get through so can you just step aside so we can pass?" Luna was trying to ignore his unkind words.

He stopped for a moment and started laughing even more than before. He held his belly as he swayed back and forth on the ground. "Oh, please stop! It hurts!"

Luna just stood with arms folded looking at the captain. He cleared his throat, "Yeah listen here! We need to get by so can you move? There's only room for one at a time, but if I have to push you aside, I will." He smiled threateningly at the man-beast. Suddenly his hooves flipped him up to his feet startling Luna and the captain.

His laughter abruptly stopped. "No, I'm sorry I can't do that. You're not allowed, strict orders from the king and queen." He ruffled his shoulders in a defensive stance.

Luna didn't try to go forward but just stared at him in disbelief, "Who are you anyways? Do you work for the king and queen?"

He started laughing again, "I am Broeder, The Great and Wonderful!" He bowed performing for his audience. "I don't specifically work for them, but I definitely am not stupid enough to let you through, I would be in big trouble for that." He started dancing on the spot. Luna thought him not only odd but doubted he had all his senses about him. The captain just shook his head.

Broeder bellowed again, "So anyways, where was I? Oh yes, laughing at how stupid you are!"

Luna's infuriation rose, "Why don't you shut up?"

Broeder started jumping up and down, "Oh this is good, it doesn't take much to get you upset, I am going to thoroughly enjoy this!" He clapped his hands.

The captain turned to Luna waving his hands at Broeder, "Come on Luna, let's sit down until we can figure something else out." She followed him and sat down feeling completely beaten up. Her mind raced about Broeder's comments about her appearance, picking apart her features, even the way she talked. Broeder's words cut deep and raised Luna's insecurities to the surface. "Pull out the map Luna." The captain held out his hand and the two sat looking for an alternative route but alas there was none.

"It's useless to look you know, you have to get by me and that is never going to happen." Broeder strutted around back and forth. "You know Luna, you should really just give up, you're never going to get by me, don't be so stupid." Broeder started laughing again throwing himself on the ground.

Luna jumped up, "What is wrong with you?! What made you so cruel and mean?" She was near tears.

"Don't cry, you little baby," He wiped away invisible tears. Luna couldn't take it anymore and began weeping.

"Luna, don't listen to him, he's just going to enjoy you crying." The captain's words gave her no comfort and made the tears fall more.

Broeder pointed and laughed at her again, "Look at the big baby!" Luna's tears shut down and she dejectedly sat back down. She and the captain sat for a long time just listening to Broeder's non-stop antics and insults. Luna was getting weaker by the moment falling deeper into the despair of her own insecurities. She wondered how Broeder got to be the way he was. What had happened to him to make him so cruel? But it didn't really matter, he wasn't about to change.

Hours crept by and the captain grew more impatient. He picked up rocks and threw them, "What are we going to do Luna?" Broeder began imitating every word they uttered. It was getting annoying and just as Luna was about to burst in anger again she stopped herself; intuition kicked in.

She smiled at the captain, and looked over to Broeder, "You're the one who is just a baby, aren't you? You're just a baby craving attention all the time. You hate everything about yourself. You're the one who can't stand the way he looks, how he talks, what he does." Luna stood firm in her conviction and she was right, it was affecting him.

He stopped bouncing and dancing, and became defensive himself, "Stop it! That's not nice what you're saying and it's not true!" He looked as though he may cry.

"Now it's your turn to feel the pain you inflict on everyone else. You need to laugh and make fun of me so you don't have to look at yourself, half man, half animal or beast, whatever it is you are. By the way, what is it that you are? I feel sorry for you." He began to contort in pain. Luna kept on and didn't let up, endlessly barraging him with the truth. He fell down writhing in pain. He began to shake, screaming in agony, and suddenly transformed into a small little boy, shy and timid. He looked up at Luna and shrieked away in fear. Luna walked up to him and held his hand, "Don't worry, everything is going to be all right." She wrapped her arms around the tiny boy, "You are actually very beautiful." The child nodded his head shyly. Luna looked around, "Stay hidden until you hear us come back." She smiled as Broeder sat down amidst the grasses. Luna and the captain continued on.

When they arrived at the third obstacle it was obvious, a man so hideous and mean, shackled in the pathway. As was the case with Broeder, he blocked the entire width of the passage. Luna approached him, unafraid, "Hello, what is your name?" He just gritted his teeth.

Luna asked again, he snapped, "Gisil! Why?"

"I think you know why I'm asking."

He sullenly glanced her way, "Go away, I don't want you here." He turned away miserable. Pity washed through her.

"Look I don't want to bother you but I really need to get through this path and you are in the way. And from what I've experienced so far my job is to get you to move."

He looked up at Captain Maskel, "You with her?"

The captain threw his hands up, "Yes I am, I don't know how I got here, but yes I am."

Luna chuckled, "Gisil, tell me why you're shackled."

He pulled at his shackles revealing his bloody and bruised wrists, "I don't know why I am, but even if I did I wouldn't tell you."

Luna sat down in front of Gisil, "Well it looks like we're going to be here a while." Luna and the captain sat trying to get information out of Gisil for hours but it was no use. Nighttime fell and they lay down in the path taking turns keeping watch as the other slept. Gisil did nothing, only stared off through tormented eyes. Luna's empathy produced kindness for him. He responded at times, but maintained his mean demeanor. "I can see you're in pain Gisil, why don't you let me help you?"

She hoped he would say yes but instead he replied, "Nobody can help me." He sat down on the ground wrapping his arms around his legs. Luna could see his self-pity and it bothered her. The captain sat bored from trying to figure out the situation, he was also feeling rather hopeless.

Luna studied Gisil, "Why are you here?"

He looked away, "The king and queen made me come here."

"Why, did you do something wrong?"

"Yeah, I did something wrong. I was born."

Luna gasped, "You don't really believe that do you?" For the first time she saw the deeply wounded soul in his eyes. Luna didn't wait for his reply, "Gisil, I'm sorry for whatever happened to you, I don't know what it is but I'm sure it must have hurt a lot. I know what it feels like to suffer and feel so alone. I was just like you, shackled. I do know one thing is for sure, we were all meant to be here, you and I as well." He listened quietly to the Bastling. "I come from a place where nobody was the same as me, I was made fun and ridiculed for being different, until they drove me out of my own world one day." Luna felt the pain all over again. Gisil and the captain were captivated by her story, "When I was driven out I thought I would die and came close to it but fate, destiny stepped in and saved me. It was then that I started on my journey to find the answers I had been asking all my life. That journey has led me here." The captain fought back tears as he cleared his throat. Gisil took in her words as Luna watched his pain reveal itself to her. "But Gisil you must understand, nobody can make you feel this pain you're in, and nobody can take it away, only you. You have the choice right now to free yourself. If I knew that before I was driven out, I would have willingly thrown myself into that Black Pool and swam to the other side. You're lucky because right now you have the chance to unlock those shackles." Her eyes followed the line of chains. She instinctively reached out her hand to him and placed it on his hand. He didn't retract his. Tears began rolling down his sullen, worn face. "It's alright Gisil, just let it out." He sobbed like a child as Luna reached over to hold him. She put her arms around him and when she did he began to shake. A crackling noise echoed through the pathway as Luna and the captain looked for its source. She felt something move within her arms and realized it was Gisil. His body began cracking and crumbling as Luna cradled him. The pieces of Gisil fell away to the ground revealing a young, vital man underneath. When it was all over Luna was still holding him.

She let go as Gisil looked around and then at his new body, "What happened? This is incredible, I haven't looked like this in years. The vibrant face looked up at Luna who was smiling, "Thank you Luna, thank you."

"It wasn't me, it was you who set yourself free." The two stood up and turned to see the Captain staring at the both stunned, "Well Captain, I guess we can go now."

Gisil asked, "Can I help you get to where you're going? Let me repay you please."

The captain shrugged, "I don't see why not." Luna agreed. The three made their way down the path towards the Castle of Wreckage, with Gisil leading the way.

When they reached the end of the path they looked up to see the castle looming in the distance. There was darkness all around. No life existed. The trees, grass and plants were dead. No other signs of life, no animals, just the sound of silence. A cry could be heard in the distance of the castle walls. Luna shivered, "Well Gisil, this is as far as you go. I don't want to drag you into this any further." He disagreed, he wanted to keep going with them but Luna and the captain insisted this was where he stopped. "I don't want anything to happen to you since you just found yourself again. You could help us in another way though, why don't you search out anyone else who may be on this island and help them."

Gisil thought about for a moment, "Alright I will. Will I ever see you again?"

Luna nervously smiled, "I really hope so Gisil, I really do." The Bastling and the captain said goodbye to Gisil as they watched him run off. Luna continued watching him, "I hope he'll be all right."

The captain looked back at the castle, "Yeah and I hope we will be too." They headed off to the ominous castle in the distance. When they arrived at the castle grounds there was no sign of guards or soldiers. Luna thought it odd but continued on anyway. They reached the enormous doors within minutes and the captain looked around, "Now what?!" Suddenly the doors opened to them revealing an empty hall. Everything was gray and black, worn and neglected. "I don't like this Luna." Hands grabbed the captain from behind as he fought, but it was no use he was outnumbered. The ghastly soldiers held him and walked away up the tower steps. Luna screamed for him and ran to chase them but more soldiers caught her and dragged her back down the stairs to the main hall. They threw her down in the middle of the floor as she cried out in pain.

"You shouldn't be so disrespectful in my kingdom, especially in my castle." Luna looked up to see two thrones upon which sat the Savage Queen and the Maimed King. The queen's beady, black eyes, reminded Luna of the Dregs.

The Maimed King sat lifeless in the throne, he didn't seem very threatening, "Guards, take the prisoner and chain her here." The queen pointed to a pair of shackles near the throne. The shackles looked eerily familiar to Luna as she recalled Gisil. They grabbed her and chained her up. The guards were told to leave.

Luna yelled at the queen, "Where's the captain?"

The queen flicked her head at Luna and glared, "Don't ever speak to me unless you are spoken to." She raised her palm, sending a shockwave that caused Luna to recoil in pain. The king sat fidgeting in his throne. The queen smirked, "You will find out quickly here Luna, I am in charge and each time you don't listen you will receive prompt punishment."

She rose and left the hall leaving Luna with the Maimed King. He looked over at Luna, "Are you all right?" Luna was surprised he could even talk, "Yes I'm okay, I didn't think you knew anything that was going on."

"Oh, I know more than you think, I just don't say too much, it's no use. She'd just as soon do to me what she did to you."

Luna was shocked by his nonchalance but felt strangely comfortable with the king, "Why are you holding the Heart Stone?"

He sat up quickly and looked around making sure nobody was within listening distance, "Don't ever bring up the Heart Stone. She'll kill you if you do. You must never speak of it in front of her." His warning was sincere.

Luna pushed, "Can I talk about it with you?"

He sat back tired, "There's nothing to tell, it's here and it always will be as far as she is concerned." He stared straight ahead.

"Where is the Heart Stone?"

"It's locked in the tower with your friend." He plopped his head down on his hand exhausted.

Luna sat figuring out what to ask next, "What are you going to do with me?"

He laughed halfheartedly, "I'm not going to do anything with you, it's her. She'll keep you here until she decides what's best." Luna looked around the hall trying to find any way of escape. The hall had no windows, they had long been cemented over as she noticed it cracking and falling out in some spots. Luna looked around the joining of the floors and the walls. It was then that she caught sight of a bizarre scene. In the middle of the room sat a small black bush, resembling a tiny tree. Its leaves were too many to count and were as black as the darkest of Dregling hearts. A spear was driven through it and from its point of entry, blood dripped. As each drop fell it scorched the marble floor. Luna sat mesmerized. Breaking free of this mesmerizing sight, she looked at the king who seemed to be going into a trance. "What is that?" She pointed to the bush.

The king rose for the first time and walked over to Luna, "That is a warning to all who live in Centros, that is the pain that can be inflicted upon anyone by the Savage Queen." He raised his leg and kicked Luna in the face. Luna fell back bleeding from her wounds. She was confused and disoriented. When she regained some strength, she noticed the king sitting back on his throne, seeming to come out of his trance. He looked over at Luna, "What happened to you, are you all right?" He sat up straighter and Luna coiled back in nervousness. "What? What are you afraid of? You don't have to be afraid of me." The king's face was full of sincerity.

Luna quickly realized the Maimed King had no recollection of his violent act. Luna didn't know how to answer him, "I fell when I tried to stand up." She put her head down and sat quiet for a long time. Soon she nodded off, exhausted.

When she awoke all was quiet in the hall and her attention was drawn to the peculiar bleeding bush. Luna watched as each drop of blood burned the floor over and over again. The king spoke, "It is hypnotizing, isn't it?"

Luna looked over at him, "What is it?"

He threw up his hands, "Who knows, I've never been able to figure that out. I don't know why she had it here but she refuses to take it out."

Just then the queen entered, her long, black gown flowing behind her, "Are you talking to the prisoner?" Her eyes grew small and squinted as she aimed her question in the king's direction.

Fearfully he replied, "No I wasn't! I was just talking to myself." He smiled hoping it would appease her.

She walked over and stood in front of Luna, "I've been to visit your friend in the tower." Luna sat up eagerly. "Don't worry he's alive…for now. And with some persuasion from my relentless soldier your horrid captain has confessed everything to me, your plans to take back the Heart Stone." The king cringed back. "I must tell you Luna, it was a very stupid decision to try this, you won't ever leave this island alive." She laughed throwing her head back. Her dark black hair glistened. Luna hated her and the queen detected it immediately, "Yes, that's good Luna. Let your heart fill with the hate, that's what I like." She leaned in towards her, "It feels good, doesn't it? The power and beauty of the dark heart."

Luna glared back at her, "No it isn't beautiful, it's weak." Luna knew she would pay for speaking but she didn't care.

The queen stood straight up and shot her hand out again at Luna causing painful waves to emanate through her body like a thousand knives. She screamed and fell back, curling up her Bastling body. The queen smiled and sat down in her throne. She then shot her hand at the king and laughed as he clenched his teeth and hands in pain, "Don't think I didn't know you were talking to her."

After Luna recovered at bit, she sat up weakly. She was beginning to understand why the king looked the way he did. The king and queen were still sitting on their thrones each watching the bleeding bush. Luna watched it as well feeling sorry for the peculiar sight.

Days passed and Luna grew frailer. The queen's routine was consistent, she would sit for a while with the king then leave for a long time. Luna always heard screams when the queen was gone believing she was inflicting pain on the captain. The king and Luna would talk a lot and every day without fail the king would fall into his daze and attack Luna, hurting her badly at times. Yet Luna felt compassion for this strange king. She knew he was good but had been assaulted himself by torment. As with the rest of the routine, day after day Luna watched the bleeding bush feeling pity and compassion for it as well. She wanted desperately to help it but knew it was no use.

More time passed, and Luna could literally feel the life draining from her body. She thought about Eldred and the Tree of Answaru and a pulse of light rushed through her. She looked at the bleeding bush and then to the king who was fast asleep. She quietly picked up her chains to see how far they would go, she wanted to get as close as she could to the bush. Every day as the king slept she would go and sit close to the bush listening to the scorching sound as its blood burned the floor. She watched it closely, her compassion for it growing daily. Luna didn't know how someone could be so cruel and knowing that the spear was causing it pain, she wanted to help the bush. If she couldn't save the Heart Stone, at least she could help this poor defenseless plant. It was as if the bush was speaking to her at times. Her compassion grew to obsession.

As it was every day, the king fell asleep and the queen rose to go to the tower. Luna went over and sat next to the bush. She laid there near to it lovingly wanting to help it. Beautiful sounds ricocheted in the hemispheres of her mind. She was convinced its source was the bush and was soon lulled to sleep. She awoke to the sound of uproar, "Get away from that bush!" Luna, half dazed, turned to see the queen's enraged approach. She looked at the bush and without thinking started to reach for it. The queen shot out her hand and inflicted her painful torture on Luna, but the faithful Bastling persisted. She fell over and over as the queen stood beating her with her invisible power. As Luna screamed in pain, she saw noticed the Savage Queen would not approach any closer. Luna moved closer to the bush reaching out to grab the arrow. The queen screeched and pushed even harder to inflict pain on Luna, but she was undeterred. The queen yelled for the king to help but he didn't know what to do, he too wouldn't approach any closer to the bush. With one last effort Luna reached for the spear as the queen pushed all her dark painful power into the little Bastling's body. Overcome with pain, Luna pulled as hard as her weakened body could and wrenched the spear from the bush. An excruciating scream came out of the bush and Luna fell nearly unconscious. The small, black shrub began bleeding profusely. The royal couple fell to their knees, overcome. Blood poured out of its small body until its life force spilled onto the surrounding floor, burning a circle into it. The torn Bastling began to cry thinking she had killed the bush. She watched as it began to shrivel, curl, crackle, shake and bounce on the floor amidst the burned rubble. It ceased for a moment, revealing its new shape, a heart.

All went silent and then with a crash of thunder, lightning, and a flash of light, there on the floor sat the Heart Stone blazing with energy and glory. As the king and queen lay on the floor nearby, Luna pushed herself up and struggled over to the stone. Leaning in to pick it up, she hesitated and then heard it speak to her, "Take me home." Luna picked it up with confidence and suddenly the ground beneath started to shake. Her shackles fell off and she instinctively ran to the tower and freed the captain. He didn't ask any questions just followed her out of the crumbling castle. The two ran as fast as they could, never looking back. They followed the path back through to where the obstacles once were, finding Gisil, Broeder, and even Rivkah.

They all rushed past the caves that housed the three witches who now stood outside as young vibrant women breathing in the air of Centros. Continuing on, the entire group of lost Sentients, the captain and Luna hurried into the Dead Forest. It started to crumble as well, as one by one their friends began to fall and be released from the trees above. The captain and Luna desperately tried to help them as they yelled for everyone to run to the ship. Once all were aboard, they set sail with nobody knowing what happened with exception of the Bastling. The captain looked out at the crumbling island with Luna, "Well we didn't get the Heart Stone but at least we can say we are the first to survive the trip." His melancholy face peered into Luna's.

She smiled, "Who said we didn't get the Heart Stone?" She reached into her bag and pulled out the glorious stone shining brilliantly with blinding pink and emerald light. The captain and crew gasped, "How did you get it? I had no idea! I just thought you found a way to escape!"

Luna laughed, "I did find a way to escape, I set the stone free!" The crew and captain listened to the tale as Luna captivated everyone with her story.

When they arrived at the shores of Centros the party was greeted with the most heartfelt welcome. They shared the story that would live forever in the hearts of every Sentient, now and in future generations to come. It was decided unanimously that Luna would have the honor of returning the stone to its rightful place. When they reached the old gateway, Luna pulled out the stone and held it high for all to see, it shone with the greatest of love and brilliance. She carefully placed it on the altar. A vast pink and emerald flash went out across the land transforming Centros back to its original beautiful state. She didn't realize there would be no chance to say goodbye as she was instantly transported to the next world.

Chapter 6

The Persecution of Time

A flash of light illuminated the corridor that lay between Centros and Vocalos as Luna came tumbling into it. She immediately began sobbing as her goodbyes were cut short by her unexpected departure. The sad Bastling turned to look behind her to see if there was a way back in, but alas there was none. Her friends in Centros stood at the gate wishing that they too could have her back. The captain fought back tears as did Cheelah and the others. The feisty Bastling had saved their world from the perilous evil that held it captive for so long. Ardor seemed to take it the hardest and left the crowd to be alone. Luna put her hand to the wall but knew it was time to move on. With grief in her heart she turned towards the next world.

The tunnel posed no threat as the hues changed from true greens to brilliant blues and in no time, she had reached the door. It stood as normal as any other with the exception of the symbol of two horizontal lines crossed with a vertical one that was scored into the center of the entrance. She wanted to stop and double check the symbol on her map, but time and her instinct would not allow it, so with resignation she opened the door and passed through, into total darkness. Luna stopped abruptly putting her hands out in front of her and then to her side finding a wall. She followed the rocky tunnel, careful not to trip or lose her way in the void, each step was methodical and tempered. After a few moments of fumbling in the dark a pinhole of light caught her eyes up ahead. She quickened her pace and within moments was standing in front of a purple velvet curtain with a long braided golden rope. It concealed what lay behind with only a glimmer of light peeking through. She had learned something on her travels thus far, never hesitate, and with that she yanked the cord.

Luna cringed, eyes shut in anticipation of what would be when she opened them, but the scene was unexpected, a tiny path that led into an ancient, plush forest alive with a palette of violets and greens. Trees swayed back and forth inviting her in to their kingdom as birds serenaded from above. She followed the path. The trail stretched far into the foliage as far as her eyes would allow her to see and then disappeared. She had never seen anything like this forest before yet everything seemed so hauntingly familiar. Her senses tingled with anticipation. Salt water filled the air as she reached the end of the path where the forest broke free into sand and water.

As Luna stood amongst the pebbles of the beach she gazed up at the mist and mountains on the other side of the water. To her right the forest revealed a hillside that echoed with voices. She made her way along the pebbled pathway following it around the slope. The air became even more alive with the sounds of laughter and music. It was steeper on second glance causing her to slip a few times. In every world thus far, approaching the inhabitants caused some anxiety, but Vocalos gave no such feeling. The only anxiety she felt was the urgency to see old friends, but how could that be she wondered, after all she had obviously never been here before.

Once atop the hill a fair vibrated with life in front of her. Carts, wagons, and booths were cluttered with food, clothing, and trinkets along with throngs of people. Music filled the hilltop with people dancing in joyous circles as children scuffled through crowds, some mischievous, while others played games. Mothers showed their babies to neighbors with pride and fathers beamed at their beautiful families. Luna began walking through the crowds invisibly, accepted as if one of their own. The Vocalans looked upon her as if she had lived there her whole life.

Once deep in the center of the thoroughfare she paused to take in everything again and as her eyes scanned the friendly faces of Vocalos, they set themselves on a figure to the right in the distance. The mountains in the background gave indication to Luna that this person was important. He sensed eyes upon him and turned around from the group of men he was talking with and caught Luna's stare. He began walking towards her and upon his arrival introduced himself, "Hello I am Sonuachar of the Keltoi and you would be?"

Luna cleared her throat, "I am Luna of the Bastlings, and very pleased to meet you."

He smiled, "Well it's obvious you're not from around here, do you have any lodging for the night?"

"No, I don't. But I'm quite used to camping by myself outside." Luna explained to him that she had just come from Centros and upon entering Vocalos, had come directly through the forest to the hill top.

Sonuachar shook his head in disagreement, "Nonsense, I will not hear of it, you won't be outside tonight, you can lodge at my parents' inn. The invitation is also for selfish reasons, I want to know how you came through the gate to this world." He smiled and Luna accepted without hesitation.

The following days Luna spent time learning the Keltoi ways from Sonuachar, a people she quickly grew to love. They too, welcomed her openly and genuinely wanting to know her Bastling ways and about the mysterious world of Elan. Of course there wasn't much to tell as she too wondered about the Bastling way of life and what it meant to be such a being. One day when Luna and Sonuachar were out for their daily walk through the grasses, they came upon a cave nestled quietly in between the grasses of two small hills. Although silent it resounded with a presence, "What is this place Sonuachar?" He explained that it was inhabited by the thousand-year-old man, a hermit who had lived there for the past two hundred years. Luna wondered why someone would want to live that way when there were so many wonderful people in Vocalos.

Her friend explained, "He is a mystic, a man gifted at birth with insights far beyond his years. He grew up to be a well-respected spiritual leader of the people seeing many generations live and die. People say he healed every one of them at one time or another. One day after eight hundred years of service he announced that he had to go away from the village for a higher purpose. The people were saddened but understood it was his way. Nobody ever bothers him out of respect for his wishes. There are many myths surrounding him now, some say he lost his powers and that old age had finally caught up with him. Others tell a story of a raven that came and warned him of a time of bloodshed that would fall on the good people of Vocalos, so he went into solitude to search for a way to stop the tragedy. Ultimately, it is still a mystery as to his departure but sometimes late at night you can still hear him chanting and singing as it echoes throughout the land."

Luna's curiosity welled uncontrollably, it was as if she was being pulled towards the cave by an unseen magnetic force. She stepped closer and Sonuachar warned, "It's better he is left alone, out of respect we must honor his wishes." His voice was stern but Luna didn't listen, her feet carried her right to the opening of the stone mound. She knew what Sonuachar didn't, she had seen this place many times before in her dreams and it was exhilarating to finally be in front of it. As for Sonuachar, he was agitated and nervous, he wanted to flee and did his best to persuade her one more time but it was too late, making his way out of the cave was the old man himself crawling on all fours.

She quickly bent down to help him but he stubbornly pulled it away, "Let go! I'm old, not feeble! It's just too short to stand up in here!"

Luna burst into laughter as Sonuachar stood in shock. The old man came out into the grasses and finally straightened up his torso. He eyed Luna and then Sonuachar, "Ha! What a sight, this is the pair I've been waiting for all these two hundred years? Hmm." The Bastling and young Vocalan looked at each other in amazement as he barked out his order, "Well don't just stand there gawking! Take a seat on the grass."

The two followed his instructions without any thought as he wagged his finger at them, "I've been waiting a long time for the two of you and I must say you are slow learners." Luna stared intently at him, his ragged old robe once white, now tattered and grayed from all the solitary time in the cave. Sonuachar thought the old man's statement odd since he had passed by the cave many times in his life.

The old hermit snapped back at him obviously hearing his thoughts, "Yes, but you two weren't together then, it needed to be both of you!"

Sonuachar, stunned by his statement replied, "I didn't say anything."

The old man laughed, "No, but you were thinking it."

He turned to Luna, "And yes, I do wash the robe at the water's edge but it tends to fade after two hundred years." It was Luna's turn to look stunned as he laughed, "Don't let the old body fool you, I'm as sharp as I ever was if not more! It's good to be alone, it heightens the senses." He gazed into Luna's eyes too intensely for her liking, "But you would know all about that wouldn't you?" The Bastling blushed with embarrassment as she realized he knew of her painfully lonely existence in Elan. Sonuachar wanted to know what he was missing and the old man answered his thoughts again, "It's simple really, she spent her whole life very much the same way as you, around many people but not really there at all, sheltering feelings, fears and a heart from those who might not treat it so kind. You really are kindred spirits." The pair looked at each other and glanced away. The old man hobbled in closer, "Allow me to properly introduce myself, I am Ceil Loch Cucuhlain, Mystic Bard of the Raven Clan and your humble teacher." Luna and Sonuachar didn't know what to say, she felt perhaps she had been mistaken for someone else and Sonuachar simply felt he could not do whatever it was Ceil wanted to teach him. The old man raised his hand, "Wait, wait don't tell me, you are Luna and he is Sonuachar!" His laughter was full of sarcasm. It was then that Luna quickly shared her belief that he had the wrong person.

"On the contrary my dear, you are exactly who I've been expecting and you look just as they showed me."

Luna questioned him, "Who are they?"

Ceil chuckled, "Why the spirits of course. Who else would it be?" He then turned to Sonuachar who had turned silent, "Snap out of it boy! Don't worry, your father knew of this when you were born, he'll not be upset. He knows that you are to do this, he knows you're chosen." Sonuachar's face was full of surprise as the two sat in disbelief as Ceil announced it was time to begin.

From that moment on, every chance Luna and Sonuachar had they spent with Ceil. He taught them so many things they feared they wouldn't remember everything. Yet the more they held this belief, the more Ceil would put them to the test. He would make them sit in the fields by his cave and meditate for hours. He taught them how to focus and harness their clairvoyance, clairaudience, and clairsentience. Ceil taught them that they could focus on any living thing and heal it by giving it their loving energy. They were an outstanding team. They complemented each other, where one lacked, the other would pick up the slack. When Sonuachar wanted to give up, Luna would encourage him to go on. When she was too tired, he would carry her. Ceil was growing quite proud of his prodigies but also growing tired himself.

On their daily trek to his cave, as Luna and Sonuachar came over the hill into the fields, they were struck with a feeling of unease, they both instinctively knew something was wrong. When they approached the cave, they found Ceil lying in the tall grasses. The two rushed to his side and helped him sit up. His breathing was raspy and he was barely able to speak, "Hello my two young bloods, I am afraid I am not feeling well and it appears our lessons are at an end. I thought I would have more time but the spirits have informed me this is where we must stop. They say the rest is for another time and place, another life." He cracked a weak smile as Luna's eyes filled with pain and tears, "Now you must both listen very carefully to what I say, very soon things will get very strange and you will not understand why they are happening, but this you do not need to know. It serves a higher purpose in which the effects will be as ripples in the water for futures yet to come. What you do need to know is that you must see it through to the end and be each other's strength regardless of how far apart you are. The others are coming and there is nothing you can do to stop it." Luna's body quivered with chills as did Sonuachar's, causing him to buckle over in pain. Ceil grabbed hold of his arm, "Boy, you must learn to block better, if you don't you will experience things far too deeply. It will cause you great distress in the future if you don't."

Luna interrupted him, "You said the others were coming, who are you talking about?"

Ceil's face saddened, "They are the ones who came into Vocalos during the Dark Storm. They have stayed hidden all this time plotting and planning to take over our beautiful lands. They are dark, darker than the storm itself." The old, frail man looked directly into her eyes, "Everyone has a destiny no matter how great or insignificant it may seem. Your destiny is with them now, you two are the ripples that cause tidal waves." He gasped for air and with another small breath his spirit let go of his body. It rushed through Luna and Sonuachar on its exit. The two sat for hours in the green of the land holding the greatest and most holy man they had ever known and their tears ran like rivers onto the old man's worn robe. After they buried him in the traditions of the Vocalan people, Luna and Sonuachar set out to fulfill the duties Ceil had bestowed upon them. For them it was the only way to keep his spirit alive. They tirelessly helped the people, healing, restoring, giving. It was the least they could do to honor the man who had given them so much. Soon people were coming from all ends of Vocalos to seek the pair's help and they lovingly obliged.

One day as Luna and Sonuachar sat in the fields near the cave they talked of a subject that had never discussed, Luna's exit from Vocalos.

"You know how grateful I am to you, Ceil and all the people, but I have to keep going. I've been here so long and it's time for me to continue, as much as I hate it, I have to."

Sonuachar turned angry, "But you know what Ceil said, our destiny is here. I don't know who these others are but if they are as horrible as he said they are, our people will need us more than ever."

Luna's heart sank as she fought back the guilt, "Please Sonuachar, why don't you leave with me? Travel to the other worlds with me? Perhaps Ceil meant for us to help others in those worlds too." Her eyes pleaded for the answer she longed to hear from Sonuachar, but it did not come.

"Luna, I can't leave my people, I just can't and I don't think this is what Ceil meant for us. He wanted us to be together as a team."

Her heart fell, "Okay I will think about it, just give me a little time." Sonuachar knew one of them would be unhappy with the outcome.

As the two rose from the grasses to head back to the hills, their silence was broken by the sounds of people coming across the hills near the mountains. It was an unusual sight to see as none of the Vocalans lived on the other side of the hills. It was barren and produced no good lands or crops since the Dark Storm. As they came closer into view they realized they were not any of the villagers, these beings were dressed far differently, the likes of which Luna and Sonuachar had never seen. Luna looked to her friend for answers, "Who are they? Do you know them?"

She was surprised by his answer, "Yes they are the Firemakers, they have stayed over the mountains in the Far East for many years, but I have never seen them come this way before. They conquered the other side of Vocalos years ago, it gives me a horrid feeling inside." He clutched his belly.

Luna felt the pangs too but did not let on to Sonuachar and wasn't quite sure why. "What do they do Sonuachar, why do they conquer?"

He waved his hand back and forth over the grass causing it to move under the energy of his touch, "They believe everyone should think and act as they do, they believe there is no room in this world for anything else but their way. They have rituals for everything and pray to an empty God that is nowhere to be found."

Luna shook her head, "How can that be? God is everywhere, all around us, in us, in everything."

Sonuachar agreed, "But not in their world, they don't see it that way. They believe the only way to see God is to conjure him by chanting and falling to their knees, yet he never appears to them even when they do."

Luna continued staring at the figures crossing the hills, "What does it mean that they are here now?"

His turned solemn, "I'm not sure, but it can't be good."

The two realized it was time to get back to the village and warn the others. Luna turned back to him, "Why are they called the Firemakers?"

He shook his head, "I never did find out why, the last time they came into these parts of Vocalos I was only a child, but the Elders managed to drive them out. I have asked my father the same question but he never would tell me." The two made their way back quickly.

The following day was Luna's favorite, Festival Day. There was a special place in her heart for it as it was the first day she ever stepped foot into Vocalos, a day when she felt an immediate connection like no other. So, with Festival Day came great anticipation. She made her way out of the mists of the morning like she always did. Luna loved to follow her pebble path through the forest where the water waited patiently to welcome her and the mist gently tapped the shoreline. Luna breathed in as if it were her first as she raised her hands into the air giving thanks for the day, sunlight, and all things living. She also gave special thanks for being able to be and experience all of it. A raven called out behind the mountains. Emerging through the fog, it perched itself atop the tree that stood beside her. A strange feeling came over her, at first it was an honor to be greeted by such a messenger but then she felt as if Ceil were there too, as a warning. She quickly dismissed it and thanked the raven for its presence, and made her way up the pebbled beach as she had done so many times before. It felt exhilarating just to be alive there on the shores of the great waters and the grasses sparkled as they softened her ascent up the hillside. Soon she was hearing the familiar sound of the festival, and music and laughter filled the air. The sounds of life were all around her and within her and she loved it.

Once atop the hill Luna scanned the crowd of faces she had come to know so well, as they smiled back at her. As she made her way through the village she felt eyes upon her and a sense of terror seized her. Luna turned to find the source of the stare, she had seen him in the village many times but did not know him personally. His blue eyes were cold and piercing, putting a knot in her stomach. He smiled oddly, nodded his head and disappeared into the crowd. She shook it off, burying another vibration and tried not to think about why she had been doing this so much lately. Spotting Sonuachar in the crowd she sent him a telepathic "hello" and he returned it back with a wave. He was standing with his father and uncles, so Luna decided to leave him talk with them for the time being. She was happy just to be standing there amongst the villagers as she always did. The Bastling glanced over to the watchful mountains standing as silent giants in the background. She wondered what it must be like to see generations live and die as they had, as Ceil had, when suddenly her thoughts were interrupted by gasps coming from the crowds. Luna stepped through the Vocalans to see what they were gawking at, stepping through the path her eyes captured what their attention was on, an image in the hills. Riding furiously towards them, The Firemakers. Luna's heart began to race as she attempted deep breaths but failed. Pressure began building in her chest as she watched the people's expressions turn to horror and fear. As the group drew closer the panic began to pound at her body like a death drum. Just then, the raven flew overhead crying out to all its warning. She looked for Sonuachar but could not see him through the throngs of people huddled closely together.

The Firemakers pulled up in front of the villagers and dismounted from their horses. The first to approach was a man whose milky white skin sat starkly against the black of his robe and his fire red hair. His blue eyes like jagged icicles. Behind him stood a large clan of men dressed in velvets and jewels. Their stares were predatory. The leader wasted no time talking, "I am Gideon and my men and I have come a great distance to see you as you are the last of your kind. Your land no longer belongs to you, it will now be controlled by the Righteous Ruler. It is in your best interests to cooperate fully so no harm will come to your families. It has been brought to the Righteous Ruler's attention that there are those of you who practice the old ways. This must stop at once. We will be kind to you all, leaving you to peacefully till and harvest in these lands with of course a small profit going back to the most gracious Righteous Ruler. We do not ask for much else with exception that you adhere to the laws passed down by him." He stopped for a moment glaring into the faces of the motionless villagers as nobody dared to react, it was as if each of them was frozen in time. He walked back and forth peering into the crowd, "Resistance and rebellion will not be tolerated! To prove this point we shall show you what revolution will get you. It has been brought to our attention that some of you here still practice the old arts of healing. The Righteous Ruler has handed down strict laws regarding these practices and behaviors. Therefore, we have come to seek out and punish those who practice this heathenish craft to set an example for the rest of you and the lack of tolerance the Righteous One has for such acts. I have been given the names of those involved in such treacherous behavior. Your own people have turned you in, so there is no use trying to run or hide. When I call your name, step forward."

Gideon began reciting the names of women of all ages and clans and yet there was not a man among them called. People muttered and cried. A rush of heat coursed through Luna as the people started backing away, as the creature called more names. Luna could see the energy around him, pure black. She shuddered with fear for she knew that for such a being to have energy in this state, no mercy lay within his walls and in that moment, she wished she was anywhere but there. She thought of Ceil as the raven circled continuously over them. She caught sight of Sonuachar as the crowd backed away. Terror was in his eyes just as much as the others. "Luna! Luna of the Bastlings, step forward!" She felt as if she was in a dream. Everything around her went hazy as the Vocalans looked at her with tears and pity. Every action took on a slow motion as she caught sight of Sonuachar pulling his sword from its sheath and yelling, although it was as if she could no longer hear, deaf to the scenes around her. All that remained was the pounding of her heart.

The men that once stood behind Gideon now stepped to grab hold of those who stood before them as accused. Luna felt hands grabbing her away from where she had stood, but stayed focused on Sonuachar. His father and uncles fought him and pushed him to the ground taking his sword as Gideon's men were now focused on the scene. Luna instinctively called his name drawing her voice one more time, "Sonuachar! No!" Her voice turned soft as she put her hand out as if to stop him,

"Leave it, I will go." His shoulders dropped, his eyes brimming with a spirit crushed. Luna smiled bravely and from her heart to his she spoke telepathically, "It will be all right." Gideon's men pushed her and the others towards the back of the carts that were hitched to the horses. They began tying their hands with rope and tethering them to the carts. Luna's back was now to Sonuachar but she could feel him staring all the same. She looked around at the women who were crying and scared. Luna felt pure hatred for the first time in her Bastling life. She vacillated between rage and numbing fear of what would come next.

Gideon began addressing the people once again, "You have seen what happens to those who do not follow the law. There are consequences for those who take advantage of the Righteous Ruler's good grace. Let this be a lesson for those who stand here now! Disrespect will not be tolerated."

With that he turned around and made his way to the carts. As he did one of the women called out to him, "Your grace, please! I have children and I've done nothing wrong. Please for the sake of my little ones, I beg your forgiveness!"

"You should have thought of that before you practiced such treacherous acts mocking our God to his face." He grinned and shot back around, "To the ship! We have already lost a great deal of time!" The men mounted their horses and began pulling the carts that were full of supplies. Luna and the rest of the prisoners began walking quickly trying to keep up with the pace of the carts to which they were tied.

For what seemed an eternity, Luna and the rest of the women were dragged behind the caravan, stopping only briefly for one of the men to fix a wheel. At the water's edge, they saw a huge ship waiting. The soldiers untied them from the cart, but kept them hitched to each other in a row. One by one the group boarded the wooden ship. One woman fell as she tried to get on causing the entire group to stumble into a pile. The soldiers didn't help them but instead laughed in their faces. When a young girl attempted to get up from the pile, she fell into the rail of the ship cutting her face wide open; the men laughed even harder.

Once they were all aboard Luna looked back to the beautiful land that had once gleamed with love and laughter. It was now silent and melancholy, as if the land itself was in mourning. Luna hoped that Sonuachar would disregard her wishes and come to rescue them, but no movement appeared in the hills. They all hoped men from the clan would come rescue them, but they did not. Their hopes and wishes were disrupted by yells as the men walked by the row of women kicking them as they passed by. One of their boots met Luna's face and the warmth of her own blood pooled in her mouth. Her head came back up to look him square in the eyes as he announced, "This is a feisty one." He leaned into her face and whispered for only her to hear, "There's more where that came from, wait until you have your confession then we'll see how brave you really are." His ominous laughter was halted as he caught sight of her Bag of Borrowed hanging from her back. Ripping it off her, he said, "What is this?"

He smirked as she screamed fighting to get up, "Give that back! It's none of your business!" Luna was near hysteria when he opened it and rummaged through its contents.

"Nothing you're going to need anymore." And with one quick swing he tossed the bag over the side of the ship as the broken-hearted Bastling watched it disappear into the murky depths of the water. She knew in that instant that Sonuachar had gotten his wish, she would not be leaving Vocalos after all.

It was an arduous journey on the ghastly ship, no food, no water, and plenty of sick women. Some women didn't make it through the journey and when the soldiers found one lost to dehydration or their wounds, they simply cut the ropes that tied them to the others and threw their bodies overboard. The sights she witnessed horrified Luna, and she began to feel she would not make it either. Fainting spells were common and reality was beginning to fade for all of them. When they arrived at their destination many women were gone and two more perished before they disembarked the ship. Silently, they followed the ropes trying carefully not to slip and bring the others down with them. This was the only piece of dignity and control they had left. When they stepped off the ship they were in another land. Across the distant horizon the only sight was gray smoky plumes. The green land was like the greens of the hills they had just come from but the land did not sing to her, instead it whispered different things, words she didn't want to hear. Once again, they were tied to carts and horses and led up the hills towards the smoky columns.

As dusk fell, the exhausted prisoners heard Gideon shout, "We are at the city walls! Take them directly to the dungeons!" Luna gazed up to see walls that almost touched the sky. Huge wooden doors creaked open. As they entered the city, smoke filled her nostrils. Some began coughing. People were lined up alongside the carts staring at them as they were led in. They looked very much like the Vocalans of Sonuachar's clan but there was something missing in their eyes, they were vacant, soulless. Luna could not detect any light in them as if it had been ripped out by invisible claws. They laughed, scowled, and mocked the women as they were dragged through the streets, throwing garbage at them while yelling obscenities. A woman who walked behind Luna spoke in shock, "Even the children are behaving this way, how could a young one be so dark and evil?"

Luna replied, "They are more frightened of us than we are of them, they've been brainwashed by darkness. They live under fear and tyranny every day, they are probably happy it is us and not them today. It's just survival." The woman did not speak again.

Led into the center of the fortified village, a huge stone castle lauded over the city. Smoke encircled the top of it making it difficult to see how tall it really was; it seemed to rise forever into the darkness. The smoke now invaded all her senses as screams from within the walls could be heard. The flames rose higher. Luna was beginning to understand why Sonuachar's father never told him why they were called the Firemakers.

They were taken towards the back of the castle where there were a set of steps leading down below the building. One after another they descended with only wall torches to light their way. Once all the prisoners were down, they were led into a large room where a foul odor lingered making Luna feel even more uneasy. She tried to keep her breathing down to a shallow inhale but it was no use. To the far right there was a holding cell made of metals melded together. It was here that Luna and the rest would be placed. All ropes and shackles were taken off, open wounds and cuts were left behind. Their prison was replaced by another as the gate slammed shut, locking them inside.

Luna stood at the front of the holding cell and peered into the huge room. There were several wooden tables with shackles and weapons of all kinds and instruments she had never seen before. When Luna's eye caught the black mask hanging over the fire pit on the wall, she suddenly felt sick again.

They all huddled together for warmth despite the smell coming from themselves and the walls in which they were contained. One by one, the women succumbed to sleep, and dreams of a place where the lands rolled green and free and they danced with friends and family. Luna's slumber was interrupted by a nudge from a woman, it was old Annie, "Bastling, there must be a way out, can't we do anything? We can't die like this."

Luna's heart ached for the old woman, "There is nothing I can do Annie, or I would have. I've been trying to think of some way, but even if I could come up with a plan, my energy is so low. I'm unfocused and so tired." Luna's guilt overwhelmed her as did her feelings of helplessness. She hated saying those words to poor Annie, it was by far the worst feeling she had known.

Footsteps echoed from the corner of the dungeon and Gideon and his men suddenly appeared. They were not the men from the ship, these men were twice their size, formidable and strong. Luna grabbed the metal bars of the cage, her hands revealing the fresh wounds on her wrists. She searched the faces of the men for any compassion but found none. They all glared at her with evil intent, "What are you going to do with us? Don't we get a chance to plead our cases?" Gideon and the men laughed as Luna continued, "Who can we speak to to prove we've done nothing wrong? Who can we talk with about our terrible treatment?"

Gideon moved closer to the cell, "You will never speak to the Righteous Ruler but you will have a hearing with one of his representatives. Once all of you have met with him each one of you will go before the council where a decision will be made regarding your fate, and then you will be given a chance to retract your wrong doings." He smirked, his eyes piercing her soul. Gideon called to one of the men, "Mattheus, bring me the list." He held out his hand never taking his eyes off Luna. He read out the first name and Mattheus came over to the cell and unlocked it. The woman who came forward was ripped out of the cell by the arm. The door slammed once again leaving them to fear their fate.

When the first woman returned, Luna noticed she was in the same shape as when she left, giving her a glimmer of hope. She was returned to the cell with the others and another name was called. Woman after woman left and returned recounting the same story, that a gentle speaking man met with them, asked the women many things about themselves and was then released back to Gideon. There was one more commonality, all the women saw that Gideon was quite uncomfortable around this man. When it was Luna's turn to leave she felt in her heart that everything was going to be all right. Luna was led back up the stone steps and outside. It was daylight although barely evident through all the smoke. The men led her around a corner and up a long flight of stairs. In her weakened condition, the walk seemed like it took forever. Once atop, the group entered a hallway finely decorated with curved stone openings to the outside. A view of the village center could be seen where the people wandered around busy with activities. Luna could not detect any happiness as she stared down at them. After reaching the end of the hall she was made to turn left and taken through another narrower passageway that contained only doors. Stopping at the fourth one on the right, Gideon knocked surprisingly gently. The door was opened by a man dressed in a long black robe. His face wore no smile as he stepped back and waved them inside. Luna's heart tingled with anticipation, it was oddly comforting. Without warning Gideon and the others quickly exited leaving Luna standing in the middle of a small white room with a solitary chair in the corner and an old round table in the center with a few neatly stacked books. A window to her left allowed a dull smoky light into the room that fell flat against the slatted wooden floor. The solemnly robed man walked over to another door rapping gently, "The next one is here my noble one." His squeaky voice didn't match his features.

A confident voice on the other side said, "Bring her forth." Luna was allowed in with a turn of the door knob. She proceeded cautiously.

Inside was a man dressed in a long red robe seated behind a desk. He was immaculately ornamented with gold and red jewels. He motioned for her to sit at the chair in front of the desk, "Please sit down." She followed his command without thinking. He looked up at his robed assistant, "Emilius, you may leave now." He pointed to the door and his assistant obligingly left, bowing as he did. He looked back to Luna and gently lifted a smile to his face, "You look familiar to me, how is this possible? You obviously are not a Vocalan, what is your name?"

She was taken off guard by his candor and replied, "My name is Luna of the Bastlings."

He curiously sized her up and down, "A Bastling? Where are you from?"

Luna sank back, self-conscious of her appearance and the odor emanating from her clothes, "I am from Elan."

His face perked up, "How in the world did you get to Vocalos? That is a long way from home."

Luna found a reason to crack a smile, "It really wasn't my home, I am still searching for that and through my searching I came to Vocalos. I must say I am still in a great deal of shock from all that has happened. My heart is so saddened I cannot even begin to explain it."

He interrupted, "I am Anamchara, most call me "Lord" but I don't care for that. If you like you can call me Anam." Luna was once again surprised at his frankness and wondered why he would be so kind in such a dark village.

She warmed to him immediately, "I will call you Anam then." Her smile was returned by his and for a brief moment their eyes locked searching for something familiar.

The energy between them was strong and Luna began to shake, "Luna are you all right? Do you feel ill?" His eyes filled with genuine concern.

"Forgive me Anam. I am ill from lack of food, water and many miles of walking, it has been a nightmare. Most of us will not see our trial if we don't eat soon."

His face flushed with anger, "Emilius! Come here this very instant!" The fearful assistant scurried through the door and waited silently for his orders, "Take this message to Gideon immediately, the prisoners will be fed and given drink at once or he will answer to me. After you have delivered this message see to it that a meal is brought here for my guest."

Anam held his glare as he motioned to Luna who sat stunned by his commands. She looked up to Anam with his forceful demeanor to see tenderness oozing from his heart and admired his nobility immensely. When Emilius left, Anam returned to his seat behind the desk looking deeply into her eyes again.

Luna questioned, "What is it that you are looking for in my eyes?" Her heart softened for him despite her own predicament. He kept the same pose but his eyes wandered above her head.

"I have been in this post for many years now, and although it has been good for my life in many ways, I feel there is something missing, something is gravely wrong here. I find myself not agreeing with the duties I am asked to perform and when I meet people such as yourself I am curious as to the nature of their beliefs and moralities. I wonder if it is the Righteous Ruler who is wrong. If God is loving, why would he want us to kill in his name? You are on trial for being you and nothing more. Yet I fear for my own life and livelihood if I dare speak up. I am a coward." Luna couldn't believe what she was hearing and wondered if it was a trick, but just as quickly as the thought arose, Emilius entered through the door with their food. The two sat silently while the strange assistant placed trays down in front of them. Luna's stomach began to growl as the smell of the food reached her nostrils, "Thank you Emilius, you may go now." Anam gave no hint of kindness towards the robed servant causing him to exit quickly.

"Everyone seems afraid of you, yet all I have seen is kindness." Her eyes filled with pools of tears.

"It must be the company I am in to make me this way." His broad smile made his eyes twinkle, "Please Luna, eat and I apologize for what you and the other villagers have been through." The two sat quietly while they ate, in companionable silence while the fire spewed outside the walls of the cozy room in which they dined. When Luna had filled her body with fuel, the two drank tea and talked for a long time. "I must say Luna, I fear the worst for this situation but I will do everything in my power to withdraw the charges put upon you and the others but ultimately it is not in my hands. Gideon has a lower rank than I do but his opinion carries weight with the Righteous Ruler. They think very much alike and his passion for blood and undying affection for the Ruler is unstoppable. If he wants you to be punished, you will be." Luna's heart sank and it was now Anam's turn to tear up, "Come sit with me in the gardens for a while." He rose and went over to a door next to his bookcase that was concealed behind red drapes. He pushed gently and a door opened to the outside. Once in the garden, she could see the entire compound. Even though the castle and fortress were immense she thought perhaps there was a way to escape after all. As if reading her mind Anam spoke as he looked over the stone wall, "It is a huge complex full of crowds that one could get lost in, however there are guards posted every five feet around the entire perimeter to ensure nobody goes free. I have thought many times of trying to disappear into that crowd myself." He hung his head in shame.

Luna followed him over to a bench nestled between two flower beds, "Anam I feel so sad to see you in this anguish, is there nothing you can do to leave this post?" Her face was sincere with concern.

Anam shook his head, "How can you care for someone else when you are facing such a terrible sacrifice? That is not the soul of someone who is consumed by darkness." Anam shook his head adamantly, "No, there is nothing I can do. Long ago when I was young I was given this position, I've seen how people were after the Dark Storm and how the blackness consumed them, the Righteous Ruler promised salvation and order but when he began taking over other parts of Vocalos it didn't seem right. He claimed they were full of the darkness but I began to see it was the exact opposite; it was him who was dark. Now I feel like it was the worst decision of my life and all else pales in comparison. I once thought I was lost and found a better way to be despite that horrible situation. Today I feel I would have been better off leading that old life, at least I would still have my dignity." Luna studied his features, he was a robust man, tall and thick. The hair on his face disguised a still youthful face despite his years. His eyes revealed his soul, one that Luna felt very comfortable with. She felt herself getting lost in them and tried to refocus.

"Who is the Righteous Ruler, where did he come from?"

He shrugged, "Nobody knows for sure. Some say he was born after the Dark Storm, some say he came from it."

"Anam, tell me what will happen after I leave here." She searched his face this time for the truth. He rose again and walked over to the wall of the garden and looked out at the mess below.

"You will be returned to your cell as the others were and tomorrow we will hold council on what each of your fates will be, that is when I will make my plea to them. After a decision is made you will be brought before the entire council and given your sentence. Once that is completed with each one of you, the punishments will be handed out." His head dropped between his shoulders.

Luna went over to him and put her hand on his back, "Don't worry, it will be all right. I'm sure of it, I believe in you. Besides, whatever my destiny is, it is meant to be. I thought I would make it to the Tree of Answaru but perhaps my destiny lies here in Vocalos. If it does, at least I know I was happy and have met beautiful beings like yourself in spite of these dark ones. I have learned one thing for sure, sometimes the mind won't hear what the soul intends." Luna was appearing incredibly brave, but was terrified on the inside. She shook her head in defeat, "Even if I could escape I don't have my Bag of Borrowed anymore, it's lost in the waters forever."

Anam raised his head and stared at her with pity, "I fear Luna that your destiny is in their hands now." His words sent shivers down her spine as she recalled Ceil's words that echoed the same sentiment. He went back to the bench and asked Luna to join him again, "Tell me Luna, did you do these things they accuse you of?" It was the first time he broached the subject with her but she felt no hesitation.

"If you are asking me if I use the gifts or charms I have been blessed with to help others, the answer is yes. I believe we are reflections of whoever or whatever created us and since that power can heal and change all things then so can we. What is wrong with helping a neighbor, a stranger, a child if it gives them peace? What is wrong with helping a being who is between life and death? I don't fear anything when I can hear, see and sense the Creator smiling when I do this."

He looked out to the smoke-filled sky, "I cannot see God here and that is what I fear more than their punishment." He swung his head back to consider her face again, "You don't belong here and I will never forgive myself if I cannot save you from them." He clutched his hands together as if in prayer as Luna sat silently watching. They shared the sense they were catching up after being away from each other for a long time. They couldn't explain it and didn't try. Luna had learned many things thus far on her journey in the Lower Worlds but she could not explain knowing the Vocalans as she did. She was grateful to have the time she had with Anam, her only hope was that she had said and done enough to make it right. When it was time for her to leave the two paused for a long moment gazing into each other's faces once again. Many thoughts and feelings were exchanged without saying a word. The time came to say goodbye. He walked her to the door that led to the outer waiting room where his assistant waited quietly. Anamchara kept his focus on the floor in great contemplation visibly upset at what he knew he could not change. Luna already knew it as well.

She turned one more time to Anam and smiled, "I'll see you again Anamchara, perhaps in another life." His head raised quickly and stared at her in disbelief. She was the most unique being he had ever met and in his heart, he knew she had spoken the truth. Luna was escorted back to the cell where the rest of the women awaited their fate. They were happy to see her as they had thought something happened because of her long absence. The rest of their time was spent wondering what their sentences would be. Luna had a pretty good idea of what it was but did not divulge it to the others. For what seemed like an eternity they waited until the sound of footsteps penetrated the cold stone steps again. Gideon and his band of thugs marched in quietly. They lined up in front of the cell glaring at the ragged women.

Gideon smirked at Luna, "Although you made quite an impression on Anamchara your fate is not his decision alone, all of you will now go before the council to hear your judgments." He looked extremely confident. One by one the women were led back to the castle. They traversed another hallway this time.

Luna searched anxiously for Anam but could not find him. The hallway was richly decorated with gold trim and blood red paint. Pictures of pious Vocalans crowned in lights of glory hung on the walls. At the end of the hall was a set of double doors which led to the council. Perched behind a long table sat the ones who would decide their fate, among them was Anamchara, who sat slumped and defeated. He could barely keep his head up let alone look at Luna. Her heart sank as she suspected he had lost the fight for their freedom. Each woman was called forth to stand before the council and handed a sentence of cleansing and purification. The sobs were endless as each innocent Vocalan was given her doom. When it came time for Luna to receive her judgment Gideon smiled as Anam sat agitated and fidgeting in his seat.

The same council member spoke, "Luna of the Bastlings, you are charged with heresy and sacrilegious acts against the Righteous One, how do you plead?"

Luna didn't need time to answer, "I plead not guilty. I have done nothing wrong except be different than you." She held her Bastling head high. Anam's head rose in disbelief as the rest of the council began muttering under their breath. Luna was terrified but kept her fear hidden.

He raised his eyebrows, "I see, so you believe it is no harm to do the things you have done?"

Luna's fear caught in her throat. She swallowed and responded, "No, I do not feel I've done anything wrong, I have just been myself. I have done what the Creator has asked of me, to help others. I am on a journey and Vocalos has been part of it. I wish to carry on, leave here and go to the next world but I am sure that will not happen. Regardless, I will not apologize for anything."

The Arch Council member's face was furrowed with anger and his voice rose in a ferocious pitch, "You shall pay for this unholy action and your words! Your penance is cleansing by purification and death!" The women sobbed louder and Gideon smiled as Anam's face paled and Luna shook with dread. "Take them away and begin the process!" He pointed towards the door.

They were all pushed out and Luna fought to turn around, "Anam, don't forget anything I said! I will see you again!" Luna felt a stinging on her head and lost consciousness. Mattheus put his weapon back in his belt after flogging her with it.

Luna and the others were thrown back into the holding cell below the castle and awaited their purification. She awoke on the dirty floor at the feet of the other women. Screams penetrated the air along with cries from inside the cell. Luna sat up slowly and turned around to see women being cleansed on the tables, it was horrifying. In the cell, the women clung to each other holding on in a frenzy of fear. One after another was taken from the group, cleansed, tortured, asked to repent for their grievous actions towards the Righteous Ruler. All the Vocalans eventually did, after being broken by pain. It did no good, however, it didn't stop their purification nor the relentless cruelty of Gideon. After the cleansing, they were left for dead on the floor of the dungeon or died on the tables. As Luna was forced to watch these horrors unfold something grew inside her from a flicker to a flame. The anger and rage took her as never before. Defiance brewed within her own walls. One of the women began whimpering like a child behind her. Luna whipped around, "Stop crying! Don't give them the satisfaction, don't let them know your fear." Her eyes were wild with anger as Gideon turned to see who spoke the words.

Pointing his finger, he lashed out, "I will save your confession for last. You can watch all your precious friends perish before you." Luna didn't care anymore; her rage was in control now. Gideon and his madmen left for a short while that seemed like forever. Luna surmised it was to prolong their terror of what lie in store for the rest of them. They had tortured, forced confessions, and killed almost all the women. There were only three left, Luna, Grianne, and Tara. When they did finally return they brought with them a different man. He was much larger than the rest and took his position near the entrance of the dungeon. Gideon began with Luna's consorts wasting no time in initiating their cleansing. Luna preferred to call it what it was, torture. It didn't take long for Grianne and Tara to lose consciousness once they were forced to confess to things they had never done. Once again, he made Luna watch and wait for hers, but little did he know she had been practicing the ways Ceil had taught her. She thought back to the old man and understood why he taught her different things than Sonuachar. He made her practice breathing techniques taking her aside on many occasions without Sonuachar knowing. On one such day he talked explicitly about pain and gave her a lesson she would never forget. Her mind drifted back to that day and his words in the field near the cave.

She had reached Ceil before Sonuachar that day as he waited outside as usual. She chuckled as she approached, "Hello Ceil! How are you today?"

He looked up from the fruit he juggled in his hand, "Aside from two hundred years of the same old berries of the field, just fine." Luna laughed with him. She noticed a peculiarity that day. He eyed her suspiciously, "Luna do you know what pain is?"

She thought that an odd question, "Do you mean physical or mental or emotional?"

Ceil rebutted, "All of them my child, all of them."

Luna felt quite certain she knew the answer, "Well, everyone knows that if we are truly alive here we will feel some pain in our life. I know the physical pain of what the Savage Queen did to me in Centros, and of course I know the emotional pain of loneliness."

Ceil breathed deep and looked skyward, "I need to teach you some things but you mustn't share this with anyone, even Sonuachar, this is for you and you alone. You will need it one day, sooner than you think." Luna didn't like it when he alluded to the future, it made her feel uncomfortable and she told him so. "What would you like me to do Luna? Would you prefer I lie to you? Perhaps you don't need this help as much as I thought you did." Ceil knew she would change her mind.

"No, Ceil I always want your help and teachings, I just feel uneasy when you tell me these things. I don't feel right about it."

Ceil persisted, "What do you feel? Try to put it into words. Pull out all the sensations in your belly and let it talk to you."

Luna sat quietly breathing as he had taught her. She closed her eyes and focused on the sound of the grasses moving in the field. She asked the sensation to show her a picture. Flashes of fire were rolling in front of her eyes. Flickers of bright blue eyes and then a howl. It scared her and her eyes shot open. Ceil was watching her intently, "Now you understand child?" Luna nodded her head as Ceil stood up, "Good, then let's begin." She followed Ceil to a lone tree in the distance where a rope sat coiled beneath it. He grabbed it and began wrapping it tightly around her wrist. Nervousness coursed through her. He tightened it more as she winced at the pain shooting through her arms. Ceil looked into her face, "Does it hurt? Can you feel the pressure on your veins and tissue?"

Luna tried twisting the rope but it only cut deeper, "Yes I can feel it and it hurts. I don't like this Ceil!"

He stepped closer, "What if you had no choice? What if it was put on you to endure? You are a warrior as well as a healer. You cannot be one without the other. Anyone who chooses to walk the path knows this suffering and sacrifice in all true endeavors." His voice had become deep and foreboding. Luna backed away from him, "Luna you must have total control of yourself in every way to get through what is to come." He raised his hand and began making a slashing motion in the air. Luna began to feel pain across her arms, chest, and legs. It was warm and tingly and she cried out when it began to burn. She looked down to her body where blood poured from all the wounds he had lashed at with his invisible whip. She looked to Ceil and begged him to stop feeling betrayed by her old friend.

"Why are you doing this?"

Blood poured into her eyes from the laceration on her forehead. "Focus, my child focus, on the pain and put it out, stop it." Confusion rippled through her like the pain and she began to cry. Ceil's face softened for a moment, "Luna you are like a daughter to me it will serve you later if you trust me, now focus on putting out the pain!" Luna's trust and spirit took hold of her conscious mind. She began to focus on the throbbing discomfort. As she put her attention to the excruciating injuries her body began to speak very clearly to her. Ceil made her bring in healing energy from above and below her. She did until she finally started to feel the intensity of the pain ease.

Slowly it subsided as the Bastling stood bleeding profusely in front of Ceil with a smile, "I did it Ceil." When he felt she had succeeded he walked towards her and placed the same hand he had slashed her with over her head and in between her eyes. Luna felt a different kind of heat, one that was loving. It emanated throughout her body as it soothed her. Her eyes remained closed yet could see the radiant light streaming into her and all around her. When it began to dissipate she opened her eyes to see the old man's face staring warmly at her. The ropes lay ripped on the ground and her body completely healed. She spoke softly, "I don't know whether to thank you or yell at you Ceil."

He smiled, "One day my child you might wish I had been more brutal to prepare you for the task at hand." Ceil's face fell with pity.

"What is this task?"

Ceil replied, "It is for many reasons you will free those who don't even know of you and help generations to come, and besides it's the only way out of Vocalos." He turned and walked towards his cave.

Her trip back in time was interrupted by Gideon's yelling. He towered over her as she lay on the table. "Do you confess to practicing the healing arts which is treachery under the laws of the Righteous Ruler?" Luna stared at Gideon, his stark blue eyes were glaring at her with madness.

Luna raised her head as much as she could, "Yes, I confess to practicing the healing arts."

Gideon smiled, "I am glad to see you are cooperating, your punishment will not be as long because of it." Luna smirked and began to pray, to all her ancestors, to the Great Mother, to all the divine spirits who would listen. She called on Eldred and even the Tree of Answaru. She especially prayed she could remember what Ceil had taught her. Gideon lowered his voice slightly and slithered closer, "Do you repent and take the Righteous One as your salvation?"

Luna opened her eyes, "I will never worship anyone who claims lordship over people's spirits. I will never entrust my soul to the salvation of a madman."

Gideon's face twisted and distorted, "Begin the cleansing!" Mattheus and the two other men came closer with their tools and instruments of torture. Luna closed her eyes again. She endured hours of torture. Her body, skin and bones broken but not her spirit. She focused her energy into the separating that Ceil had taught her. She brought in the energies above and below. It was working, but she felt herself growing tired and weak as spirits began to take form in front of her. Hovering over the men and Gideon, were black forms. They would lash out at the bright ones that encircled Luna. She knew they were her allies and she smiled faintly. Gideon noticed her smile, "Stop! Perhaps the prisoner wishes to speak!" Luna raised her head once more as he leaned in to listen.

Her voice barely audible, "I will never worship you or your perverse, sick ruler." Gideon backed away in shock and rage that she would not surrender. Mattheus asked if he should finish it. Gideon refused, he had something else in mind.

"Take her and the other two off the tables. Call the people to the square and prepare the fire." They lifted Luna's limp body and tossed her on the ground of the dungeon. Her eyes closed again. Soon, her Bastling ears heard footsteps. She tried to move but couldn't. She tried to open her eyes but only one would obey, the other was swollen shut. Her eye could see forms and shadows descending on the wall along the steps. Luna scanned the dungeon for life. She could see what was left of the women of Vocalos whom she had come to love. Their spirits now hovered above her. She spotted Grianne and Tara writhing on the floor in pain. They were in better shape than she was as they had confessed. It was all they could do to stay alive, little did they know it was all in vain. The men approached them taking them up the stairs and out of view. Luna lay alone amongst the dead.

After a few moments passed, she couldn't feel pain, cuts, even emotions. Her thoughts were interrupted by the sensation of being dragged. Mattheus and another man were dragging her crushed body up the steps. Her head bounced off very step but thankfully Luna could no longer feel it. Once at the top they stood her up and forced a red gown over her head. It had etchings across the front, two horizontal lines with a vertical line through them. Her arms hung loosely and bloody, barely connected to her body. The two men had to hold her up the whole time. She could see the smoky sky for the first time since she had returned from her visit with Anam. A crowd was gathered at the foot of a platform a few hundred feet away. The bigger man picked Luna up and slung her ragged body over his shoulders, stepping onto the platform and swinging her down and around as if a rag doll. The crowd cheered feverishly. He dropped her down in front of them pretending it was an accident causing their laughter to pitch to a frenzy. As Luna's body lay slumped on the wood slats of the platform, her eye caught sight of the faces jeering at her. She was picked up once more and thrown into a wood pole. While Mattheus held her almost lifeless body against it, his partner tied her with rope to the pole. When they finished her head slumped forward unable to support itself as she caught sight of the dried grasses and kindling piled at her feet. To her left Tara stood roped to a pole as well, shaking uncontrollably. She looked to Luna, "I'll see you in the light my Bastling friend." Her head dropped and did not come up again.

Gideon came onto the platform and the crowd cheered even louder. He raised his hand, "My good people! Look behind me, what you see here are three evil ones!" Luna turned her head slowly to her right to see Grianne there in the same position. Gideon continued, "Three who were given the opportunity of forgiveness by the Righteous Ruler. They chose to stay as they were, refusing salvation from our all-powerful God! They are truly hopeless! Therefore, after days of trying to help them find repentance we proclaim it a useless effort. Instead they have chosen to burn in the fire that they lived in!" The crowd screamed as Gïdeon raised his hands to the smoke-filled sky, "Let the burnings begin!" Mattheus lit a torch and walked over to Luna. Her eye saw the flame but it didn't matter anymore. His torch dipped down and touched itself to the grasses beneath her feet. As the kindling began to spark with red hate, Luna looked out to the crowd one more time. For a brief moment, she hoped to see Sonuachar riding up to save her, but there was nothing but the vengeful crowd. She searched for Anamchara hoping he too might rush down from his room in the castle and put a stop to this madness. She lost control of her reality thinking it was a dream and would awaken soon. The only thing that came running for her was the flames as their red claws grasped and reached higher. Luna couldn't feel them; her spirit was no longer holding her body. She could see far and wide again with both eyes and floated freely as she watched her body burn with no recourse. She watched all of it making careful memory of it in her soul. Then a brilliant light coursed behind her, so bright it was blinding. Someone called her name and beckoned her towards it but Luna hesitated. Turning around once more she watched the scene of what was once her body now consumed in flames and embers. A voice called out her name again but still she would not answer. Her spirit scrutinized her death as the crowd cheered her demise. At that very moment Sonuachar sat by the water's edge where Luna had trekked so many times before. He slumped, his sword sitting lifeless in his hands by his side. The water softly slapped back and forth against him. Guilt and anger coursed through his veins as he fought to make sense of what had happened to his dear Bastling. His father and the other men of the village refused to fight, deciding it was better they lose a few than all. Sonuachar argued intensely with all of them and when he tried to go on his own they stopped him, forbidding him from ever doing so. Tears pooled in his eyes and as the first tear dropped to the water below, he gave up, sick from grief, and his spirit released his body.

Back in Anamchara's chamber he walked out to his private garden. He leaned against the stone wall as he often did looking out at the smoke rings that encircled the village. He knew all too well what it meant. He could hear cheers from the crowds below as the flames roared higher. He dropped his head into his hands and began sobbing. Pain squeezed his chest and arm just as the ropes squeezed Luna's body to the pole. The pain was unrelenting and as he reached for his heart Luna's face flashed before him. She was the last vision he saw as he let his soul slip away. His body fell to the ground and his knightly red robe rustled in the soft breeze and lowered gently to cover him.

Luna turned once again to the light and the echoing voice that emanated from it. She felt a pull on her spirit, taking her away from the fire. Soon she was immersed in the most beautiful presence she had ever known. It loved her and she loved it back.

Chapter 7

The Representative

Luna felt her spirit rise higher and away from the flames. The more she tried to focus on the life behind her, the faster she accelerated upwards. She turned her vision ahead to see two fireballs coming towards her, one was red, the other blue. They raced to her side, each morphing into androgynous beings with an explosive energy that expanded around them, giving the appearance of wings. They grabbed hold of Luna's spirit. The three moved quickly through the tunnel of light as it curved and spun them through the vortex. Ahead an entrance awaited, emblazoned with ultraviolet light. The three spirits came swiftly upon a set of double doors that swung open. Beyond the entrance was a great palace, and in the center of its grandeur stood the figure of a man. So much light flowed from him Luna lifted her hand to shield her eyes from the brightness. The man had a youthful appearance despite his long white robe, flowing long hair and beard that were speckled with the dark hairs of his youth. He stood with arms crossed and had a smile as if he'd been expecting her. The two heavenly escorts gently let go of Luna, enabling her to get a better look at them. One stood stoically to her right blazing in blue energy. Compassion streamed from him as he looked at her with a nod and a smile. The other, to her left, glowed with red embers of strength and courage. Notty and the rest of the Bazers would have been very excited to meet such an outstanding red creature. He too smiled and quickly gazed back ahead as the man standing before her addressed them, "Thank you Uriel and Raphael." He smiled at Luna, "Welcome to the Starlight Palace!" He held out his hands, very proud of his domain. He bowed down, "Allow me to introduce myself, I am King Solarus, The Representative." He bowed slower this time, "How are you dear? It's been a long time, hasn't it? Well, not really but in time down there it seems like forever!" He laughed at his own joke taking note of Luna's serious demeanor, "Come now, it's not that bad! I know you've had a rough go of it, but before you know it you'll be right as rain!" He smiled again, but Luna still did not respond. Instead she unleashed all her anger on him.

"What happened? What is this place? Where am I?"

"You're in Browand." He danced a little jig as he chuckled.

Luna thought him mad, "Browand?"

"That's right."

Luna retorted defiantly, "That cannot be, that is the next world above Vocalos! How did I get here? I just died!" Luna pointed and looked behind her only to see the door had disappeared. When she turned back, the glorious man was seated on his throne and began to laugh.

"Of course, you died! That's what you wanted. Besides, it's the only way to get into Browand."

"What?!"

"That's right, it's-the-only-way-in."

Luna became very upset, "But I didn't want to die! I didn't want to go!"

He scoffed, "Of course you did. It'll be all right, there's plenty of time to go over all that."

Luna's frustration persisted, "Well who are you? What exactly do you represent? And who are they?" She pointed to Uriel and Raphael.

"They are your highest guides and I already told you. I am The Representative, King Solarus." He stared at her with solemn pride. Luna was so utterly dumbfounded, she could do nothing but stare blankly. "Whoa! We got a tough crowd tonight, boys!" The two escorts looked at each other and then straight ahead in their sentry stance. "Look, I understand you're upset. You've been through a great deal and it takes time and love to heal these things. Of course, a few dolphin realignments can't hurt either." He wiggled his eyebrows up and down.

"Dolphins?" Luna's voice shrilled with frustration.

"Yes, you know, nice little fellows, swim, eat fish, and dance a lot for humans." He was making swimming motions with his hands. Uriel and Raphael began to laugh. Luna didn't find any humor in it at all as the Representative stopped motioning his hands, "That's right, you wouldn't remember what they are. Well they're very sweet and they do this healing circle with…"

Luna cut him off. "I don't mean to be disrespectful but who are you again?"

He stood and bowed again, "I am the Representative."

The Bastling threw off her energy in irritation, "The Representative?"

"Yes. You were expecting someone else?" "What exactly do you represent? And what am I supposed to be doing here?"

"Well I can see that you're still a bit cranky. That's all right, you're allowed, besides, once you have your realignment you'll feel as good as new." He cleared his throat, "Ah, yes well to answer your question, I represent the big guys, you know, cosmic parental units, mom and dad." He smiled again.

Luna was even more confused, "Mom and dad, what mom and dad?"

He looked surprised, "You know, the big spirit in the sky so to speak, where we all came from, the big bang and all. The whole made you in my image stuff." He was using his hands to make quotes in the air, "Boy you really do need realignment." He rolled his eyes.

"That's another thing! What's this realignment? What exactly is going on here? In case you haven't noticed I was just burned alive and condemned to hell by those ignorant brutes in Vocalos! Not exactly what I was hoping for you know! That was the happiest I'd ever been until they stepped in! Now it's all gone, and I'm standing ...no floating here ...and I'm really mad ...and all you can do is make jokes!" Luna's energy was shooting out everywhere and was as red as the fire she had just come from. The Representative just stood there, arms folded and smirking. "What is so funny?" Her heart swelled as it prepared to cry.

"I just like your fire. No pun intended! It's good, very good indeed."

Luna went on as if he hadn't even spoken, "So what now? What do I have to do now?" she demanded, pushing down the tears.

"What do you mean?"

Luna's impatience was growing, "Well in every world there is always something I have to do, something I have to find, fight or get rid of, so what is it this time?" Luna's sarcasm was at its height. Her spirit began to rise and fly around in fits of anger. The Representative watched silently, he was trying not to laugh but he couldn't help it. Luna had not yet become accustomed to her new body, or lack thereof and so much of her temper tantrum was thwarted by endless bumping into walls. Finally, she gave up and threw herself down to the floor in a heap and began to cry as she slowly floated upwards again.

King Solarus put his arms around her and whispered in her ear, "There, there now my dear, everything is going to be all right. I'm here and so are your master angels, and there's plenty of others to meet. It just takes time, I believe in you; we all do. Besides you have a great task to accomplish, you mustn't let a few heartless people destroy that." Luna had never felt so much compassion and loving vibrations from an embrace, it calmed her completely. She looked up over her shoulder to say thank you when she noticed he was still sitting on his throne.

Bewildered, she bounced up, "Hey! How did you do that?" She was unnerved but impressed at the same time.

"I'm The Representative my dear! These positions don't come without perks you know. You'd be amazed at some of the things I can do! Isn't that right guys?" He looked over to the escorts as they nodded in agreement. He leaned in and whispered, "Better yet, you would be amazed at what *you* can do." He smiled genuinely then quickly moved on to the next topic at hand, "Well shall we get on with things? I suggest first that you have a rest in the dolphin room." He stood up clapping his hands together. "They really are very nice and they always make you feel at home, shall we go then?"

Luna suspiciously followed him, unsure whether it was just another joke on his part. She loved the way his energy shot out in every direction, welcoming her into its embrace regardless of distance, but his sarcasm was perplexing, it wasn't the sort of thing she had expected from a spiritual representative. Luna walked behind King Solarus, and her two angels. The palace halls were extremely long and seemingly endless. Everything glowed of the same warming ultraviolet color as the entrance when she first arrived. After what seemed an eternity they stopped in front of a door where a blue watery opening shimmered.

"Is this door real, or is it water?"

Luna looked over at the Representative who was grinning, "It does appear to be a tiny bit fluid, doesn't it? Why don't you see for yourself?" He waited for Luna to touch it, "Go on then, give it a go." He folded his arms. Luna apprehensively put her hand out to touch the door, and it slipped through to the other side as watery electricity shivered up her arm. King Solarus laughed, "Isn't it amazing! That's always a personal favorite of mine!" He clapped excitedly as if he were experiencing it for the first time.

Luna laughed at his child-like response, "What is it with you anyway? Everything excites you and makes you happy."

He turned serious, "Luna, you really must learn to lighten up. It's fun time here in Browand! There's no pain here, no chaos, it's simply divine!" He threw his arms up into the air for emphasis. Luna fought with herself, wanting to relax and see things his way but she still felt so heavy from all that had just happened in Vocalos.

"Can I ask you something? Why is it if I am dead and on the other side, that I still feel the pressure, the heaviness of all that has just taken place? I mean, shouldn't I be in high spirits and lighthearted like you?"

The Representative's face softened into a compassionate gaze, "Luna, the soul doesn't forget what the body has experienced and we carry those things within us like a complex pattern of signals and waves within the spirit. The soul, emotions, mental state, and body all work together when we are in the third dimensional reality, they are interconnected and woven together. That is why all souls come here to the Starlight Palace. It is here we heal and prepare for the next leg of the journey. Until you repair and adjust yourself to not being in a body and the effects of your recent life, the pain remains with you and must be worked through in the next life. There is nothing wrong with you, in fact you're quite normal. Once you are done all your healing work, you will be ready to go back in again. That's just the way this process works." He smiled and waved his hand around her as a light peacefulness washed over her again, "Don't worry sweet child, it's all for the best." His demeanor quickly changed and he was back to his bubbly, funny self, "Now get in there and swim with those little fellas! Show 'em who's boss!" He laughed at his own joke again. This time Luna joined in with him as well. She turned and headed towards the watery door not really knowing what to expect. As she passed through the waves she heard King Solarus yelling, "I love you! Always have, always will." She was warmed by that love as she felt his hands push her reluctant spirit through to the other side. Once past the threshold, Luna was still in the watery substance except now it was more than that, it was like a kind of jelly. Yet she had no problem moving through it. Everything shimmered in blues and greens with streaks of gold and silver threads. Noises echoed through the waves. Beings raced through the huge room from every direction. She was startled and tried to find somewhere to get out of the way but there was no place to hide. They feverishly raced in circles around her. They were fast swimmers, speedy and light. Blue and green sparks flew from their bodies as they swam by her. Clicking noises emanated through the entire room as well as laughter that echoed, creating orbital patterns through the water. Luna was caught up in the middle of this whirlwind and could do nothing but wait it out. She became disoriented a few times as these beautiful creatures sped by so quickly.

They began speaking to her telepathically, "We are the race of beings known as the Dolphins. We have been here with all of you since the beginning of time on the Great Mother. We love, have fun and we heal. Our divine porpoise," they all broke out in a high pitch fit of laughter, "is to ease you gently through to the next level of consciousness on your journey. In the Upper World we exist in physical bodies to teach, and to send waves of love and light through the earthly waters in the hopes of changing the frequency of the planet and of the humans. It is part of the next phase of evolution for them up there."

Luna's curiosity peaked, "Evolution? What do you mean?"

They swam even faster, and as they did, tiny fibers of light began forming as strings around Luna who was oblivious. "Yes, that's right, evolution. Every species has an evolution of some sort. This one just happens to include the entire planet and every species within her. There is a great force in the universe pulling all planets in this solar system into what is known as a vortex. Each being must adjust accordingly or face great problems. Every life form needs to function and operate at a higher frequency level and that is where we come in. It is not entirely our responsibility, it is the species' ultimate responsibility if they are to survive, but the ones who have asked us to help we do in this way."

Luna retorted, "But I never asked you for help."

The dolphins broke into fits of laughter again, "Of course you did! That's why we're here!" Amidst Luna's confusion they now swam so fast they could only be seen as flashes of brilliant blue and green light. As their speed increased, so did Luna's dizziness. Strings of gold and silver wrapped around her as a high-pitched hum emanated through them. A flash of light and explosion of energy surged, and suddenly all was still. The dolphins were no longer spinning furiously around her, she was floating in a beautiful cocoon of shimmering, watery light. Nothing disturbed her, there were no thoughts in her mind, no feelings of pain, it was simply being in the moment. Tiny fibers were filling her spirit with glorious light. Happiness, love, and compassion washed through her and remained there. Images flashed before her, star clusters, galaxies, nebulas, planets, and solar systems. They became deeper, no longer was Luna seeing them, she became these magnificent images, imbued with a hazy stardust, feeling the new life forming within it, within her. She rushed into galaxies only to feel them rush into her, uniting with stars in her veins of energy. Over and over again her soul merged with these life forms bringing a oneness she had never known before. It happened continuously until they flew so fast they began to all melt together. A burst of energy exploded shooting through her like lightning, bringing silence and serenity once more to the walls of the cocoon. Soon the weave of silver and gold began to unthread, leaving her spirit hovering carefree amongst the dolphins. They gently waded around her in a circle of light welcoming her back from her sacred journey.

One of the divine creatures approached her, "Well, do you feel better now?"

Laughter echoed again as Luna smiled, "I feel so calm and peaceful, I don't know how you do it, but I am grateful. Thank you so very much."

They all did back flips in response, "As long as you are happier, we are pleased. We wove new light filaments into your soul matrix again, making the next time around easier. We also cleansed your spirit of the traumatic experiences from Vocalos. However, when you return to the Great Mother in physical form, you will have to cleanse the rest of the lessons yourself. After all, we can't do it all for you, what would be the fun in that?! This is what we do every time a soul comes through here, hopefully making the next trip into the Great Mother, a little less difficult."

Luna marveled, "You mean every time I leave the Great Mother I come here to see you?"

They all chimed in unison, "Yes and we love having you!" Luna danced in the watery gel laughing with her new friends. They all circled around her giving off loving vibrations once again, "It was so wonderful to see you again, but we're afraid it's time for you to go to the next healing room."

Luna's laughter faded, "Really, I have to go now? Can't I stay with you a while longer?"

The dolphins swam in closer, "It's time now Luna, but don't worry, we'll see you again, next time around."

They escorted Luna to the door. As she stepped out of the watery doorway, the love of the dolphins followed her. Once again in the hall, Luna found herself alone. She began to float down the corridor looking for the next room when a low humming caught her attention. Ahead on her right was another door that held the source of the sound. Luna looked up, forcing her spirit to knock, "Come in Luna."

Luna stepped into the next room where a vast, dark twilight place filled with ferns, trees and bushes awaited. Sounds of birds and animals loomed overhead, their locations unknown. It was strange and eerily familiar.

A voice echoed throughout the jungle, "Luna welcome, we've been waiting a long time for you." She peered into the shimmering twilight for a body to match the voice. "Please Luna, come down the path that lies before you."

Trusting the inviting voice, she moved ahead on the trail at her feet as it stretched into the dark ancient forest of time. As she made her way deeper in, the misty ferns bowed down tickling her arms and face as she walked through their world. Water droplets rained upon her from the towering trees above. Looking up she could see their waving limbs as if greeting her to a familiar place.

Once completely immersed inside the forest the voice echoed again, "In order to meet at the council fires Luna, you need to ask to speak with us."

The voice remained silent as Luna searched her thoughts to understand what this meant. When the answer didn't come from her mind, Luna searched her heart. There, the answer of faith replied.

"Alright, I will just believe that I am meant to be here right now to speak with them, whoever they are." Luna stopped at a clearing in the forest. Gazing upwards, she called out, "I ask you to help me now, be here so that I may speak with you and sit among the council fires."

Suddenly a circle of flames appeared, as the torches revealed a ring of silhouettes. All were meditatively staring into the fires that began to blaze in the center of them as they held their stoic positions. One of them finally stood, illuminating its true nature, up on his hind legs, a bear towered over the rest. Its roar commanded Luna who was filled with fright as the forest shook.

He spoke, "Come sit with us in the circle, the council is waiting to speak with you." Luna recognized his voice immediately, his had been the voice of initial invitation.

She took a place among the silent ones. Once seated, they all turned their gaze towards her as she smiled awkwardly not knowing what to say. They all smiled back and nodded their heads in acknowledgement and Bear said, "Luna allow me to introduce you to your divine council. Chosen by you, and for you, they have waited with great anticipation of this meeting since the last time we were together. We are very proud of you for the work you did in all the worlds, especially Vocalos, and we grieved your pain as well. Your grandmother will begin."

He directed her attention to the old lady who sat on Luna's direct left. Her ancient face was as cracked as the hidden caverns and rocks of the many worlds below. On her forehead, withered by time yet still visible was the same symbol Luna bore. The old lady appeared frail, yet carried a face full of strength and light as it reached out to her.

As she began speaking in a tongue foreign to Luna, the words were transformed, as if in midair, so Luna could understand, "My dear granddaughter, I am your grandmother of many generations past. I lived many times back in the Great Mother, and yet even as I sit here now, not of that world, my blood still lives through you. Our people come from a faraway place, far from the Great Mother and lived in the Upper World for a great long time."

"Where did our people come from?" asked Luna.

The old woman chuckled, "That is for another time of understanding. For now, I will remind you of what you have already been told in the last lifetime you sat with us here."

Luna spoke again, even more surprised, "I have been told these things before?"

Her ancestor laughed lightly again, "Every time you make another circle through a life you are reminded of what you forgot while in the earthly realm; that is the way. The goal is to one day remember consciously in a lifetime all these things we tell you." She paused for a moment, giving Luna a chance to think about her statement, "We lived peacefully for and with the Great Mother, but when a horrible thunder loomed in the Upper World and shook our people, many died but the ones who lived, traveled below. We did so to preserve our ways, our people, the very essence of our blood line. It was there in Elan we stayed a great long time, and again we kept to ourselves, and stayed peaceful and free. Until one day a sickness came upon us, many died again, but most lost the greatest thing of all, our charms. Soon we became like a fireball turned inward, and we began to live in selfish, harmful ways. Eventually less and less of the clear ones, the seeing ones, and the knowing ones existed. Our race was then taken over by the Dreglings. They spoiled everything within Elan. But the one truth remained, a prophecy of our people that one day a clear one would be born amidst the dark to restore our people and our bloodline, to right the wrong. I am here not only as your grandmother, your elder and your teacher, but as an ally. Any time you have needed help, I have come." The old woman's face cracked with a smile. She patted Luna's spirit gently, "You are a sparkle, you have so much of your people's light in you." Luna swelled with pride, its light so intense that it burst from within and extended all around her. She beamed at the old woman and saw her own reflection smiling back.

A voice to her right spoke in the same language as her grandmother, and it too was transformed for Luna's understanding, "My dear granddaughter, I am your grandfather from a different line, yet of the same Bastling heritage." Her eyes fell upon the same Bastling birthmark on his forehead. "As your grandmother explained, we came from a world far from the Great Mother and in time came to live in the lower worlds. The surviving few that were not taken over by the Dreglings left Elan and came to reside in the world you know as Yellao. In time, the people divided into two groups, the Huma and the Kumrai. Although a good deal of the ways and charms of the Bastlings remained with both groups, there is much that has been forgotten, especially that they were once one race." Luna peered into the old man's face, she could see Dewin's reflection there as well as her own. Like her grandmother, his eyes danced with life as his frail spirit body revealed his age. Luna's heart overflowed with contentment for being amongst her own kind. He smiled weakly, "I believe you are the prophecy fulfilled Luna."

Bear continued his gaze into the fire as he spoke, "Next Luna, you will see how much power and help you had all along."

Bear pointed to each member of the council, "The doctor, a great healer and helper for many in the Upper World long ago, now your personal spiritual assistant."

A focused being sat next to Luna's grandmother, never taking his eyes off the burning flames of the fire, "I am one of your healing helpers. Any time you needed my assistance for such a purpose, I have come in to help."

Luna was puzzled, "A healing helper?"

"Yes, you see, being who you are and the bloodline you carry brings strong charms. You have lived many times before, and not always in the lower worlds, many times you were in the Upper Worlds working as a healer. It was decided in the last incarnation, that I should be one of your guides. You and I have worked together before, but I had completed my journey on the Great Mother many lifetimes ago. I am sorry to say however, that this life you have had a great deal to work through, as you decided this was the life that you concentrated on clearing all blocks from previous visits to fulfill your true divine purpose." The man continued his steadfast gaze into the flames as he perched a smile, "The souls' travels are not a simple case of understanding. When we enter a life, we carry all memory of it to each following life. Think of the memory as being like a sticky string or substance that goes where the soul does, stretching from its point of origination or source, like little dots in time and space following the soul. If there is pain from a previous life, we tend to gravitate away from memory triggers of it, in the next life. Yet at a soul level, the deepest yet lightest part of who we are wants us to remember, for the soul knows what our fear doesn't want to, that in order to be free we must trust and overcome that from which we want to run. When we are in bodies, the mind is like a trickster, constantly telling us to stay away from all things that are not easy and quickly gratifying. Yet the heart knows this is a lie unto the self. When you chose not to have faith while you lived in Elan and lived in your fear, you stayed stuck in your pain. It was only when your faith had been restored, and clarity was upon you, your true journey to yourself had begun. So here you are, among us now, gaining insight into all the things your mind helped you to forget, that your soul already knew."

Luna sat astounded at the profound words of the quiet, still man who never looked her way once. "You said you are my healing helper, what does that mean?"

He smiled gently, "You have a divine charm of healing passed down from your Bastling heritage, to help those around you, to hold their hand as they travel their own path. Whenever you did healing work in Vocalos, you called for help and assistance and I came. By placing your Bastling hands in near proximity, you have eased the burden of many and that is worth far more than what you have endured." He glanced over at the Bastling spirit as his words held their own healing properties over her.

Bear introduced her to the next spirit in the divine circle. He looked at her directly, never taking his attention away. "In the Upper World, I would have been considered a scientist of the mind. My work consisted of healing of a different sort, a philosopher to some. I analyzed and thought deeply about matters of spirit, science and the natural world. It is a very tricky thing, the mind. If used openly and freely it can draw great conclusions on matters of all worlds and life; when used in negativity, it is a cage, a burden to be locked in. As a philosopher, I used the mind to expand awareness, not only of the self, but of the environment around us. True thinking is a difficult exercise, yet one that should be practiced often. A marvelous tool the mind, a perfection of creation I worked with properly. It is the bond and holder of all currents in the third dimension, connecting all layers of who we are together." He finally returned his stare to the flames of the center fire.

Bear spoke once more, "This is your saint." He pointed to a small figure seated on the other side of the circle from Luna.

Her face peered across the flames, "I am the nature of all spiritual matters. I was not only your helper but a constant reminder of your soul's true nature and knowledge. My purpose was to help you remember the truth of the universal principals while in the Lower World dimension. As explained to you before, the mind can be a grace or a hindrance. When fear and stagnation stopped the flow of this knowledge, I was your reminding helper to bring it forward from the ethereal realm to the earthly realm." Luna watched as this tiny being sat gracefully emanating an enchanting vibration. "In the Upper World, many cycles ago I perfected my being with strict spiritual discipline. I became what they call a saint. I do not call myself that, I was simply a student of the divine teacher, the universal consciousness."

Luna was impressed to know such a being was one of her council, "I had no idea I was surrounded by such powerful and noble souls." Luna fell quiet again.

The giant bear stood again on hind legs, "I am Bear, I have been with you since your birth. I am a guide, a helper. The charm I bring to you is strength. All you needed to do was ask. In dreams I often came to you and you came to us. But in your waking life you were forgetful of who we are. Many times I frolicked with you in green meadows, and vibrant forests, we have waded in cool waters together. I am a keeper of the west wind."

"What do you mean 'I came to you in dreams'? How could I have known to do that in dreams and not in my waking time? And what do you mean west wind keeper?"

The bear's roaring laughter filled the jungle air. "My dear Luna, everything is connected, be it of the Great Mother, ghostly or other realms. We are all related as many spokes of a wheel to a great hub. When one enters the dream time, they are not constricted by their earthly bodies, they go back and roam. The soul knows all, knows it is part of everything and all is part of the soul. When you sleep you allow your soul to take over, no longer hindered by the physical, it endeavors to communicate with the light and many other things that will be explained later in your journey. The soul spends a great deal of time accessing the mind to help it break free of its confinement. The only way to encourage this is to let your mind go and be in your heart. You have a great deal to learn Luna, but you have a great deal of strength within and if you ask me for help it will be tenfold."

"So, when you are asleep you are awake and when you are awake, you are asleep." Luna took in the giant being's words very seriously.

He sat back down among the council, "Now it is time for you to continue on your way into the next room of Browand.

It has been good seeing you again, and we hope you remember everything you have been told here."

Luna stood up and looked at each member of the council, "Thank you for helping and guiding me through my journey in the Lower Worlds. I am deeply grateful to have met with you again. I love you all." The council gazed back at her, each one nodding in recognition of her thanks.

Bear roared, "Go now Luna to the next door down the hall and be well on your journey. Remember we will always be with you."

Luna turned and walked back through the deep forest trail finding the door she had entered through. She made her way down the hall of the Starlight Palace finding an elegant golden door to her left. She stood in front of it for a moment, contemplating her council's words again. When she was ready, Luna opened the next door and it burst forth with splinters of light towards her, as if a million schools of fish were swimming by. When the splinters subsided, seven beautiful creatures stood before her. Luna gasped, stopped in her tracks. She was confounded by the splendor that beheld her. Each of the seven stood very tall and thin, shimmering with blues, greens, and silvers just as the dolphins had. They all stared at Luna smiling, each one holding a symbol in their hands. As Luna's eyes scanned the room, waves of energy continuously poured forth from an unknown source. There was music, a melody playing of the likes she had never heard before. The music echoed not just through the room but through her as well, as if every part of her essence glowed and pulsated with each note.

The first of the seven beings stepped forward, "Hello Luna! Greetings and welcome, we are the Seven Mystics. We ask that you make yourself comfortable, please sit anywhere you like."

Luna looked through the twirling watery lights to find a semicircle bench in the middle of the room. The Seven Mystics' eyes followed her as she made her way to the resting area. Turning towards her, the first one spoke, "We will join you now."

Luna watched in amazement as everything changed before her, the floor became marbled black and white checkers and pillars of white stone encircled the entire room. As Luna looked behind her at another set of doors, they opened revealing another vast room where millions of books lined the walls. Inscribed inside the top of the door were the words, *The Great Mother's Library.* Turning back once more, she found the seven mystics already sitting on the stone circle bench across from her.

The mystic sitting on the far left began, "My name is Nana." She held open her hand to reveal a pyramid with a pair of eyes looking out. "We are your ancestors, from a great long cycle ago. We are from another dimension, the fifth to be exact. We seven come from a different star a very long way from the Great Mother Ahki. A long time ago we lived here and our grandchildren inherited our place. They stayed in the Upper World for many moon cycles, and they eventually became shadow people in the Lower Worlds, becoming the ancestors that you come from, some of which you have met in Yellao. Now in this time of the Mother's great cycle, we are back to assist and help, not in earthly form, but in spirit, however it is only given if asked. We can never overstep our divine laws. We must be invited in to assist any of our grandchildren on the earthly journey."

Luna responded, "Just as my guides explained as well."

Nana smiled as she glimmered, "Yes, Luna that is correct. Spiritual helpers mustn't and won't break universal law, none of us really can. There is a rhythm to the universal law that is unchangeable."

Luna looked into Nana's hands, "Will you help me now?"

Nana smiled, "Of course child."

"What is that?" Luna's eyes never left the object in the Mystic's hands. Nana raised it high for her to get a closer look.

"What do you think it is?" Nana waited for her reply.

"Well it's a pair of eyes so it probably has something to do with vision." Nana moved off the bench and stood directly in front of her.

She held it in front of Luna's face, "Look into the eyes Luna and think of what frightens you the most." Luna's mind jumped from one thing to another, her thoughts fell to her loneliness and suddenly the eyes distorted into a black misty figure. Luna saw herself sitting down alone, the misty figure reached down its hands around her neck and began choking her as she began to struggle to breathe and grasped her own throat. "Okay Luna that's enough, stop thinking of it." Immediately the eyes resumed their mysterious stare and became clear again. "Now Luna I want you to look into these eyes again and think of the happiest memory you have." Luna's mind rushed back to Yellao and the people there, the ceremony, the smell of food, music and community. Suddenly the eyes of the pyramid lost their shape again, but this time they arched into a beautiful rainbow, exploding with light. Luna felt a surge of love and happiness as it filled her entire body. Nana's voice broke the Bastling from her beautiful spell, "You see Luna, your world around you is exactly how you believe it to be. If you believe the world is a scary place, then it will be. If you believe it is loving and warm, your world becomes a rainbow of light." Luna sat dumbfounded as she was completely in awe of the truth she had just witnessed. Nana sat down beside the other Mystics, "There is no mystery or secret Luna, which is the simple truth, the world is how you see it. That is all." Luna sat very still, her eyes fell to the black and white floor beneath her feet that seemed to be moving. Pulling her away from what she had just witnessed, she shook it off and looked back to the Mystics as Nana sat quietly again smiling at her.

The second Mystic spoke, "I am Palena. Nana has already explained who we are, but what I wonder is, are you learning who you are?" The question hit Luna hard. It had not been posed to her since she came to the palace in Browand.

"Well I don't know, I realize that I am far more than what I once believed in Elan. I look back at that time which seems so far away now, yet not long ago at all, and I see I am so much more than that little Bastling."

Palena laughed throwing back her head so her long flowing hair waved in the watery light. "Do you know that you are limitless? Do you know that anything you want to do, you can?" Luna was at a loss for words, unsure if she was being mocked or not. Palena sat down beside her, as her energy overwhelmed Luna. She felt strength and freedom coming at her that was so powerful it was frightening. "Look into this." She held up a cube of blue aqua light. Within the cube sat an eagle. It cried out and ruffled its wings as if daring Luna. "Do you think this eagle has limits Luna? Do you think it flies with fear? Or do you believe the eagle's spirit knows no bounds?"

Luna smirked, "I am sure the answer is, he flies with no fear."

Palena smirked back, "Ask him, go on, ask him to show you."

Feeling somewhat strange Luna posed the question, "Okay, do you fly without fear?" The eagle turned its majestic head and peered into Luna's eyes. It lifted off the mountain top upon which it was perched, and began flying towards her. It saw the containment of light that was the cube, but continued flying, smashing the limits of the cube on impact. It relentlessly flew at Luna, and upon contact with her, she was soon flying in a swooping circle high upon the mountains. The clean, crisp air danced in her nostrils as she looked to her side to catch the beautiful expanse of wings. Above her, the sky opened, revealing the sun's light. Luna's spirit soared as she dove straight down and back up again to greet the wind. There was no fear in her, only freedom, and a sense of oneness with everything. A voice called out to her as she turned around. Blue light exploded and the hazy voice buzzed in her ear, and in an instant, she returned to her seat next to Palena. Luna looked down at her position on the bench and then to the eagle perched on the mountain, still within the cube in Palena's hand.

"You see Luna, the mind is the only limitation we really have. Truly there are no restrictions, only the ones we set for ourselves. If one is capable of knowing this, the possibilities are infinitely endless to what we can do, be and create, the only limit is us." Palena's laughter sent ruffling energy waves throughout the entire room. She got up and walked back over to sit amongst the maidens, still laughing.

Luna was still trying to take in what she had just experienced, "The place where I was flying, was that the Upper World?"

"Yes, Luna it was, did you like it?" Her face was serious and genuine.

"It was the most beautiful, wondrous place, I wish I could go there still."

Palena's voice softened for the first time, "That decision will be up to you in the end." Luna wondered what that meant but didn't ask. She felt she would come to understand soon enough.

The third Mystic sat smiling gently while she tossed an orb back and forth between her hands. "My name is Kahe." She stood up and walked behind the others roaming to the center of the room, surrounded by the pillars of stone. She raised her voice loud enough for Luna to hear, "Tell me Luna, have you ever seen the power of your own creation? Come, come with me and let me show you the wonder of who you are, the nature of your power!" Luna jumped up and walked over to where Kahe stood. She propped herself facing the maiden eagerly awaiting her lesson. Kahe held an orb up to Luna's heart, "Come let's join the dance." Luna looked into the orb only to see flickers of light dancing and bouncing off the walls that contained them. Their movement was chaotic and mesmerizing. Kahe snapped her fingers, "Let us see." The orb expanded becoming the size of the entire room until all was contained within it. Luna watched as the chaotic light bounced off the room, pillars, her and the Mystics.

"Luna, have you ever wondered how things happen? Regardless of what it is, the circumstance, the thought, the action, it is creation. Look around you everywhere, all you see is potential for creation, little dancing bits of light waiting for birth. Come Luna, see what I am talking about." Luna moved closer to Kahe and as she did the dancing particles moved aside. A straight stream of light formed, turning into a cord between Luna and Kahe. She stopped in amazement. Luna glanced around her watching as all the dancing particles diverted themselves from her glance.

"Why do they do that?" Luna kept trying to catch them with her eyes.

Kahe started to laugh. "Energy is boundless and abundant, but when the looker is focused on one particular thought or piece of information it is caught, and transformed into an energy link. That is why when you focused your attention to be close to me, that source, that energy reconfigured itself to your creation, your thoughts." As Kahe spoke, and explained this to Luna, streams and cords began flowing from Kahe to several different particles at once.

"Is this true? Is this real? How can it be?" Luna shook her head as if trying to reject this new way of seeing the world from her brain. Shoots of light exploded from her head.

"It is the truth Luna. This is the matrix of the universe, it is the substance that we are made of. Try something for me, look towards that pillar behind you." Luna swirled around as the dancing particles diverted her glance again. Luna's eyes found the pillar, and focused on it. Particles immediately began gathering in line from her to the pillar. Within seconds, a stream of consciousness and light hung between the two. Luna couldn't believe how quickly the action took place. Kahe smiled, and authoritatively directed her, "Now Luna, imagine that the pillar is crumbling." Luna looked deeper at the pole. "Picture that it already happened Luna." She visualized the pillar crumbling into a million pieces. It began to crack the cement beneath her feet as she watched it race to the pillar base. Kahe broke the spell, "Very good little Bastling." She raised her hand to the stone post creating streams that returned the cracks and the pillar to its original position. "So, you see Luna, whatever you focus on, you try, so as it goes with your life, your journey. If you feel sadness, all energy turns to sadness, and you not only radiate this, but create it all around you as well." Kahe closed her eyes and soon the room of energy began sparking and returned to the orb from which it came. Luna looked around her, looked at her hands, took everything in and saw her whole world in a different way. Kahe returned to her seat leaving Luna in the middle of the room. She looked over at the Mystics wondering what would be next.

The fourth stood up and glided over to her. "Now is the time of power Luna. Truly I say there is no yesterday and no tomorrow, it is all contained in this moment. Past, present and future are all here together." Luna listened, opening her mind to the new information that felt so true and natural to her. "I am Manaua and I too want you to see your universe in a different way. Explaining this concept is never an easy one, but I will do my best." Luna hung on to Manaua's every word.

"Think back Luna, to a time you had on your journey, take any memory you've had." Her mind began to wander back to all her experiences along the way and Notty flashed before her face. Manaua raised an object, three pyramids intertwined together. Each was a different shade of purple. It was mesmerizing as the three colors pulsated in sync with each other. Manaua smiled, "Grab a memory and let us look at it closer." Luna's memory of Notty remained fixed. Suddenly the colors shot out of the object and swirled around the two figures. Revealing their mystery, they were instantly transported back to the moment when Luna discovered the truth of the symbols in Redios. She watched herself in action as an onlooker. It was enlightening to be in such a position, to see herself in this way. Yet she wondered why she was observing it. "Look Luna, look at how you acted, full heart and in the moment. The truth was before you, as it always is for any of us and because you were in that moment, not in the past of fears or the future of uncertainty, you were able to seize your power, focus it, and transform past, present and future.

"How is it Manaua, that the action changed the past, present and future?"

Manaua stepped closer to Luna, "This is a very good question but not so easily answered. To most Luna, the past seems to take precedence, it appears unchangeable, yet it is as watery and uncertain as this moment is now and in the future. The scope of reality is ever changing and can be bent, so to speak to allow those changes." Manaua's hands crossed behind her back as she watched Luna, awaiting her reply. Luna contemplated Manaua's words, her heart tingling with the truth they revealed. Thinking back to that moment in Redios, she realized there was a distinct possibility that even though she could not look back to the past before Redios, perhaps there was a change that had occurred, and even further, the future could be entirely different now that she had acted in a place of truth. Perhaps her journey would have ended right there in Redios had she reacted from a place of fear. Surely she would not be standing with Manaua, contemplating her new teachings. Luna began to understand why it was so important to grasp the moment of now, as the moment of power. The truth of what Manaua was trying to teach her began to seep into Luna's soul, as if a drug awakening her to what lay sleeping in some forgotten place within. Awareness began to burn as an ever-steady growing flame.

"How amazing and wondrous," Luna thought, "that in every moment a balance, so delicate, it hangs waiting be equalized." In that second of her awareness, the room holding the scenes of her memory collapsed back into the triple pyramid.

Manaua triumphantly walked back to the bench, satisfied Luna had a new understanding.

The fifth Mystic arose, and Luna walked over to her, knowing she too had much to share. Malu approached the Bastling smiling. As she did, a million sparks of light followed her. They resembled butterflies. She opened her arms to Luna as the butterfly lights leapt towards her enveloping the expectant Bastling. Luna welcomed them knowing they would greet her lovingly, "Luna! Where is your happiness?" Malu opened her hands again only to reveal a gleaming flower. As the petals opened, a thousand pictures and images came towards Luna, all reflections of joy along her journey.

Luna was perplexed, "I'm sorry?"

Malu asked again, "Where is your happiness? Do you know? For wherever that is, so too is love." Luna was taken aback. All along she had never really thought or reflected where her happiness was, yet she knew in her heart she had experienced it.

She thought deeply then replied, "I was happy when I was helping others, Bazers, the Sentients in Centros, all the worlds I've been in."

Malu smiled, "That is beautiful Luna, why did it feel so good to help?"

"Well, because it helped me to forget about my problems. It gave me great joy to see someone else happy, knowing they succeeded and knowing I played a small part in it; I felt I had a purpose."

The Mystic released more butterfly lights, "That is what you must always remember, for love is truth and truth is the way back home to the soul." Luna smiled lovingly at Malu as she twirled around and returned to her place among the others.

The sixth Mystic came towards Luna, "Do you know where true power comes from?" Luna stood perplexed by the question. The Mystic waited for a moment and then continued, "I am Mana, and I urge you to think deeply about the words I have said." Mana raised her hand to reveal a vortex sitting within the heart of her palm continuously flowing with energy from the bottom up. Luna followed its path becoming hypnotized by the endless cycle it traced. Mana smiled, "It is useless to look outside yourself Luna, all power comes from within. It is fruitless to seek the source of power from anywhere else. Notice the path it takes of initiation, always flowing up and outwards from its true source. It emanates outwards, because creation, intent, and thought once released follows the pattern of this universe itself. Think about it Luna, what if you had waited for someone else to release the Heart Stone from its captivity in Centros? Why you might have died there alone in that horrid castle, but instead you directed your power of compassion and released not only the stone but yourself as well." Luna knew full well it was the truth. Mana poised her head and peered into Luna's face, "This is what you must always remember Luna, that your destiny lies in your hands, not anyone else's." The beautiful mystic jiggled the spinning vortex in her palm, breaking Luna's hypnosis.

Luna looked into Mana's eyes, "Thank you, I am once again grateful for the insight you have given to me."

Mana pointed to Luna's heart center, "Never forget where your power comes from." Turning around, Mana took her place with the others.

The seventh and final mystic sat staring at Luna as the Bastling wondered why she had not yet risen. Instead, she began speaking from her spot on the bench, "My name is Ana, and I will not rise to greet you until you answer my question."

Luna giggled, "Alright I'll bite, what's the question?" Ana showed no signs of amusement as Luna became uncomfortable.

"How can you measure truth?" Ana sat calmly watching, as Luna pondered this difficult question, but regardless of how she tried to find an answer it would not come. "Take your time child, there is no hurry, we have an eternity." All seven Mystics began chuckling which inflamed Luna's embarrassment. Ana held up both her hands as a stream of white energy began to weave itself around them in a figure eight, "Can you do this for me Luna?" Ana's eyes became wide with anticipation as Luna wrestled with attempting this feat. Not wanting to let Ana down, she raised her hands and focused her thoughts on creating the same figure eight pattern. Yet the more she tried, the greater her resistance came to achieving her goal.

Frustrated, Luna dropped her hands, "It's no use, I can't do it!"

Ana smiled warmly, "Of course you can do it, but the trick is to know how." Her answer did nothing to dissipate Luna's disappointment. The seventh Mystic continued, "Tell me Luna, do you want to know how to accomplish this task?"

The Bastling threw off her energy to show her irritation, "Of course I do!"

Ana laughed boisterously, "Well then we are halfway there! You see effectiveness is the measure of truth, your intent is everything. Whatever you desire, regardless of what it is, must come from a place of true knowing within you. Once that connection has been made, your intention is the key, and once that has been established all that is left is manifestation. Now would you like to try again?" Luna smirked and raised her hands once again. She looked at each Mystic and focused on the teachings each one had given to her, and remembering especially that all power comes from within, she gazed down to her hands once more. Trickles of white energy began tracing circles around her hands. At first, they were mere flickers, but as her confidence increased the force became stronger until at last the form was a brilliant translucent white light traveling repeatedly in a figure eight pattern around her hands. Ana finally rose to greet her, "Very good Luna, you have answered the question well."

The Bastling looked up to Ana and back down again marveling at her creation in her hands, "This is incredible, I had no idea I could do this." She began to cry, wrapped in sheer joy from knowing such freedom.

Ana drew closer to embrace Luna, "Congratulations my dear Luna, you have passed on to the next place in Browand, having learned all that we Seven Mystics needed to reveal to you at this time." Ana released her from the embrace as sparks of light shone between them. "Now Luna, go back out this door and find King Solarus, he will guide you the rest of the way." Luna looked around at the Mystics and all their surroundings. She would never forget this place, regardless of how much her mind would try to interfere with her spirit's remembrance. Making her way to the door, Luna turned to say goodbye once again. The Bastling spirit closed the door and made her way down the hall to where King Solarus sat waiting on his throne.

"Ah, there you are my dear, how was it? Feel better now?" He clapped his hands together feverishly.

Luna's laughter resounded through the halls, "Yes I feel much better now, thank you."

She sat down in front of him on the floor, "Oh come now Luna, let me get you a chair." King Solarus waved his hand and Luna looked down to find herself upon a chair.

"Why, thank you so much!" She chuckled as the Representative bowed his head in acknowledgement.

"Now my dear, it is time we had a little chat."

Luna was surprised by his unusually serious demeanor, "You're not kidding or joking, it's the first time I've seen you this way."

Luna fidgeted in her seat as he twirled his finger in the air, "I like to keep it light because I know the journey and transition is hard. I can see how different you are, lighter and calmer. I understand how hard it can be. I was once in the Upper World, they judged me harshly but there were and still are many who loved me. It is these ones we must remember, not the negative ones. I will tell you this as well, if you find yourself in the Upper World one day, you may encounter many who claim to know me, but you must remember at a soul level who I am. They may say this or that, recite words I didn't say, but you must allow your mind to hear the whisper of this moment and know that it is the truth. What I speak to you now is who I really am. Let this moment between us now speak louder than the voices of those fools above. Many will say I am returning one day but they will be waiting a long time, for I will not be returning as one man but as a spark of light in every heart waiting to born with the greatest power there is, love." Luna sat glued in awe to every word as King Solarus continued, "I have a few pieces of advice for you before you leave. Remember in the Upper World money will seem like everything out there, but really it is nothing, an illusion created to distract you from what is important. You don't need money to be happy, what you need is yourself and not just a fraction, but all of you. If you can achieve this then you are rich beyond compare. Remember as well how infinitesimally small we are in this vast universe so that the big picture seems so much clearer. Never let yourself be carried away by arrogance. Remember, humility is the cornerstone of any foundation. Also, know this, when you weep in pain and anguish, loneliness, or sadness, you will find peace. The tranquility and courage that comes from feeling your own pain, your own feelings are tenfold in abundance to the actual pain itself. In facing and embracing it we find comfort. Oh yes, and always keep this in mind, follow the path less taken, the middle ground, not so that you aren't leaning towards one side or the other, but because if you follow the middle path, you can always see both sides clearly, and then you will know all that is yours.

Never stop believing when you see or experience injustice or persecution. Have faith that all things follow a course and play a role in time, and remember that at any given moment you have the choice to see how to deal with it. The power is yours. Be kind and treat others well and bless every one of them with the best of who you are. Never judge another, for you never know when you may be on their path. We are after all, a reflection of each other. Remember as well, that when you are in your truth in your heart, loving, taking everything in, yet knowing the illusion it can be, that you truly will see the face of your creation. Try always to make the best of any situation. If you can help others in a battle to make amends, then be swift with your action to do it. When you do this, your face will reveal who you really are, a daughter of creation." Luna began to cry as King Solarus smiled and raised his hands gently to Luna's face. The tears instantly dried and tranquility flowed through her.

"Maybe I shouldn't go on, maybe I should just stay here."

The king laughed heartily, slapping his hand on his knee, "That is always the situation with you isn't it Luna? You always find somewhere to call home for a while but then you realize you must keep going, and it's true Luna, you must keep going, until you find your true home." He smiled and put his finger to her heart.

Luna replied, "So I must keep going, but where, what do I do now? I am dead in the physical, no longer part of that world, the third dimension. There is still another world to go through before reaching the Upper World even if I could." Her eyes fell dejectedly to the floor of the great hall, "I was so close."

King Solarus shook his head, "Ah, come on now, it's not so bad, besides haven't you learned anything here? I thought you did!" Luna looked up at King Solarus to see a beaming smile across his sunny face. "Remember now is the moment of power. In Browand if you ask a question, you will be given an answer." He raised his eyebrows repeatedly, "Come on give it a go!" Luna laughed, still confused. The king bellowed, "What? What? What? Okay someone has to stop this craziness!" He morphed himself to a likeness of Luna, including his voice. He clasped his hands together humorously imitating her, "Can I finish the journey? Can I continue on to the Upper World? And the answer to the forty-four million light years question is, *Of course you can!*" He slapped his hands together.

"Really, I can?" Luna asked in naivety.

"Yes silly, oh sorry," He morphed back to his original body and voice. "Yes silly, all you had to do was state your intention. It is yours for the taking."

She was confused, "But how?"

The king smacked himself in the forehead, "Sorry must have slipped my mind what with all that other stuff I was telling you, plus I have a lot of other beings to attend to, crying, pain, all kinds of…" He was interrupted by the sound of Uriel and Raphael clearing their throats as they entered the room. King Solarus briefly greeted them with a quick flick of his hand, "Ah yes of course, anyway, where was I? Did I forget to tell you?" He turned his head scratching it as if that would reveal the answer, "No, no, you came into Browand, dolphin thingy, seven Mystics, now you're here. Nope! I guess I must have forgotten!

You see Luna, we all go around and around until we complete the circle. We just keep diving in until we get the big catch." He stood excitedly holding out his arms in measurement of a huge fish. "We go again and again until we have reached a place of true consciousness, knowing we are complete. I won't bore you with all the details, they'll be plenty of that later in your journey, believe me!" Luna nervously laughed half confused and bewildered. "Well then, I'll just see you off and wish you luck at the door!" He prompted Luna to follow him back to the front doors of his palace that were now once again visible. All those she had met and learned from, the dolphins, her council, and seven mystics were all waiting in a line. "There we are! All waiting as expected!" He looked back and forth between Luna and her council, putting his hands behind his back, "Well Luna it looks as if you're all set to go." They all looked at King Solarus with confusion. Again the angels cleared their throats. The king threw his hands up, "Oh yes of course, silly me again!" He waved his hands and in an instant Luna was back in her body. "There we go, much better!" She stared down at her body in amazement. She touched herself, and held out her arms in front of her. It was indeed real.

She looked up to see everyone smiling at her, "No marks, no breaks, intact and healthy. Now what happens?" she asked the king.

"Well now you walk out my palace doors, go up the staircase, take it to the top until you reach the white door. That is the entrance to Crownland. Take it easy up there, lots of things to learn up there, but relaxing all the same." He touched his

nose as if Luna was supposed to understand, but she didn't. She didn't have a clue what he was talking about.

She embraced each of her new and longtime companions, "Thank you so much for everything and I promise that when I get to the Upper World I will remember this and all of you."

The king rocked back and forth on his toes and sarcastically mumbled, "Hmm, that's what they all say." The others chuckled.

Luna waited to say goodbye to him last, "King Solarus, you are so incredible I have no words for how you make me feel." She reached up and kissed him on the cheek.

He blushed and looked to the others, "Did you see that? She likes me, I told you I'd win her over in the end." He smiled proudly as she waited for him to say something else but he didn't, he seemed lost in his own happiness.

"Well I guess I'd better be off now." She looked back one more time as she walked away hoping for another word from the king.

She was all the way to the top of the stairs, when he startled her, appearing at the top before her. "I forgot to tell you, anytime you need me all you have to do is call, and I want you to know I love you very much. I always have and I always will." The two embraced for a long time before letting go. Luna wanted to stay but knew she had to go, and so did the king. She opened the door and walked through. As she closed the door, the king called out, "I'll see you next time around! I love you!"

Luna called back, "I love you too!" gently closing the door behind her. She turned to face the new world of Crownland with a renewed sense of purpose.

Chapter 8

The Children of the Lotus

Luna stepped into the final world of what lay beneath the Great Mother. Upon her arrival Crownland seemed quiet, except for the sound of the beating of her newly born heart. Without noise to interrupt, her eyes were left to take in the splendid beauty of this last lower world, a place visually stunning with opalescent streams of light that sparkled with all the spectral colors. It was by far the most dazzling of all the worlds so befitting that it was the highest. Walking ever so slowly as if her footsteps might affect the show of light, she entered on to a solitary path that lay ahead of her. Luna watched the dancing light, not in the least apprehensive about her new surroundings. As she neared the end of the path, light coupled with sound, as a soft heavenly low frequency hum resounded through everything, down to every cell of her body. Luna stood on the brink of the most unimaginable sight, a set of seven circular paths, ranging from largest to the smallest being at the center. Along the perimeter of the outside circle laid thousands, if not millions of paths leading into this center. Mouth agape, she studied the vastness of the circular wonderland, trying to comprehend its magnificence. The central core shone with a light so bright that it suggested the same light that had drenched her spirit on her journey from Vocalos into Browand. Yet even the glory of this brilliant light, Luna still could not see any life forms to speak of. There were no Bazers or Keltoi, no dolphins or Huma, just simply the light. She stepped forward towards the first circular path glistening with white energy. Suddenly a mist began to form above her and all around this outer path. The figure of a young boy came to life right before her eyes. His color was translucent white and yet still held the originality of the mist within him.

Brilliant was his light as he placed himself before her, announcing his arrival, "Greetings, I AM Wyllan. Thank you for asking me to be here." He laughed casting arrows of crystal light from his body.

Luna immediately began her barrage of questions, "Who are you?"

"I told you I am Wyllan."

Luna continued, "Yes, but do you live here in Crownland?"

He smiled, "Yes I am one of the Children of the Lotus, born from the consciousness and breath of the flower itself. I am one of the seven original children. All else came to be after us."

His words piqued Luna's curiosity even more, "What do you mean, 'the flower and all else'?"

"I mean all beings at one time or another came from us seven children, all life in the universe." Luna was taken aback by his statement as his discourse continued, "I am the purpose, power and will of the lotus." He pointed down one of the straight paths that led to the center of all the circles. Sitting quietly was the most beautiful flower Luna had ever set eyes on. Its petals surely numbered a thousand and its shine was that of a most incredible lavender.

Luna clarified, "So what you are telling me, is that beautiful lavender lotus flower sitting ever so still in the middle of Crownland, is the center of the entire universe as we know it?!" She chuckled as she threw up her hands.

"That is exactly what I am saying. Why is it so hard for you to believe Luna?"

"I guess because it's a flower!"

Wyllan smirked cocking his head to one side, "Yes, it is a flower, a powerful symbol indeed. The choice was yours to make it so." Luna stared into the young boy's eyes that glittered with the same light as the lotus. He continued, "Each being chooses out of free will the way in which they will walk their path each time they participate in the seeding. You learned that in Browand, did you not? Regardless of what path they choose, as you have seen here upon arrival, all paths lead to the one."

"You said 'participate in the seeding', what did you mean by that?"

Wyllan explained, "It simply means dispersing of the energy or what they call in the Upper World, souls. Just as a seed from a plant or tree will be released and carried on the wind, a soul once through from the previous journey will be released and carried on the wind of the universe to its destination."

Luna smugly replied, "But when a seed is released it doesn't know its destination."

Wyllan smirked, "Doesn't it?" He turned and began his walk towards the center as Luna followed, "You chose this path we are walking on right now and the way we just met."

Luna was still filled with doubt but continued in spite of it, "Where are we going?"

Wyllan retorted, "Going to meet the rest of the children." As they crossed the threshold of the second circular path a dazzling sapphire light appeared.

With laser point precision, a girl was suddenly transformed in front of them, "I AM Luba." She smiled innocently at the stunned Bastling, "And yes I know who you are Luna."

The Bastling found her voice, "So you are the first seven children, what do you mean by that?" Luba laughed.

"Exactly that, we are the first seven children created from the Sacred Voice."

Luna cocked her head inquisitively, "What is the Sacred Voice?"

Wyllan chuckled, "It is known by many different names in all worlds, The Creator, Great Spirit, Prime Mover, Eternal Force, Wakan Tanka, The First Breath, but they all mean the same, The Sacred Voice."

Luna peered around her and wondered if she was being fooled, "You mean to tell me that The Great Mother and all worlds came from that lavender flower?"

She burst into a fit of laughter and Wyllan chimed in, "Why do you find it so hard to believe Luna? Why can't The Sacred Voice reside in a flower?" His look was stern and serious.

the Sacred Voice in our hearts and we understand that we are part of the oneness with the Creator, with all."

Luna pondered her words for a moment, "Yes, but what about when we are angry or in fear? What happens when we are not in a place of love?"

Luba reached out for her hand, "Sometimes it is necessary to sit in these places of fear or anger for it is those moments and afterwards we realize what we are not, that which is not love. And how could we ever really know what love is unless we experience what it is not." Luba smiled again as Luna peered down the path to the center where the closed Lotus sat.

"So, the Sacred Voice willed creation what it is, by feeling what it is not."

The three walked towards the next circle glowing fiery greens and watched a third child manifest, "Very good Luna, very perceptive. From the will to understand, love was identified as the source of all that is, and from that desire love took form, me. I AM Cast, the third child of the Sacred Voice. I am all things that have ever been born of the dream of creation." Luna's mouth fell open as she watched Cast change forms, a tree, a flower, mountains, planets, races, and even Luna herself.

She cried out in surprise, "Oh, how did you do that?"

Cast returned to his original form, "I am all forms of creation. I threw you in there too because you are also a part of the infinite creation of the Sacred Voice. You have spent your entire life feeling separate, so alone and distinctively apart from all things, especially the Sacred Voice and what an illusion that has been. Truly I tell you it is the furthest from the truth. You

"Well it can't be a flower, I mean it should be something much larger, I pictured something much grander in design."

Wyllan's sarcasm surfaced, "Well obviously it is exactly as you pictured because you are seeing it this way. Besides, who are we to criticize how our divine parent reveals itself to us?" He wiggled his eyebrows up and down, "But that is another conversation, let me instead tell you about who I am. I am the first thought or awareness of the Sacred Voice. Our divine Parent said I AM, and so became aware of its existence. Then one day The Sacred Voice desired to know more of what it meant to be 'I AM' so it decided to create aspects of itself that would flutter away and discover exactly what it was and what it was not. So, Luna, the first child or offspring is will. There must be a desire, a will for there to be anything at all, and I AM that child, the force and nature of will." He beamed with pride knowing exactly who he was.

Luna was enthralled by this new enlightenment, "Tell me more! What else is there?"

The second child exclaimed, "Then I became! Luba, love and wisdom." Light poured from her as a waterfall from a never-ending chalice. "I AM the understanding from the Sacred Voice of what will became, a passion for the will to create and in the notion of love and what that truth really means, comes wisdom. It is an understanding of what it is and what it is not, for only in love can wisdom reign."

Luna questioned this beauty, "How can there only be wisdom in love?"

Luba smiled compassionately, "When we are in a true place, in love, then we understand all of the life force, we hear have been and always will be a child of the fire light, a daughter of the Sacred Voice. Yet you have lived as separate your whole life to understand that which you are not, inseparable."

Tears welled in her eyes as his words pulled at her heart and curiosity peaked again, "Why are you in the form of a boy? Why aren't you in the form of a lotus flower like your creator?"

Luna watched as he shape-shifted into a lotus flower before her eyes, "Who says that I AM not?" His laughter reverberated through Crownland as his lotus petals shook with joy. "You see Luna, the Sacred Voice appears to you just as we children do in the easiest way you can understand, in the way you have chosen to see us."

Filled with doubt Luna replied, "So what you are saying is that I created you to look like this? That I chose to see the Creator as a thousand-petal lotus flower?"

She crossed her arms defensively as Cast took his youthful boyish form again, "That is exactly what I AM saying. You were made in the image of the Sacred Voice, you too are a creator. Did you so quickly forget the teachings of the Seven Mystics in Browand?" Luna let her arms fall to her sides humbled as they all moved forward together towards the next concentric ring of dazzling orange hues.

Her eyes stared down the path towards the lotus again. Its petals shimmered and glowed with a light like no other, "It is beautiful, isn't it?"

Luna's eyes came back to the ginger path before her. Standing in the path to her right was a beautiful girl of the same hues as the path she stood on. Luna responded, "Yes, it is far more beautiful than I could ever imagine a flower to be. I don't understand though, how could I have created this flower to represent the Sacred Voice if I have never seen such a flower?"

"Hello Luna, I am Verity and to answer your question, you knew what the lotus flower looked like the moment you were born in the light of the Sacred Voice. All life and creation exist simultaneously just waiting to be seeded by the children of the light."

Luna warmed as Verity stared soulfully into her eyes as she waved her hands in front of Luna creating pictures and images as if with a magic wand, "I AM the beauty of harmony, I pull creation from the chaos and balance it perfectly." Luna didn't understand. "Perhaps it is a great deal to take in, but it is your soul's wish. I am the beauty of all paint brushes, the words of all poets. Every time these things are done, I am there." Verity's laughter was that of a coo of a dove, "Any time an artist of any kind dreams a dream, dances a song, paints a picture, writes a word, or carves the wood, they are pulling creation from the chaos that is life. The essence of everything and nothing at all is indeed chaotic, just waiting to be plucked and chosen for the mark of creation."

Bewildered, Luna responded, "I never thought of the universe or the Creator as chaos, it all follows a straight line to me."

Verity slapped her knee gently creating sparks that flew in every direction, "That is how many beings see things in their realm. The divine universe is so incomprehensible, it is easier to cope with your reality when you see everything in a linear fashion. Yet it is far more complex than that, upside down planets and

galaxies, top is bottom, left is right. It is so incredibly complex to the conscious mind, yet perfectly natural to the soul. Therefore, an artist of any kind has a great responsibility, they allow the Sacred Voice to work through them to remind others of what the truth is, love. Since we all are creators, everything we do is significant. Naturally once form has taken shape and begins to experience, beauty will be found, and when it is, there is also the chaos." Luna contemplated her words carefully as she watched the young girl smile, "Every world has its artists and mystics who can walk between worlds and bring back the secret of creation."

Luna queried Verity, "What is the secret of creation? What does every artist bring forth with their work?"

Verity clapped with applause for Luna's questions, "Why, the whispers of the Sacred Voice of course!" Luna laughed despite not seeing the obvious answer. They continued walking again.

"Now you are ready for me!" A child stood ahead jumping up and down and waving frantically. Yellow auras surrounded his form and shone like gold. Luna and the others approached still mesmerized by his light, "We take ourselves too seriously, don't you think?" He smiled at Luna, "I AM Matih, it's very nice to see you."

Luna felt warmed by his presence and smiled back, "Hello, I'm Luna."

Matih laughed, "I know. I AM the child of focus and intellect."

Luna interrupted, "I'm sorry but you just said we take ourselves too seriously, so why should we stay in the mind, a place where all thoughts come from?"

Matih rolled his glowing eyes, "See that's a great example, you don't need to analyze everything to death! I didn't say go ahead and doubt me with your wit! You only use your mind for certain things and forget that the intellect is your connection to the Sacred Voice." Matih sat smiling wryly at Luna.

"I must say I am far more confused by you than any of the others."

Matih laughed, "Your mind is an amazing creation, it can form armies, move mountains and conceive the greatest of feats. It was meant to be used in every way, not just to speak or add numbers. Long ago races used their intellect to connect to the Sacred Voice, a bridge so to speak, much the same way Verity explained the artists. There have been some who have held the secret of the intellect in both the Lower and Upper Worlds becoming masters at it. Yet so many more have forgotten their way and instead get lost in the regrets of the past and fears of the future, but as you have been told before, there is only now. It is in this moment of now where all the potential for true intellect lies. All the synapses of the brain are merely electrical impulses and what is electricity but energy. And energy is the source of the life force itself from the Sacred Voice."

Luna was slapped with the reality of Matih's words, "So the mind has become a prison of repeating memories and fears when really it was meant to set us free?"

Matih became very excited, "Exactly! Well done! If I could teach any of the beings in any of the worlds it would be this: contemplate all things, yourself, others, what is around you that is seen and unseen. Do not use one of the greatest gifts you have for worry or fear, but instead harness that power to set you free." Matih closed his eyes signaling his words were done. The group of glowing colorful children continued walking through the hum of the circular paths until they reached the outer edge of the sixth ring.

A glowing garnet form began to take shape in front of her, "Hello Luna, I AM Pash and I am so delighted to meet you." The Bastling watched as this garnet-faced girl smiled sincerely at her. "I am the child of devotion brought forth from the Sacred Voice. Many beings call me into being because of religious devotion. Yet devotion takes on many forms doesn't it, Cast?" The two smiled in recognition of one another, "One can be devoted to a child, a cause, a truth, a way of life. Take yourself for example Luna, you have been implicitly devoted to your journey to the Upper World. So much so that not even death has deterred you, quite impressive. With blind faith you have made it your life's vision to reach the Tree of Answaru, unaware of the end result. Such devotion will surely lead to at the very least self-love, the truest of love." Luna hoped that Pash's words were true and stated so. Pash smiled warmly "Not to worry Luna, stay focused and live the rest of the journey with the same devotion you have had and I'm sure the result will be wondrous." Pash raised his ruby hands skyward, "Devotion is fearlessness in spite of fear, and the truest of love and certainly by now, you know that love is the true spirit of the Sacred Voice." Luna's face reflected her heart, full of hope once again. "Be devoted Luna, even when it seems that it should be the last thing you should be doing. Remember what Verity said, 'Nothing is as it seems, bottom is top, left is right.'

Luna was filled with inspiration, "I will do that in honor of you Pash."

The sixth child laughed and garnet-colored energy splashed through the air, "Come on Luna, you have one more child to meet." They all approached the last and smallest circle that enveloped the center where the beautiful lotus sat. The path vibrated with the same lavender splendor of the lotus. A mist came upon them and through it walked a violet child glistening with energy.

"I AM Meridian and I would like to know what you will do when I am in your path again Luna?" She stood puzzled by the oddity of his question. "I am upon you when the moment of realization is at hand and transformation is inevitable. It is heavenly." Meridian smiled as the others giggled including Luna who relished his passion for his own existence.

"I'm not sure what I will do," she shrugged her shoulders.

"That is entirely correct, you won't know until you are in that moment. She has learned well, hasn't she?" Meridian said with a chuckle. "Because you are a Bastling, you will not know what your shift will be until the moment it is upon you, but whatever it is you mustn't fight it, just let it happen." He swooshed his arms in the air as violet lightning charged forth from his fingertips.

Luna was amazed, "It would be really cool if I could do that!"

They all laughed as Meridian became quite serious, "The time is at hand to hear the Sacred Voice, are you ready?"

Luna's laughter fell silent, "I don't know, I'm not sure what I should do."

Meridian drew closer, "Well first it depends on if the seeker is ready." He peered into her face as she studied the lotus pulsating with light.

"How do I know if I am? How do I get it to open and what do I do if it does?"

Luba put her hand on Luna's shoulder, "You simply ask to speak the Sacred Voice, it is ready at all times, it just depends on whether you are ready to listen. Once it does you must sit in the center of the lotus."

Luna nervously asked, "What happens after that?"

Wyllan giggled, "You will be put into a sleep state as your body will be unable to hold the frequency of the powerful energy of the Sacred Voice."

Matih chimed in, "Yes, you will be communicating with your mind." His eyebrows lifted up as he answered. All seven children stood silently in awe of their grand heritage as Luna silently watched them.

"Well then I guess I will give it a try." She stepped closer to the lotus that sat humming in the water that encased it. Tiny ripples were being formed over and over again from the sound. Closing her eyes, she spoke with her mind, "Sacred Voice I wish to speak to you now, I wish to hear your words." Her eyes opened to see the lavender petals opening up and the children smiling.

Luna's nervousness caught her in the stomach as Meridian reminded her, "Just let this happen Luna, do not fight it."

His words calmed her as Wyllan escorted her to the inside of the lotus, "Here, sit down and focus on your breathing. Close your eyes and relax." The anxious Bastling turned her attention to her breath and followed the rest of the instructions as the petals began to close around her.

She stood on the outskirts of the circular paths not knowing which path to journey down, "They all seemed to lead to the center, but why so many? Surely one must be the true path, the correct one."

A voice suddenly echoed through the vastness of light, causing everything to vibrate with each word, "There is no one true path, Luna. All paths lead to the one, the center. It is only true because you choose it."

Stunned by the invisible oration, Luna said, "Who is that? Show yourself!" She waited with a defensive stance.

"I have shown myself to you, always, even in this moment now."

Luna again revisited the question, "Who are you?"

The voice echoed again through the vast light of Crownland, "I AM. I am you, you are me. I am all things and yet I am nothing at all." Luna released her clenched fists. "Pick a path Luna, and follow it with your heart." Reluctantly she took a step forward scanning the paths for an indication of which one to choose. Each one was shaded slightly different than the others, although all contained the same glimmering energy. Instinctively she moved to the path whose hue radiated blissful lavender. As she made her way towards it, its color magnified in intensity setting forth lilac against a backdrop of the opalescent white. Stepping onto the pathway, the other paths to her left and right had distinct and continuous blurring movements that raced by at the speed of light. Her own movement along the lighted trail became mechanical as her eyes peered to the right, left and then back again as she tried to distinguish these blurring figures. So concentrated was her attention on these other paths, that she had unknowingly reached the center with great speed. As her eyes caught up with her final destination they fell upon an exquisite sight, a lotus flower drenched in the same light-filled lavender and nearly as large as the center itself.

"I AM glad to see you have made it here Luna." As her body shuddered with the vibrations that emanated from the voice once again, she peered around the center for its source again. Yet all that was revealed was a thousand-petal lotus with its dazzling light. "Welcome to Crownland Luna."

Luna was pulled from her hypnotic stare on the lotus, "Where are you?" She inquired again.

"My child, I have already told you, I AM everywhere, and yet I AM nowhere at all."

Luna's frustration mounted, "Okay that's fine, if it's going to be riddles, just get on with it! Just tell me how I get out of here, I need to get to the Upper World."

Laughter reverberated throughout the entire world of Crownland, "Ah yes, the Upper World, one of my finest creations."

Luna squinted in doubt, "You created the Upper World?"

The laughter ceased, "Not just the Upper World, all worlds, everything, everywhere. Of course, so did you." The voice retorted softly, "Never mind, that's for later."

"Why don't you come out where I can see you?"

The voice's tone softened even further, "My children, always full of doubt and disbelief. I AM showing myself to you, right now in this moment, everywhere you look."

She swung her head back and forth, "I don't see you anywhere."

"Yes you do, it's just difficult for you to understand. You are being blocked by many things again."

Luna huffed, "Well, why don't you help me to understand?"

The voice replied lovingly, "That is the very key to understanding, the desire to know. So you are going to the Upper World? It is a beautiful place and what will you do once you get there?"

Luna quickly answered, "I am going to the top of Answaru to find the owl, but I still haven't found out how to get out of Crownland." She looked above her head to see mammoth tree roots flowing down through the walls of the world she stood in. Shock rose in Luna as she understood what they were.

"Yes, they are exactly what you are thinking, they are the roots of my beautiful Answaru, and as far as leaving Crownland, you are free to go whenever you choose. It was you who created all this including right now." The Sacred Voice's echoes caused the walls in Crownland to shake including Luna.

"Wait, I created this? That's impossible!"

The Voice resounded, "You did, but like many other things you don't remember creating this moment, you are sleeping as well, sitting ever so softly in the center of the lotus. Trust me child, take my word for it." Laughter echoed throughout the land causing everything to hum. "I made you in my image therefore you too are a creator of all your experiences. These words are what you need to hear right now, therefore you do. Each being will dream in their own way that suits them best. Once you are in the Upper World this conversation will be forgotten as well. Let me rephrase that, this conversation will not be remembered on a conscious level but your spirit will always know. Unless of course you reach enlightenment in which case all things are known in a single moment of clarity."

The voice chuckled softly this time as Luna sat down crossed legged staring up at the roots, "It is so amazing, I can't believe I'm almost there."

Her pride swelled as the Sacred Voice continued, "The Upper World is a much different place than the Lower Worlds. It is vast, teeming with life and of course great revelations if you allow it. Although the roots seem close the tree is still far. It is massive and has only been estimated by those in the Upper World how far the roots go. If they only knew the roots contain all worlds and all worlds contain the roots. The tree is sacred among all others. It shares seasons with you all, never the same, always changing, yet ever constant. She holds life when before there was none. She holds the keys, the memories of all time, she is the keeper of time. My children of that realm have forgotten many things including that they need each other, more than they know."

Luna spoke up, "That sounds very sad."

The Voice replied, "It is for many of my children. If they would only realize they are eternal, but they must first wake and realize they exist at all!" Luna's body shook from the reverberation of the Voice. "All that is needed is a reminder that everything is theirs and what is theirs is everything. Imagine if you could all wake from slumber and realize you are being whatever you desire in that moment. The possibilities are endless and so is time, and as new dreams come, new existences are birthed. This is essential for you to remember Luna when you are in the Upper World. There is no judgment, only the ones you place on yourself. Remember my dear Bastling, at any time you can wake up and be free."

With that said, Luna opened her eyes only to find herself lodged in a tunnel of earth and mud. Above her head a tiny pinhole of light, giving her cause to proceed. She wormed her way slowly through the muck as the moist dirt permeated her nostrils. She followed the light. Within moments the light became a large enough opening for her to fit through as she attained the destiny of her dreams, the Upper World.

Chapter 9

On The Backs of Friends (Weaving the Web)

Luna popped up through the earthy hole that led to an extraordinary world unlike any in the lower realms. Squeezing and pushing, Luna forced the rest of her body out and plopped herself down on the outer edge of the gateway amongst the thick carpet of grass. All that could be seen from this vantage point were green lush hairs towering overhead reaching as far as the eye could see. Lifting her head skyward, she breathed in long and deep, the air was different up there. Her nostrils took in the scent of soils and greens. She lifted herself up again, this time to stand and take in the scenery. From her vantage point, she could see an enormous tree not too far away. Her eyes followed the stretch of it as it seemed to go on forever into the sky, she knew it had to be Answaru. Beyond its giant foliage was the Sky of Wonders. Its familiarity beckoned Luna. The brightness of the sun made Luna's eyes water. As she shed the tears from her eyes a movement was caught out of the corner of her periphery, bobbing up and down repeatedly. Turning her head towards it, it seemed real and not a creation of her tear-blurred vision. She shuddered, scared of what might happen if it caught sight of her and considered going back down in the hole, but quickly realized, the passageway to Crownland had disappeared.

She peered over to the base of Answaru standing ready, but cautious. Just as she was about to make a dash, a voice echoed through the grasslands, "Who's there? I know you're there! Don't hurt me please! I can hear you!" It was coming from the same direction as the strange bobbing motion.

Luna called out, "Hello there! I'm over here! I'm not going to hurt you!"

The terrified voice answered back, "Please! I'll do anything just don't hurt me!"

Luna's frustration rose, "I'm not going to..." THUD! Luna stopped to listen for another sound but there wasn't any. Calling out to the stranger once again, Luna waited in anticipation for his response, "Can you hear me? Excuse me, over here!" When her words found no reply, she started off in the direction of the sound. Parting the grasses, she discovered a creature laying passed out, belly up on the ground.

He opened his eyes, and looking her way, jumped up and back on all fours, screaming at the top of his lungs, "Oh my gosh, oh my gosh. Don't hurt me! What are you? I've never saw anything so strange! Ah!" With his last shriek, he ran in three circles and fell belly up again, passing out cold. Luna rolled her eyes. It was an odd response from someone who looked as he did, long green scaly body, four legs, and eyes that twirled constantly in his head.

She mumbled under her breath, "I'm Luna of the Bastlings you silly thing."

The creature jumped back onto his feet again. "Well it's about time you answered!"

Luna's temper rushed through her, "It's a little hard to speak to someone who keeps passing out!" Luna's face was set in a pucker with arms crossed.

There was silence for a moment and then laughter, "Raha-raha-raha! That is funny! That is bloody funny! Passing out! Wow you have a vivid imagination! Ha! I'm a lizard, we don't pass out! What nonsense!"

Luna couldn't believe what she was hearing, "So you're the body behind the voice." Luna tried to hide her smile.

"Yes, I am. Lenny's the name, and your name is?"

Luna looked away from his swirling eyes. It was just too much for her to hold in, she began laughing, "I am sorry Lenny. It's been a long journey and my laughter is merely a sign of fatigue." She didn't have the heart to tell him of his frequent memory loss, besides it wouldn't do any good. He would forget she told him.

"My name is Luna of the Bastlings. It's a pleasure to meet you."

The lizard tilted his head to one side. "You're sure you aren't laughing at me, right? Cause I would be very upset if you were. I just don't think I could handle that kind of teasing. I'm very sensitive you know. I just couldn't take it." Lenny slapped his claws over his face. He started to pretend to cry as he peeked out through his scaly sharp toes.

Luna cleared her throat, "Sir, I can assure my laughter is just fatigue." Luna tried everything in her power not to laugh again. It was very difficult when those eyes just kept twirling in infinity.

"What are you doing here? Don't you know we could get run over here? Not a good place to be perched, definitely not good." The lizard shook his head and trotted through the grass to a large rock. Luna followed him making certain she wasn't in the way of getting smashed by one of his fainting episodes. He threw himself down against the rock to get some sun. It was the first time she had seen him belly up and awake, "So Luna, where are you headed?" He put his arms behind his head.

"Well not very far. I'm going to the Tree of Answaru." She pointed to the mammoth tree in the distance.

"What?" Lenny jumped up and began running in circles, eyes twisting and turning feverishly, "Oh no, oh no, this isn't good. Nope. Not good at all. Too much going on there in that tree! No sir, no way." Crossing his arms back and forth in front of him and shaking his head, Lenny finally showed confidence.

"It can't be that bad," Luna retorted.

Lenny stopped his antics and looked at Luna. "There are THINGS over there you don't want to see. Thousands, no millions of them all shuffling around, working, and collecting just waiting for something to go and snatch!" He wrung his hands as he paced furiously. Luna grabbed Lenny to calm him down but it didn't work. Her attempt caused a panic, Lenny screamed and passed out again, belly up of course. Luna waited patiently until he came around again. He opened his eyes and they began turning as Luna watched him, attempting not to laugh.

"Lenny, I understand that these things cause you to be nervous, but just because something makes you feel uneasy doesn't mean you should stay away from it. Some of the best things we do in our lives come from things we fear. The best thing you can do for yourself is face it. Besides I need a friend to show me the way to the tree." Luna smiled and Lenny's heart melted. It was either that or the blood was finally being pumped back to it again after fainting so many times. Lenny reluctantly decided it was best if he escorted the Bastling to the base of Answaru. It was a relatively quick and uneventful journey. As the two came out of the grass and entered into the clearing, their eyes scanned the land that stretched out forever in the distance beyond. The blue of the sky seemed to round behind everything. Without any doubt, none of the beauty of the Lower Worlds could have prepared her for the overwhelming splendor of this one. There were flowers of red and yellow hues swaying in the breeze releasing an intoxicating aroma of blooms into the air, and the birds! Their melodies wafted across the sky in an electrifying dance of sound.

Luna wanted to sit down and take in the entire goings on, but Lenny would have no part of that, "Oh no! You can't just sit here! We'll be captured, attacked! We're sitting ducks right here!" Lenny was getting worked up again.

"Okay, okay Lenny. We'll keep moving, it's just that the tree is right there and I thought we could stop to admire some of this beautiful scenery." Lenny shook his head adamantly and Luna tried to take it all in, as if savoring the experience for later.

The neurotic lizard started trotting and talking to himself aloud, "Listen Lenny, you have to get a hold of yourself. It's no good. It's no good to just sit here spinning in your mind! Get a grip. It'll be okay. You just need to remember what your clan taught you, what was that anyways? Hmm, oh yes, always look both ways at centipede crossings? No, no that's not it. Oh, I know ...always bob up and down when holding your own territory? No. No, I do that anyway. Uh, what was it? Oh yeah! Always give up your tail in a dangerous situation! That's it!" Lenny pointed his scaly finger up in the air, quite proud of his revelation. But three legs is no way for a lizard to balance himself, so he keeled right over again. Luna burst out in a fit of laughter. Lenny however had scared himself right into a fainting spell again. When he came to, Luna had to explain to him that it was all his doing and nobody in any uncertain terms had tried to overtake him. He reluctantly believed her. In no time, they reached the base of Answaru. It was a colossal tree, far more daunting once viewed from the ground directly below it. Luna wondered how she would be able to climb this great tower. Lenny just shook his head.

"How long do you think it will take to climb her Lenny? Have you ever tried before?"

Lenny looked at her as if she had completely lost her mind. "Are you talking to me? I would never climb this tree! No, no! There are too many things to get snarled up in, no way!" He stood up on his two hind legs, crossing his arms and tapping his foot. "It would take an army to get me up there!" Just then a sound in the distance caught their attention, "Hup, hup, left right left. Hup hup, left right left." Luna peered to see who it was but could see nothing as the sound continued. Lenny had already keeled over again. She wondered if all lizards behaved the way Lenny did, she was about to find out. "Hup! Hup! Left right left!" To her direct left Luna could see a dark trail, a moving line in the distance. She turned to Lenny but he was still belly up on the ground. She was feeling vulnerable with no place to hide, but decided there wasn't much to do but stand there exposed and hope for the best.

The moving line came closer, "HUP! HUP! LEFT RIGHT ...HALT!" Luna froze. The little creature stopped the line from moving and scurried forward. "Excuse me! Are you going to eat that?"

She looked behind her, "Eat what, that?" She pointed to Lenny still flaked out.

"Yes, that's right, because if you're not, we'll just be on our way with the carcass."

Luna stepped back, "Carcass? No, no! He's not dead, he's resting. It's been a very trying day," she whispered so as not to stir Lenny.

"You mean he's still alive? RETREAT!! Come on boys and girls! No time to lose before this big Lizzie makes us dinner!" The leader yelled back to the troops. They all began shuffling the other way.

Luna stepped in their way, "No, no! You don't understand. Lenny wouldn't hurt you! He's a softy, besides he's scared of his own shadow," she whispered. They all looked back at the sleeping giant.

The leader spoke up, "Well that would be a first. A lizard afraid of us! HA! Wait until the rest hear about this one!" Just then the feared giant began to stir. He opened his eyes slowly panning the sky. He turned his head to see Luna and a long trail of army ants standing to his side. He scurried to his feet, tripping several times in the attempt.

"Oh gosh, oh gosh! I knew it! I knew it! I knew it would end like this one day!" Lenny dramatically put his claw over his face again. "Please don't hurt me! Please!" The ants crept backwards unsure of what to do. Luna was trying to think of a way to calm the situation as Lenny backed up falling into the trunk of the tree, "Please! Take my tail, take my tail just leave me with my life! Ahaaabhaa!"

The leader of the ants moved forward a little, "Well if you insist, I mean, how could we say no? I sure..."

"ENOUGH!" Luna stepped between Lenny and the ants. "Nobody is taking anyone's tail. We are all going to be civilized. There's no need for either side to be afraid of the other."

The leader stepped towards Luna, "You're not from around here, are you?" Everyone started to laugh.

"No, I'm not but that's beside the point."

The leader ant cleared his throat, "Well usually around here, guys like Lizzie eat us for breakfast and if someone eats him, we take the leftovers."

The leader smiled as Luna's stomach churned with repulsion, "How hideous! That's the most horrible thing I've ever heard!" She was feeling quite queasy.

"Hey, I don't make the rules, I just follow 'em."

Luna regained her composure, "Well today we'll have none of that. We're all going to be nice and nobody needs to get hurt."

"Well, okay if you insist, I guess if that's way you want it." The leader stepped forward, "The name's Artie. This here's my fifth battalion. Good bunch, hard workers, so if you don't mind we'll be moving onwards. We have a lot of ground to cover today."

Luna was impressed with his fortitude for such a small creature, "Well actually before you leave I was wondering if you could help us with something. You see, I need to get to the top of Answaru but I don't know how I'm going to climb up there, any ideas?" The ants all started to chuckle and whisper.

Artie spoke up, "Well you got that big lummox over here! Why don't you ride him up the trunk! That is what lizards do, you know. They climb up trees! Lizzies are great vertical climbers, I once saw a lizzie scale a three-hundred-foot vertical wall in two seconds without blinking. And you know how hard it is for them to not blink!" He nudged one of his fellow battalion, and they all started howling. Luna looked back at Lenny who was standing on hind legs again tapping his foot and whistling pretending not to hear the conversation.

They all shifted their eyes to him. "What? I'm sorry did someone say something?"

Luna was now standing with her arms crossed, "Lenny, why don't you give me a ride?"

His arms pointed to his chest, "Who me? No. I can't! Please don't make me! Please!"

Luna knew it was fruitless to keep asking. "Well he's out of the question. What about you guys? Can't you help me?"

Artie spoke up, "Well now little miss that's something that has to be cleared by the general. We don't do a thing without strict orders from her." He too crossed his arms.

"Can we meet with her?"

Everyone went dead silent, "Ah, yeah about that, you see the only way for you to meet her is to come into our bunker and I don't think that would go over too well, if you know what I mean." He flicked his head in Lenny's direction.

"Lenny wouldn't hurt anyone, you know that." Luna didn't understand what the problem was.

"Yeah well…you see, he's a lizzie and we're ants and ah well, usually they're eating us. I mean could you imagine the hubbub if he was in our bunker? There would be chaos! Anarchy!"

Luna wasn't giving up. "Can't you just ask the general? Better yet, why don't you let me ask her?" She felt confident she had found a good solution.

"No can do! No unauthorized personnel in the bunker unless warranted by the big chief herself!" Luna's shoulders fell in hopelessness. She only had a little farther to go to reach her destination and yet it seemed so far away. "Tell ya' what little miss, I'll radio the chief and see what she says. I'll explain the whole situation but just don't start bubbling on me, I can't stand crying!"

Luna jumped up and down, "Thank you so much, I really do appreciate this."

Artie turned to face his army as she tried to sneak a peek at what he was doing, but all she could make out was all their antennas coursing together at once.

In no time at all, Artie had his answer. He pivoted himself back around to face her, "Okay little miss, I've explained the whole happenstance to the general and she said for you two to follow us. She's alerted the troops not to panic when they see wiggly eyes here enter the base and she wanted you to know that she's been anxiously awaiting your arrival." Artie looked perplexed by the last part of his orders but followed them strictly regardless of however odd they seemed. Lenny started getting nervous and Luna knew he was going to pass out again unless she intervened.

"Listen Lenny, I know this is going to be hard for you, but I really need your support and help right now. I believe we'll be okay just as long as we abide by their rules. Besides they're more afraid of you than you are of them." Luna wasn't sure how much she believed that but said it anyway. The panicky lizard reluctantly obliged. She was the first real friend he had made in a long while and regardless of his anxiety, he wanted to stay true to her. Lenny and Luna followed behind the army until they reached a spot which was just on the other side of the base of the tree. It didn't seem too far at the time, but looking back Luna realized just how thick the roots of Answaru were. Lenny was excited as he had never gone around that side of the tree before. The two stood, wondering how exactly they would fit into the tiny opening surrounded by all those tiny dark pebbles.

"Don't let the opening fool ya' little miss. Our underground complex is huge! We here in number five battalion boast the biggest barracks in this neck of the woods! Normally we would try to tear ya' apart but since you're still alive and all, we'll just squeeeeze ya' through. Once inside, you'll have plenty of room!" For the first time since meeting Artie she wasn't so sure about him, and Lenny well, he just went bottoms up from the excitement. Once Lenny came to, the troops began pushing the two newcomers into the hole. It was an incredibly uncomfortable fit but when they did finally make it to the other side, it was just as Artie had said. The hole did nothing to reveal what lay beneath, a full-size labyrinth that stretched miles underground. Luna assumed it lay literally on top of Crownland. Thousands and thousands of busy army ants scurried feverishly back and forth. It was quite an amazing sight. Artie stood looking out quite proud of the entire operation. The ants were so busy they hadn't noticed the two strangers among them, that is until Lenny let out a loud howl and keeled over again. The ants stopped their work and just stared, frightened and extremely untrusting. Artie yelled out to the workers. "Well what are you all staring at? You've all seen one of these before, wiggly eyes here is harmless! They're here to meet with the general so get back to work!" With Artie's command, they all began furiously producing again but keeping their attention to the new members of the battalion. Luna hauled Lenny up to his feet again and followed Artie down a long winding steep path. She could feel the downward motion of the trail. It reminded her of Elan, dark passages that wound around and around, except there were no Dreglings to speak of here. When they reached the end of the tunnel they stood staring at a soil wall just like any other. Until Artie pressed on a certain spot and... BAM! The walls parted to reveal a glowing room with a Queen Ant sitting on the throne, regal and dignified. At her feet sat thousands of glistening iridescent eggs, babies ready to be born.

She motioned the three into the room, "Hello, please come closer." Her voice was sweet as honey. Luna stepped forward with intimidation for such a stately sovereign, while Lenny was more nervously concerned over the thousands of eggs at his feet. "You may leave us now Artie. Thank you for helping our friends." Artie saluted, clicked his feet together and swung around to leave. "Oh Artie, be a dear and give our Lizzie friend some food. I'm sure he must be starving, he looks a bit rattled." She smiled.

"Yes general!" Artie motioned towards the door to Lenny.

"Aren't you coming Luna?" Lenny nervously asked.

The queen put her eight legs forward and spoke in a motherly tone, "Don't worry she'll be along shortly. I just wish to speak to her alone for a moment."

Luna reassured the anxious lizard, "It's all right Lenny. I'll be there before you know it." Luna gave him the bravest smile she could muster. She was feeling a little nervous herself. Lenny and Artie left through the door and closed it behind them. Luna looked for a place to sit but there wasn't one.

"Please excuse the children. They are due any day now and take up an enormous amount of room. If you like I can part a place for you to sit." She thought it was kind but Luna insisted on not disturbing them, she would stand. "It is nice to see someone so trusting as you to come down here. Although I am not so sure your friend feels the same way." The two laughed breaking the tension. "We are a very misunderstood race, us ants. There are many kinds of us, all industrious and great problem solvers. Most do not see us that way however. The ant nation has a reputation in the Upper World as being pests and problem causing. This view is held mostly by the two-legged nation, although there are some who do appreciate our presence here in the Great Mother. Most other races understand the importance of our existence. They know that we are an intricate part of the web of life. Things would not be the same if we didn't exist to help them along with our great sacrifices." Luna questioned her use of words, "Yes Luna, any race or being at any given time can choose to sacrifice for the good of others. It is the ultimate service of love. We queens are a living example of sacrifice. While others search for wings we are born with them and when we are ready to serve our community we let them go. Once they are gone we can birth the children, future generations and our legacy." Luna listened intently to her every word. "I explain this to you as a sacrifice, but really it is an honor. To be chosen to birth new life is a gift. It is essential regardless of what world you live in. We all have a legacy, a creation or gift to birth so to speak, once you know what it is, the sacrifice is easy."

"When I think of my life and what I have been through so far, it makes sense."

The queen smiled softly. "An ant never questions its responsibility, it just does, for the good of the race and the cycle of life. We not only serve our community, we serve all. I believe every member of every race at some point in their existence is faced with question, 'How shall I serve?' They ask themselves what we know from birth, that whatever I choose it will have profound and lasting affects upon all." Luna decided to nestle down in a tiny spot amidst the unborn children after all. The queen nodded her head, "We mustn't ask, 'Why should I serve?' but instead ask, 'How may I?' Whatever truth betters the individual in turn benefits the race and in turn brings evolution to us all. You see my dear, whether queen or worker, lizard or Bastling, the call is always floating out there in the cosmos waiting to be pulled down." Luna stared mesmerized by the queen, sitting on her throne, all arms outstretched pointing upwards to the world that lingered over their heads. She was beautiful in her own right. For the first time since she had begun the journey, Luna wanted to know who she was not only for her, but for everyone who might benefit, as a renewed sense of hope and peace filtered through her. Clearing her throat, the Queen Ant rose from her gloriously tiny throne, "Well having said that, I do believe you have a journey to complete."

Luna humbly smiled as she bowed slightly, "How do you know about my journey?"

"Come now child, don't you know by now that everything presented on your path is very distinct and part of the divine plan?"

Luna's lack of response gave the queen an assurance the Bastling understood what she was saying. The two carefully treaded through the new life that lay waiting for birth on the floor.

The queen and Luna entered the busy chamber of workers who were tirelessly building. They reminded Luna of the Bazers, functioning with focus and purpose. She wished she could tell Notty and the others how much she had realized about them and all the worlds since she had left the lower realms. In the corner was Lenny, laughing hysterically as the ants trekked across his belly. His big lizard body had blocked their way, so they worked around him, or over him. Lenny was in heaven, he loved belly rubs. The two spent a long while with the army learning their ways, and as much as Luna enjoyed her time there, she knew it was time to complete her journey up the mighty Answaru. The queen assured Luna she would have the army's help getting up the tree, and that's exactly what they did. Battalion Five pushed, prodded, and squeezed Luna and Lenny through the opening once again. They popped out just in time to see the first rain clouds roll in. Lenny wasn't fond of the rain, but Luna enjoyed it thoroughly. She sat right down in front of Battalion Five's hole, allowing the cool water to wash over her. Lenny chose to hide under some nearby ivy. Artie popped his head out to announce that they would be leaving at 0600 hours. Luna didn't have a clue what he was talking about but told him she would be right there waiting.

She looked over at Lenny, his eyes closed but still rolling around underneath his eye lids. "Lenny, are you asleep?" she whispered. "Lenny?" The rain pelted down on the leaf above him.

Suddenly he jumped up and started yelling, "Yes it's all right! I'm here! I'm here! Where am I? Yes, that's right, I'm here!" He was running in a circle on the spot where he had been laying.

Luna laughed and shook her head, "Lenny you are a funny one!" The comical lizard stopped dead in his tracks and looked over at Luna. His eyes were filled with sadness.

"Luna, you know I can't come with you right?" He smiled awkwardly as Luna's heart filled with sorrow. She had come to love that crazy lizard in such a short period of time but also felt guilty leaving him.

It was a mystery how he had survived this long without someone to help him, "How come you can't come with me Lenny? Are you scared? Because if you are, we'll get through it together. We'll be fine." She smiled back quite sure that was it, but Lenny surprised her.

"No Luna, that's not it, I truly cannot go with you. This is for you and you alone." His somber expression remained unchanged as he continued his stare. She realized how serious he was, "Luna do you know the difference between when you are sleeping and when you are dreaming?"

She laughed nervously, "Lenny what kind of a question is that?"

The lizard wasn't laughing, "Can you? And tell me how do you know the difference?"

Luna's serious demeanor suddenly matched her friend's, "I can just tell, it's hard to explain, its different realities I guess."

Lenny stared at her. "Okay, so when you were in the lower worlds you knew this world existed right?"

She shrugged her shoulders, "Well I hoped it did. I had never been here before so it was purely speculation, a hope."

He clicked his head to the side while his eyes swirled crazily, "Okay then let me put it another way. You are sitting up here but you know the Lower Worlds still exist even though you're not in them right now, right?"

"Yes, I'd say that's true."

"Well sleeping and dreaming are the same thing. You can wake yourself in your dreams, you can tell yourself that it is exactly that, a dream. It's not easy but it can be done. That's a charm of the lizards you know."

Luna was surprised, "Really! I didn't know that, what a fascinating charm to possess."

Lenny finally smiled lightening the mood, "Yes, it is pretty cool." He stood up on his two hind legs and quickly fell over. He regained his composure and carried on as if nothing had happened. "Anyway, I just wanted to make sure you knew that! Very important details you know."

Luna started laughing at him again. "I am definitely going to miss you Lenny! You wacky lizard! It has been an honor sir." Luna stood up and bowed down before him as Lenny's face flushed with embarrassment.

He clapped his claws over his face. "Stop it, you're too kind!" The two sat together waiting for the rains to stop. Side by side they talked about the Upper and Lower Worlds, sharing their knowledge as Luna wrapped her arm around her friend's leathery shoulders. The rain did finally stop and as promised, Artie and the troops came out of their hole immediately after.

Luna stood up, "Hello there, fellas! I hope this doesn't cut into your work time too much."

Artie marched over to her, "Nonsense little miss! We got plenty of soldiers to cover the ones that are away from the base!"

Luna turned to Lenny to see tears welling in his whirling orbs. "I'm going to miss you Lenny. What are you going to do when I leave?"

Lenny smiled bashfully, "Well, while you were talking with the queen I had a little talk with the troops down there. Turns out they need someone to help them with detecting food over long distances. Since I'm so good at it, I was the obvious choice. I can even stay down below with them, so long as I don't get in the way." Luna felt happy for Lenny that he had finally found a place to belong.

"That's great Lenny! Maybe I'll come back and visit you and tell you all about the top of tree."

Lenny changed the subject and came closer to Luna, "Let me just do a traditional lizard goodbye." He began dancing and bobbing up and down. After doing this several times he ended it by touching his tail to Luna's forehead on her birthmark. As he did this, a tingle rushed all the way down her spine. "That's so you're always with me, and I'm always with you." Lenny came back once more this time for a hug. The two embraced, "You be careful up there and remember what I said about sleeping and awake." There was genuine compassion in his eyes.

"I will Lenny. Thank you so much for everything." She hugged him again as Artie stood behind them uncomfortably.

He cleared his throat and pretended to be busy examining his baton.

When the two finished their goodbyes, Lenny went over to the ant hill. "I'm ready!" With that he was pulled back down to help his new friends.

Luna turned to Artie, "Whenever you're ready guys!"

Artie swiveled around to the troops, "Okay boys and girls! Let's move 'em out!" The ants marched up to Luna and started sliding in position underneath her. "It's better if you just trust them and their leg work. Let them pick up your weight! They won't drop ya!" Artie was hollering as he led the pack underneath Luna. Before she knew it, they were hauling her sideways up the trunk of the great tree. Everything looked so different from her higher vantage point. She could see so much more and they weren't even halfway up the trunk of the tree. Beautiful fields of green could be seen in every direction. There were other trees too but none compared to the grace and poise of the great Answaru. The ants kept time with their senses led of course by Artie. "Won't be long now little miss! We'll have you up there in no time!"

Luna wrestled with pangs of guilt for leaving all the work to Battalion Five. "Are you sure there's nothing I can do to help?"

Artie laughed as they scurried underneath her, "Nonsense! This is what we do best!" On their way up they passed a moth sitting on the bark. It made no movement as they cruised by. Luna thought it was a beautiful creature. "Look boys! Dinner!" Artie started laughing and soon the rest joined in. Luna didn't find it funny. She thought it was far too fascinating to eat and tried eagerly to put it out of her head. "Alright troops! Start unloading!" Luna felt herself being turned to the left then the right. Soon she was sitting upright on the first limb that stretched out of Answaru. Artie and the rest marched out from under her and ceased the procession once everyone was accounted for. The tiny leader looked around for any signs of trouble, "Well looks like this it kid. We'd take you further but we can't take the chance. Too many enemies up ahead for us, but you'll be fine."

Luna didn't like the sound of that. "Anything I should know before I head up?"

Nervousness pinched her stomach as Artie stood scratching his head with his legs. "Let me think...hmm ...oh yeah there is one thing. Be careful climbing when it's wet. The rain makes willow leaves and bark really slippery."

Luna was disappointed in his answer. "Well, all right I guess."

Artie faced the troops, "You guys ready to move out?"

"Yes, Sir!"

He faced Luna once again. "Little Miss, it's been a pleasure meeting you and all that stuff. I'm not one for goodbyes, makes my throat all tight." He rubbed the back of his neck with his legs. Luna knew he was feeling extremely uncomfortable again.

"Well I just want to say thank for all your help. I don't know how I'll ever be able to repay you, but I appreciate this more than you know."

"No need, no need at all, the best thing you can do is make it to the top in one piece!"

Luna smiled insecurely, "I will. I promise."

Artie turned and prepped himself for the march down, "Let's move out!" Luna watched as her tiny friends walked down the trunk without her, which left her feeling very alone. Artie stopped and yelled back to her, "By the way! Give Serendipity my warmest regards!"

Luna strained to hear him." Who's that Artie?!" He didn't answer. Luna watched Battalion Five march out of sight. Everything was quiet. She sat for a long time looking out into the distant lands. She could see tall buildings all clustered together. Tiny objects moved to and fro, and although she couldn't make out what they were exactly, it seemed like a very busy place. Her eyes panned the landscape to see the sun shining brightly over rolling green hills, making their way past the clouds that were trying to cast rain again. She turned to look in front of her, to the east and saw heat rising in golden waves like water from Centros. To the south the red lands called out from beneath the sky. She gazed to the west as it revealed huge glorious mountains nestled in the distance. The north held white covered lands glistening with diamonds from the sun's rays. It was surreal to be sitting in the Upper World nestled in the Tree of Answaru. A dream she held for so long that the reality of it was almost too much to take in. Peering straight above her the tree seemed dormant. There was no movement except that of the willow itself hypnotically swaying in the wind. Bewilderment filled the Bastling as she could almost see clear to the top. There was no owl, only blue sky and diamond sun drops peeking through the leaves. Her thoughts and fears began pounding fast and furious, "What if I get to the top and there is nothing? What if did this all for nothing? What if the answer I'm looking for doesn't come and this whole trip has been in vain? What if I have to go back to Elan? No, I won't, I can't. I cannot go back there. There's no place for me there now, there never was. I couldn't live in that same world after changing so much. Then again maybe I haven't changed so much at all. Maybe I haven't learned as much as I think I have." Then she remembered a lesson learned along the journey, "You're constantly worried about whether you're in the right place or not...whether you're on the path. You are, because you're here. This is your path, this is where you are supposed to be." Luna felt frustrated with herself. Every time she felt positive, a negative thought would pop up and set a series of insecurities in motion. Self-awareness bombarded her revealing how much of these insecurities were her own sabotage. She shook it off and focused upwards again. There were a great many branches to climb before reaching whatever sat at the top and she decided it was time to pick up and move on. At first the climbing was fairly easy. One foot at a time, she carefully made great strides until she found the branches getting wetter closer to the top. Her footing slipped quite a bit and she was getting tired from hanging on so tightly. Reaching three quarters of the way up, Luna decided to rest a while. It was from this higher vantage point that life inside the great willow was exposed. Birds flew in and out of the great willow's hair, as nests of other creatures lay tucked away, hidden from view. She leaned her head on a branch to rest and to observe the activity above as she enjoyed the melancholy sounds of life in the tree. She soon dropped off into peaceful slumber. Luna hadn't been asleep long when she was stirred by a voice humming a tune. Her eyes opened just in time to catch sight of a huge black spider swinging past her as quick as a flash.

"Hmm...hmm, hm, hm, hm, hm, oh hello. I'm sssoo sssorry dear, did I wake you?" The voice was uncomfortably sweet. The eight-legged acrobat swung up and down, side to side as if sporting an invisible pair of wings. "I'm jusssst putting sssome finishing touchesss on my web. I hope you don't mind," she said coyly.

Luna wanted to get up and run, but since there was nowhere to escape to, she did the next best thing and pleasantly replied, "No, I'm sorry. I must be in your way, I'll just be going." She reached the branch above her head and pulled the weight of her Bastling body up, accidentally catching the web with her hand and pulling a large section of it down. Luna frantically tried to get it off, but to no avail.

"Oh, now look at what you've done." The spider hissed. As quickly as her voice had accused Luna it softened again, "Well that's alright, I can fix it up in no time." She smiled most insincerely. Although Luna's first instinct was not of a friendly kind towards the spider she did feel very badly about the web.

"Can I do anything to help you fix it?"

The spider just smugly laughed, "Ah, no dear, I am sssure that you cannot." She dangled in front of Luna studying her more closely, "Where are you from?" She innocently cocked her head. It was difficult to look into the spider's eyes, so Luna kept her focus just below the fuzzy black stranger.

"I'm from Elan, the first of the Lower Worlds."

Luna tried to slide back and away from the spider, "Oh Elan, that isss very interesssting. Although I would highly diss-sagree that Elan is the firssst world." She snickered underneath her breath. Luna wondered what she meant but didn't dare ask.

She wanted to get away from the creature as fast as she could, "Well I really must be going. I've already set myself be-hind." She put her foot up to the next branch, feeling relieved to be farther away.

"We haven't even introduced oursselvesss yet, how impo-lite!" Luna liked her less and less as each moment passed.

"My name is Luna."

The spider swung around in a circle, "Luna, that's a very interesssting name. I am Ssserendipity. Most everyone knows around here that thisss is my part of the tree, however sssince you're not from around here it would be hard for you to know that."

Her sarcasm gritted against Luna's nerves, "Well I don't want to take up any more of your time in your part of the tree, so I'll just be on my way," Luna bit back with her words.

"Look, letsss try to get along here. Theresss no need for hossstility. Sit down up there and talk to me a while. Itsss not often I get visitorsss." The spider's voice melted into sweet-ness once more. Luna reluctantly sat down again as Serendipity slid up next to her again. She swayed back and forth from her single strand of webbing again. Luna couldn't stand looking at Serendipity too long, yet there was something that drew her closer. "Ssso you are going to the top of tree, how very interesssting, it isss a very unique place. Tell me, what do you want to go up there for?" Serendipity kept swinging back and forth.

"I am seeking the owl, I need his advice on something." Luna turned her head out into the distance refusing to divulge too much.

"Oh, the owl, hmmm ...he is a wise one." Serendipity secretly snickered. "I bet he'll have all the answersss for you when you get there."

Luna perked up, "Yes I hope so, I've come a long way to meet with him."

Serendipity rolled her eyes, "I've never understood that, everyone always wants to ssseek out the owl, I'm just as wise, if not wiser, yet nobody will ever come and assk for my advice."

Luna sensed her jealousy but said nothing as she folded her arms indignantly. She turned her head as if completely uninterested in what the spider was saying. It was easy to become offended in the presence of Serendipity. The spider sensed this and as if to irritate even more, moved a little closer. "What do you need advice with? Perhapsss I can help. After all, the owl is an owl, nothing more, but I am far more than jussst a sspider. I am a creator and dessstroyer, that in itself is the meaning of wisdom. What owl can boassst that, a spider knowsss the true meaning of life, look at my body, a perfect figure eight, representing the infinite and beyond. Notice my legsss, eight beautiful limbs, again the numeric representation of infinity. I am the eternal, my creations of lovelinesss aren't jussst a work of art, they are the cycle of life itself. The intricate patterns of circlesss, anglesss and intersssectionsss are what the universe itself is made of. All life is creation, a sssystem of crossroadsss formed, broken down and rebuilt over and over again." Serendipity's anger mounted as she carried out her passionate discourse.

Luna didn't want any more problems as she was so close to her destination but couldn't help but ask, "If you are so wise, which I don't doubt you are, why does nobody come to see you? Why do they go to the owl?" Luna smirked, confident she had ensnared the arrogant spider.

She hissed, "Becaussse they are weak, afraid to admit the truth. You see dear child, most like to sugar coat life, the owl is a fabulous symbol of that, beautiful, soft, and quiet, confident flight, an illusion of life. However, I am the truth, yet others want to turn a blind eye to me, life is both birth and death, creation and destruction. That is the truth I offer, not pretty feathers and soft cooing. That is why my webs are beautiful creations and destruction and death, my webs harbor reality, not illusion."

Luna shuddered at Serendipity's hard, cold words knowing there was truth in them, "Well Serendipity I am here with you now, so why don't you impart some more of your wisdom to me. Tell me what you long for all to hear."

The spider crept closer to Luna, "Are you sssure child? Are you certain that you are ready to face the knowledge I have to offer?"

Luna reluctantly replied, "Yes I am." Her uneasiness spun through her body like webbing itself.

Serendipity slunk back again, "Well dear, I'll tell you what, you get a good night'sss rest since dusk is upon us, and in the morning, I will tell and show you everything." Luna agreed willingly as she was tired from her conversation and her arrival into the Upper World.

"Where should I sleep Serendipity?"

The spider slinked across the air to the other side of her web, pointing one of her legs above, "Right here child, you can lie down where I am doing my lassst bit of work on my web. I'll sssave that for tomorrow, tonight I'll work on another project I've been waiting to do."

Luna was satisfied, eager to cease her conversation, "Okay then, I'll get some rest." As the sun fell to its death in the west, Luna wondered how she had lost so much time. She perched herself above the dazzling display of silken webbing. It was impressive, vast lines connecting for what seemed like miles around her as the glossy threads dangled happily in the air suspended by talent. It truly was a work of art. Luna hoped the spider's intentions were as sincere as her craftsmanship. The top of Answaru was much closer now, visible from the center of the spider's golden threads of her home. Serendipity scurried over to a spot in her lair that sat unfinished. It was the only area like it.

"Please excuse this part of my web, this is where I am making room for something and it isn't quite finished yet." She laughed hastily and scurried over next to Luna, "There wasss a time in my young life when I did not understand the beauty of my own webs. I was foolish then. Now I see the power they hold and I understand the intricacy of their place in the circle of all things. It takes time to see this. Tell me, what do you undersssstand to be true for you?" Luna pondered Serendipity's question deeply, it wasn't an easy question by any means. Serendipity grew impatient for her answer.

"Many things have changed for me since I started the journey. I know that we are given everything we need on our path whatever it may be. I believe, for me I have had to always remember to have faith, not only in others but especially in myself. I've learned that anything worth having or achieving comes easy yet the lessons are incredibly hard. I've come to love who I am despite my flaws. I can far more easily forgive others and myself, although sometimes it doesn't come immediately."

Serendipity cringed back when she said this, looking at Luna as if she had three heads, "Forgivenesss, why do you need to forgive yourssself?" The spider shook off her astonishment, quickly changing the subject, "While you are resssting, I'll just work on my project. We'll discuss this issue of forgivenesss tomorrow." She smirked and swung over to the unfinished section of her glistening home. She began weaving immediately while Luna rested, finally falling into a deep slumber.

During her sleep, in Serendipity's lair, Luna's dreams were strange and wondrously scary. Images zoomed in and out of her focus, repeating themselves over and over again, from Elan to the Upper World. Each time the dream sequence repeated it was always the same, the Dreglings, Eldred, Notty, Crone Morel, Mediwin, Dewin, Ceil, King Solarus, the Voice of the Lotus, the Queen Ant, and Lenny. Each would speak to her but it was never audible; as if being muffled by a hand. Lenny's words were the most frantic to communicate to Luna.

As Luna lay sleeping her body shuddered as reflexes twitched her legs. Serendipity smiled and hummed as she marveled at her latest creation. Swinging carelessly from a single golden thread she looked out to the goings on outside the great tree. Glancing back to her new artwork, a smile creased her dark face as she admired a perfectly woven cocoon, "Ah, my dear child you wanted to know the truth and ssso you ssshall have it firsssthand." Serendipity swung over to the golden cocoon, releasing her fangs. Slowly and steadily she injected her sleep potion into its inhabitant, Luna suddenly plummeted into a deeper sleep, oblivious to the world outside. Her heart rate slowed as her dreaming repetition raced into a frenzy of cycles. Lenny's face remained the most vivid in her dreams, wild eyes spinning, as her conversation with him increased in intensity. All her friends remained ever-distant except for the loving lizard. Days passed and Luna's body began to weaken and thin inside her new slumber-filled home. What Luna had worked and struggled so hard for had disappeared in an instant. Serendipity passed her days waiting for her cocoon to be ready, when its sleeper would finally succumb to the deadly potion forever. As long as there was movement from Luna's bodily reflexes, the spider knew it wasn't time yet. Luna's dreams persisted as did Lenny's communication, louder and louder his voice rose as his eyes swirled. His words were broken, "Luna!" Soon the rest of the dream sequence disappeared along with her friends, only Lenny's face remained repeating his broken words at an alarming rate. In the dream Luna reached to understand the lizard, but fell short on every attempt.

With one last succession Lenny's voice pierced through the Bastling's unconscious state, "Luna, wake up now!" Again, Lenny's words were clear and crisp, "Luna wake up now!" Slowly, she began to realize his expressions in her dream. She writhed inside her warm chamber as she awoke in her dream, the cycle slowed and Lenny continued to speak, "Luna wake up, you are dreaming?"

Confused, Luna peered into his swirling eyes, "I'm dreaming?"

Lenny smiled, "Yes Luna, now you have to wake yourself. Help your body and mind to realize that you are sleeping and wake them up! Now, before it's too late!"

Luna did not understand, "I don't know how, I've never done this before."

Lenny retorted firmly, "Yes you have Luna, you've done it every day of your life. Think back to our talk before you went up the tree, you know that the Lower Worlds exist even though you are now in the Upper World. Just because you aren't there doesn't mean it isn't real. Think back to Browand, what did Bear tell you? That we must understand that when we are sleeping we are awake and when we are awake we are sleeping." Lenny turned and flicked his tail hitting Luna's birthmark as he did before she left him at the base of Answaru, this time with full force. Sparks flew in every direction as Luna instantly became aware of her alternating realities. With all the strength of spirit she had she forced herself from her sleep state. Opening her eyes, she panicked seeing the soft down of the golden cocoon. She began to kick frantically as she gulped for air. Pain radiated from her shoulder blades as her fingers scraped away at the inside of her fuzzy prison. Her foot ached from Serendipity's sleep potion that coursed through her veins. Her weak body flailed as blood trickled down from her fingers as she clawed in panic for air. With one last painful grip, her red stained hands ripped a tear into the spider's spun tomb. The coolness of fresh air rushed into the Bastling's nostrils through the tiny opening as the pain in her back and shoulders throbbed. It tightened her entire body thrusting her forward towards the gap in the warm wall of the cocoon, her body's weight fell into the tear ripping it wide open. As she fell forward, her stiff body released itself from its prison with her Bastling mind knowing full well the impact might end her life.

Serendipity screamed as she watched Luna fall from her work of golden art, "No, no, that'sss not fair! I'm not done with you yet!" Luna's ears took in the spider's words as she watched herself fall through the great Tree of Answaru. A flash of light exploded from the Bastling and expanded out into the vastness of the Upper World as Luna's fall slowed and the pain in her back eased. Suddenly Luna's direction was curving slightly upwards, as if lifted once again by invisible hands just as in the Black Pool. Soon she was coursing back through the limbs and leaves of Answaru, heading towards the top. Upon reaching the highest branch she landed gently. Luna's body felt light and free. Her limbs were no longer stiff and yet although the pain in her back had subsided, a small weight bared down between her shoulder blades. She sat down securely and tried to reach around to her back, but before her hands reached her skin, they were met with something else. Luna turned her head behind as far it could go. She let out a gasp as long and deep as her journey had been, on her back, where there once was so much pain was a pair of the most exquisite wings she had ever seen. Luna's eyes welled with tears. Bastling laughter filled the air.

CHAPTER 10

Talking Trees, White Owls

AS LUNA'S LAUGHTER filled the tree with delight, a change occurred within her and all around. She peered out at the vastness of the Great Mother as energy and light coursed through her and shot forth. Everything was filled with this magnificent energy, just as she had been shown in Browand by the Seven Mystics, all was in harmony flowing in circles and streams, beaming with this electric light. A movement behind her caught her attention, a change in frequency and pattern.

The force was warm and positive as Luna welcomed it closer. "I have been waiting for you a long while. I am so happy to see you here." The voice was filled with an unforgettable softness as it echoed through the majestic air of Answaru. Luna circled around to find herself face to face with the Great White Owl. Its feathers ruffled as his wings opened revealing their extraordinary width. "A job well done little one, you have made it." The voice was hauntingly familiar as his green eyes danced with the light of a thousand fireflies. "You have come to realize there are no limits, no expectations, only what our minds perceive as such, and only what your heart will allow." Her stare fell deep into the eyes of the great feathered one as many things were found there: teachers, friends, moments, words, and deeds.

She knew instantly and whispered softly, "Eldred." The realization warmed her spirit, "I knew I would see you again." The Great Owl transformed before her very eyes morphing into the gentle Sage and Magician.

The power of Eldred's changes moved through her in waves as he smiled brightly, "I have been with you all along, every step of the way. Do you realize what you have done?" He didn't wait for her to answer. "You have changed everything. Remember, one person changes many things, all things. Thoughts, feelings and actions can alter worlds and universes. For example, do you know what Elan looks like now?" She shook her head. "Come, I'll show you." Luna wondered how Eldred would make this happen. He grabbed her hand, "Remember Luna, just be there."

She thought of Elan and suddenly they were standing at the entrance of the first world below. Once closed off it was now open and glorious, stars and orbs of lights danced by them as they gazed at its splendor. The Dreglings once hideous and ugly were now beautiful creatures of light. Everywhere she looked there was an abundance of life and love. Another entrance that had once been blocked off and barricaded long ago, was now open and through it could be seen a constant uncoiling serpent of fire. It was coming from the Rivers of Fire deep within the Great Mother. There was a sound that penetrated the world of Elan that hadn't been there before, it was hypnotic and beautiful. Everything was in perfect harmony, unflawed and moving without effort.

When the Dreglings saw Luna and Eldred they came running over to meet them, "Greetings! We have been waiting for your return." Each one stood tall and proud, much different from the once hunched over miserable, short Dreglings. Seven rays emanated from the center of their bodies. They all carried dignity, no longer the shame or guilt that Luna had become accustomed to. Their bodies were shaped and thin, even their teeth were clean and healthy and were surrounded in serene smiles. Their eyes had lost their blackness revealing an earthy chestnut color. Their hair waved gently from the waves of light. Luna stood staring in awe of their beauty. "We have been set free, a peaceful race now because of your sacrifice Luna and for that we are eternally grateful. Once you set us free, the walls of Elan began crumbling and cracking. At first we were all terrified, fearing our world was at a close, but once the walls broke and caverns began falling, we saw the truth, the world of light that had been underneath the gray walls all this time. Our memory returned to us instantly, a memory of Times Before Times, a knowing of our true beginnings, knowledge of our first breath, our first existence. We were all simultaneously transformed to what you see before you. We are no longer the Dreglings, we are the Light Carriers, your true ancestors, the Bastlings. We are no longer lost from the ravages of the Dark Storm."

Luna's eyes fell to their foreheads that now wore the familiar Bastling birthmark, a flame encircled by a crescent moon.

"We love you so much, and thank you, for now we are all one again." The old Dreg now a Bastling extended his arm behind him and stepped back revealing a statue in the center where the old broken ones once stood. It moved and changed in color, texture, light and water. The image itself was remarkable. It was Luna, with light rays shooting in every direction from her marked forehead, as the River of Fire coiled around her from her feet to her head. Her right hand held a sword and in her left palm exposed for all to see, a white star. Aligning the center of her body was an orb of energy representing each Lower World with cords stretching and reaching out to all things. Behind her head and above was another string of energy, gold with speckles of light reaching and connecting to the source of all power. Beneath her feet there were roots of a tree firmly planted in a patch of light that was the Great Mother Planet Ahki. Wings expanded from her back, moving and always flowing.

Luna began to cry tears of joy and happiness that comes with knowing the love she felt, "It is so breathtaking that I have no words. Where are the old statues that used to be there?"

From within the crowd two voices chimed in unison, "We are right here." The stone Bastlings that Luna used to visit and sit with in her darkest hours now stood before her. They were exactly as Luna had imagined them to be if they were alive.

They extended their arms to her and embraced her lovingly, "Luna our child, we are so proud of you."

As she held on to the two Bastlings a revelation encompassed her, "You are my parents?"

They smiled as they gazed into her face, "Yes and we have missed you so much. We owe everything to you, thank you."

Luna flooded with a flurry of emotion and grabbed hold of them again, "I knew you were real! I just knew it. But how did I stay alive if you were gone? I have never understood that."

Her father spoke, "It was Eldred who took care of you and made sure you were safe. He knew when the time would be right for you to start your journey." The Bastling stood dumbfounded.

Eldred proudly looked at Luna, "You have done exceptionally well, your greatest wish has come true, and you have your answers but we must go now, this is not the end but merely the beginning."

The Bastling didn't want to hear his words, "But I want to stay here, I want to be a Bastling here in Elan with my own kind, with my family."

Her mother lovingly kissed her cheek and held her face in her hands, "Luna, we will be here waiting for your return, but for now you must go. Find out what there is in the Upper World. We must know why the Dark Storm happened so it is not repeated. Be our representative, and teach others what you know. We will never be far from you and will always be in your heart as you are always in ours."

Luna looked around at her new family and race. She didn't want to but in her heart, she knew she must, "I will do it, but I will be back to tell you everything I find and then we will celebrate." She unwillingly said goodbye. Luna said many blessings and thanks to the Bastlings, promising to stay in communication with them always.

One of them spoke up, "We will always know where you are by the ever-flowing and changing statue of your life." Eldred and Luna walked toward the opening where the River of Fire flowed freely. They stepped inside its parameter and let it take them away. They went through the center of every world:

Redios where the Bazers happily worked away with the Serpent.

Orangelis, where Morgan and the Wonderlings sang as she flew by.

Yellao, where the Huma and Kumrai sat together for the first time.

As they passed through Centros, they saw the ship Luna had once sailed on, rocking slowly, adorned with Emeralds of great luminosity anchored in the pink waters of Donloom. Luna peered down to the shores to see all the Sentients, Cheelah, Captain Maskel and the crew, waving lovingly.

Faster they traveled moving higher into the world of Vocalos where they watched as Ceil, the Keltoi and those who lived amongst the Firemakers were happy and free, no longer their captives. She even caught a glimpse of Sonuachar and Anamchara looking up and smiling at her.

Upon entering Browand she waved to King Solarus, the Seven Mystics, the Dolphins, and her divine council. She slowed to look at the beauty of life there and then continued on.

Again they went higher, even faster than before into the center of Crownland where she saw the cosmic glory of the

Children of the Lotus as they stood around the Flower of the Sacred Voice. Finally coming up fast into the Grasslands, she recognized her friends Lenny, Artie, and even Serendipity. Yet she no longer saw a lizard, an ant, and a spider, she saw what they truly were, energy and light.

It was a reality far greater than she could have ever imagined, and it was glorious. As they rose higher they both aimed for the top of the tree where they had been reunited. As they guided their bodies onto the branch, they turned to face one another, "Well done, and now I have one more thing for you Luna, it is a gift. It is the greatest gift you have." She looked at the being as she chose to see him, as Eldred. His appearance became the magician she had come to love so dearly in the dark passages of Elan. His eyes were soft and swirling with cosmic images, yet clear, "Tell me little one, what has been the one constant through your entire journey, from Elan to the top of the tree?"

Luna thought for a moment, seeing images being released from her heart, Eldred, Notty, Morgan, Mediwin, Dewin, all the way to the owl. She thought of the end result, the revelation that they had all been Eldred. That was the one constant. "It has always been you Eldred."

"Yes, my child, but it is even deeper than that. Tell me what have you learned on your journey?"

Luna looked back in her mind and recalled with heart, "I have learned that I am far greater than I ever knew. I started out searching, not only for answers to my questions, but for myself. I found strength and survival, and found them in the deepest mystery and beauty. I realized that I am only as good as my mind will perceive and that my mind, spirit, body, and emotions are intertwined and must be balanced as long as I choose this earthly domain and I realized that I do choose. My sorrow, losses and heartbreak have become my sword, my shield and my power. I have seen the gravest of situations become beacons of hope because I chose to see them in this way. I learned that my voice is my power while on the Great Mother and I must always remember to tread carefully with that. I know that I can change things with my words, I can create with them like Serendipity and I can also destroy with them. I understand that I must never violate the spiritual laws that are within me, but if I do I am forgiven only by the measure of how much I love myself. I know that another sister or brother's strength is my strength and their sorrow is my burden to carry for them until they gather their own power to rise up again. I also know that everyone and everything in this universe is connected. I know truly in my soul I am never alone. How can I feel lonely for one moment of my life when stones and trees talk? How can I ever feel an ounce of separateness when my friends are the spirits and my allies that walk with me and are all around me? It is impossible for any sadness when I see the waters that flow through the Great Mother, the Fire Rivers that bubble in her belly is the same water and fire that flows through my veins. When I see the wings of the sky nation, I see the wings behind my shoulders. How can I ever feel anything but part of it all? I am in everything and everything is me. We are all one blood, one nation, regardless of race or world."

With that Eldred smiled warmly. Suddenly more understanding and awareness came over Luna as her mouth fell open. She spoke slowly realizing more with every word that came from her mouth, "Oh my, it's been you all along." Eldred knew she was finally becoming. Luna melted within herself. The tree took in the waves of love and understanding and shimmered. "You have been me all along, waiting for me to see with eyes closed. You are the parents I searched for, the child I was, the truth I am." Luna began to cry tears of joy.

She held out her arms to embrace Eldred, as he moved to do the same, "I am you and you are me. I am your highest self and I am here within you always to guide you back home, to you."

As they embraced they melded together, merging into one powerful source. Luna's light grew in brightness and capacity. She turned and spread her wings to fly.

From within Luna came the magician's voice, "Let us go now and spread the teachings of what we already know and the things we will find out." Luna flew from the top branch with a trail of butterflies flittering behind. She was off to tell all who would listen, to remind everyone of what the magician in each of us already knows. A new journey awaited.

THE END...OR...TO BE CONTINUED...